THE ITALIAN ROSE I
MAFIA SERIES

REVENGE

REVENGE

THE ITALIAN ROSE MAFIA SERIES

C. R. Mitchell

COPYRIGHT

TheItalianRose

TheItalianRose

@TheItalianRose

TheItalianRose.com

papillonebooks.com

DEDICATION

MY LOVING HUSBAND
DAVID

IN LOVING MEMORY

OUR BEAUTIFUL DAUGHTER
LIZ

MY FURRY WRITING COMPANIONS
SAM, PEPPER, MIZZOU

ACKNOWLEDGMENTS

Revenge, Part I of *The Italian Rose* Mafia Series, is my first book to write and self-publish. Bringing it to fruition has been an exciting adventure tainted with enormous hurdles.

This book's storyline rattled around in my head for years. Every aspect, scene, emotion, and character formed a vivid movie. As exciting and straightforward as that sounds, converting such images into words is a real challenge, especially for a newbie. But by the grace of God, I had help.

My wonderful husband, David, was the first to encourage me to write this story. He inspired me with a simple phrase: "Just write it down, don't worry about the rest!" David is my biggest supporter, constant creative consultant, editor, and cheerleader.

Every thread of life starts with a mom, and God gave me the best. Mom's infinite love, encouragement, mentoring, and support are incredible. She taught me the value of unconditional love, the power of harnessing life's lessons, and the significance of one candle in the darkest days. In this book, I use many of her phrases and teachings. They are gifts far too valuable to remain hidden. Her wisdom is a spark ready to ignite an individual's transformation to find inner peace.

My sons, Jack and Luca, are vibrant sunsets casting soothing hues and endless happiness on my soul. Being an author is cool, but nothing is as extraordinary as being a mom. Their love and support are a tremendous fuel to propel me forward. They are the most amazing blessing in my life.

Liz, my (step)-daughter, was a bright, talented, and beautiful woman. No matter what the occasion, she was always willing to jump in and help. When I published the first edition of this novel, she introduced me to a dear friend who created The Italian Rose's original cover. Liz, too, was a beautiful sunset in my life. I only wish she were here in person, not just in spirit. I feel her love and encouragement every day. She is forever missed.

Cindy Ellis is my enduring support when chaos strikes. From losing a very dear employee nearly twenty-five years ago to my husband's cancer, my health issues, and most recently, Lizzie's death, Cindy keeps me sane. She was the first to read my book cover to cover, not just once - *several* times. For that alone, she deserves a medal of honor! I am eternally grateful for her honesty, encouragement, support, and friendship.

Some friends help you grow. My conversations with Lori Briscoe about day-to-day struggles fuel my desire to write about managing the adversities in life. Lori has an inspirational presence. Her honest feedback on my writings, including this book, is invaluable. Lori also read this book a dozen times. She is an amazing, beautiful soul; I am blessed to be her friend.

Dr. Joann Mariano is my *super-fan who tells everybody, including book clubs, friends, and neighbors,* about The Italian Rose Mafia Series. I can't express my gratitude for her support, encouragement, & avid belief my books are worthy of an HBO series. She is a loving soul & a joy to be around. I am grateful for the tremendous gift of her friendship.

I extended my gratitude to those I mentioned and the many I have not. Thank you for believing in me and supporting me in my dream. I thank God for blessing me yesterday and today until the end of time.

CHAPTER 1

As the eerie morning fog slowly lifted, a soft glow from the sun illuminated the beige and gold walls of the city. Roberto peered out the window of his apartment above his cobbler shop. A shadowed figure on the metal balcony across the street made a quick movement. A loud pop echoed around him. He jumped back and closed his eyes, his hands searching for the entry wound. He drew a deep breath. There was no blood seeping out, saturating his tweed vest. Hesitantly, he peeked out the window again. The figure was only a woman hanging the linen, not the assassin. With a gulp, he returned to his task.

"You must go!" Roberto's eyes pleading his case.

Intermittently, he glanced out the window to examine the people walking along the street. Soon, two tall, ominous figures would appear at the front door of his cobbler store. A pair of ruthless men who enjoyed collecting past-due payments in money or life. Today, Roberto, a modest cobbler, would pay with both. But he was not ready for the devil's servants to arrive, not yet. He had one last thing to do. He prayed he did not botch his last act as he did with his family's four-generation-old business.

"No, I will stay!" Francesca said defiantly.

"Please, my love!"

Roberto kneeled beside the mattress and frantically shoved the overflowing mountain of silk, cotton, and wool into the old suitcase.

"Stop! Stop, you will ruin them if you treat them so!"

Francesca rushed over to pluck her favorite red silk dress from the disheveled pile of fabric.

"My Love, it is no longer safe for you here. You *must* go!"

"Why? The war is not coming here!" Francesca pressed the ruby-red fabric against her body and elegantly twirled around an imaginary ballroom. "Besides, that evil Hitler will soon fall from power."

"That is not the danger that concerns me."

Roberto's veins bubbled with anxiety. Like a paranoid prairie dog, he popped his head out the window every ten seconds to glance at the sidewalk.

"Who are you watching?" Francesca demanded, stomping her foot.

"My love, please go to my family in Alessandria. I sent them a letter. They are ready to receive you."

Roberto's caramel-brown eyes emitted the glowing plea of a lover to his Athena, but his wife ignored him. Frustration won over his temper. He ordered his wife to obey her husband's command.

"I will not leave without you," she huffed and twirled out of his reach.

Roberto disregarded his wife's coy tantrum and returned to the closet to gather her shoes. In the back, he spotted an old, ragged pair of two-tone pumps. A tear rolled down his cheek as he pulled them from the darkness. These shoes brought his love into his life. She was on holiday with her mother, or so they said. Hundreds had traveled south from Germany to find safe havens from an evil tyrant. Every month, dozens of weary travelers stopped at Roberto's shop to have their shoes repaired, and Roberto's business boomed.

One brisk April morning, heaven opened its gates to allow his beloved to enter his store. Francesca stood in the doorway, an angelic vision of grace and beauty. Her long, golden curls cascaded down her shoulders, and her radiant blue eyes sparkled in the morning light.

"You kept them?"

"Why would I not?" She smiled. "They led me to you!"

Roberto squeezed the shoes, and his stomach turned with guilt. He placed his faith in one man. Yet, instead of buying a better life, it condemned his family to hell. Roberto cringed at the breadth of destruction his choice made. He shoved the shoes into his overalls. He would keep them as a reminder of Francesca's beauty. The thought of her love would carry his spirit into the next world. With a heavy heart, he prayed God would forgive him so they could reunite in the afterlife.

"Francesca, I do not want them to harm you. I order you to leave!"

The men after him would do horrific things to Francesca; he had to protect her. It was his mistake, not hers. She had no part in it except to enchant him into Athena's web. Her boundless love compelled him to provide all the finery money could buy. Francesca was a goddess, *his* goddess, and he wanted to give her a life worthy of her radiance. A life free of the past's haunting demons.

Roberto jumped when Francesca placed her hand on his broad, muscular shoulders. The contrast of her soft, loving hands against his muscles bound by fear was stark.

"Roberto, what is the matter? Why are you so tense?"

The cobbler struggled to voice an explanation of his crime. His wife was not from Italy and did not understand the cultural nuances. For Don Salvatore, a ruthless mafia boss, to control the rich and poor through physical threats and exorbitant taxes was inconceivable to a foreigner. So, any explanation would only confuse his wife.

Because the Salvatore family's power started two decades *after* Roberto's great-grandfather repaired the first pair of shoes, Roberto felt the hefty burden of disappointment from his ancestors. *He* fell prey to an evil, which those before him evaded. As an heir, he failed. As a husband, Roberto refused to let his Athena live under the thumb of this corrupt overlord. She deserved a better life.

He glanced at the clock; it was almost 8:00 a.m. He had only a few minutes before the devil's henchmen arrived. He peered at the street below, his breath heavy on the glass. He would soon open the shop door for the demons to enter the peaceful sanctuary he called home.

"Roberto, please tell me what is wrong. I am your wife!"

"You will be safe in Alessandria."

"But I will not leave without you!"

"You must! They will do terrible things to you."

"You will not let them! I know you, you will not," Francesca insisted, but the quiver in her voice belied her level of certainty.

"For as long as I live, I will protect you. It is when I am gone that I fear for you!"

A tear ran down his cheek as he gazed into her sapphire eyes bobbing in a welling pool. She blinked, breaking the dam that held the trail of her salty tears.

"Francesca deserves to know," a voice echoed in Roberto's head. *"She is your wife. Do not leave her in such darkness. Lies will fester and cast a grim shadow across her memory of you."*

Gently, Roberto urged Francesca to sit on the bed. He bowed before her and passionately kissed her soft hands, savoring the heavenly scents of lavender and sandalwood sweetened with a hint of citrus.

"I am sorry, my love."

Francesca wiped the tears from his cheeks, pressed a kiss to his forehead, and urged him to free his thoughts.

"This is hard to explain, but I hope you can forgive me."

"There is nothing you could do to upset me." Her smile was pure adoration.

"I have offended Don..."

"Oh, Roberto, you could never..."

He interrupted, pressing a finger to her lips.

"I broke Don Salvatore's law, not maliciously, but..." Roberto sighed. "This is not how I wish to spend my last moments with you! What I did was for love, for you *and* the child you carry."

Her eyes danced with joy. "You know?"

"Si, my love, I know because your skin glows like the morning sun."

"When the time was right, I planned to tell you."

"I know, my love. You and our child must leave this place. A ticket for the 8:50 train is in your pocketbook. You *must* be on it! Take the back alley to Severino Street. You know the rest of the way?"

Choking back her sobs, Francesca nodded.

"Good! Now let us speak of more important things," Roberto smiled. "If you have a girl, name her Josephine, and if you have a boy..."

"I will name him *Roberto!*"

"Thank you, my love. I could ask no more of this life. Tell my child I was a good man."

"I will tell him you *are* an honorable man!"

Roberto smiled at his bride, then kissed her soft crimson lips while his hand roamed through her silky, golden curls. Kissing Francesca was heaven, and he swore he heard angels singing in the distance. He embraced her until the clock chimed the eighth hour.

"I do not wish this to end, my love. But I must open the shop, and you must hurry to the station."

Roberto grabbed the suitcase and rushed her down the steps. He cracked open the back door and peered along the cobblestone path. It was vacant except for a black and gray cat pursuing a tiny field mouse.

"Do not look back..." His eyes expressed what he could not.

She leaned in and kissed his lips once more before scurrying down the alley. He listened to her footsteps echoing off the brick walls for a moment. He leaned against the closed door and made the sign of the cross, praying for her safety.

A knock at the entrance ended his prayer. He gulped and walked toward the front door, where two shadows loomed. Roberto looked out the front window and saw a dozen shop owners scurry like mice to avoid the devil's soldiers. Their actions did not upset him. No one dared acknowledge the devil's existence out of fear he would call at their door next.

Roberto's trembling hand unhooked the chain. He turned the handle and slowly pulled the door open. The old, rusty hinges screamed in protest, making a shiver race down his spine. This ancient door was once a gateway to heaven. Now, it was a portal to hell.

"Antonio and Bruno, good morning!" Roberto greeted the cloaked demons.

"It *is* a good morning for *us*!" Antonio said with a chuckle.

The mafia boss's henchmen shoved Roberto out of the way, and they strolled into the shop. Antonio acted as Don Salvatore's hand, punishing any man *or* woman who did not obey. His horrific methods of torture, done on behalf of The Don, were no secret.

Roberto's life was charging for the finish line with the speed of a racehorse. He pulled back the reins with small talk, hoping to buy Francesca time to reach the train station.

"What brings you in this morning? Do you need your soles mended?" Roberto asked, stepping behind the counter.

"No, today we only take a *soul*!" Antonio chuckled at his clever duplicity.

"Your name is Antonio," Roberto asked, "But they call you *'Demone de Fuoco,'* the fire demon, si?"

Roberto's fingers nervously tapped the century-old wooden counter. His great-grandfather hand-carved the intricate trim and a claw-foot base. It reminded him of his failure. He glanced at the brown cash register to his right. The night before, knowing his fate, Roberto stuffed the till's contents into Francesca's purse. What use was money to a dead man? He hoped that last act of love reduced some of the shame in his ancestors' eyes.

"You have done your homework!"

"You could say."

The casual banter unnerved the cobbler. It prolonged his inevitable death, but he was adamant about giving Francesca more time. With the thought of his bride's soft hand in his, Roberto swallowed his fear and continued chit-chatting with the devil.

"Do you know *why* they call me Demone de Fuoco?"

A swell of fear slowly rose to the cobbler's throat, making his words tremble. "Because you like to burn things?"

Antonio leaned close and exposed his yellow teeth. His sour breath and evil snarl made Roberto recoil.

"Ahh, close!" Antonio mused. "I enjoy burning *people*! The crackling sound of their flesh as it melts from the bone, the tortured scream. Ahh! It is more pleasing than a harlot's moan!"

The implication that Roberto's flesh would be the fuel to destroy his family's legacy horrified him. Soon, his family's business would tumble in a heap of flames and rubble at the feet of an unworthy heir.

"Bruno. Pour!"

Antonio's counterpart opened his long, black trench coat and unstrapped two tall cans that sloshed when they hit the hardwood floor.

"Take a seat, Cobbler."

Antonio guided Roberto to a nearby chair. Roberto backed away, but an impatient Antonio grabbed the cobbler's collar and flung him into the chair.

"Put your arms on the table!" Antonio told Roberto.

The cobbler refused. Inpatient, Antonio grabbed the cobbler's right hand and slammed it on top of the workbench.

"Bruno, hold him still."

Antonio grabbed a handful of nails from the rusty can on the nearby counter. Roberto struggled to get free. The effort to escape was futile. Bruno was twice the cobbler's size.

"Isn't that cute? The cobbler is excited," Antonio mocked as he jostled the nails in his hand. "*Or* are you afraid? Sometimes, I confuse the two."

Roberto noticed his grandfather's hammer a foot away. He contemplated racking Antonio's balls and smacking Bruno in the head with it. The heroic act would give him time to run, to be with his lovely bride, and watch his son grow into a man.

Distracted by his vision, a visceral scream pulled Roberto back to reality. He glanced around to find the injured soul but saw no one. His search ended when a debilitating pain radiated up his arm. Antonio had driven a nail into the cobbler's hand. It was Roberto's shrill of agony that echoed around the room.

"I am not a violent man. I do not believe in torture," Antonio professed. "Do you believe me?"

Roberto shook his head.

"See, I knew you were not stupid!" Antonio snickered, driving another nail into the cobbler's right hand.

Writhing in pain, Roberto released a long, chilling scream.

"That didn't hurt!" Antonio grinned. "But *this* will!"

Antonio drove two more nails into Roberto's other hand and one into his wrist.

"See what happens when you wiggle. I wanted that nail to go here," Antonio scoffed as he drove a nail into the meaty part of Roberto's thumb.

"Please..." Roberto sobbed.

"No!" Antonio replied, driving in another nail.

Roberto wailed from the intense and unending pain.

"Oh, hush!" Antonio scolded, shoving a rag into Roberto's mouth. "That is better! I swear people can be so dramatic."

Antonio removed a large silver flask from his breast pocket and drizzled the liquid up the cobbler's arm. The pungent smell of gasoline made Roberto's lungs revolt. In a fit of coughs, the rag launched out of his mouth.

"Oh, you want a drink? It *will* make the process go faster!" Antonio chuckled. "See Bruno; I am not a violent man. I am a man of mercy!"

The two devils laughed in unison.

Bruno threw the cans aside and announced, "It's done."

His focus on Antonio, Roberto did not realize Bruno had returned to pouring gasoline along the shop's perimeter.

Antonio removed a second flask from his other breast pocket. After a long inhale of the fumes, he poured the liquid from Roberto to the door.

"Oh, and sorry, we cannot stay for your *finale*. The Don requested we give your beautiful bride a proper sendoff!" Antonio glanced at his watch. "Ahh! Plenty of time to catch the 8:50 train to Alessandria!"

Roberto's face ran pale. He struggled to free his hands from the table, but every movement caused a surge of agonizing pain and an eruption of blood. The crimson river flowing from his wounds spilled off the table's edge into the puddle of gasoline at his feet.

Antonio bit off the end of a cigar and, with a grin, spit the tip at the cobbler.

"Any last words, Cobbler?" Antonio asked. "No? Probably for the best."

Antonio scraped the slender stick across the matchbox. The flame surged, and Roberto shivered in horror. Not because of his impending death, his fate was irrevocably sealed. It was *what* the dancing yellow and red flame illuminated. Inside Antonio's demonic eyes, Roberto saw the gate to hell's fiery inferno.

Antonio held the match to his cigar, drawing air through until the end turned red. A trail of smoke rolled from his nostrils, and a grin curled his lips. He winked at the cobbler and released the match.

Roberto transfixed on the tumbling stick, braced for the ensuing fire. An invisible cloud of fumes ignited one foot above the floor, sending a raging river of red and yellow toward him.

"Are you hungry?" Antonio asked Bruno as they casually left the cobbler's shop.

"Sure," Bruno grunted

"There is a nice café across from the train station."

The sweet sound of death's scream came from the cobbler's shop, engulfed in flames. A snarky grin curled Antonio's lip.

"Ahh! An exquisite melody! Ehh, Bruno?"

CHAPTER 2

Rosario Beretta proudly stood on the hilltop overlooking his vineyard. He drew a deep breath and enjoyed the view of vibrant green lines flowing over the rolling hills. Even though his stout body only cast a small figure across the rocky point, he felt like a giant. The two decades of toiling outside had aged his handsome face and cultivated the strands of grey in his thick, black hair. Though arduous work matured his features, Rosario, like the vines below, was healthy and full of life.

Few, especially during the trying years of a world war, could make their dreams come true. Rosario had it all, a thriving business, a house filled with his children, and he married the love of his life, Sofia.

He allowed his mind to drift back a few years to the day his eldest son, Marcus, left to serve in the war with Germany. He shivered at the memory of battle, having served in World War I. The faces of his fallen comrades played like a film in his mind. Each memory left a scar that would never heal. He said a silent prayer for Marcus, who was experiencing the same evils. In his heart, Rosario hoped the young man would face his demons with honor and return home soon to his family, where he was sorely missed.

Now, the tides had shifted, and Italy fought with the Allies against Hitler. Changing sides and Mussolini's fall stirred rumors of the war ending by summer. Rosario knew what came after a war, celebrations -for *everything*. And no party was complete without wine. Excitement filled his chest in anticipation of the booming post-war commerce. Life was good, but soon it would be even better. His wife would have her son home, and he would see his dream become reality.

As Rosario made his way down the hill from his perch overlooking his little kingdom, he smiled at his handy work. He had turned the modest estate his wife inherited into a thriving winery. At the base of the trail was his expanded villa, his castle among the clouds that he spent the last twenty-five years building.

When he and Sofia first arrived in the early 1920s, the house and outbuildings were overrun with weeds. The few remaining vines were scraggly and produced small, bitter grapes. Together, they worked as a team to rebuild what her uncle had let fall to decay.

The once small house required several additions before it could accommodate their four sons and two daughters. Though it was not the grandest house in town, it was a castle to Rosario and Sofia. It was perfect in every way.

As he climbed the stairs leading to the kitchen, he heard his wife sobbing.

"Bella Mia?" Rosaria asked.

Though he spoke softly, his voice made Sofia jump. She quickly wiped away her tears, hoping to hide her grief.

"What is the matter, Bella Mia?" Rosario moved to her side and enveloped her in his strong embrace. "Why is my love crying?"

Rosario gently stroked Sofia's shoulder, patiently waiting for her to speak. He caught sight of the blade that pierced her heart and knew it would be some time before she could utter a word. He sighed. In Sofia's trembling hand was a letter stained with fresh tears.

"Did Marcus send you another letter?"

Sofia nodded and looked up at him with her eyes filled with tears. Black smudges of make-up, bloodshot eyes, and the deep lines of worry imprinted on her forehead tugged at

Rosario's heart. He suppressed his emotions to be a pillar of strength for his wife.

"And what does a loving son say to his angelic mother?" Rosario asked, removing the message from her tight grip.

Dearest Mamma,

I miss the smell of your home-cooked meals. The food here is terrible, and the wine, when we find it, tastes more like vinegar. I found some grapes during our march north last month and made a small amount of grappa. Do not tell father. He would be ashamed of how horrible it tasted. However, it was better than what they usually serve.

I have stopped counting the days since I left home. After the second Christmas away, I lost hope of ever seeing my family again. The distance between reality and home seems too far to reach. Keep praying for me, my dearest mother. Pray God keeps me safe and delivers me home soon.

Please send more home-baked goods, a new book, and some cigarettes. Your letters and care packages keep hope alive in a world that grows darker and lonelier each day.

Give my love to all.

Love,
Marcus

"Ohh, Bella Mia," Rosario held Sofia tightly. "He will come home. I promise! We have switched sides. The war will end soon. I know it feels like forever for us. It is for him, too, but look how lovingly he writes. Your boy, your *sweet boy*, is still alive."

Rosario lifted Sofia's chin, and gently, he wiped her face with his handkerchief. Only a few fine lines of age accented her eyes, yet she was as beautiful as the day he first saw her.

"I miss him so."

Sofia sniffled as a stray tear cascaded down her cheek. Rosario cupped her chin, brushed away the tear, and kissed her forehead.

"I know, Bella Mia. Marcus will be home soon. They cannot keep him forever." Rosario rocked her slowly and asked, "What were you thinking about when I startled you?"

"The day he left."

"Ahh, si. What part of that day?"

"How he set the others afire, saying he is my favorite."

He smiled at the memory. "That made you laugh, no?"

"He always made me laugh," Sofia replied.

"Then let his words return the smile because he would want that for his Mamma!"

Sofia sighed and nodded.

"He never liked to see you cry. Even as a baby, he would try to make you laugh!" Rosario chuckled. "You remember when you fell and broke your arm? You were crying in pain. He wanted so badly to make you happy, so he filled his mouth full of grapes and walked toward you like a growling monster. His little voice was barely audible." Rosario laughed again from the vision. "I can still see juice dripping from his lips as he mumbled."

Rosario continued to talk about Marcus as a young boy until he felt Sofia's tension fade away. After a few minutes, Sofia was smiling, remembering good memories. He quietly tucked the letter into his shirt. He would add it to the box of Marcus's letters after she was asleep. Though the letters caused pain today, Rosario believed they might be needed to bring Sofia from the darkness of sorrow in the future.

"Now, do you feel better?"

"A little," Sofia said, drying her eyes.

"It is hard to be away from family, Bella Mia. We are his lifeline. You should write to him right away. Write about happy things. Tell of his siblings and what they are doing. Make him feel as if he is here with us, living among the family. Later today, I will buy him a book and a case of cigars. By tomorrow morning, we will have a care package fit for a king. It will brighten his spirit and yours!" He kissed her forehead again. "We all must remain strong for him and pray for his swift return. Have faith in God, Bella Mia."

"You are wise. I am lucky to have you. I shall bake him fig cookies," she said, pulling her limp body from the chair.

"Make your lemon biscotti, too. Those are his favorite."

"Si...and yours." Sofia winked.

Though the pep talks and redirection of thoughts helped, only one thing could remove the weight on her heart and return her vibrant energy; the safe return of her oldest son.

Rosario watched his beloved saunter out of the room. He lost count of the number of reassuring conversations he shared with Sofia. It was his duty to keep her happy, yet he worried his words' effectiveness would fade. The chances for the worst to happen increased with each passing day. It was heartbreaking seeing his beloved tortured by Marcus's absence. But a mother grieving the most significant loss of all -*life,* would be soul-crushing.

Rosario paced the floor, thinking of the atrocities Marcus must endure. It would take Marcus many years to recover from the haunted dreams of battle. Even now, many years later, if Rosario heard the loud sound of a car back-firing, a flood of neatly tucked memories would emerge and open the door to weeks of nightmares. He sighed, longing for the war to be over and his family reunited again at a table filled with Marcus's favorite dishes.

Rosario walked to the window and gazed down the long, dusty drive. His thoughts, too, traveled a meandering road of memories. The day Marcus left, along with his personal experiences from World War I, floated around in his mind. Rosario's gut wrenched; he would never wish the horror of war on even his worst enemy.

A vision of one man's face filled Rosario's thoughts, making him retract the blanket wish over all foes. One man was a devil in the flesh and deserved the wrath and suffering inflicted by war. In a fiery rage, Rosario's clenched fists ached to bludgeon the worthy target again and again.

"Some people deserve the misery of war," he mumbled. "Some deserve a slow, painful death."

Rosario looked back at the chair where the love of his life was seated. Her sweet perfume danced in the air, enchanting his senses with lust.

"And she was worth it!"

CHAPTER 3

"They are here, Signore," Antonio announced.

"Who?" Don Salvatore asked absently as he inspected a flower hanging from the magnolia tree. He drew in the sweetness and savored it. A grin dimpled his cheeks. "Si. Si, I remember."

Antonio remained silent while The Don continued his pensive inspection of Mother Nature's beauties. Only the rustling leaves and the squawking birds fighting over the grain scattered on the stones were allowed to fill the void. Don Salvatore slowly wandered around the elegant garden filled with fruit trees and colorful flowers. It was a place of serenity, an irony since the owner was never known as a man of peace.

After a few minutes, The Don muttered. "I am in no mood for a long meeting. So many come asking for more than they offer. I am tired of people wasting my time. See to it they know they must be brief!" His youth gone, Don Salvatore grunted as he sat in his chair. "Despite your recent failings, Antonio, you may stay for this meeting."

"Si, Signore, if you wish," Antonio replied.

Don Salvatore reached into a small can and retrieved a handful of grain. He scattered it around his feet to attract his feathered friends before returning to his peaceful reverie. The Don absently waved his dismissal toward Antonio.

With a slight bow, Antonio backed out of the peaceful courtyard and into the expansive mansion. The lavishly decorated home was an elegant display of wealth. Priceless art covered every stucco wall, and each room contained well-preserved century-old furnishings. Almost everything The Don owned was inherited or earned by aiding the right political people. Of course, some items were payments from an insubordinate debtor. The building itself was by far the most expensive in the region, and its contents were worth nearly triple.

Antonio knew this was not an appropriate time for a new business offer. But the Don never passed an opportunity to make more money. After all, what else was there in life?

As he entered the round, domed foyer, Antonio cleared his throat, interrupting the two visitors' conversation. The younger man was tall, well-built, and good-looking. Antonio guessed his age to be mid-to-late twenties. The older man was short, with grey hair and deep age-lines across his brow.

"Probably sixty, give or take a couple of years," Antonio thought of the old man.

Their stylish clothing and gold jewelry dripping from every limb conveyed they were not the usual hustlers searching for money. Perhaps they were only seeking The Don's blessing for a business idea.

"A bonus in your favor," Antonio thought. *"But it takes more than fancy clothes to convince me you are more than a piece of shit!"*

Antonio nodded toward Bruno in the room next to the entry. It was his signal for Bruno to pull his gun. Bruno loaded a round into the chamber, causing the two men to flinch. Their eyes widened as the instinct for danger alerted the rest of their senses. The hair on their arms raised, the calm repetition of breathing accelerated, and muscles tensed with anticipation of their fate.

"I understand you are here to visit with The Don. He is a busy man. He asked me to inquire more as to the purpose of your visit today," Antonio demanded.

"We have a business proposition for Don Salvatore," The young man boasted.

"That is not an unusual request. In fact, you are probably the fifth person this week, and it is only Tuesday afternoon. But I am sure your business opportunity is different," Antonio pulled a box of matches and a cigar out of his pocket. "Somehow, you will help the Don amass a wealth unknown to him," Antonio professed, waving his hands at the luxury surrounding them.

The old man followed the gesture and drew in a slight breath. The high arched ceiling painted with frescos and gold filigree-trimmed pillars accented the four archways that led to other areas of the expansive estate.

"I am sure The Don would find himself destitute if not for your offer of tremendous wealth." Antonio flashed Bruno a mischievous grin. "So, let me ask you again, and please do not waste my time any further. What is the nature of your business with Don Salvatore?"

The young man scoffed and rolled his eyes at his interrogator. Bruno stepped closer and placed his gun against his head, and the young man laughed.

"Does the cat have your tongue? Speak!" Antonio demanded.

The younger man's expression was unmoved, and his posture did not change. Antonio admired the calmness in the face of death. A quality typically not found in their usual visitors.

"Tell The Don the son of Victor, his late brother, is here to introduce himself and offer an opportunity to exact revenge."

"Ohh, sure! Long-lost relatives looking for a handout ain't an original tale." Antonio cackled. "How can I believe you are... who-the-fuck's nephew?"

"The Don's nephew!" The young man growled, puffing his broad chest, ready to fight.

"Yeah, sure! I will ask one more time. How do I know you are The Don's long-lost...was it *dead nephew*?"

Antonio and Bruno exchanged laughs. They loved antagonizing anyone who crossed their path.

"Wow, so The Don has an ignafuck as a watchdog. That is disappointing!" The young man said to his companion.

"Who the fuck do you think you are, you little prick!" Antonio growled and moved inches away from the young man's face.

"Since you are such a fucktard, I will spell it out for you..."

"Easy! Easy!" The old man interrupted, slowly moving his much smaller stature between the two young men. "Please, Signore. We are here to bring peace to a troubled heart. We mean no harm or insult to the house of Don Salvatore." Calmly, the old man smoothed Antonio's shiny black lapels. "Please, Signore, we are merely family wishing to reconnect with family. That is all!"

Antonio straightened his tie. He glared at the young man for a moment, then waved for Bruno to step down. Bruno grunted and took two steps back.

"You are lucky your old man has manners." Antonio's eyes burned with a fiery aggression.

"Yeah, really lucky!" The young man rolled his eyes. "Look, if The Don does not recognize the similarities." He pointed at his face. "Then perhaps he will recognize this..."

Bruno saw the young man reach into his front pocket. Instantly, Bruno's gun was firmly pressed against his opponent's temple, his finger curled around the trigger. He was ready to splatter the young man's brains across the creamy white wall.

"Easy!" The young man slowly raised his hands into the air. "I have nothing to harm The Don. I am not an idiot!"

"Nor am I!" Antonio, reacting as fast as his associate, held his gun against the old man's head. "Bruno, check them for weapons."

Bruno put his gun away. His giant hands aggressively patted along their arms, legs, and torso.

"Clean," Bruno said with a nod.

"What is in his pocket?" Antonio asked.

Bruno reached into the young man's right front pocket to retrieve the evidence allegedly proving his relation.

"Are you enjoying yourself? Keep your hand there a little longer, and I will give you something you'll never forget!" The young man laughed. "A little more to the left. Ahhh, that's it, baby! Bring Papa home!"

Bruno growled and retrieved his hand.

Antonio resisted the urge to punch the arrogant piece of shit for fucking with his partner. But that was what the prick wanted. Antonio and Bruno were being played. If this punk is The Don's nephew, touching him would be considered an insult to The Family.

"It was good for me!" The young man laughed. "Hey, now. Come on, baby! You enjoyed it too... right?"

"Are you trying to get us killed? Be a little more respectful!" The older man insisted. "I have no desire to make The Don an enemy!"

"Well said old man! What is your name?" Antonio asked.

"Please, take no offense. However, I... *We* would prefer to remain anonymous in name," The old man responded.

"Well, if you do not trust Don Salvatore with your names, he will not trust you with his blessing!"

"I understand. If The Don will just hear us out, we..." The old man stammered.

"It seems you don't understand the nature of your situation. If I disapprove of your presence, you will not proceed any further!"

"My apologies. We do not intend to agitate you, Signore," the older man replied.

"Oh, come on! I am The Don's nephew! I am family, and your idle threats mean nothing to me! I will see my uncle. *Now!*"

The young man's deep voice bellowed into the courtyard, causing the birds to stir into a flight of disgruntled squawks.

This time, Bruno stepped in front of the young man. Two bulls standing face to face, nostrils flaring, eyes locked, ready for a fight. Each silently willing the other to make the first move.

"Antonio, where is my wine?" A deep voice beckoned from the courtyard.

"So, you are really just his bitch, not his watchdog!" The young man laughed and pushed Bruno out of his face. He glared at Antonio as he walked past.

"You will regret your insults. You should choose your next move wisely," Antonio warned, grabbing the young man's arm.

"For the record, I'm not impressed by you or your little Rottweiler. Why don't you fetch your Boss his wine and take the dog for a walk while the grown-ups get acquainted?" The young man, unmoved, matched Antonio's fiery gaze. "You coming, old man?" He added before brushing Antonio's grip away like a pesky fly.

"Sure," the older man said, straightening his white cuffs.

A large gold and diamond ring on the old man's finger sparkled in the light, catching Antonio's eye.

"You have five minutes to make your case, or Bruno will have you for lunch. And I will happily take that fine ring for my own."

"You really should work on your social skills. The Don truly deserves better!" The old man locked his black eyes with Antonio's. Shedding the meek façade, his malicious tongue launched his acidic words at Antonio. "I suggest you bring the wine and make it snappy. I don't have all day! Oh, and if you ever threaten that young man *or me*, I will personally kill you and your puppy! Do I make myself clear?"

Clenching his jaw, Antonio allowed the old man to pass. This was the first time anyone forced their way past Bruno, only seeing him as a puppy. Enraged, Antonio needed to burn something to soothe his mind. His partner instinctually handed him a lit cigar, and the two walked into the courtyard behind the unwanted guests.

"I can't wait to kill that prick," Antonio grumbled.

"After we rip out his tongue!" Bruno added.

Antonio watched from the doorway as the two men greeted The Don. The younger man bowed in respect and kissed Don Salvatore's ring. After a few words of respect, the young man presented a small gold coin.

The Don staggered back, and his hand gripped his chest. Antonio rushed into the courtyard to aid his master, but the young man had already grabbed a chair and was lovingly helping The Don into the seat.

"Are you ok, Signore?" Antonio asked, but The Don waved to ward off any assistance.

Don Salvatore stared at the coin, gently stroking it with his thumb. A tear rolled down his cheek as he mumbled a few words. After a long pause, he gripped the coin tightly, closed his eyes, and pounded his fist against his chest.

"Are you a ghost to haunt me?" Don Salvatore questioned, his voice cracking. He traced the young man's chiseled face. "I knew a man with a square chin, dark eyes, and thick brows, much like you, but you are not him."

The young man smiled sincerely and opened his mouth to respond, but The Don stopped him.

"How did you come to possess this coin?" The Don's trembling hand held it before the young man's face.

"It was given to me a long time ago."

"Not by me!"

The young man wrapped his hands around The Don's and peered up at him.

"I knew someday I could use it to exact revenge."

"I've done nothing against you!" The Don recoiled, his eyes burning with anger.

"I know," the young man said respectfully.

"Then why are you here? Why do you bring back the past and the dead? A past that has caused me much grief?"

"Because I know who killed him!"

CHAPTER 4

"Two tickets to Alessandria," Antonio said to the cashier.

She was a young girl with a round face, probably thirty pounds overweight. Not his type, but it had been a while since he had fun.

"You have pretty eyes," he lied.

She was not pretty at all, at least not to his standards. But complimenting an ugly girl was equal to giving a beautiful woman a strand of diamonds.

"Thank you, Signore." Her cheeks flushed, and her hands shook nervously as she took the money.

Good, he thought. *I like them nervous.* "So, why is a pretty girl like you working in a place like this?"

The young girl smiled and gave a little giggle. "Here are your tickets, Signore."

"Thank you."

Enjoying his game of cat and mouse, Antonio captured her plump hand in his. His eyes danced seductively as his thumb caressed her skin.

"Is there any chance I could take you to dinner?"

"Signore, you are going to Alessandria."

"Well, there is nothing as beautiful as you there, so I guess I will just have to come back."

"Hey! Keep the line moving!" A voice shouted, "I got a train to catch!"

Antonio's blood boiled, but he kept it hidden. He turned around to find the man who interrupted his game. It was a short, fat guy in a long trench coat, and his hair was combed over to cover his semi-bald head. Antonio mentally noted the guy's features and returned his attention to the ugly girl.

"So, what do you say, my sweet little angel? Will you have dinner with me?" Antonio begged. "Please, or my heart might break."

"I leave in an hour but will be here tomorrow until seven," she whispered.

"Then tomorrow night shall be a night you will never forget! I promise!"

Antonio, grinning with satisfaction, kissed her hand. With a flirtatious wink, he tipped his hat and strolled away. Waiting for the fat man to reveal his final place of resting, Antonio fantasized about torturing the cashier. He enjoyed stalking his prey; however, his frustration begged for a more immediate act of sadistic gratification. Since Francesca was only to be silenced and his date was not until tomorrow, Antonio decided this...*pig*... would satiate his hunger.

"No one pushes me, especially an ugly, bald fucktard!"

Leaning against the crumbling plaster wall, Antonio listened to the fat man purchase his train passage.

"One ticket to Alessandria." The fat man grumbled, fidgeting impatiently.

Antonio smiled. This trip would be better than he planned. He watched the man waddle toward the platform: his worn, dirty attire disgusted him.

"It'll be a service to society to get rid of this piece of shit."

"Ya got our tickets?" Bruno asked, walking up to Antonio. "Who ya watchin'?"

"A dead man." Antonio nodded toward his target. "See the fat guy getting on the number two car?"

"Yeah, who is he?"

"An ignafuck heading to Alessandria."

"You think he helped the cobbler's wife escape?"

"No, he just said the wrong thing to the wrong man!"

Antonio's intense scowl warded off any ideas of challenging his focus. Bruno followed his partner across the platform. The warped planks squeaked beneath their feet, filling the silence between them.

"Tickets, please?" The steward asked as they climbed the stairs to the number two car.

Antonio handed the tickets to the man but did not make eye contact. He was too busy searching for his first victim of the day. The fat man was sitting in the eighth row next to the window. Antonio chose a seat three rows away. A perfect spot to watch the man and contemplate his plan of attack.

When the fat man gets up to take a piss, I will give him a push -right off the train. The thought of watching the round body bounce and roll along the tracks made Antonio grin.

The whistle screamed twice, and the train lurched into motion. Antonio and Bruno settled into the dilapidated boxcar, tattered from overuse during the war. Of the twenty passengers, most were businessmen, except for three well-dressed ladies draped on the arm of an equally dressed man.

"What'd your guy say in Alessandria?" Bruno asked, pulling a newspaper out of his coat.

"He'd seen her with the cobbler's family two days ago," Antonio replied absently.

"Ya gonna stare at that man all day?"

"Only until he is dead!"

Bruno released a low growl and flicked open the paper.

"Let me know when ya ready to talk business."

Antonio looked at his partner. He was the only person besides The Don who was allowed to scold him. And Bruno only did it when Antonio deserved it.

"You know it would be more believable if you turned the paper right side up?"

Bruno scowled. Antonio's mocking shrug in reply irritated the big man. He rolled his eyes and turned the paper.

"Vito said she was living with the cobbler's family. She arrived two days later than she was supposed to."

"That explains why we lost her. How'd The Don take it?"

"He's pissed, but luckily, he is focused on his nephew."

Antonio removed a pack of cigarettes and offered one to his friend. Bruno lit his and handed over the matchbox. The exchange was a habitual routine performed by the pair a thousand times.

Bruno released several smoke rings and asked, "Did The Don ever tell you what the deal is with them?"

"Only a little. Personally, I think it's a con job."

"You think *everything* is a con!"

"They're grifters peddling a crap story. A pure swindle."

"But he had the coin."

It was Antonio's turn to scowl at his partner. "Who gives a fuck! So, the kid has a coin like the one the Don carries!"

The whole scenario pissed Antonio off, and it could not have come at a worse time. This was the first time he and Bruno had failed on a job. They lost track of a woman, of all people, and The Don was less than pleased.

"Great story, though. I'll give'em that! Shit, if we thought of that tale...ssizzziss!" A roll of smoke accompanied Antonio's whistle.

"So, what's the big deal about the coin?" Bruno asked.

"It was a gift or some tear-jerking crap!"

Bruno grunted his agreement.

"Guess the boy's mother died when he was young, forcing him to live in the streets with the sewer rats. Boo-hoo!" Antonio mockingly rubbed his eyes. "He didn't find out his father was a Salvatore until recently."

"Wasn't The Don's brother killed in the Great War?"

"That was one story. The other was he was murdered."

"By who?"

"No one really knew," Antonio said with a shrug. "The Don's brother, Victor, was a real asshole. A sadistic fuck."

"Sounds like a Salvatore."

"Yep. Not exactly a jolt to the sack, ehh?" Antonio stated, grabbing his crotch. "Guess Victor shoved the nephew's mom out the door 'cause he found a new piece of ass. A rich one to boot. He did not know the bitch he tossed out was pregnant. Even if he did, Victor probably didn't care. His new conquest would inherit well."

"Good move!"

"The Salvatores didn't get rich by marrying poor cunts!"

"That ain't no lie! Did Victor get the money?"

"Come on, Bruno! Is life ever that easy?" Antonio savored a drag from his cigarette before adding. "The nephew said a lot of babbling crap. She refused, 'cause she loved another man.' Blah, blah blah!"

"She refused a Salvatore? Did he kill the bitch?"

"Nah, he was more methodical than that. Salvatores exact revenge on their own time frame. They like being devious."

"I'da killed the bitch,"

"You and me both. Sometimes, getting it done quick is the best, but that ain't the Salvatore style. You know what I mean?" Antonio asked rhetorically. "Before he had a chance to fuck up her life and get the dough, bam! Victor was murdered!"

Antonio tapped the hot embers from his cigarette into his scarred palm. The smell of burning flesh gently wafted up to his nose. He inhaled, filling every open space in his lungs with the pleasurable smell. It was as soothing as sex to him. He savored the erotic smell, forcing Bruno to wait patiently for the rest of the story.

"Don Salvatore described the boy's mom as 'a tart piece of ass,' but no money, no honey!"

"Bills over skills!" Bruno joked.

Antonio's boisterous laugh caused the passengers to crane their necks in search of the rude culprit disturbing their peaceful ride.

"Nice!" Antonio said with a pat on Bruno's shoulder

"I know I can be a thick pot of sugo, but what the fuck does the coin have to do with anything?"

Antonio shrugged as he pulled the last hit off the cigarette.

"Don't tell me. A con?" Bruno rolled his eyes.

"Give the man a meatball!" Antonio laughed and retrieved another cigarette. "The rest is hazy bullshit, too. A total fucked up con. The Don's gone soft if he is wooed by a tear-jerking story about a raped cunt and an orphan. Boys get abandoned every day, and women are raped. What the fuck difference does it make. Somebody raping somebody is a sport, not an epiphany!"

"It's the best way to take a cunt! Bend her over and enjoy the ride! Kinda gets me goin' just thinking about it," Bruno said as he adjusted his pants.

Antonio scowled. "Thanks for sharing!"

"What? You can't tell me..." Antonio held up his hand to stop Bruno, but he persisted. "With all the sick shit you do?"

"I don't need to know what sizzles your sausage! Disgustoso pezzo di merda!"

"*I'm* disgusting?"

"No, *you* are an ignafuck! Your sausage is a disgusting piece of shit!"

"Ya know those things are gonna kill ya!" Bruno nodded toward the pack of smokes.

Antonio handed one to his partner. Their habitual exchange complete, Antonio let the smoke roll out his nose, and a wicked smile pressed his lips. He chuckled.

"Somethings gotta get ya!"

CHAPTER 5

Rosario crouched down to examine the soil near the base of a vine. The earth was dark and rich, but the hot, dry month was taking its toll. He looked to the heavens and asked for the gift of rain. At the end of his prayer, he gave thanks for all he had been blessed with over the years: his beautiful wife, four healthy sons, two beautiful daughters, and, of course, a growing business. Rosario was filled with pride. His heart was full. And why not? In everything life could offer, he had an abundance...life was good. A tingle of excitement surged through his body. It was an omen, a gift of foresight...more blessings were coming.

"Thank you, God!" Rosario rejoiced to the heavens with a smile. "Thank you!"

His prayer was interrupted by a vehicle racing up the long drive. The car screeched to a halt, and a large dust cloud enveloped it, temporarily reducing Rosario's visibility. The plume of grey quickly dissipated, revealing the two men climbing out of their Mercedes 540k. The black car with chrome trim glared in the sunlight. It was an incredible piece of machinery that displayed a level of wealth and luxury Rosario had not seen in many years.

"Buon giorno, Signore," Rosario said, cheerfully greeting his guests.

"Beh, buongiorno anche, Signore. We are seeking the owner of this property."

"How can I assist you?"

"Ahh! You? Wonderful! We have some business to discuss with you," The old grey-haired man said, removing his hat.

Suspicion crawled up Rosario's spine. Their accents were unique, and they dressed unlike any businessmen he knew.

"What kind of business?" Rosario asked.

The old man waved his hat, fanning his round face. The mid-morning sun was intense and caused beads of sweat to form on his brow. However, his younger, thinner companion stood still, silently watching the conversation unfold.

"It's a sweltering day!" The older man said, hoping for the hospitality of a refreshing drink and some shade.

"Makes for good healthy vines," Rosario replied, uninspired to be a gracious host.

They seemed an unlikely pair: one tall and well-built, the other short and stout. Rosario wondered if these men, like many others, came with an offer to buy his land or his wine.

"I'm told you make the best wines in the area, no?"

"I like to think so, but I am biased."

Rosario's eyes lingered on the young man's sharp features. His chiseled chin and cheekbones were as bold as the stone bust of a Roman warrior. His facial structure appeared similar to that of someone from another region in Italy, yet Rosario felt he recognized him.

The older man walked toward Rosario, interrupting his mental search to place the young man's face.

"You're a humble man, Signore Beretta," The old man said, extending his arm. "Please excuse my manners! I'm Mario Giovannese, and this... this is my son, Giorgio."

"Please call me Rosario, Signore Giovannese," Rosario replied, accepting the hand of friendship. "Tell me what I can do for you."

"Ahh! Si. Please, call me Mario. Formalities are so... formal!" He laughed at his joke and smoothed his wet, grey hair back before replacing his hat. "I own several upscale restaurants and hotels in the region. Soon, I'll have one here, in Brusnengo. Of course, that means I'll need the wine to serve my guests."

Rosario listened, occasionally nodding as he escorted the men toward the large stone building at the top of the hill.

"We cater to the rich and those who, shall we say, need... well... *discretion*."

"Discretion for what?"

"So, they may fulfill certain...ah..pleasures." Mario grinned, bouncing his eyebrows and thrusting his hips to drive home his meaning.

"I see," Rosario replied plainly, hoping his distaste went unnoticed.

He was not thrilled with the prospect of selling to a whorehouse. However, money is money. And with the war ending soon, a business such as Mario's would boom.

"It's my unique design. On the first level is an elegant restaurant serving food prepared by a fine chef. Many of our guests are traveling businessmen, such as myself, and we desire a high-quality meal with certain... accommodations to match. At the Hotel Bella," Mario beamed. "A gentleman may retire from an exquisite meal to his lavish quarters and enjoy the rest of the evening with the company of a beautiful woman... or two." Mario, chuckling, elbowed Rosario's side.

"So, you sell food and women?" Rosario half-heartedly joked.

"Of course, all this dining and a... talking... makes for very thirsty guests." Mario flashed a smile at Rosario, but it was not reciprocated. "We need some variety of wine. You have white and reds?"

"Si, we grow all our own grapes. Unlike other vineyards, we do not need to acquire grapes for flavor. As you can see," Rosario motioned toward the rows of vibrant green, "we have many acres of healthy vines. The quality and quantity to mass-produce."

The Giovannese men gazed at the rolling land. It was beautiful. The perfect lines of healthy, tall plants were breathtaking.

Rosario continued to describe the wine operation and each building's use as he led the two men on a tour.

"This building is where we make the wine. It is a process I take very seriously. Only the best grapes make it into the barrels. Of course, we sell substandard wine as grappa. I am no fool; money is money, and I will not waste what could be sold. There is a market for everything," Rosario said confidently.

"Ahh, very smart!" Mario agreed.

Rosario continued the story of Beretta Vineyards as they walked up a cobblestone path toward two large buildings with steam billowing from their turrets. The dark green ivy spanned the walls in pursuit of the precipice, hiding the old caramel-colored stone. Rosario shared how he rebuilt and constructed additions to accommodate the growth, turning it into the grand production facility it was today.

"Sofia inherited a portion of this land shortly after the great war. Her family had owned it for many years. They were unwilling to do the hard work a business such as this demands. Thus, the buildings decayed, and the land was decimated by pests and drought."

"We worked every day from sunup to sundown. It took nearly ten years to revive this place to its natural beauty. Now, this beautiful land repays us with the best grapes. Many have tried to buy this land, but it is our other child. Our first, really!" Rosario chuckled.

The memory of spending hours together in the sun, planting the new vines, filled his thoughts. On hot sunny days, they would eat lunch by the river, cool off in the water, then make love on the bank. For a moment, the vision of her lying naked on the green grass, her golden olive skin and long black hair glistening in the sunlight, enchanted him.

"Papa!" a voice cried from the window, releasing him from the visual spell. "Papa, come quickly before Anton fills the last bottle. This is the best wine yet!"

"Well, well! What light through yonder window break!" Giorgio mumbled to his father.

"Indeed, my boy! But, *her* beauty far outshines fair Juliet!"

The look exchanged between the men was not lost on Rosario. How could he blame them? Angelina was stunning. And the comment, 'the best wine yet,' was an intentional ploy to stoke the embers of a sale. She knew when to light a fire under a business deal. A skill Rosario took pride in grooming, though he wished he could say she took after him.

"Ciao, Papa!" Angelina, slightly winded, greeted him with a kiss on his cheek.

At nineteen, she was a beautiful young woman with long, silky black hair, captivating dark eyes, smooth caramel skin, and a curvy figure. Her wine-stained dress and hands did not mar her looks. She was breathtaking, just like her mother.

"Angelina, this is Mario Giovannese and his son, Giorgio."

"A pleasure to meet you, gentlemen." Smiling, she batted her long eyelashes and extended her hand.

"I believe the pleasure is truly all mine," Giorgio said, stepping in front of his father.

Turning the common greeting into a flirtatious maneuver, Giorgio held her gaze and suavely kissed her hand. Angelina bashfully giggled at the gesture, only allowing the eye contact to last for a moment.

Rosario rolled his eyes at his daughter. *He* could read her like a book. She always used her beauty and charm to lure them in, like a spider to its web.

"Would you gentleman like un bicchiere di vino?" she asked, guiding them towards the tasting room. "We have a semi-sweet red! The mellow flavors linger on the tongue with just the right amount of sweetness to accent the full body of the wine." Her hips swished as she walked, adding duality to her words.

Mario was enchanted. "Sounds tantalizing."

As one who indulged himself with wine and women, Mario was captivated by her description.

"Angelina, along with my other children, help make the wine. It is a family business from plant to bottle. We all contribute." Rosario boasted proudly. "That young man up there is my son, Anton."

Rosario pointed at the well-built man in the loft. His jet-black hair was covered in dust, and his shirtsleeves were rolled up, exposing his massive biceps. Rosario turned their attention to the thin young lady helping him. Her mahogany brown hair was pulled back tight in a bun, though a few strands had escaped and dangled around her pretty face.

"Next to him is my other daughter, Catalina."

The machines' roar prevented them from conversing, so Rosario guided them into the sorting room past the tables.

"And this young man stringing the grapes is my youngest son, Rosario Jr., or RJ."

A thin, wiry young boy, unaware of his audience, was busily weaving string through the grapes' stems.

"He's a diligent worker for so young," Mario said. "You say he's your namesake?"

"He is a good boy. He may have my name, but he is more like his mother than me."

"How is that?" Giorgio asked

"Ornery!" Angelina answered, not allowing her father a second to respond.

The group released a roar of laughter. RJ looked up, his face flushed in embarrassment, thinking they were laughing at him.

"RJ, come let me introduce you to these men," Rosario shouted at his son over the loud machinery.

"Si, Papa!" The young boy scurried, wiping his dirty hands against an apron that was just as filthy. He extended his hand. "Pleased to meet you."

"You as well, young man," Mario said in a formal tone and accepted RJ's hand. "Wow! A firm grip for such a young man. How old are you?"

"I will be ten next month, Signore," RJ said and peeked out of the corner of his eye to see his father's face.

Like all the Beretta children, RJ wanted to make sure he spoke in a fashion that pleased his father. He received a gentle smile from Rosario, which encouraged RJ to continue his conversation.

"Are you gentlemen here to taste our wine? We grow all our own grapes, and as you can see, we process everything here ourselves!" A smile exposed RJ's dimples. "Would you like to know how we make our wine so much better than everyone else?"

The comment made Rosario tense, and he gave his son a reproachful glare. The men responded in chorus with a resounding yes.

"I tell you what, you try to guess what it is after you have tasted our wine. If you guess correctly, I will tell you," RJ joked, his grin broadening.

"Well, Giorgio, I think we should taste some wine!"

"Right this way!"

Angelina smiled and slid her arm into Mario's. She guided him through a stone archway, stopping at the top of a dark stairwell. Near the first step, in a shadowed alcove, was a box of matches and some candles. Angelina struck the match, holding it steady to the wick. The candle hungrily accepted the flame. A momentary surge of light illuminated their surroundings, then faded. The soft glow danced around Angelina, drawing Giorgio's lustful stare.

She led the way down the curved staircase to the pitch-black cellar. Rosario and Angelina moved around the room with ease. It was an effortlessness formed over years of moving in the cold, dark space. She lit the remaining candles around the room. Each additional flame gradually banished the darkness and revealed the rows of wine bottles stacked to the ceiling. Some were covered in dust and cobwebs, while others appeared freshly placed about the expansive room.

"Are these all wine?" Giorgio asked, pointing to the endless rows of shelves that filled the long cavern.

"Si. We have wine from every year since we started bottling in 1927," Rosario replied, guiding the men down a small walkway toward the end of the room.

"This is only one of our four cellars," Angelina said.

While Rosario took the men on a brief tour of the cellar, Angelina and RJ prepared the small rod-iron table for the wine tasting.

"Very impressive, Rosario!" Mario glanced at his son, and they exchanged greedy gazes. "How much wine do you make each year?"

Mario's continuous stream of interrogating questions thickened the tension in the room. But not as much as Giorgio's lustful stare hovering on Angelina. He caught her eye and smiled. She instantly blushed and turned away. She never displayed anxiety around businessmen. This one, however, was considerably more attractive than most.

"Papa, shall we have them taste?" Angelina motioned them back toward the table, hoping to shift Giorgio's attention away from her. "Shall I pour?"

Rosario held up his hand as he finished his thought. When Mario plunged into another series of questions, Angelina's uneasiness surged.

"RJ, go get the others!" Angelina whispered.

RJ, scurrying out of the room, his tiny feet slapping the stone steps, pulled Mario from his curious interrogation.

"Papa, shall we?"

"Si, Bella. Let us not tease these men any longer," Rosario winked at his daughter.

The men joined Angelina by the table. Enchanted, they watched her remove the wax, then skillfully pry the cork from the neck. Her strong hands and well-defined muscles flexed as she worked.

Rosario watched the Giovannese men closely. Both men were drooling and not over the wine. He had seen those looks before; hell, he gave them to his wife every day! His daughter was beautiful but too young for a young man who appeared to be in his late twenties to early thirties. Giorgio was well past the age of finding a bride. Rosario's growing concerns about these two unusual men fostered many questions. Rosario would need to know more about them if they were to become regular buyers.

"So, Giorgio, tell me about yourself," Rosario asked.

"I work with my father. We are usually gone for several days at a time, traveling from one restaurant to the other, and these days traveling in pairs is much safer."

Angelina handed him a glass, and he promptly switched the wine to his left hand.

"So, you are a lefty?" Rosario said as he noticed the switch.

"Actually, I am right-handed. However, I was shot three months ago, and the wound still feels fresh. Each week, I gain a little more strength, though." Giorgio lifted his glass to salute, "To new friendships!"

Rosario and Angelina swirled the wine in unison, then drew in the full aroma through their noses, allowing the subtleties to penetrate the senses. Satisfied, they sipped the crimson liquid and savored the richness as it slowly bathed their tongues. The men watched the spectacle and tried to emulate them but were clueless about the process.

"Ahh, very nice!" Rosario said, twirling his glass between his fingers, "The wine is excellent, almost the best. Though, I think our 1932 is still my favorite, Bella."

"Hmm, perhaps. But this one has a balanced floral taste with a light earthy undertone. It would be exceptionally good with a pork cutlet or, if one is lucky enough to find a thick steak!" She looked at the men fumbling with their glasses. "What do you think, Signore Giovannese?"

His response was postponed by footsteps coming down the steps. Rosario flashed his daughter a quizzical look.

"Ah, that must be my other siblings," Angelina said. As if cued, three faces entered the lighted area. "You have already met my brother RJ. This is my sister Catalina and my brother Anton." While each child took a turn shaking hands with the Giovannese men, Angelina whispered to Anton, "Where is Ricardo?"

"He is making a delivery with Fernando," Anton muttered. "You never have us come down... *why* this time?"

"I will explain later," Angelina whispered.

"A pleasure to meet you... all of you," Mario greeted each one of them. "Quite the brood, but I heard your wife is a beauty, so I can understand." Mario bounced his brows and gave Rosario a playful wink.

"Thank you!" Rosario replied, trying not to puff his chest too much in front of his children. Smiling, he added, "This is not all of them. I have two others."

"Anton, Cat, taste this," Angelina interrupted and passed them each a glass.

Her eyes fixed on Giorgio, Catalina nearly dropped her glass. Embarrassed by her lack of grace and the possibility of Giorgio noticing, Catalina's cheeks flushed bright red.

"He is a loser, Cat, don't pay attention to him," Anton whispered to Catalina. "Look. He is not married. He is a lecher! See how he stares at Lina?"

"He is like all the rest," Catalina sighed. "Nothing in my world will ever change. I am the ugly sister."

Rosario observed his other daughter for a moment. Without hearing what she said, he knew Catalina thought Giorgio was extremely handsome. But like most men, Giorgio only had eyes for Angelina.

His concern for Cat quickly shifted.

Why did they join the tasting session? That was Angelina's strong suit. Besides, the others were not interested in selling the wine. They were perfectly happy just making it, Rosario thought.

The rumble of planes vibrated the building, and dirt sifted through the ceiling, distracting everyone from the wine. Rosario noticed the fear increase in Mario's eyes. The man was uncomfortable in the small space, and the roaring planes made it worse.

"Would you prefer to discuss business in the house?" Rosario asked in a soothing tone, hoping to ease the growing anxiety.

"Perhaps. I do think you have excellent quality wine," Mario said as he dashed toward the stairwell.

"As you can see, we can manage the demand that a business like yours would command," Rosario said, following them up the dark staircase.

Breathless from the climb, Mario said, "Let my son and I discuss things. We'll get back to you."

"Here is a bottle of white. I am sure you will enjoy it." Angelina, with an angelic smile, offered the bottle to Mario. "It would make a perfect pairing with fish."

"Thank you," Mario said graciously, his countenance calmer in the light of day.

"In fact, Friday is the first Friday! My mother prepares the best fish dinner. Perhaps you could join us?" Angelina said as she looked toward her father for added encouragement.

He understood and said, "It is a meal you would not want to miss!"

"Come at sunset! We will sample a few other wines before our meal!"

"We would love to," Giorgio replied, extending his hand.

Angelina placed her hand in his. He swiftly lifted it and kissed her soft skin.

"We'll see you Friday," Mario said as he extended his farewells, a little less suave than Giorgio.

The two men walked toward their car side by side. Mario's hands moved about as if he were in a heated conversation.

"Nice save, Angelina!" Rosario said to his daughter. "But why did you call the others down?"

"I became uneasy. They were..."

"What? You are never uneasy!" Rosario said in shock.

"Look on Giorgio's back," Angelina said timidly.

Rosario looked at the men walking away. His eyes squinted. "I see finely tailored suits."

"No, look at the bulge in the small of his back!" Angelina's voice quivered slightly, "Why would you need a gun to buy wine?"

"Good question, but what did you think? All of you would jump on top of him if he drew it." Rosario chuckled, trying to make light of the situation.

Angelina shrugged. "I suppose you are right. I guess I thought Anton and Ricardo would be stronger than him."

"You did fine, Bella, do not worry. He did not run because everyone was in the cellar. He was claustrophobic, and the sound of the planes only heightened his thoughts of being trapped down there. There is still much fear from the war."

She nodded, accepting her Papa's summation. Timidly, her chin tucked, she asked, "Should I tell Mamma I invited guests for dinner?"

The expression reminded Rosario of her as a little girl, begging to get out of trouble.

"I will tell her," he said and kissed her forehead.

His love for his daughter swelled in his heart.

Angelina is a woman, and the men know it, Rosario thought. *I must learn to accept my daughter is no longer my Little Lina. ...I am not ready for this part of her life.*

CHAPTER 6

"He was very handsome!" Catalina said to her sister.

"He is nice-looking but not my type."

Angelina's reply was nonchalant, her mind busy contemplating why Giorgio would bring a gun to buy wine? Who shot his hand, and *why*?

"Really?" Anton caught up with his sisters and draped an arm around their necks, "You could have fooled me! You were flirting with him the whole time! Of course, he couldn't stop drooling over you, Lina."

"I was enticing the sale," Angelina said firmly.

Anton laughed. "Enticing the sale? Ohh, that is what you call it? It looked more like flirting!"

Angelina slipped out of his arm. "Look. I do what needs to be done to help Papa make the sale. I don't see either of you pressing the flesh to keep the family business rolling!"

She knew Anton was only having fun, but his comments made her feel like a whore, not a businesswoman.

"I bet Giorgio would like to 'press the flesh' with you!"

"Ha-ha! You are hilarious, Anton! I only provide what all pig-headed men desire."

Angelina's face flushed; her brother was right. Well, partially right. She flirted but not for the reasons Anton claimed. Her actions sold more wine, so why stop. Besides, it made peddling wine feel more like a game and less like work.

"Not all men are like that," Fernando said, joining the quarreling siblings.

Fernando avoided Angelina's gaze by looking at his best friend, Anton. Occasionally, he braved a glance at her from the corner of his eye. Fernando was too shy to look directly at her, but his words were meant to influence her heart.

Fernando did not look related to the others. Although he was pure Italian, his fair complexion with blue eyes and golden brown hair reflected a lineage from several European countries. He could easily pass for a German or Austrian.

Fernando's parents, Carlos and Carmella, worked for the family for years. He was born at Beretta Vineyards. Carmella brought him with her every day and raised him with the Beretta children. Rosario and Sofia cared for him like he was their own, and Rosario insisted he, too, should be taught how to make wine. It was natural for Fernando to consider this place home and feel brotherly love for the Beretta children. He did love them as siblings, all except Angelina.

"He is right, Sis. Not all men want sex alone," Anton said. He cleared his throat and winked at Fernando.

"Good morning, Fernando," Angelina said in a softer tone.

Fernando's inability to look at her did not go unnoticed. It was a habit she never could understand. Especially since everyone said he loved her with all his heart. If that were true, he should at least make eye contact with her.

"Fernando, tell us, what *do* most men want?" Catalina asked, stoking the fires.

"Love!" Fernando's eyes finally reached Angelina's. For a moment, their gazes locked.

"You are right, my friend!" Anton admitted with a playful smile. "I look for more than a flirtatious woman, too."

"Really, Anton? Then why are you constantly out at the bars drinking and chasing women?" Angelina asked, seeing an opportunity to change the direction of the conversation.

"Because love is like finding the perfect grape. You must fondle many full, plump bundles before you find the tastiest one!" The comment sent the group into laughter.

Angelina noticed Fernando pretended to be amused. His fake smile screamed his disapproval at Anton's impression of dating. At her core, she knew Fernando loved her and longed for her to reciprocate.

"Come on, Nan, we need to load the truck for tomorrow's run." Anton draped an arm over Fernando's shoulder. Once out of his sisters' earshot, he asked, "Why so down."

"Do you really think she liked that man?"

"No! No, you know my sister. She likes to flirt, and she thinks it sells more wine. And unfortunately, she is right. The men seem to return more frequently just to see her in action. She definitely has the skill to read people. She always has. You know that!" Anton gave his friend a reassuring smile. "That girl has been manipulating people since she was little."

"True."

"I tell ya, Nan, she is going places. If you want to be with her, you better hang on for the ride!"

"For what ride? She has no feelings for me!"

"Sure, she does!"

"I doubt she feels for me as I feel for her."

"Now that is where you are wrong, my friend!" Anton said in an upbeat tone to brighten Fernando's mood.

"What do you know? Did she say something?"

"Not in words, no. But my Sis ain't the only one who reads people. I see how she is around you. If it erases that gloomy look, I will talk to her and help her see what she is missing."

Fernando silently contemplated the offer. They did not see women in the same way, which concerned him. Anton's typical methods of persuading women did not always generate a positive response. However, Nan's impatience for a relationship with Angelina overwhelmed his concerns.

"At this point, Anton, I will take all the help I can get!"

"That's better! Now, enough about her. Let's get to work. I have a girl I want to see tonight!"

"Who?"

"Maria! Angelina's nurse friend. She and her Father are joining us for dinner tonight."

"I didn't know you liked her." Fernando released a grunt as he lifted a case of wine.

"You may be in for love. I am in for fun, and she looks like a good time!" Anton climbed onto the truck's bed and began stacking the cases in a row.

"I hope that is not your pickup line!" A deep, thundering voice barked.

From inside the building, Ricardo heard the chatter about Anton's conquests. He couldn't pass up the opportunity to pick on his brother. Even though Anton was younger, he was taller, stronger, and considerably better looking. Ricardo hated Anton for it and constantly found other ways to overpower his younger brother.

Anton groaned and rolled his eyes, "Of course not!"

Ricardo and Fernando shared similar perspectives on women. Romance and chivalry filled their veins. Anton, on the other hand, planned to enjoy life before handing his heart over to a single woman.

"Good! Maria is a sweet girl. Too good for the likes of you!" Ricardo said as he puffed his chest.

"I suppose you think you are better suited for her?"

Anton instantly regretted his response. It was precisely what Ricardo needed to perpetuate the argument.

"No doubt I am!" Ricardo, always in the mood for a fight, deliberately argued to ignite his brother's temper.

Anton and Ricardo were constantly at odds with each other. A natural sibling rivalry that evolved from boys fighting over toys into two grown men challenging each other for a woman's affection.

Ricardo confidently presented himself as a gentle and kind knight to women. His old-fashioned charm won the hearts of many, an accomplishment Ricardo loved to rub in his brother's face.

Anton never let his brother's ego deter him from any challenge. Anton had his own talents. Aside from attractive looks, his calm, cool demeanor gave him patience. He believed waiting was the best part of a challenge and could do so for days or months. Yet, somehow, Ricardo, always seeking a fight, effortlessly disabled that patience, bringing Anton's temper to a boil.

Anton slammed the case of wine on the truck bed. His brother had crossed a line. Assessing their skills with women was fine, but they never attempted to charm the same girl.

"Aw, now, brother. Do I detect a bit of jealousy? Could it be, Nan, that Anton has a soft spot in his heart for this fair maiden?" Ricardo ended with a taunting laugh.

"You really like this girl, don't you?" Fernando asked quietly as he hoisted another crate onto the truck.

"I like her, but I am not in love with her!" Anton tried to remain calm and hoped his brother would drop the subject.

"Good, then she is fair game! How about a wager? Hmm? Let's see..." Ricardo, deviously tapping his lips, paused in pseudo-thought.

Anton wished his brother would either start helping load the truck or go away. He had no desire to duel over a woman, especially with Ricardo. And the idea of placing stakes made the entire thing distasteful.

Ricardo's face lit up. "Ah! I got it! The better man wins the girl!" Ricardo said as he extended his hand toward his brother. "Nan, you can be the judge of the winner."

Anton huffed; at that moment, he hated his brother more than anything.

"Unless you prefer your older brother show you how to lure a woman into the arms of a real man!"

Anton rolled his eyes again and continued working. He had no intention of placing a bet over a conquest, especially for a girl he only wanted to date, not marry.

Ricardo's laughter traveled down the hill to Angelina and Catalina. They rushed to join their brothers' conversation.

"What is so funny?" Catalina asked.

"Nothing!" Anton's face flushed red in anger.

"Just a friendly wager." Ricardo puffed his chest, enjoying the moment.

"Wager?" Angelina asked.

"Ricardo and Anton are going to try to win Maria's heart," Fernando said.

"What?" Angelina asked incredulously.

"I did not agree, Lina!"

"Then, I win!" Ricardo announced with pride. The grin on his face reflected his pleasure for his victory.

"Ricardo, you are too old for Maria," Angelina said, glaring at him, partly protecting her friend but largely in distaste.

"Too old? You were flirting with a man almost twice your age only a moment ago!" Catalina added.

"He is not twice my age!" Angelina's flushed red with embarrassment.

"You admit you were flirting?" Catalina asked playfully.

"No! I was not flirting with him."

Angelina looked at Anton for help, but he just smiled. He was glad to move to a different subject. Plus, he knew his sister could easily manage Ricardo and Catalina on her own.

"Angelina, you lie!" Catalina's emphatic statement made her hop in the air. "She was flirting! Wasn't she, Anton?"

Everyone stared at Angelina, waiting for her to confess.

"What? I was working!" Angelina said.

"You are a winemaker's daughter. You sell wine, not a..." Ricardo began but was interrupted quickly by Angelina.

"Wait, how is this about me? The two of you plan to attack my friend at dinner!" Angelina said, steering the conversation back to its previous point.

"We will not attack. I merely plan to show our brother how to properly woo a woman!"

"You wish!" Anton said under his breath.

"Do you think it will help your case if we tell her you placed a bet on her affections?" Angelina asked, pleased with herself for effortlessly redirecting her brothers' attention.

Ricardo towered over her. "No, because you won't tell her, *right*?"

Angelina laughed, "I am immune to your charm, Ricardo!"

He smiled with an air of superiority. "No woman can resist my sweetness!"

"Oh, shall I list a few recent failures?" Angelina asked.

"That will only take a second, but I could spend a day listing your lost loves, Lina!" Ricardo tried to say in a serious tone but then broke into laughter.

Laughing, the siblings continued teasing each other about the opposite sex. One by one, all of them became the tormented target. Soon, the original subject was forgotten.

A loud bell rang from the house, pulling them from their loving, yet humorous, roast of each other.

"We better hurry, or Mamma will make us feel guilty for being late for lunch! Last week, she claimed we took so long she thought she was dead and only a ghost in the house," Anton said, hustling toward the cellar.

They quickly hoisted case after case of wine, filling the truck bed. Wiping their brows, they paused to catch their breaths before heading to a much desired meal.

"Now, about the bet." Ricardo extended his hand.

"Really?" Anton replied.

Ricardo, waiting for his brother to cave, didn't move. After a long moment, Anton reluctantly shook his brother's hand.

Angelina's jaw dropped. "I can't believe you! You are a piece of work, Ricardo!"

Ricardo grinned. He did not care. He won the first fight.

"She won't fall for it!" Angelina said, glancing over her shoulder as she walked down the hill with her sister.

"You are forbidden to tell her!" Ricardo's command echoed off the buildings, adding weight to his words.

Angelina and Catalina, unmoved by his attempt to control them, replied in unison, "Ohhh, forbidden?"

"Si! It must be a fair fight!"

"Very well, Ricardo, but she is not an idiot!" Angelina said with a hearty laugh before whispering, "Ohh, Cat, this will be fun!"

"Why?"

Angelina took several more steps before she glanced back to ensure the men were out of earshot. She giggled deviously

"The joke is on them! They don't know *why* Maria is coming!" She leaned close and whispered into Catalina's ear. They erupted in laughter. "We shall enjoy entertainment with tonight's dinner!"

CHAPTER 7

"Look, Cat, they are preening themselves like birds!" Angelina giggled.

"You are cruel not to tell them," Catalina whispered.

"You are enjoying this just as much as I am!"

Catalina giggled. "More than I should."

Angelina's brothers fought over the small mirror on the wall. Ricardo pushed Anton out of the way so he could watch his comb slowly pull through his well-oiled hair. The light shined off the moist black locks that refused to part with their natural wave. He smiled at himself in the mirror, admiring his good looks.

"You both look dashing!" Angelina said, barging into the wash closet. "Now leave so we can have our turn!"

"I 'm almost finished," Ricardo said, yanking his arm from Angelina's grasp. "Your turn will come when I'm done!"

"You spend more time than a girl in front of the mirror! Papa only has two daughters; if you were wondering, you are *not* one of them!"

Anton laughed at Angelina's comment, which intensified Ricardo's aggravation. It was a short walk for Ricardo; his temper was always quick to flare. He tried to compose himself but could only force a weak smile.

"Angelina, you are so beautiful you do not need to brush your hair!" Ricardo said, trying to sound sincere, but his temper rang through. He growled at his lack of control.

"Awe! How sweet!" Angelina smiled. "But what does that say about your looks?"

Ricardo's mouth dropped open, but no retort came to his lips. Angelina used his dazed state to her advantage. With both hands, she pushed him out of the room. He turned to scold her, but Angelina slammed the door in his face.

"Angelina!" Ricardo pounded on the door. "Angelina!"

When she cracked the door slightly, Riccardo's red face, burning with anger, glared at her.

"What?" She asked, keeping a tight grip on the doorknob.

"I'm not finished in there! You can't just push me out!"

"I can, and I did!"

Angelina tried not to laugh at her brother's childish attitude and pouty lip. It was almost enough to make Angelina feel sorry for him.

"You want a hint about Maria?" She asked with a mischievous smile.

He hesitated for a second, then placed his ear to the opening. The thought of telling him the truth entered Angelina's mind. But Catalina's begging not to spoil the evening's fun persuaded her to hold her tongue.

"What?" Ricardo asked hungrily.

"She does not like vain men!"

Angelina giggled and slammed the door. She looked at Catalina, and they both erupted in laughter. Their conversation about their brothers and men perpetuated their giggles throughout the lengthy beautification process.

"Is Maria's fiancé joining us for dinner?" Catalina asked, pulling the brush through her sister's long black hair.

"No, he is working at the hospital. He told Maria to pick whatever she wanted. He will be happy if she is happy."

"How romantic!"

"He loves her very much. She is completely spoiled by his affections."

"I will never find a rich man to spoil me." Catalina, shoulders slumped, released a heavy sigh. "She is lucky to find a handsome doctor to give her everything she wants."

"Oh, Cat. You will find someone to fawn all over you."

"Not likely."

"Why do you say that?"

"Not when men only have eyes for you!" Catalina avoided her sister's disbelieving stare. "Let's face it, I am nothing in your shadow."

"That is not true! You are beautiful!"

Catalina ignored her sister's rebuke and changed the subject. "Nan would spoil you if you let him."

Angelina scowled, "Was it Anton's idea to corner me?"

"No, but he knows too. *Everyone* knows Nan is in love with you." Catalina said as she twisted a lock of Angelina's hair. "The real question is, why do you push him away?"

"I do not."

"Ohh, really? Your actions speak otherwise. You flirt with every man you meet but never with Nan."

"We were talking about Maria. My love life is not important."

"You could at least try to reciprocate his affections."

"Are you about finished?"

"No! Not even close!" Catalina forcefully pinned another swirl of curls to Angelina's head, intentionally inflicting pain. "You must endure this a bit longer."

Angelina cringed. Catalina would drag the conversation out until her point was made, whether by pin or tongue.

"Why does everyone care about Nan's feelings for me?"

Catalina pulled the hairpin out of her mouth to answer, and Angelina flinched. Enjoying the dominance over her older sister, Catalina smiled and continued making her point.

"We live in a small town with few options. You don't want an arranged, loveless marriage. Nan is in love with you!"

While her sister continued to list the reasons for the match, Angelina looked at her hands. She would enjoy a ring on her finger, a wedding to plan, and the prospect of a family of her own. After all, she was nearly twenty. Most of her friends were married or engaged. Yet, she was the only one not seriously involved. Marrying Fernando for that reason was tempting, but at what price? Was it fair to either of them?

"Are his feelings the only important aspect of the match? What about how I feel?"

"Don't be silly! Your feelings matter, too. What I don't understand is why you fight it." Catalina forced another pin into her scalp.

"Ouch!"

Catalina blushed. This time, the pain was unintentional.

"Please, the conversation is torture enough!"

"He is a good man from a good family. His mother and father work for our parents. Heck, they practically raised us as well!"

"Exactly! Can't you see why it's wrong? He is more of a brother than anything!"

"Nice try! I have seen you look at his chest when he is in the fields, his body hot with sweat!" Catalina grinned, playfully fanning herself.

"Sounds as though *you* have the crush!"

Catalina gently pinned the final ringlet to Angelina's head. The silky black strands, masterfully placed in layers of braids and curls, were beautiful.

"You are truly an artist! My hair looks gorgeous!"

Catalina ignored the compliment. "What keeps you from accepting his love?"

Angelina sighed. "Well...What if we do not have the same dreams? Fernando would never leave his parents *or* Brusnengo. I do not want to stay here. I want to travel, see the world, experience life. If I settle for Nan..."

Catalina stepped away, glaring in disgust. "You are cruel to think or even say such about Nan! Perhaps you prefer someone like Giorgio?"

"You thought more of Giorgio than me! Why doesn't anyone understand my side? I have dreams and ambitions. Besides, Fernando was raised with us. To think he is more a brother than a suitor is not unreasonable!" Angelina's harsh, escalating voice made Catalina back away. She took a breath before continuing calmly. "Please, Cat, let me choose the right man at the right time."

"At least date him."

"I will think on it."

"You think too much! Sometimes, you have to jump without worrying about where you will land!"

"You sound like Mamma! I said I will think on it, I promise!"

"Ohhh! Fine! You have won...for the moment!"

Smiling, they sealed their truce with a hug.

"Enough about Nan. We have a fair maiden to rescue," Angelina said with a wink.

CHAPTER 8

Angelina followed Catalina down the back stairs to the kitchen, where their mother, with Fernando's assistance, was laboring over the meal.

Fernando hoisted a heavy pot from the sink to the stove and asked Sofia, "Put it on this burner?"

"Si, thank you. You are better help than my children. Maybe I should adopt you," Sofia said sweetly.

Sofia teased Fernando as she would any of her children. Angelina watched the familial exchange between them and wondered if her parents thought the same way Catalina did.

"You look beautiful...as always," Fernando said when Angelina joined them in the kitchen.

"Thank you." Angelina searched for an adequate reply. "umm...you look handsome. I...a...like your shirt!"

Angelina brushed a piece of lint from his broad shoulder. Years of lifting wine crates gave him a muscular body. Catalina was right. He was a sight to see with his shirt off.

"Where is everyone?" Catalina asked her mother.

"They are showing Maria and her Father the courtyard."

"They are already here?" Angelina asked.

"Si. They arrived an hour ago," Sofia replied.

"Sorry, Mamma. We did not notice the time!" Angelina grabbed a stack of the dishes. "I will set the table."

"Let me help you. They are heavy," Fernando said, taking the plates from Angelina's hands.

His hands touched hers. In a brief second, time stood still. Angelina felt the blood rush to her cheeks, and a warm tingle flowed through her. Shocked by the sensation, she quickly released the dishes into his hands.

"I will get the napkins," Angelina mumbled.

She turned her gaze away and hoped he did not notice her body's response to the encounter. She chided herself for the lack of control over her senses.

What is wrong with you? You reacted like Nan was Giorgio! The reflexive comparison with Giorgio startled her. *Ugh! Why him? He is arrogant and untrustworthy! Nan is...well...Nan.*

Angelina pushed away the thoughts. She would discuss it with the only trustworthy person she knew. Someone who had more experience dating. Her best friend, Maria.

Angelina decided to take her sister's advice. There was no harm in being open to his affections and perhaps a little flirting. While Catalina and her mother were busy putting the hot food into the serving bowls, Angelina decided now was as good a time as any to start.

"Who do you think will win the bet?"

"Neither!" Fernando replied, avoiding Angelina's gaze. "She is engaged to a wealthy doctor. Why would she sway?"

"You know?"

"Of course! I have known for several weeks. My mother told me about it when they arranged the visit."

Angelina's jaw dropped. "But you said nothing today."

"No way! I told your parents about the bet, and they agreed to play along, too." Fernando finally looked at her. Grinning, he added, "Ricardo and Anton need a lesson in arrogance; this was a perfect occasion!"

Angelina giggled. Fernando never instigated anything mischievous. And the last time he smiled like that was years ago when they chased the frogs along the river bank. He laughed at Angelina's facial expressions when the slimy, green blob launched out of her hands, narrowly missing her chin.

The thought reminded her that, occasionally, they did have fun together. Perhaps she could fall in love if she could remember more of the playful times.

He would need to be a lot less serious, she thought.

Her adoring smile caused him to flush and look away. Frustrated by his timid nature, Angelina rolled her eyes and marched over to the wooden cabinet, grumbling in agitation.

How can I flirt with someone so meek? I'm not that intimidating! Angelina thought.

Angelina tucked her frustrations behind a fake smile. She attempted to flirt again, but Fernando refused to make eye contact. How can he love her and fear her at the same time? His lack of congruency angered her, and she snapped.

"Why are you so shy with me, Nan?"

Fernando flushed beet red. He opened his mouth to reply, but nothing came out. Catalina overheard the harsh question and hustled to break the tension by placing a steaming bowl of pasta between them. She flashed Angelina a scowl before looking at Fernando sweetly.

"Nan, do we have enough wine from the cellar for dinner?"

"Uhh...no... I should probably go get a few more bottles."

A faint look of relief emerged from his red face. He gave Catalina an appreciative smile, then scurried out the door.

"Lina! What are you doing?"

"Following your advice! But he acts like a scared rabbit in my presence. If he loves me, *as you say,* he should be a little less frightened of me!"

"It is your eyes," Sofia interrupted, placing a basket of fresh bread on the table.

The girls gazed down at the wicker basket overflowing with warm loaves lovingly tucked under red towels. The golden aroma accented with rosemary was enticing.

"For dinner only!" Sofia commanded, wagging her finger at them. "The smell is tempting, but dinner is nearly ready. You can wait, like everyone else."

Sofia's glare defeated their begging eyes. Seizing her triumph, Sofia unleashed one of her parables on life.

"Your eyes are beautiful. They are dark and powerful, too. You bat them around when you want something...both of you!" Sofia's brow arched at Catalina and Angelina's look of confusion. "Don't play innocent with me! I have seen you use your beauty and charm to manipulate men—*especially you*, Lina." She wagged her finger, silencing Angelina's protest. "It is true; you have the gift to sell. But! You have batted those long lashes and dark eyes since you were a baby. Men are captivated by you. Of course, this is nothing new."

Catalina giggled, enjoying the tongue-lashing directed solely at Angelina. The noise captured Sofia's attention.

"Catalina, you have these charms, too. Your sister is a few years older than you. Therefore, she has mastered them. You are still learning to use them, but worry not. You, too, will master them. It is in your blood." Sofia winked and returned to stirring the pot of sugo with her favorite weapon, a wooden spoon. "Women have what all men want. And I am not talking about sex!"

Hearing a quiet groan of protest, Sofia snapped her head around, catching her daughters' disgusted looks. Her brow cocked, Sofia removed her wooden wand from the sugo and cast a spell. The single word compelled them to unconsciously obey.

"SIT!" Sofia continued to wave her wooden wand, only more emphatically. "Now listen close, my little rosebuds."

The sisters tried to avoid the flying droplets of sauce, but a blob smacked Catalina's forehead.

"Ouch! That is hot!" Scowling, she wiped it away before it scarred her face.

"Mamma, do we..." Angelina started but stopped to dodge a glob careening for her head. Luckily, it barely grazed Catalina's masterpiece.

Pleading for mercy was useless, especially when Sofia wanted to make a point. The listener was better off dodging the delicious red ammo being hurdled their way. Should one be fortunate enough to receive Sofia's enlightenment without the danger of projectiles, taking notes to prove their attentiveness was strongly encouraged.

"Do not interrupt! This is important, and *both* of you are old enough to hear it. I may not be here forever, so I must teach you while I can."

The girls rolled their eyes. It was an Italian mother's duty to inflict guilt because death's looming fingers could, at any moment, snatch her from the earth. She would commit the most heinous of all sins if she did not impart the knowledge of a thousand years of motherhood before she succumbed.

"Mamma..." Angelina tried again but was met with her mother's wagging finger.

"Women have what men want!" Sofia's sharp tone warded off any other attempts to interrupt. "It is not sex! So you can wipe that look from your face! This is important. Sit up and listen. You will need this someday, soon!"

The obedient girls obeyed. When Sofia turned to place the wooden spoon on the stovetop, they exchanged looks of relief. It was one thing to listen to their mother. Doing so while dodging drips of hot sugo was far more terrifying.

"You possess all you need to enchant a man. Some will love you for your looks, others for your mind. If you are lucky enough to find the man who does both and respects your talents, he is the one to cherish!"

Angelina and Catalina squirmed in their seats, fearful of the men overhearing the lengthy lecture. Ruffling their feathers only encouraged Sofia to continue. She relished their discomfort.

"Angelina, you are good at sales, but why? It is because you use what they crave to lure them to the prize. You manipulate them with your looks *and* your tongue."

Angelina opened her mouth, but Sofia held up her finger.

"Do not disagree with me. You know the truth!"

"It's true, Lina. You are like a siren on the shores luring in the sailors," Catalina giggled.

"Careful, Catalina! You manipulate men, too! You use your beauty and pretty eyes to ensnare them. But! You also play the damsel in distress who longs to be rescued by a hero!"

Her mother's verbal slap made Catalina bow her head. She could not argue with her mother, even if she disagreed.

"Chin up, Catalina. How you act is not a bad thing. You act as the maiden, and Lina acts as the siren. Both accomplish the same. Both traits are desirable." Sofia smiled softly. "You see, my rosebuds, it is not just sex, but the enticement of its possibility! Some men want a maiden, a heart to save from danger. Others want a powerful woman who is worth the challenge. In the end, it is the adventure they relish. If sex were all they wanted, the oldest profession would not be called old... it would be called the most profitable!" Sofia chuckled, pleased with her cleverness. "You wait and see. One day, *when I am gone*, you will look upon this conversation and realize I spoke the truth today!"

Sofia noticed Fernando walking toward the door with an armful of wine. She huffed; she had not finished her teaching. With her finger drawn, she rounded on Angelina.

"Angelina, Nan is a good boy! Be gentle with him. He is not like the men you sell wine to. He is a romantic, and you must be willing to be romanced."

Sofia put away her wagging finger and smoothed her apron before opening the door for Fernando.

"Thank you, Nan," Sofia said sweetly, her tone completely opposite from seconds before. "Did you see our guests?"

"They were heading toward the front door," Fernando

replied, slightly winded. "Would you like me to open these so they may breathe?"

"Thank you, Nan," Sofia smiled. "Cat? Lina? Please fetch the wine glasses!"

The girls scurried away, grateful class was dismissed.

The front door creaked, and muffled voices filtered down the hall to the dining room. Sofia removed her apron. In her reflection in the window, she inspected her hair. Satisfied, she waited by the dining room to greet her guests.

A wide stone archway separated the large dining room from the kitchen. Beyond the ivory and golden stones was a beautifully carved wooden table stretching the length of the room. The left wall was a large, soot-stained fireplace framed with the same ivory and golden stone as the archway. In the corners on the right side of the room were curved wooden cabinets, perfectly crafted to match the table. The beauty of the glistening chestnut and finely carved details paled in comparison to the wall opposite the archway. Nearly the length of the table, a picture window framed the setting sun's golden glow over the rolling vines. It was a breathtaking, majestic backdrop for any meal.

"Isn't the view beautiful?" Maria asked her father.

Maria's father, Jasper, a carpenter in his youth, noticed the handcrafted woodwork in awe. Understanding the labor to make such a remarkable piece, he did not hear his daughter nor notice the glorious sunset.

"Rosario, this table is beautiful!" Jasper said with a slur.

"Thank you. I built it." Rosario pointed toward the right wall. "And the matching cabinets."

"You are a talented man! You are a maker of delicious wine. A builder of a fine estate. A maker of beautiful furniture. Can you fly, too?" Jasper boisterously chuckled and stumbled to the chair Rosario offered.

Maria, embarrassed by her father's drunkenness, blushed

63 | P A G E

and tugged at her father's arm. "Papa, please!"

Sofia gave the blushing bride-to-be a comforting smile.

"Signora Beretta, may I help you with..." Maria glanced at her father. "...*anything*?"

"Si. Come help me carry the rest of the meal to the table." Sofia winked, acknowledging the young girl's discomfort.

"I am deeply sorry." Maria dropped her chin. "My father drinks a lot when he is nervous!"

"You are his only daughter. This is an important occasion for a father. Do not worry. All will be fine."

Maria brightened when she saw her best friend.

"Hello, Maria!" Angelina gave her a big hug. "Did I hear you say your father is nervous?"

Maria nodded.

"How drunk is he?"

"I'm so embarrassed! He promised not to drink, but..."

"Papa will see it as a compliment. Do not give it another thought!" Angelina reassured Maria with another hug.

"Where are my brothers?" Catalina asked.

"They have been acting strange since we got here! When we came into the house, they were still arguing." Maria accepted a tray of fresh fruit from Sofia. With a shrug, she added. "Maybe they are still outside?"

Angelina, Catalina, and Fernando waited for Maria to turn away before exchanging mischievous smiles. Sofia interrupted them with a harrumph. She handed Catalina and Fernando a dish, then shooed them out of the kitchen.

"Angelina, go fetch your brothers," Sofia said.

As she walked down the hall, Angelina struggled to suppress her smirk. Anton and Ricardo, still ignorant of the purpose of Maria's visit, were making fools of themselves, and she loved it!

As she walked down the hall to the front door, Angelina heard her brothers arguing, one slinging insults as fast as the other. She paused to listen at the door and laughed.

"Wow, you guys are really fighting!"

She stepped outside and waved to catch their attention, but they did not look at her. She slammed the door, but they still ignored her.

"Are you two done?" Angelina stormed down the stairs and placed herself between them. "Both of you stop! Now! Mamma says it is time for dinner! And she wants you on your best behavior!" She headed back inside but stopped and glared back. "Oh, and for your information, Maria thinks both of you are acting strange, so knock it off!"

"But!" they responded in unison.

Angelina took a page from her mother's book and wagged her finger to silence them. Without another word, they tucked their chins and marched inside.

"Wow, can't believe that worked! I'm gonna remember that the next time they argue with me!"

CHAPTER 9

"Nan, we need eight more cases of red," Ricardo said as he reviewed the order form.

"I have two of them," Anton shouted to Fernando.

Anton hoisted the heavy crates onto the bed of the truck. Thoughts of the previous night continued to flit around in his mind. The evening was a disaster. Not only did he embarrass himself, but he also humiliated his family. Of course, he knew he was not the only one responsible. Ricardo played his part in the mess, too. Anton wanted to blame it all on his older brother. However, by accepting the bet, he was complicit.

"Then get a case of white and red if you are man enough to haul two cases, Nan!" Ricardo hollered.

"Do you always have to be an ass?" Anton asked, arranging the two cases of wine. "He is my best friend. You could be a little nicer to him."

"He did not act like your best friend last night! He could have told us Maria was engaged to Dr. Leonardo! But instead, he let us look like fools!"

"*You* looked like a fool!" Anton replied. "At least I didn't try to kiss her!"

"Ha! You were vying for her affections as much as I was!"

Rolling his eyes, Anton scoffed and returned to his work. He was exhausted. This was the second truck he had loaded this morning while Ricardo pretended to be busy matching the cases of wine to the manifest. Anton's back ached, and he was ready to get out of the blistering sun.

"Are we finished yet?" Anton asked, wiping his brow.

"No, we still have six more cases to load."

"*We?*" Anton glared at him. "*We* would be, Nan and me. *You* have spent the morning picking on Nan! And me, for that matter!"

"I am supposed to pick on you. Consider it part of my job," Ricardo proclaimed, counting the crates on the truck.

"Well, you're an over-achiever! After embarrassing the entire family with your 'suave moves,' you think your mouth would be full of humble pie!" Anton grumbled.

Anton jumped off the truck's bed and made his way toward the cellar. As much as his body craved a break, his nerves begged for sanctuary from Ricardo's inflated ego. And the only place he would find that was in the cellar.

A few minutes later, their faces covered in dirt and sweat, Anton and Fernando resurfaced from the cellar, each carrying two cases of wine.

"Are we...delivering this load, or will...Ricardo?" Fernando asked Anton between breaths.

"That's a silly question. We know Ricardo doesn't work!"

"Carlos and I will make the run to Alessandria," Ricardo corrected Anton.

"Damn, how could he hear you?" Fernando mumbled to Anton.

"Because I have good ears," Ricardo replied.

"Well, you and Carlos can have the run. I, for one, am exhausted. A cool shower sounds like heaven to me!" Anton said, hoisting the crates onto the truck bed.

"I would prefer Carlos be close by," Their father's voice instructed as he approached them. His long legs and broad shoulders emphasized his towering muscular build.

"Who do you want to go to Alessandria?" Anton asked respectfully.

"If you and your brother could refrain from fighting, I would prefer the two of you go. Unless you intend to continue your stupid antics, which almost cost us a large order!"

"What antics?" Ricardo's argumentative tone exposed a belief of his innocence in the previous night's debacle.

"The embarrassing ones you displayed at dinner last night," Rosario reprimanded. "You upset your mother, and I fear you caused quite the scene with Maria."

"In all fairness, Papa, we did not know she was engaged!" Ricardo puffed his chest.

"Engaged or not, you should not attempt to kiss a woman while I am giving her a tour of the vineyard!" Rosario, two inches taller than his son, appeared to tower over him.

"She lingered in the cellar with me while the rest of you left. I merely seized an opportunity. Besides, it was only an innocent kiss!"

Rosario's temper bubbled to a red-hot boil. His hands punctuated his words as he continued his beratement.

"Innocent! You trapped her in the cellar, blew out the torches, and attacked her in the dark!"

"I didn't attack her!"

"That's a matter of perspective, son!"

Rosario and Ricardo continued to argue back and forth while Anton stood quietly by the truck. Fernando disappeared into the cellar for the last few cases of wine. When he reached the top of the stairs, Rosario was scolding Anton for his part in the fiasco.

"And what do you have to say for yourself? Did you place a bet on a woman's affections? Have I not taught you better?"

"I am sorry, Papa. It was wrong, and I should not have accepted the wager," Anton replied remorsefully, his head slightly bowed.

Over the years, Anton learned that fighting with his father was unwise. It was an impossible battle to win. The more effective way was to speak calmly, as if he were taming a wild horse—a technique he learned from his mother.

Anton remained silent and remorseful, even though the redness faded from his father's face, and the throbbing vein in his temple retreated. To apologize further would only prolong his father's disapproval, if not cause it to resurge even more intensely. All Anton needed to do was wait for his father's raging storm to pass.

After a long pause, Rosario released them from the torturous silence with a sigh.

"Ricardo, you would do well to learn from your brother." With a slight grin of pride, Rosario patted Anton on the shoulder.

"Here are the last two cases," Fernando interrupted, placing the heavy boxes on the truck. "Good morning, Signor Beretta."

"Are they making you do all the work?" Rosario asked.

Breathless, Fernando held up a finger as he struggled for air. After a moment, he pulled his body upright and removed a tattered rag from his back pocket to wipe his brow.

"No, Signore. Anton and I carried up the brunt of it while Ricardo counted the load." Fernando replied with a small smile towards Anton.

"The men do the actual work and leave the paperwork to the weak," Anton said.

He winked at Fernando and nodded to watch the volcano of anger that threatened to erupt from Ricardo's mouth. Within seconds, Ricardo's face flushed bright red, a warning of his intention to punch his younger brother.

"I am not weak!"

"Easy, boys!" Rosario stepped between them. "This is exactly what I am referring to! Both of you, stop your constant fighting!"

The sound of a horn blaring interrupted the impending skirmish. With similar expressions of curiosity, the four men watched as the car, followed by a billowing white cloud, raced up the winding drive toward the house.

"Wait here and try not to kill each other while I go see who this is!" Rosario instructed with an arched brow.

Rosario reached the bottom of the hill just as the car stopped at the house. A young man bounced quickly from the driver's seat of the black car covered in white dust.

"Beretta residence?"

"Si," Rosario replied.

The young man removed an envelope from his satchel. Inquisitively, Rosario stared at the sender's address for a long moment. Lost in contemplation, he reached into his pocket for a few coins. The courier paid, Rosario slowly turned toward the house, his eyes locked on the envelope.

When the dust settled from the courier's departure, Rosario opened the missive. Each letter chiseled away at his broad shoulders until they slowly crumbled into a heap. He looked to the sky, mumbled a few words toward the heavens, and sighed.

The three boys watched Rosario intently. Subconsciously, their bodies mimicked him. Their father never showed defeat unless it was something terrible.

"Oh shit!" Ricardo gulped back his fears.

"Come on," Anton stated.

Fear filled their hearts. There was only one thing that could cause such agony.

"Papa! Papa!" Anton, the first to reach him, asked, "What is wrong?"

Rosario's natural olive complexion turned chalky white, and his dark eyes danced in a pool of tears.

"You and Nan make the run to Alessandria," Rosario ordered coldly. "Be home tomorrow, and do not waste time. Do you understand me?"

"Si...Papa." Anton gulped, his heart racing with fear.

"Ricardo, you will take one of the workers with you today. Carlos took Angelina and RJ to the market." Rosario looked down at the letter again. His powerful grip slowly crushed the paper. "They will not be back in time. You must leave now to be finished in time for supper."

"Si, Papa." Ricardo glanced at Anton for an explanation that did not come. His tongue was a barren desert, and he struggled to ask, "Is everything ok?"

"Get your deliveries done. I expect you home by dinner." Rosario patted Ricardo's shoulder but did not make eye contact. In the same lamenting tone, he instructed Anton and Fernando to be careful. "Be swift, but use care."

Rosario hugged his sons and gave Fernando a consolatory smile before walking into the rows of grapes. Slowly, the vines enveloped him, and his body vanished amongst the green foliage.

"What did the letter say?" Ricardo asked.

"He didn't say. Whatever it is, it was not good news," Anton gazed at the green arches that swallowed their father. "Papa only walks through the vines when he is upset."

"He walks them when he is happy..." Fernando said, but Anton and Ricardo's glares shifted his position. "But...you are right. He looks very distressed."

"Ya think!" Ricardo's harshness made Fernando cringe.

"Hey -easy!" Anton held up a hand in Fernando's defense. "He is only trying to be positive. Nan may be right. Maybe it is not the worst. Papa would have gone straight inside to tell Mamma if it were news about Marcus!"

Anton did not believe his own synopsis; he only hoped for it. Deep inside, Anton feared Marcus was dead, and his father struggled to tell the woman he loved she lost a son.

"Now look who is trying to be positive? You don't believe your own bullshit, Anton!" Ricardo loomed over Anton.

"It doesn't matter *what* I think, Ricardo. We will know the truth when Papa is ready to share it! You will probably know tonight. Nan and I have to wait until tomorrow!" Anton met his brother's glare with equal bitterness. Satisfied that his point had been made, he walked away.

"Where are you going?" Ricardo shouted at him.

"To get our lunch pail." Anton pointed toward the kitchen. "We need to get on the road, and so do you!"

Ricardo and Fernando continued to discuss their concerns while Anton hustled up the steps to the kitchen. Anton opened the door to find his mother, Sofia, happily fixing breakfast.

"Good morning, Mamma!"

He kissed his mother's cheek, then snatched a chunk of cantaloupe from the mound on her right. "How is the most beautiful mother in the world?"

"I am well," Sofia replied, shooing him away from the pile of cantaloupe. "What do you want?"

"Whatever could you mean?" Anton teased, snatching another bite.

"You only flatter when you want something!"

Assuming her usual interrogation pose, left hand on her hip, arched brow, the blade's tip pointed at Anton, Sofia asked, "What do you want?"

"Ok. You caught me, Mamma!" Anton held up both hands. "Could Nan and I have some meat and cheese for the trip? We need to leave for Alessandria."

Though her tone was harsh, a smile peeked out the corner of her lip as she continued to harass Anton.

"Looking like that?"

"We will wash up at the barn before we leave. We wouldn't want to make a mess in my mother's washroom!"

"Blah!" Sofia scoffed in disbelief. "How long will you be gone?"

"We should be home tomorrow afternoon." Anton maintained a look of adoration for his mother, knowing her bravado was a ruse to extract more love.

Sofia's eyebrow remained arched for a moment before the smile that begged to be free spread across her face.

"Aren't you charming!"

"I get it from you."

Anton planted a peck on her cheek again and stole another bite of cantaloupe.

"Bring me your lunch pail," Sofia ordered with a sweet smile.

She hummed a little tune while filling the bucket. She was happy to do things for her children, and feeding them made her the happiest.

Ricardo, with Fernando on his heels, walked into the house. Ricardo greeted Sofia with a kiss, but Fernando only smiled.

"Do you need lunch too, Ricardo?"

"That would be wonderful, Mamma," he replied meekly. "I will be upstairs getting my things ready."

Ricardo walked toward the stairs with his head hung low. He could not effortlessly tuck his feelings away like Anton.

"Are you going to Alessandria, too?"

"No, Mamma, I will be home for dinner."

Sofia spun around and placed a hand on each hip.

"Well, you better be on your best behavior!"

"I promise, Mamma. I will be better tonight," Ricardo replied dutifully.

"Where are the girls?" Anton asked to distract his mother from Ricardo's mood.

"Catalina is over helping Carmella. She is not feeling well," Sofia explained. She looked at Fernando. "Is your mother better this morning?"

"A little. I am sure Cat will revive her. She could bring a ghost back from the dead with her nurturing attention."

Anton glared at Fernando for the untimely analogy.

"Sorry," Fernando mouthed to Anton.

"Si, she could!" Sofia replied, oblivious to the exchange of concern.

Happiness beaming from her smile, Sofia wrapped the

cheese, bread, fruit, and meats in separate napkins. She did the same task hundreds of times and effortlessly arranged everything to fit perfectly into the metal container.

"Did Lina go with her?" Anton asked.

"No. Carlos took Lina and RJ to the market. Since she invited more mouths to Friday's dinner, Papa made her get more food!" Sofia chuckled at the thought. "Like adding mouths to *my* dinner table is a challenge. I always cook enough to feed three families: the mice, the birds, the cats, and any other mouth nearby. If you are hungry when you leave *my* table, it is your own damn fault!"

"Will they be home this afternoon?" Anton asked.

"I am hoping they will be home before lunch."

After placing the last items into the pail, she released a slight harrumph of satisfaction, then handed the masterpiece to Anton.

"Thank you, Mamma, you are the best!"

"Oh! Wait!!"

Sofia scurried to the cabinet in the dining room. She removed a large porcelain container and placed it on the counter. Carefully, she wrapped several items from the jar in a napkin and put them gently on top of the pile of food.

"What is it?" Anton asked.

Sofia's smile, beaming brighter than the sun, said, "Fresh fig cookies!"

Anton's face lit up. He wrapped his arms around her, plucked from the ground, and twirled her in a circle.

"You are better than the best!!!"

Anton ended her flight with a kiss on her cheek.

"Thank you, Signora Beretta," Fernando added, giving her an awkward hug.

"Why do you insist on calling me Signora?" she asked, pinching his cheek.

Sofia had posed the question many times before, but

Fernando never had a suitable answer.

"We better get rolling if we want to get there before dark!" Anton interjected to save his friend.

"Thank you for the food," Fernando mumbled before scurrying out the door behind Anton.

"Did you call her Mamma?" Anton elbowed Fernando's ribs as they walked up the hill.

"No."

"You are such a coward. You know that, right?"

CHAPTER 10

Deep in thought, Rosario wandered through the vines while he waited for the two trucks to leave. It was best his sons found out the news after he had time to console her.

Rosario replayed the words on the missive as he walked back toward the house. It baffled him how one short sentence tore his heart apart. But part of his heartache was for her. Rosario knew he could not hide the news for long. Yet, the thought of crushing her spirits plagued him. In the past few days, she finally returned to being happy and hopeful. He clutched the pain in his chest. He knew how this note would squelch her laughter. Her laughter was the source of joy and love in his home. Without it, a dank gloom hung in the air.

The serenity of the vines comforted him. The branches arched together, and the sunlight glistened between the leaves. It was a majestic cathedral. Rosario stopped to gaze down the symmetric rows that provided him the sanctuary for his soul. This vineyard was his church; the vines were his flock to tend and love. He prayed the *Our Father* as he walked the last few yards of vines. With each step, he let go of the grief the missive would cause.

Three plants from the end of the row, he plucked a bundle of grapes from the vine. The branch released its tension and bounced vigorously with its newfound freedom. Rosario smiled; after his walk through the vines, he also felt relief from the heavy burden on his shoulders.

The plump purple spheres begged to be eaten. Rosario

popped one into his mouth and enjoyed the sweet flavors rolling across his tongue. Next week, they would begin harvesting and crafting yet another superior vintage of wine.

As he reached the house, he tucked the paper into his pocket. He would deal with this after breakfast. For now, he had something sweet to share with an angel.

Rosario stood silently in the doorway, staring at his beautiful wife washing dishes. Her long black hair glistened in the morning sun. His heart still raced at the sight of her. She was the love of his life.

From the moment he first laid eyes on her, he knew she was everything he ever wanted in a woman. And Rosario would stop at nothing to make Sofia his bride.

"Are you going to stand there all morning or come to the table for breakfast?" Sofia teased, glancing over her shoulder.

Sofia's smile still warmed his heart, as it did the first time he saw her at St. Agatha's Church. She was attending Mass with her Uncle Lorenzo on a chilly day in March. A shy and quiet young girl far from her home in Sicily. Brusnengo was a different world than her warm, sunny birthplace.

Lorenzo Veruso, a wealthy and powerful man, inflicted his authority on many, especially Sofia. Lorenzo's immediate distaste for caring for his niece was well-known all over town. His abuse began the day she arrived. Many whispered prayers for the Saints to protect her from his evil. No one dared run to her aid, or they, too, would experience his wrath.

Two days after her sixteenth birthday, Sofia's parents died in a house fire. She, too, would have perished had she not left that morning for the convent. Sofia attended a retreat every month at her mother's behest. Some whispered that Sofia's mother, Chiarra, did not love her and wanted her gone. Such words were lies. In fact, the opposite was true. Out of love. Chiarra used the retreats as a refuge from a drunken father. Sofia enjoyed her peaceful time of prayer and reflection at the convent. With the sisters, she found temperance of the mind and spirit. They provided the love Sofia needed to discover her own beauty, inside and out.

"Your breakfast will get cold." Sofia smiled seductively.

"Breakfast, huh?" Rosario returned her countenance.

"The meal I have been working on all morning. I made your favorite, le tue omelette preferite, con pecorino e saleme," Sofia explained, setting the plate on the table. "I gathered the eggs fresh this morning."

"Sounds delicious!"

Rosario embraced her and nibbled her neck. Sofia giggled.

"Rosario, eat your breakfast, then we can..."

Pulling her in close, he silenced her with a passionate kiss.

"I made your favorite, too. It is hot as well!"

Rosario plucked her up and gently placed her on the long wooden table.

Sofia giggled again. Rosario's passion, even after bearing six children, never abated. He always wanted her. Skinny or plump, he did not care. Her beauty surpassed all women.

"Your breakfast! Do not mess it up! I worked hard on it!"

Rosario reached behind her and picked up the plate so his beautiful bride could lean back without fear of destroying her masterpiece. His eyes fixed on her lovely face, he mocked her.

"This does look perfect!" With his free hand, he raised her skirt. "Si, very delicious! Here, hold this."

He placed the plate on Sophia's belly, flashed her a mischievous grin, then dropped to his knees. Tenderly, he began kissing her ankle, slowly moving up her leg.

"Rosario, stop, stop! We cannot do this here!"

Sofia intended her tone to be that of an emphatic rejection. But his lips tenderly caressing her skin overpowered any fiber of refusal in her body. Her proclamation to stop transformed into moans of exhilaration.

"Oh, Cara Mia!"

Her hand released the plate, and it fell, spilling the hot eggs and fruit onto the table beside her. She arched her back in pleasure, causing the dish to fall to the floor and shatter into several pieces. The crashing sound was a void noise to the lovers' ears. Their desire for each other was the only sound to be heard.

Rosario paused and looked up at her with a smile. "I love my breakfast. It is delicious!"

"Don't stop now!" She commanded breathlessly. "Finish! Finish! You..."

Sofia gasped for air. She collapsed into a puddle, her heart the only thing still able to move.

"Oh, my love, you *do* know how to devour a meal."

"Who says I am done, Bella Mia?" Rosario unbuttoned his trousers and grabbed her hips.

Rosario looked down at the beautiful woman lying in front of him. Sofia unbuttoned her blouse. The silk material fell to her side and revealed the delicate lace bra that accentuated the curves of her breasts. He moved his hand toward her chest. With a lover's grin, she smacked his hand. He smiled at her playfulness. They always had fun together, and their passion was endless. The warmth of her body and supple skin was intoxicating. Breathless, he collapsed against her belly.

"I love breakfast! It is my favorite meal of the day!"

Sofia giggled. "You certainly know how to heat up the kitchen!"

She stroked his hair gently, enjoying the comforting weight of his body on hers.

"Do you remember the first time we met?" Sofia asked.

"Of course, my love. It is a day I will never forget," Rosario said, standing up. He extended his hand to help Sofia. "You were like an angel coming into St Agatha's." He twirled a strand of her hair and gazed into her sparkling brown eyes. "I fell in love the instant I gazed upon your beauty."

"I asked about when we met!"

"Ahhh, you did!" Rosario tucked a strand of hair behind her ear. "But I saw you the first time, weeks before we met. Surely I have told you?" Rosario plucked her off the table and placed her on the cabinet.

"Again?" She asked incredulously.

"No, my love. You are barefoot, and there is glass on the floor. I would not want those precious toes to get cut!"

"Oh my, I didn't notice!" She laughed. "Oops!"

"You were a little busy!" He soaked in her captivating radiance for a moment. "Don't get down. I will clean it up."

"How did I get so lucky?"

"I am the lucky one! You are my everything!" He kissed her hand. His gaze landed on the soft curves of her breasts. "But you should put those away, or there *will* be a round two!"

Sofia looked at her exposed chest. "Well, if you insist!"

"Wait!" He leaned over and ravished them for a second. "Ok, now you can tuck them in." Walking toward the closet, he said, "Magnificent! Si, they are both magnificent!"

Sofia giggled at him, happily sweeping up the glass.

"Tell me the story of the first time you saw me."

Rosario stopped sweeping to hold Sofia's adoring gaze.

"It was March 3, the air was cold, and the ground was still frozen. You were wearing a dark green dress and a matching hat. The black fur of your warmer matched the trim of your gloves and long, hooded coat. Your cheeks were red from the cold, making you look like a porcelain doll. Your perfect skin," he glided his hand across her cheek, "was glowing like an angel from heaven. I watched you walk to the front row of the church. You followed your uncle like a well-trained dog. He barked an order at you, and you immediately obeyed." Rosario kissed her hand, then held it to his heart. "I vowed two things that day: One, I would make you my bride, no matter the cost. And...no one would ever treat you the way your uncle did."

"And you have fulfilled both promises." She gently kissed his forehead. "I saw you that day as well."

"Oh, you did, huh? And what did you think?"

"I thought you needed a haircut and someone to dress you!" She snickered, her legs swinging with delight.

Rosario grabbed her waist and tickled her.

"Stop, stop!" She tried to wiggle out of his reach.

"That is not what you were saying a minute ago."

"Stop, stop!"

"Needed a haircut, huh?" He said, laughing, still poking her sides. "Is that all you thought?"

"And someone to dress you!"

Sofia yelped when his finger found a new spot. He launched into another round of tickling, making her jump and squirm. Another roil of laughter ensued.

"You are a feisty little filly!" Grinning, he stopped the torture and enveloped her in his arms. "But that is what I love about you!"

Winded, she wrapped her legs around him and pulled him in. She ran her hand through his hair and smiled tenderly.

"I saw you in the pew with your untidy hair and turned-up collar. Our eyes met for a brief second. I felt like we were the only two people in the room. Time stopped, and I wished we could be as we are today: together, happy, and in love." She paused and allowed her love to radiate from her eyes before adding, "I thought you were a vision of perfection wrapped in imperfection."

Rosario's eyes welled with tears. "I never knew you even saw me that day."

"Nor I, you." She leaned toward him, and they embraced in another passionate kiss.

CHAPTER 11

Their tender embrace was cut short by the deep honk-honk from a car screaming up the drive. The short toots were immediately followed by a third, long blare that sent the chickens into a frenzy of cackles and squawks.

"Good timing!" Rosario winked at his glowing bride.

"*Very* good!" She glanced out the window. "That is not Carlos. I wonder who it is?"

Rosario plucked her from the counter and placed her away from the broken glass. He swept the shards into a pile.

"Wow! That omelet looked perfect. Sorry to have ruined your delicious breakfast, Bella Mia!"

"Oh, I am not sorry, not in the least!" Sofia giggled. "Darn it!" she exclaimed.

"What is the matter?"

"I miss buttoned my shirt! I hate it when I do that!"

Sofia unbuttoned her shirt, and Rosario watched for a quick peek at her plump treasures. She noticed his eager gaze and laughed at him. Before she could scold him for his glutenous desires for the flesh, a loud boom from a hand pounding on the front door made her jump.

"Rosario, you greet them. I need time to fix my blouse!"

"I think you look ravishing! Or at least as if you were just ravished!" he teased and patted her butt.

"You are so ornery!"

"It's what you love about me!"

"Cara Mia, give yourself credit! It isn't the *only* thing I love about you!"

Sofia finished re-buttoning her shirt, then turned her attention to returning the kitchen to its normal state. During their passionate tryst, Rosario's enthusiasm moved the table several inches. She looked at the heavy table that held her while her husband sent her to a heavenly realm of ecstasy. It was far too heavy for her to move, so she decided it looked fine in its new spot.

"I wonder if anyone will notice?" She chuckled to herself. "Oh well, it looks good to me!"

Sofia ran her hands through her hair and adjusted her skirt and blouse. Once her reflection in the hutch's glass doors reflected a suitable appearance, she joined Rosario.

"Sofia!" Rosario hollered over his shoulder.

"Si!" Sofia replied from behind him.

"Oh! That was fast!"

"Really, I didn't think so," Sofia said with a wink.

Rosario flashed her a playful smile.

"Sofia, this is my friend, Vittorio Fiori, and his son, Maximilianus," Rosario said, beaming with pride. "Vito and I served in the war together."

"It is a pleasure to meet you. Rosario has told me many stories about you." She extended her hand to greet them. "Please come in. May I offer you a cup of espresso and something to eat?"

"That would be wonderful! Grazie!" Vittorio replied, entranced by her charming nature.

"Please make yourselves comfortable while I fix some breakfast. It is my favorite meal to prepare. In fact, some days, I find myself fixing it twice." Sofia said playfully.

"Thank you, Mia Bella."

Once his wife was out of sight, Rosario patted his old friend on the shoulder. Having Vittorio in his home filled him with uncontainable joy.

"Brother. Brother!" Rosario repeated in a happy chant. "My brother!"

They hugged again. This time, Vittorio clapped his hand on Rosario's right cheek. For a brief second, the brothers in arms matched gazes. Vittorio kissed both of Rosario's cheeks.

He was an inch taller and slightly slimmer than Rosario. Evidence that neither had let the past two decades pass by while sitting behind a desk.

Maximilianus stood beside his father, his back straight and his chest broad. His muscular build filled his expensive suit perfectly. His dark hair, chiseled face, and dark eyes reminded Rosario of Vittorio many years ago. However, Maximilianus was at least a head and neck taller, and his body was significantly more muscular.

The young man's eyes constant examination of the surroundings was slightly unnerving. Because he was his oldest friend's son, Rosario tried to take the inquisitive behavior in stride.

"Forgive my son. He has a habit of letting his eyes wander. It is a good habit, one that someday will keep him safe." Vittorio turned to his son. "We are among friends, relax!"

Maximilianus looked around one more time before he sat on the sofa against the wall.

"It is so good to see you again, brother." Rosario sat in the chair near his friend. "Tell me, Vito, what brings you to Italy? I thought you moved to America!"

"Si. Si. we have. We have made a good life there. It is a beautiful country. Beautiful! Of course, nothing matches the beauty of Italy, you know."

Rosario watched his friend smooth his tie against his shirt as he examined the room. It was a habitual motion for Vito, one Rosario had seen often during their service. The memory of Vito as a young man nervously petting his tie brought a glint of happiness to Rosario's eyes. His old friend had not changed, at least not much.

As his friend's eyes took in the lavishness, Rosario realized for the first time how wealthy he must appear with expensive furniture scattered about the room. The hand-carved dark wooden arms of the furniture added a striking elegance to the gold thread woven into the silk upholstery. The walls, freshly painted not a month prior, matched the decorative curtains adorning the window. The crystal dishes and porcelain figurines scattered about the room gave more proof of a healthy financial situation.

"It is a good life in America. You and your lovely bride should visit. Stay awhile. You may decide to move. Although it appears you have done well for yourself here!" Vito commented as he continued to admire the decor.

"I would love to visit, but this is home. My heart is here among these vines."

"I would think it should be among those!" Vito chuckled, nodding toward Sofia, his hands tracing her curves. He winked, and the brothers laughed at the insinuation. "Wow, molta bella! You are a lucky man indeed!"

"She is the love of my life!"

"I can see why."

"So, what brings you to Brusnengo? Your family is from Alessandria, no?"

"Si, they are! How good of you to remember. But this time, we are here on business. You see, my son is in the import-export business," Vito said with a proud smile.

"Good for you!" Rosario still did not understand the purpose of a journey so far from home.

"Don't look so confused, my friend! Wine is a big commodity for his company, and this," Vito's hands gestured, "is the land of Vino. Ehhh!"

"And my vines produce the best! You should take some of my wine to America and make us both wealthy!" Rosario's hearty laugh at his joke echoed around them.

"That is precisely the purpose of our visit." Maximus's deep, rich voice was filled with sincerity. "Please call me Maximus."

The young man's every movement and word conveyed a level of professionalism Rosario had never known.

"You mean, you came all the way from America to do business with me? That seems too good to be true."

"In truth, this trip was an unexpected necessity. We only decided to make the most of it while we were here. I can understand your surprise. If I were in your shoes, I would question the idea, too. Perhaps I can ease your mind if I expound on our intentions."

Maximus possessed a certain charm. Every word, every hand gesture, and the calmness in his eyes set one at ease. He explained how he intended to import wine to America. He made the task seem as simple as watching the sunset. Rosario's head nodded as if he understood every word, but in fact, he was lost in his own thoughts.

"Signor Beretta, my Father, has spoken highly of you for years. We felt we were close enough that we should at least discuss the option of adding your wine to our list of imports. Is this something you would be interested in?"

"I am honored by the gesture. But..." Rosario's tongue went dry, and he became speechless.

The offer came out of nowhere, yet it was an answered prayer. Rosario dreamed of his wine being loved and sought after by people all over the world. He could feel his stomach twist and turn. Dreams and reality do not always mix well.

"Signor Beretta, you look ill. Are you ok?" Maximus asked.

"Um... Maximus," Rosario stuttered as he searched for a response. "Please... a... call me, Rosario."

His mind was turning with questions, fear, and concern. He was at a loss for the right words to convey his thoughts without appearing disrespectful to an old friend.

"Is there something I have said that disturbs you?"

Rosario felt the penetrating gaze of Maximus's eyes. He knew the look. He, too, used the same technique to gather information. To allow your heartbeat to slow while you observe your target. Every detail was cataloged; the pupil's changing dilation, the color fading from the skin, the acceleration of inhalation, and the repetitive twitch of a body part. All of it was registered and weighed. This gift was one of the reasons he became successful at an early age.

Rosario knew part of this skill was innate, yet it needed to be fostered. Although Vito was a bright man, he did not possess such talent. The question of 'who taught him' added to the swirling dialog in his mind. He knew only one other person to possess such a gift, and he was almost certain they had never met, or at least he hoped.

"You are very perceptive," Rosario replied, more to stall than acknowledge Maximus's astuteness.

He and Vito were brothers in the war, but a decade had passed since they last spoke. So why now? Why did a ghost from the past appear unannounced and offer Rosario what he had always wanted? Fear filled Rosario's heart, and his head pounded with questions.

Rosario always feared the day Don Salvatore would find his weak link. Give an order to an unsuspecting friend, perhaps a brother from the past. If Rosario were to accept this dream-come-true without The Don's permission, it could lead him down a path of destruction.

With his heart in his throat, Rosario looked at Vito.

"You are my friend, Vito," he paused. "No! Not just a friend, a *brother*! My *only* brother! We have seen many good times and lived through events that were too terrible to share. We have survived the destruction of so much in this world." Vito's head shook in agreement. "I have a wonderful family; they are my life, and I fear for their safety."

Vito interrupted his friend with a wave of his hand.

"Brother, we do not come to cause you or your wonderful family harm."

"I do not mean to imply such." Rosario sighed. "I am a simple man who is sometimes still afraid of the darkness."

Maximus scooted to the seat's edge and leaned forward.

"I know you struggle to believe me now, but I hope, in time, you will trust us. We come in good faith, and your concern for offending the local Don is... Well... Shall I say, very respectable. It shows me you are a man worthy of doing business with, someone *I* can trust." His soothing tone seemed to ease the tension in the room.

"How did you know *he* is what caused me concern?"

"You are an honorable man, and I am a well-educated one. I understand the ways of business and La Mano Nera... A practice very much alive in America."

Rosario shook his head in understanding. For a moment, he felt foolish. He should have known the Italian ways continued, even in other lands.

"If you accept this proposition, I offer my protection for you and your loved ones. As for Don Salvatore's approval. I can be very persuasive when needed."

Maximus's grin caused a chill to race up Rosario's spine.

"You are a very astute businessman, but how can I be assured my family and I will not pay a heavy price to Don Salvatore? That man's hand reaches a far distance, and he thrives on the chance for a fight."

"Good to note," Maximus replied, rubbing his chin. "Do you know what Maximilianus means?"

"No."

"It means Greatest Adversary. I am not a man to back down because another thinks he ranks above others. We are all created equal. It is what we do with our life that makes us different." Maximus stood and slowly paced the floor, deep in thought. "Don Salvatore is someone with power, and believe me when I say I have done my homework. By that, I mean he already has a vendetta against…"

Rosario held up his hand to silence Maximus. He glanced over his shoulder before he gave Maximus a slight nod of understanding.

"Well, it seems he has the same for a few others in town, and I intend to make friends with those he opposes."

"So, you do not want my wine because it is good. You only desire to squeeze the Don?" Rosario's face became pale at the thought he was to be another toy in a game of kings.

"My apologies!" Maximus professed. "It was not my intention to give you that impression! First, I only know what I am told of your wine, so my opinion of its greatness is irrelevant. Second, I extend my hand in friendship and business because of *who* you are to my father. I understand he owes you a debt of gratitude that could never be repaid."

"His friendship is repayment enough," Rosario affirmed with a pat on Vito's hand.

"You saved my life, Rosario, and took a bullet in the process! How is that shoulder of yours? Does it still ache when the weather shifts?" Vito asked compassionately.

"Like an old barn door needing oil."

"I asked my son to consider your vineyard because I knew your wine is the best. And because I believe in doing business with those you can trust. I trust you more than any friend I have. This was my idea, Rosario. I want you to accept this as a gift from a brother." Vito drew a deep breath and placed his hand on Rosario's shoulder. "How many nights did we lay awake listening to the distant explosions and gunfire?"

"More than I care to remember."

"What did we do to keep our minds sharp? We dreamed of the future. Women, food, what we want our lives to be after… *if* an after ever came." A soft smile pressed Vito's lips. "You know how many times you told me the same dream? I thought you were crazy, thinking it was even possible to sell your wine to the entire world! Now, by God's blessing, I wish to help you achieve that dream! This is your chance, old friend." Vito held his hands open as if presenting a gift. "Please accept my gratitude for your friendship."

"He speaks the truth, Rosario. You present yourself as a gentleman and a worthy business associate."

Rosario stared at Vito. The scar across his throat had faded into the fine lines of an aging man. Capitalizing on an action such as what happened that day seemed dishonorable. Yet, what Vito said was true. This could be his dream-come-true. Every beat of his heart seemed to press against his chest. This opportunity had great potential, but at what cost?

"Perhaps you should discuss this with your lovely bride before you give us an answer," Maximus suggested when Sofia entered the room with a tray of coffee.

Rosario looked at Sofia, her silky hair draped across her shoulder. Their eyes met, and he longed to hear her thoughts.

"That would be appreciated," Rosario replied.

"How long will you gentlemen be in town?" Sofia poured the espresso into three small cups. Handing one to each man, she asked, "Do you have a place to stay?"

"We are in town for the day, Signora. We travel tonight to Bergamo for another business meeting," Maximus replied.

"Ah, such a shame. If you could spare yourselves an evening, we would be honored to have you as our guests for dinner." Sofia smiled sweetly, trying her best to encourage the men to accept the offer.

Rosario wrapped his hand around hers and gently squeezed, recognizing the scheming wheels turning in her mind. Sofia was always on the lookout for a suitable match for her daughters. Maximus was well-educated, charming, and incredibly handsome. All qualities Sofia hunted for in a suiter.

If Rosario were honest, Maximus appeared to be a perfect match for Angelina.

"We would love to join you for dinner. Next time we are in town, we will schedule more time here. This was an unexpected visit to Italy, so we are doing our best to make the most of it," Maximus replied.

"Well, I am sorry to hear that. I was looking forward to hearing these two old men tell some tall tales!" Sofia giggled. "Breakfast will be ready in five minutes. Rosario, will you show our guests to the dining room?"

"Si, Bella Mia."

Hypnotized by her grace and beauty, they watched her leave the room like an angel floating away.

"You do not need to give us an answer today. Think about the offer for a few days," Maximus said.

"I appreciate your patience. A day or two to think this over would be helpful. Perhaps over breakfast, you could enlighten me of your ultimate plan for Italy, especially Brusnengo," Rosario jested and winked at Vittorio. "Or at least your plan for Italy's best wines."

Maximus forced a small laugh. His mannerisms and dress made it obvious he was used to being in charge. He made it look natural with his expensive tailored suit, gold watch, stylish cufflinks, and classy wingtip shoes. He exuded he air of a very wealthy man. Rosario understood power and money came hand in hand, no matter where you lived.

"Are you

hungry? My wife is an excellent cook. And our eggs are fresh," Rosario exclaimed, leading them down the wide hallway.

The wall was covered in family photos. As Maximus walked alongside Rosario, he examined the portraits, taking a moment to notice each unique feature on every framed face. Rosario saw his interest and began introducing each person as if they stood before him.

"These are my sons Ricardo, Anton, Rosario, and Marcus," Rosario said as he pointed to each photo. "And these are my two daughters, Angelina and Catalina. All except Marcus, who is serving our country, work with me here. It is wonderful to have them at home. Seeing their smiling faces every day brings joy to my heart!" Rosario gently tapped his chest. "When Sofia and I were young, we spoke of having a home filled with children and eventually grandchildren. God blessed us with six healthy children."

"A fine-looking family," Vito said as he patted Rosario on his back. "Fine looking! Of course, I can tell they all take after their mother! And that is a blessing!" Vito and Rosario roared with laughter.

"You have a beautiful family. What are their ages?"

"Son, he is family. Say what you mean!" Vito patted his son on the back. "You want to know the age of the man's lovely daughters. I see your eyes lingering on those angelic faces," Vito chuckled. "My boy has yet to choose a bride. He approaches thirty, and he refuses to settle down. His mother goes to church daily praying for an angel to be sent from heaven so she may have grandchildren!" Vito placed his hand on his old friend's shoulder and leaned in with a big grin. "Perhaps we should negotiate a wife *and* some wine!"

Maximus's face hardened. He did not share in his father's humor.

"Blah! I see the look you give me, Maximus," Vito said before returning to his friend. "He feels differently about women. He enjoys their company, yes, but none has met his desire for intelligence and grace. Beautiful women fall all over him, but not for his affections. He says they are easy, loose women in search of money. None possess the ability to have an intelligent conversation. So, my son vows not to settle down until a woman stimulates his mind *and* his body. For now, he only enjoys women who can satisfy the latter."

"I have more respect for this man and his daughters than to negotiate a deal like they are a case of wine," Maximus admonished his father.

The distaste the son had for his father's comment was apparent. It lingered in the air like a dense fog. Vito's chin dropped, and he removed his hand from Rosario's shoulder. As Vito turned away, Rosario noticed the shame that flushed his friend's face. In front of a friend, such a verbal attack, especially from his son, would deflate any man.

"You have raised your son well, Vito. He is a respectable man." Rosario wrapped his arm around Vito. "A good man indeed. And he will be a fine choice for any promising woman." Rosario turned to Maximus. "You are a man after my own heart! We feel the same about marriage, Maximus. Perhaps we *will* build a wonderful friendship, just as your father and I have done."

"To answer your question, though, Marcus is twenty-eight. Ricardo is twenty-three, Anton is twenty-one, Rosario is ten, and my daughters, Angelina and Catalina, are nineteen and seventeen."

He paused, watching to see if they reacted to the age range. Both men merely nodded as they examined the details of each child's face.

"Ah, it has been too many years since we have seen each other, ol' friend," Vito mumbled.

It was almost three decades since Vito and Rosario were forced from their families by the draft to serve their nation. For some men, they felt it was unfair to be removed from their ways of life. For others like Vito and Rosario, they believed it was an honor to serve.

They knew the war would bring a better life and more freedom from the Austro-Hungarian influence over their country. Like many, the hopes of an Italian Republic were the ultimate goal. Such a goal is sometimes only achieved with war.

Many brothers in arms lost their lives in the fight for an Italy free of Vienna influence. The Great War and an alliance with the Allies achieved their separation, allowing Italy a permanent seat in the Council of the League of Nations. All were steps toward the long-sought-after Italian Republic. Unfortunately, another war and the removal of the current Fascist regime were required to achieve the desired government.

It was a long road filled with difficulties, loss of life, much sadness, and hardship. Now that it appeared the second war was closer to an end, life gradually returned to a sense of normal. Many businesses could see the tides turning as sales improved. Men returning from service found the loving arms of a woman, perpetuating the creation of new life. Citizens left their homes more often as the fear of a bomb strike trickled into a distant thought. In all, it was progress toward healing the deep wounds caused by the horrors of war.

The sun rose every day, the moon set in the night sky, and the memory of loved ones lost soon would settle further into the distance, allowing the birth of each new soul to bring the joy of life again. It was how the living marched on from war.

"Please have a seat. Sofia will bring in breakfast."

She appeared with a tray of food as if she had been waiting for Rosario's introduction. Sitting at the head of the table with his friends, Rosario watched his talented wife serve the meal. She loved cooking for company. She took pride in every aspect of the meal, especially in the presentation.

Sofia set a plate in front of each of the guests and noted the expression on their faces. She beamed internally when wide eyes of amazement flashed across their faces.

"This looks amazing!" Vito grabbed his fork.

"You have created a masterpiece, Signora Beretta,"

Maximus added with the refined etiquette of royalty. "Thank you for your generous hospitality. I am certain you had other plans for your day. We are grateful for accommodating us on such short notice."

"Some days, when you rise, the wind takes you in a different direction than you planned. I prefer not to resist the shift and am usually well rewarded for it," Sofia replied.

Sofia flashed a devilish grin at her husband. In return, Rosario gave her a seductive smile that made her blush.

Maximus's never-ending sophistication endeared himself even more to Sofia. The more he talked, the more enchanted she became. Though Sofia outwardly remained demure, Rosario knew his bride wished Angelina were home, as did he, but for different reasons. Angelina was his right hand in business. Her input on the opportunity would be invaluable.

"You are very skilled. This is delicious," Vito said between bites.

"So glad you like it!" Sofia replied. "Maximus, tell me what you do for a living. I heard something about importing?"

"That is one of our family businesses."

"Oh! *One*?" Sofia exclaimed. "What are the other ones?"

"We have a printing company, but the import-export business is the most glamorous."

"We have a fine restaurant, too!" Vito added between bites. "But he is right; a printing company is not very exciting."

"God has been good to us," Maximus added.

"What an interesting mix of businesses. But I disagree. I think printing is fascinating! Do you make the newsprint?" Sofia asked before taking a bite of eggs.

"Some."

"What else can you print?"

"If you think about it, almost everything you see has something printed on it; advertisements, theater tickets, receipts, even money must be printed. We have the best equipment, allowing us to print for various clients. We can replicate nearly anything."

"Well, I never thought of it! The things we take for granted. I will be more mindful when I am out and about!" She twirled her fork between her fingers like she was spooling her spaghetti. "You said money. Do you print money, too?"

The directness of the question caused Vito to drop his fork and his chin. Maximus stared at his food. He moved a piece of fruit across his plate in contemplation.

"Signora Beretta." Maximus began, slowly raising his gaze.

"Please, call me Sofia."

"Very well, Sofia. To print money is a dangerous business. Not the process per se, but the nature of having control over something so valuable," Maximus stated firmly. "Typically, I lie to people who ask me something so direct."

"I am sorry. I..."

Sofia's face went pale. Her fork visibly shook from her trembling. Maximus was not her uncle, but his commanding voice hurled her back in time. As a young girl, she asked too many questions about her uncle's work. For her impertinence, he scolded her for an hour. His harsh words berating her into a tiny, terrified mouse. When his tongue was tired of flinging insults, he whipped her like a mule.

Rosario placed his hand on Sofia's and gently stroked it with his thumb. Sofia opened her mouth to apologize again, but Maximus, smiling calmly, explained his business.

Gently, Maximus held up his hand to stop her apology.

"You asked out of pure innocence. You meant no harm. Therefore, you do not need to be embarrassed," Maximus assured her. "Because I know you will not betray us and will keep my business dealings quiet, I will answer you honestly."

"We have a contract to print money for the American government. They have exacting standards in every detail. As I said, we have the best equipment. Thus, we can uphold such standards. It is a profitable arrangement." He paused to sip his espresso. "Of course, we do not discuss this with anyone. It is a dangerous business."

"Oh! I am sorry to pry!" Sofia's face turned bright red.

"It is ok. I would not share the information with you if I thought it was placed in unsafe hands."

With a smile, Maximus raised his cup and winked at Sofia. His genuinely charming effect did nothing to assuage Sofia's embarrassment. From time to time, between stories, Maximus flashed a gentle smile in her direction or made a simple comment to include her in the conversation. It was a valiant attempt to show Sofia he was not upset with her.

When the meal came to a close, Maximus helped her clear the dishes. The two old war buddies lost in the conversation did not notice they were left to themselves, quibbling over details of a story several decades old.

"They will talk all day," she said to Maximus as she smiled at her husband, who was happily enthralled in conversation.

"I know," Maximus replied, removing his cuff links. He rolled up his sleeves and plunged his hands into the water to wash the plates before Sofia had a chance to stop him.

"What are you doing?"

"Helping!" He grinned, picking up a dish. "I shall wash since I know not where to put the dishes when they are dry."

Sofia was speechless. Was this man sincere? Rosario was the only man she ever met who would help wash dishes. At that moment, had she the courage, she would have begged him to stay forever and marry Angelina. Her racing heart flushed her cheeks. Sofia had already overstepped once; she dared not press a second time.

Drying the dishes, she occasionally peered out the window, hopeful for Angelina's return. If Maximus and Angelina met, Sofia could approach the subject of a union at a more suitable time. Sofia would never arrange a marriage for her children since she had experienced such atrocities herself. However, she was not opposed to planting a seed to encourage the desired result.

When the dishes were done, and the kitchen returned to its normal clean state, Maximus interrupted Rosario and Vito's conversation.

"Papa, I hate to interrupt, but we must leave if we wish to make it to Bergamo tonight."

"Ahh, si! I know, my son. Forgive the rambling of an old man," Vito groaned as he pried his stiff body out of the chair. "It has been many years since we last visited, Rosario. Yet we picked up like it was yesterday!"

Vito and Rosario hugged.

"I do hope we can visit again soon, brother!"

Rosario and Sofia walked their guests to the door.

"Can I pack you, gentlemen, any food for the road? You will need to eat along the ride."

Rosario silently chuckled at his wife's attempt to stall their guest for a little longer.

"Your hospitality is beyond words, Signora Beretta!" Maximus tipped his hat to her. "We dare not impose on you any longer."

Not the desired response, a visible sadness washed over Sofia.

"Perhaps we may be allowed to return soon and enjoy another wonderful meal," Maximus added.

"Only if I get a hug before you leave," Sofia smiled. "You are family, and family never leaves without a proper hug!"

CHAPTER 12

Angelina's stomach growled. The trip to the market had made her hungry, as did the tray of freshly made cannoli on her lap. The delicate pastries dusted with a blanket of snow-white powdered sugar, and the candied orange peel in each end completed the vision of perfection. She wanted to eat one on the ride home but knew the repercussions. Her impromptu invitation to Giorgio and Mario for dinner had already incited a long-winded tongue-lashing from her mother.

"We are already hosting guests tonight!" Angelina recalled her mother's response to Giorgio and Mario attending dinner. "We are not a restaurant for everyone to dine for free! Do you think we are so wealthy we can feed every soul who crosses our threshold?"

Sofia slammed the dishes, making the incident more than it really was. Carmella had been ill for several days, and all the household duties had been left for Sofia to tackle. She was exhausted, and the idea of another feast had overwhelmed Angelina's mother.

"I am sorry, Mamma, I was only trying to capture the sale. They were going to leave, and I wasn't sure they would return without a worthy cause," Angelina apologized.

"Our wine is good. It is better than good! If they are not willing to buy it, then a meal will not change their minds. Neither will a wiggle of your hips!"

The acid on her mother's tongue stung Angelina's heart. She did not flirt as hard as everyone accused her, and her mother knew it. Sofia had gone too far and apologized instantly. But the wound was already made. Angelina could not hide her look of defeat.

"I am sorry, Bella, I did not mean that! You do not wiggle your hips." Sofia wrapped her arms around Angelina. "My little angel. Your beauty is more than an exterior wall around you. There is an inner beauty, too. Any man would be a fool to refuse you!" Sofia cupped Angelina's cheeks. "And whoever wins your heart will be the luckiest man alive! God bless him, though. He will never defeat you in an argument or squelch your desire. You have the gift to charm anyone when you are set to action. Especially when selling our wine! Truly, no one stands a chance against you."

"I am sorry I invited them without asking, Mamma."

"It will be fine. Carmella should be well by then. But you will go to the market for me and pick up the extra food we need," Sofia replied with a gentle smile.

Angelina's stomach growled, returning her to the present moment. She gazed down at her little brother sitting silently next to her. The jostle of the car gently soothed him. His head was heavy as he struggled against the lure of slumber.

"Are you sleepy, RJ?"

"No, I'm looking out the window." He rubbed his eyes.

"What were you looking at?"

"I am watching for the planes to come over." He sat up.

"What planes?"

"The warplanes! I am going to be a fighter pilot when I grow up!" His eyes widened at the prospect.

"Why?"

"I want to see the world from up there!"

"Won't you be afraid of falling?"

"No!" RJ's eyes widened in disbelief at his intelligent sister's ridiculous question. "You don't fall when you are in a plane! You soar through the clouds and can see a thousand miles away. Life is different up there. Real quiet, too! Well, except for the engine. But you get used to that."

His enthusiasm was contagious. Angelina could not help but smile at his vivid description.

"How do you know so much about planes?"

"I read about them. One time, when I was with Papa at the bookstore, I saw pictures of what the ground looks like from up there. It is beautiful!"

"I think I would be afraid."

"When we get home, I will take you to the top of the house. You can see for miles up there. You will see there is nothing to be afraid of! I bet after that, you will want to fly like a bird, too!"

He was on the edge of his seat, his big brown eyes wide with excitement. The catnap that approached moments ago was banished from his thoughts.

"Oh, RJ!" she laughed.

Her little brother had the best imagination. He could spin a tale that would make you laugh or cry. The words spilled off his tongue as if the story was one he lived. His animated facial expressions and lively hands illustrated the story. Your mind had no trouble envisioning every detail.

"Hey, who is that?" RJ asked.

He pointed to the expensive, shiny car heading down the drive toward them. The sunlight shimmering off the polished black hood.

"I don't know. Do you, Carlos?"

"No. I have never seen that car before," Carlos replied, inspecting the passengers as they passed. "I don't recognize their faces either."

"They sure are rich!" RJ exclaimed, peering out the back window.

"RJ! That is improper to comment on things like that." Angelina admonished him.

"He's right, Lina. That is an expensive automobile! Not even Don Salvatore drives in such luxury!"

"Who do you think it is, Carlos?" Angelina asked.

"I do not know!"

Sofia and Rosario were still outside, watching their guest drive off when Carlos approached the house.

"I knew it! A few more seconds..." Sofia whined.

"Who was that?" Angelina asked, pointing at the plume of dust settling on the drive.

"I wish you were home thirty minutes ago." Sofia's mischievous grin broadened. "You would have fallen in love."

Angelina rolled her eyes and handed her the cannoli box.

"Did you get everything?" Sofia asked.

"Si, Mamma."

"Papa, who was the..."

"Carlos, may I have a word with you?" Rosario asked, ignoring his daughter's question.

Angelina watched as they walked up the hill toward the wine cellar. She was curious about the mysterious guest, but her father completely ignoring her was far more perplexing. It was unlike him not to at least greet her with a kiss.

"Mamma, what is wrong with Papa?"

"Nothing is the matter with him!" Still smiling from her exhilarating morning, Sofia hummed as she unpacked the items from the market. "Are you going to help or stand there looking like a ghost?"

"Who were the rich people, Mamma?" RJ asked as he carried in the last sack.

"They are Papa's old friends. Well, *one* was old. He served with your Papa in the war. The younger man, however, was his son. He is *very* handsome!" Sofia grinned at Angelina.

"They were rich, right, Mamma?

"Very rich!" She smiled at her youngest child and kissed him on his forehead.

"Told you!" He stuck his tongue out.

"Why did they come by?" Angelina ignored her mother's insinuating remarks and her brother's tongue.

"To see your father. They are in town for a few days and decided to stop for a quick visit." Sofia kissed her son's head again. "RJ, you best get started on your chores!"

The vivacious boy stuck his arms out and roared like a plane as he flew outside. The youthful display made Angelina and Sofia chuckle.

"Mamma, did you know they were coming?"

"No. I would not have sent you to the market."

"Is it not odd for someone to make a surprise visit?"

"I suppose," Sofia replied dismissively and returned to her cooking. Her mood was too good to worry about civilities. "They were charming. You would have liked the son." She grinned. "And *he* would have loved you!"

"Oh, Mamma!" Angelina rolled her eyes.

"What? He is handsome, charming, and intelligent. I think he would be perfect for my little Angel-lina." Sofia said, pinching her cheek.

"Don't let the others hear you say that! They think Nan is a perfect match."

"He is a good choice, but this man is a much better match."

"Well, since he doesn't seem to have the manners to schedule a visit, I guess we will never know!" Angelina quipped as she crushed several cloves of garlic for the sauce her mother was cooking.

"I am not so sure about that. They may stop by on their way back to Alessandria in a few days."

When Carlos and Rosario returned, they spoke for a moment on the steps to the kitchen. Rosario nodded several times before issuing his response and dismissing Carlos. Rosario straightened his shirt and entered the house alone.

"Angelina," he said gently. "Sofia, I need both of you to

please sit for a minute." He ushered them over to the table, placing them side-by-side.

"What is the matter, Papa?"

"I received this telegram this morning."

"You did not tell me about any telegram!" Enraged, Sofia tried to snatch the paper. "What does it say?"

Rosario held it out of reach. "I will tell you, but please be patient." He unfolded the note, rereading every word.

"Is it about Marcus?" Tears formed in Sofia's eyes. She grabbed her chest as the enormous sorrow seized her lungs. "How...could you hold this from me! You—"

"Sofia! Remain calm. I am trying to convey this as best as possible," Rosario insisted. "I understand your fear for your son's life, but this is not about Marcus!"

Sofia's lungs, free of the constricting horror, filled with air.

"Then what is it, Papa?"

"It is from the men who came by the other day. They are canceling their dinner plans with us this evening."

Angelina, shocked, tried to still her trembling hands. The sting of rejection pierced her heart, but the idea she failed to capture the sale was mortifying. Her mistakes haunted her. She steadied her feelings before looking at her father.

"Does it say why?"

"No, Bella. I am so sorry. I know you were counting on them coming tonight. This has to be hard for you to hear."

"It is unfortunate." Angelina stated dryly.

Though she pretended to be unmoved, a pinkness flushed her cheeks. She made a fundamental error. She overplayed her hand and was too eager, costing them the sale.

"It was my fault. I am sorry, Papa."

"Angelina, do not blame yourself." Sofia placed her hand on her daughter's thigh.

"Do not worry, Principessa. They seemed a little... I don't know... Perhaps they are untrustworthy," Rosario reasoned.

With an expressionless stare, Angelina listened as her parents did their best to console her. She was, however, a perfectionist. Life requires structured and measured actions, not reactions. When these rules were ignored, disaster always followed.

"Then it is for the best," Angelina mumbled. "What may I do to help you with dinner, Mamma? I know you have been busy all morning."

"Nothing, Bella. I will not fix everything as planned."

Angelina pushed away from the table and stood to leave.

"Where are you going?" Sofia asked.

"For a walk. I could not go this morning."

Angelina grabbed her wide-brimmed sun hat off the hook and turned to open the door. If flung open before she touched the handle. Catalina rushed in, nearly knocking Angelina out.

"Oops! Sorry…Lina… You are pale. Are you ok?"

"Fine, just going for my walk."

As she walked out the door, Angelina heard her parents' exchange of concern.

"Do you think she will be ok?" Sofia worried.

"She will be fine. I took the news the same. A walk through the vines seemed to soothe my spirits, too. Almost as much as my breakfast!"

CHAPTER 13

"It is your move," Don Salvatore gulped the wine. "Mmm. This is good! Where is it from?"

"The Beretta vineyards." Antonio eyed the chessboard.

"I like this red. It has a bold flavor." The Don took another swig, this time allowing the notes to roll across his tongue. "What progress have we made with acquiring that property?"

He knew no progress had been made but wanted to goad his minion into a fight. The chess match was fun, but he desired a more tantalizing battle to stimulate his mind.

"He refused the last three buyers," Antonio said calmly.

"I hear he grows wealthier. Too wealthy! I will not have him usurp me! Men with money become hungry for power. I am the *only* power in this region!" Don Salvatore growled, slamming his wineglass on the table. The sloshing red liquid splattered onto his hand. He snarled at the mess for a moment before wiping it up.

"Word around town is..." Antonio paused to move a chess piece. He held his hand on it, eyeing the board. Secure in the move, he said, "He has no intention of selling."

The Don inwardly scoffed at Antonio's stupid move. Without a thought, he took Antonio's knight. The action was driven by retaliation toward the subject rather than strategy.

"Perhaps we should give him a reason!"

"What do you have in mind?" Antonio pulled the slender white stick from the half-empty packet. He tapped the end of the cigarette against the package. A devilish grin emerged with anticipation of another job.

"You can wipe that look off your face. I have a plan that does not involve you! And put that shit away. Disgusting habit! I hate breathing your nasty air."

Antonio tried to hide his displeasure but was unsuccessful.

"Stop pouting like a little girl! You'll have your turn. I need Rosario Beretta alive." The Don cut a piece of cheese from the brick and slapped it on a chunk of bread. He smiled. "At least, for now, I need his heart to beat. But do not worry; you will see your part soon enough."

Don Salvatore's hand firmly gripped his sandwich, and he waved his hand for Antonio to move.

"What is your plan?"

Typically, The Don would never leave his right hand in the dark, but things had changed. Antonio had grown too strong-willed. He spoke as if he were The Don and became feared as much. But his recent disgrace, allowing a weak, pregnant woman to outwit The Don's right hand, was unacceptable!

"You have been quiet the past few months. Hardly a peep since our visitors! Have you turned shy on me, Antonio?"

"You have not requested my services in the matter."

"True." He took one of Antonio's pawns. "Check."

The Don's minion visibly struggled to decipher his next move. A moment too delicious to pass up. He enjoyed knocking his hired help back into place. This minion needed to understand he could not usurp his master at work or chess. Don Salvatore took advantage of Antonio's weakness. Focusing on more than one thing at a time was tough for him. The Don, however, thrived at manipulating multiple moving parts simultaneously. A rare gift, he knew, but one he rarely did *not* use.

Antonio moved his king out of the line of fire.

"Well?" The Don prodded him. "Maybe you have no opinions on the matter?"

"I have an opinion."

"That is nothing new!" The Don savored some wine. "Well, speak your mind."

"I do not trust them. The younger man is uncontrollable. He does not understand his place."

"Like you?" The Don cackled, enjoying the chance to antagonize Antonio with a verbal smack.

"He does not respect you and only looks to his own gain. The older man is more respectful. However, he is not from around here. He could easily pack up and leave rather than be controlled."

"Ah! But he would leave behind a profitable business, no? Which could be a fair price for his exit?"

"One that requires skill and..." Antonio paused.

"And?" Salivating, he leaned in close, his breath heavy from the wine and sharp cheese. He had Antonio trapped.

"And we do not have someone to take his place."

"There is always someone to take *your* place." Cackling, The Don leaned back. It was his turn to move, but he lingered more on his thoughts than the game. "I have wanted that vineyard for a long time!"

"How would you like me to get it?"

"It will not be you. I need your face to be a ghost for now. Your turn will come if our new young friend fails. But let us hope he is better than you!"

"You send a stranger to do your bidding?" Antonio's temper bubbled up his throat, forcing his voice to crack.

The Don was thrilled he finally triggered Antonio's temper. He pretended to contemplate the situation, intentionally making Antonio suffer in his own stew of curiosity. He finished his cheese sandwich and drained his glass. Grinning, he waggled it in his minion's face to refill.

"He is a man with a large family, no?"

"Si. Four sons, two daughters."

"That is a man who has much to lose. Si, many precious things." Don Salvatore played with his chin while he dreamed of his moment to squish a bug that had grown fat. "You are fat because I am patient."

"Signore?"

"Have the two new businessmen approached him?"

Antonio nodded.

"Watch them, but do not engage with these men, only observe. Their deaths have consequences that would be... less than desirable!"

Antonio's chin dropped. "Si, Signore."

"Must you pout like a bitch! I know you prefer more gruesome jobs than—"

"These pussy-ass surveillance assignments?"

"Mind your place, *boy!*" Don Salvatore snarled and held Antonio's gaze for a moment. "Have Bruno monitor the Beretta family and their workers. I want to know everything about them. Tell him to listen outside their windows. Tell that big ogre to become a fly on the walls of that home! Sleep among the vines if he must, but I want details. I even want to know when Rosario Beretta takes a shit!"

"Si, Signore."

Smiling into the distance, his eyes danced as the vision of his plan unfolded in his mind.

"In the meantime, I will work on acquiring the ownership of the vineyard! A birdie has revealed a secret that Rosario's wife does not know." Don Salvatore curled his fat fingers into a fist. "He will sell me that vineyard, or I will take *it! It* and *everything* he loves!"

The Don cackled for a moment before moving his queen five squares across from Antonio's king.

"Checkmate!" Don Salvatore gloated before releasing a burst of triumphant laughter that echoed around the room.

CHAPTER 14

The crisp autumn air settled across the rolling hills, keeping the workers cool as they picked the grapes. Harvest was in full swing at Beretta Vineyards. Dozens of extra hands were hired to work from sunup to sundown to ensure all the grapes were collected. It took weeks of long, grueling days. But on the final day, after the last bundle of grapes was plucked, they would celebrate with food, wine, and music. A fabulous party to erase the memory of the aches, cuts, and bruises collected during the long days.

"Angelina! Come quick!" Rosario yelled across the rows of vines.

Her face, splattered with dirt, was flushed red from hours of exertion. Several strands of her long black hair had escaped the burgundy ribbon on the back of her head. The locks not plastered to her neck and brow whipped wildly in the breeze.

"What is it, Papa?" Angelina asked, wiping her forehead with a rag stained with purple splotches.

"We did not lose the sale!" Rosario beamed.

"What do you mean?"

"Mario Giovannese sent a telegram. They would like to come for dinner one night at the end of the month!"

"Why wait so long?!"

"Oh, Angelina, have some patience for once. These men travel. Look, it comes from Bergamo." Rosario showed her the telegram. "They wish to finish our business discussion upon their return!"

"That is wonderful news, Papa!"

Rosario scrunched his brow for a moment as he gazed at the telegram.

"What is the matter?"

"Nothing, Bella. Nothing! I will send a reply with the courier now. Keep the men moving. I will return directly."

Rosario kissed his daughter's dirt-smeared forehead before hustling back to the house.

Angelina laughed. She had not seen her father attempt to run for a long time. The years of toiling in the soil had given him arthritis in his knees and wrists, though no one would ever know how much he ached. He never complained.

"Why is Papa running?" Anton asked Angelina.

"I don't think you can call that running. That is more of a trot." She giggled. "He is excited. The buyers, the father and son, have requested another meeting. They wish to conclude business and purchase our wine."

"I didn't think Papa liked them because of their type of business?" Anton asked.

"He didn't! Neither do I, but business is business. They want our wine, and the customer gets what they want!"

****

It took three weeks to complete the harvest. The crop was significantly larger than the previous year, and so was the party. After the well-fed and exhausted seasonal workers left, the Beretta family continued their long days of work. To make wine, picking the grapes was only one step of many.

The family was tired, but there was no time for rest. Mario and Giorgio were coming for dinner, and Sofia had planned an extravagant meal.

After a long day stringing the grapes, Angelina headed for the kitchen to help Sofia and Carmella prepare the meal.

"Don't you want to shower before our guests get here?" Carmella stopped Angelina.

When Carmella calmly asked a question, it was more of a sugar-coated command. The plump woman had a nurturing mother's auro, but her expression left no room for argument.

"I will, but I thought I would at least set the table before I head upstairs," Angelina said, picking up the plates.

"You need a hot bath and a nap!" Carmella snapped as she pulled the plates from Angelina's hands. "You are not allowed to push yourself anymore!"

Angelina was grateful Carmella did not take no for an answer. Her body desired the warmth of the bathwater surrounding her like a loving hug.

"She is right, Lina." Sofia agreed. "Go rest before dinner. Catalina should be finished getting ready. She can help us."

Angelina pulled herself up the staircase. Her legs ached from the long hours of arduous labor. Though her body was done working, her mind was busy wondering how Catalina could be ready for dinner. As far as Angelina knew, no one had quit until Rosario dismissed them ten minutes ago. When Angelina reached the top of the stairs, her temper flared. Coming from Catalina's room was a cheerful tune.

"Cat, why are you singing?"

Catalina, obviously well-rested, was wearing her best dress. Her hair was perfectly adorned atop her head as if she were going to the opera. With her makeup and nails perfectly groomed, she looked stunning.

"And why are you all dressed up?"

"We have guests coming tonight, remember? I wanted to look my best." Catalina blotted her lipstick with a tissue.

"Well, you look better than that! When did you come in?"

"About an hour ago. Maybe more." Catalina admired her hair momentarily, then checked her makeup to ensure its perfection. "You can stop trying to ruin my mood. You should save your energy for getting cleaned up. You look dreadful! Unless you plan to lose the sale twice!"

Angelina's brow furrowed.

"Are you done primping? Mamma needs help."

She was exhausted but gladly spent what little energy she had to spit acid-laced words at her lazy sister.

"If you would like, I can come up later to fix your hair?"

The thought of Catalina poking her head with hairpins made Angelina's head hurt like her body.

"We shall see. At this point, I just want to go to bed and wake up next spring."

"Suit yourself!" Catalina smiled and floated down the stairs, taking her soft singing with her.

Angelina sank into the tub of warm water, leaned her head back, and closed her eyes. The fragrant rose oil filled her nose while the aches from her laborious day faded. She wished she could relax there for hours, but the water would grow cold. Besides, their company would arrive long before she had her fill of the refreshing soak. She allowed herself a few more minutes of luxury, then reluctantly pushed her mind back into work mode. She mechanically washed her hair and body. She finished scrubbing the dirt and grime from her skin and pulled her body from the tub. Ignoring the lingering aches, Angelina dried herself and wrapped the soft cotton towel around her body. She sat in front of the mirror and gazed at her drained reflection.

"You are strong. You are confident. You are beautiful."

She removed the brush from the drawer and pulled it through the long black strands while repeating the mantra. The past three weeks of labor, from sunrise to sunset, had left both her mind and body numb. Barely able to muster the energy for basic grooming, every movement she made was done without thought.

"Angelina, are you almost done?" Anton asked through the

door, his voice exhausted as well.

"Neither of us has the energy to be anything but *done*."

"That is the truth!"

"I will be out soon."

"Knock on my door when you finish." Anton yawned.

Angelina finished the last touches of her makeup and looked at her hair, still weighted by the water. It would be an hour before it was close to dry. She would have to wait to make anything of it. If there was any time left before the guests arrived, maybe Catalina could work her artistic magic. But for now, Angelina did not care.

"I am what I am. They can take it or leave it. Besides, the customers buy the wine because it is good, not for my looks!"

"Anton, you awake?"

"Barely." He opened the door and yawned. "You ok, Sis?"

"Exhausted, like you."

"Hang in there. You will be spectacular, as always. If I know my sister, and I do." He cupped her chin. "You will have them eating out of your hand before the main course!"

He smiled and kissed her forehead.

"Thank you, Anton. I think I will lie down for a bit. Will you wake me if I am not up in thirty minutes?"

"Sure. Get some rest."

Angelina collapsed onto her bed and closed her eyes. In seconds, she slipped into a peaceful slumber. But her sleep was abruptly interrupted by a fist pounding on her door. She groaned her displeasure at the intrusion.

"Can I not sleep for five minutes!" Angelina grumbled.

"Lina, Lina!" Anton hollered through the wooden door.

"Huh? What?"

"Lina, our guests are coming up the drive!"

Her heart and head pounding at the same tempo, Angelina pried herself from her mattress.

"How long was I asleep?" Angelina moaned, trying to pull

her mind from her slumber.

"About an hour, maybe longer. I am sorry, Lina. Mamma needed my help, and I forgot!"

"Alright. Alright, I will hurry!" Angelina wanted to scream at him, but her mind was not awake enough to articulate a single thought, much less a lecture.

"I brought you an espresso!"

Angelina flung open the door. Instantly, her nose drew in the soothing aroma wafting from the small white cup in Anton's hand. The piping hot black gold made her smile almost as much as her brother's charming grin.

"Will you forgive me?" He offered her the cup as a token of his apology.

"Of course!" How could she be mad at him? After all, he was her favorite brother. Angelina inhaled the steam coming from the cup and released her tension with a happy sigh. "I will be down in a few minutes." Angelina took a small sip of the heavenly nectar and gave her brother a sweet smile of gratitude. "Thank you!"

Luckily, her makeup had not smudged during her nap, and her hair was dry enough for her to make it look almost presentable.

"It won't be as good as Catalina's masterpiece, but I will have to do my best," Angelina told her reflection. She brushed out the tangles, made a few small braids and pinned them to the back of her head.

"That looks... lovely...? Oh! Who am I kidding? It looks pathetic! Well, at least I didn't suffer a dozen pinpricks in the process!"

She finished the last sip of espresso, drew a deep breath, and told her reflection.

"It's time to shine!"

The sound of laughter and merriment wafted up from the dining area. But it was her sister's playful laughter that echoed the loudest. Angelina rolled her eyes. It finally donned on her; Catalina has a crush on Giorgio. The inflection in her voice made it clear she was flirting with him. In her heart, Angelina wished her sister had better taste in men. Yes, the man was handsome and charming, but something about him unsettled her—something besides the Giovannese business model. Throughout the evening, Angelina hoped to discover why Giorgio made her quiver.

That night, for once, Catalina was center stage. She was by far the prettiest woman in the room. Her hair and dress were even more elegant than Sofia's. Her beauty had everyone's adoration. Everyone except Giorgio, who only had eyes for Angelina.

"You look lovely tonight," Giorgio whispered to her.

"Thank you."

She maintained a professional tone and was cautious not to seem flirtatious. Especially since she caught his eyes undressing her several times. His behavior intensified her uncomfortable feelings about him.

"How was the harvest?"

"Good."

"Do you help them?"

Giorgio pointed toward her brothers on the opposite side of the room. Ricardo and Anton were chatting and laughing together. A sign they had already overindulged in drinking the wine. The atmosphere was more like a party celebrating a special occasion than a simple business dinner.

"We all help in every step of the production of our wine." Angelina arched her brow at his offensive tone.

"But surely they do not make you lift the crates and spend the long hours in the sun cutting the fruit from the vine?"

Her disgust for him rose to a boil. She was miffed by his insinuation of being a slave to the male master.

"Can you not see my skin is just as brown as theirs? I work

as they work, but not because someone *makes* me."

"You are a woman. You should be cared for, not made to break your back with man's work." Giorgio puffed his chest. His attempt to be gallant sounded chauvinistic.

"I disagree!" Angelina huffed and walked away.

She did not look back to see Giorgio's reaction to her comment. She did not care, at least not much. She hoped her acidic attitude toward him would not cost them the sale.

"Dinner is ready!" Sofia announced with open arms.

The hungry souls migrated into the dining room. The feast on the table would cause even a full man to salivate.

Giorgio pulled back the chair next to him for Angelina. She looked around the room for Catalina. Reluctantly, she gave him a half-smile and sat down. After everyone was seated at the table, Catalina appeared with a basket of warm bread. Two seats up and across from Giorgio was the only empty chair. Catalina was visibly devastated. The entire evening, Catalina had been doing her best to impress Giorgio. Now, she could only watch him from a distance. Angelina would gladly trade places with her sister. However, it was a direct invitation to sit next to him. Angelina needed to play the role of a gracious host.

Rosario assisted Sofia with her chair and gently kissed her.

"Thank you for this lovely feast, Bella Mia!"

"Catalina was most helpful," Sofia smiled at her daughter.

"It was my pleasure, Mamma. You know how I love to cook."

"And you are very good at it, too!"

Rosario extended his glass to add to the compliment. He eyed the two women who, by their staged comments, were up to something.

"It smells delicious," Mario salivated.

"Please eat up!" Sofia beamed after reciting a short blessing. "It will not get any warmer!"

Each person picked up a dish, taking a portion before passing it down. Platters of sliced meats and cheese, bowls of fresh vegetables tossed in garlic-infused olive oil, steaming dishes of pasta, bowls of olive salad, and baskets of bread were passed until everyone had an overflowing plate.

Between bites, the conversation varied from politics to war to weather. Gradually, it meandered to business. Angelina could not hear Rosario and Mario's discussion with Giorgio's incessant yapping. She tried to keep the mood light with a nod or smile. Inside, however, she screamed at him for being such a self-absorbed jerk.

"My father and I have traveled all over Europe, stayed at the finest hotels, eaten at the best restaurants," Giorgio bragged. "What is your favorite food?"

"What do you mean?" Angelina asked while thinking. *Was there any other food than what we are eating now?*

"Well, have you enjoyed any food other than Italian?"

"Italian food is delicious. I need not seek any other."

She kept her eyes on her plate, silently praying he would choke on a piece of meat.

"Ah! You should venture out. Experience life!"

Angelina rolled her eyes. She was the one in danger of choking...on his expanding ego.

"Sure, I will get to that next week."

"Haha! You have a sense of humor! That is amusing," Giorgio chuckled before shoveling pasta into his mouth.

"Glad to entertain."

Angelina wished her sister had not insisted on playing the good little housewife. Catalina could have situated herself next to this arrogant beast. At least she would have enjoyed his boastful stories of conquering the world.

"You are an interesting woman. You prefer the labors of the outdoors while your sister works on her womanly charms and cooking. Are you sure the two of you are related?"

"Quite!"

She was starving before the meal began, but Giorgio's obnoxious voice soured her stomach. She only forced food into her mouth to prevent a rude retort to his chauvinism.

Giorgio took the liberty of picking up Angelina's hand.

"Your hands are rough. You should care for them better."

She quickly retrieved it, drawing a glare of disapproval from Rosario. She gulped down her pride and lowered her head in submission to her father. She had screwed up this deal once and would not repeat her mistake.

Anton, tortured by Giorgio's hot air, whispered to Angelina. "Are you ok?"

She nodded.

He leaned over to pick up his accidentally dropped napkin.

"Try to be your usual charming self. You do the talking so that pompous ass can't!"

Angelina giggled for a moment. Her brother was so wise, and his plan was worth trying. She smiled at him in gratitude.

"Giorgio, have you traveled all over Europe? I bet you have seen some really amazing sights. Oh, and the people must be interesting," Angelina said, babbling. "I think watching people is very entertaining. Seeing who is with whom and wondering how they met? The market is a great place to watch people. It is amazing how some of the oddest couples are walking about. A tall, thin man with a short, fat woman. Or a dark-haired man with a redheaded woman. It is all so fascinating!"

Angelina chatted on and on about much of nothing for nearly five minutes before she paused, conveniently at the moment Giorgio had a mouth full of food.

Anton chuckled under his breath.

"That's my Sis. Now, maybe I can enjoy my dinner!"

Ricardo, seated directly across from Angelina, waited for Giorgio to look in another direction to mouth a 'thank you' to Anton. He, too, was another soul disgusted by the blowhard.

Rosario gave Angelina a slight nod of approval for her recovery of spirits. She returned the nod and continued to purge her nonsensical thoughts. Giorgio now played the part of a bored listener, only nodding and smiling, looking for a way out of his prison.

Catalina, however, was as unhappy as Giorgio. Her gaze fell on him longingly many times. It was apparent she wished she were the one carrying on a conversation with the handsome guest. Catalina tried to chime in, but Angelina refused to relinquish the conversation. She continued chattering over her sister's comment, earning her a dirty look. She felt terrible for Cat but did not want Giorgio to spew his rubbish.

As the meal drew to a close, Angelina tired of her banter. She picked up several dirty dishes from the table and sweetly excused herself.

"It was nice to visit with you, Giorgio. Please excuse me. I have women's work to tend to." She added a devilish grin to her acidic tone, ensuring he did not miss her displeasure with his chauvinism.

Giorgio opened his mouth. Angelina eagerly awaited his eloquent apology. She was quickly disappointed.

Giorgio, puffing his chest, said, "Indeed you do. It was an interesting visit, but I must discuss business with the men."

He pushed his dish aside and waved as if commanding her to remove it so he had room to think. Angelina picked up the dish and envisioned smashing it across his head. Her face must have given evidence of her thoughts because her father gave her another disapproving look. She smiled at him and walked into the kitchen, where she stayed for thirty minutes, taking her aggression out on the dirty dishes.

"Angelina!" Rosario called.

Angelina returned to the dining room, drying a plate with a yellow dishtowel. "Si, Papa?"

"Please bring in the wine for tasting?"

Angelina carried a tray with three bottles of wine and nine wine glasses. Out of habit, she explained the flavors of each wine as she opened the bottle and poured. Her words painted a captivating picture that entranced Giorgio and Mario. The details of each bottle's unique characteristics flowed from her lips like poetry. This was what she loved about being a winemaker's daughter. *This* was the moment of the sale she loved most of all.

Rosario relaxed back in his chair while his golden child turned the men into putty. Who would not buy from this remarkable young woman? Angelina's charisma and intelligence made her shine brighter than a simple vintner's daughter. She was a professional businesswoman, versed in every aspect of making wine. No man could deny her skills.

After each wine had been tasted, Angelina stepped back from the table and went quiet. This point of the sale was the most challenging, waiting. She called it the void—the silent pause that bridged the pitch to the close. No one liked silence; it was an uncomfortable space. But the awkward void always flushed out the weaker party. The person to break the silence subconsciously submitted to the other. If Mario or Giorgio spoke first, Angelina won the sale. If she spoke, they would manipulate the price in their favor.

Rosario understood this rule and trained Angelina. Now, years later, she was the master of the void. She was patient and could wait all night. Tonight, Angelina did not have to wait long. Giorgio and Mario nodded at each other, then Mario broke the silence.

"You were right. These are the best wines!"

"They *are* better than the other vineyards we have visited."

"We will order fifty cases a month to start. Giorgio will be by next week to pick up the first load."

"We can deliver," Rosario offered.

"No need." Mario leaned closer to Rosario. "I think my son

has an eye for your daughter. A visit from time to time might foster a loving relationship!" Mario winked.

Rosario forced a smile.

The comment was spoken too quietly for Angelina to hear. Given Mario's mischievous grin and her father's false smile, she had a good idea. To be sure, she would ask her father about it later.

After Mario and Giorgio left, Angelina's energy evaporated. Sleep was more important than asking her father anything. She helped close the biggest sale in the vineyard's history, and that was all she wanted to dream about.

"An excellent job, Bella," Rosario congratulated Angelina.

"Thank you, Papa."

"Get some rest. You have worked hard today. Carmella can finish cleaning. You need not worry about one more chore."

"Thank you, Papa," Angelina smiled. "Sogni d'oro, Papa."

"Sweet dreams to you, too, Bella." Rosario hugged her and gently kissed her forehead. "I am incredibly proud of you!"

Angelina dragged her body up the stairs but sat on the top step to watch her parents interact. It was a habit formed as a little girl in awe of the lover her parents shared.

"Sofia, come. I think Carmella can finish up on her own. Thank you for all of your hard work, Carmella."

"I am nearly finished and will be out of your hair soon," Carmella promised. "And I will get these three to bed, too."

Sprawled out in the living room, snoring away, were Anton, Ricardo, and RJ.

"Let them sleep there. It serves them right for drinking too much!" Rosario chuckled.

"You are wonderful," Sofia hugged the woman who was more of a friend than just an employee. Over twenty years of cooking and raising children together had bonded the women into sisters of the heart. "I appreciate you!"

"And I, you," Carmella replied, smiling. "Now, do I need to

tuck you in, or can the two of you manage that part on your own?" Carmella asked with a wink.

"We are going to sit by the fire and have a glass of Anissette before we head to bed." Rosario grabbed two small glasses while Sofia got the liquor.

"Your mind causes wrinkles to form on your brow. What bothers you, Cara Mia?" Sofia asked, handing Rosario his drink. "You should be happy. You closed a sale and a fine one! This is good for our family. Good for us!"

"Hmm, perhaps."

"What do you mean, *perhaps*?"

"Nothing."

"You are not very good at lying."

"So you have told me!" Rosario chuckled.

"Confess, what is troubling you."

Like Angelina waiting through the void, Sofia fell silent. The question was asked. Rosario would have to break the silence.

"I do not trust these men," Rosario replied after a few minutes.

"Why? They are nice men."

"They *seem* to be, but..."

"Rosario, why do you hesitate? We have been married for a lifetime, yet you refuse to speak your mind? Perhaps I should go so you can think."

Sofia's miffed tone did not match the smile on her face.

"Woman!" Rosario barked. As soon as he looked up, his anger dissipated, and he laughed. "I am going to spank you!"

"No, you won't! Not until you tell me," Sofia teased, continuing their frisky banter. "Once you have freed your thoughts, I will free mine!"

"How about we skip to the celebration part?" He winked.

"It is only me! You can tell me anything. It is part of a wife's duty."

"Si, a wife's duties..." Rosario grinned, grabbing Sofia and pulling her close.

"Nice try! We shall get to *those* duties *after* you tell me what furrows your brow!"

Rosario released a sigh.

"Fine. I am concerned Giorgio has an eye for our daughter. I don't know if he is the type of man I would choose for her."

"It is not your choice! We discussed this; we would not choose for our children. We would let fate choose."

"I know, but how do I protect my girl from a man I believe to be... well... unworthy!"

"Oh, Rosario! We have taught our daughters how to determine if a man is worthy of their love. If they did not listen, then it is their destiny to learn by living."

"I cannot see it so!"

"You *will* see it so! And you will avoid meddling in our daughters' love lives," Sofia snapped.

"Oh, like you?"

"Si, like me!" Sofia put her hands on her hips, her classic pose for being right.

"My love, you meddle with Angelina and Nan constantly!"

"I do not! Well... not anymore!"

Rosario roared with laughter. "Since when?"

"Since Vito and his son stopped by. *He* is perfect for her!"

"You don't meddle, huh?"

Rosario picked Sofia up and carried her to their bedroom. "I will show you *how* to meddle."

"You *are* a professional meddler," she giggled.

"I will show you what I am a professional at!"

CHAPTER 15

"Giorgio, good to see you!" Anton waved.

Anton choked back his disgust for the man. The flagrant display of chauvinism and arrogance on the previous two occasions was enough for Anton to size up Giorgio's true nature. Giorgio considered himself superior in everything, most especially his social standing.

"Anton, right?" Giorgio asked, looking down from the truck's cab with a smug grin.

You condescending prick, Anton thought. *Could your ego get any bigger? If I could beat that self-righteous look off your face.*

Anton was not a materialistic man and enjoyed his simple life. However, his lesser social standing did not mean he was a fool. Allowing personal differences to rule his actions was bad for business. Anton swallowed his pride and shoved the satisfying image of pummeling Giorgio's face from his mind. Their interactions were merely momentary transactions, not playtime for egos.

"Si, and that is my brother, Ricardo." Anton pointed at the brawny man on the top of the hill. "If you pull your truck up there, we will get you loaded. I am sure you have a busy day ahead of you."

"Thanks!"

Giorgio put the truck into drive. It jerked and sputtered, exposing Giorgio's inexperience in driving a big truck. Anton laughed. The pompous ass spent most of his energy trying to be something he was not. And he was not a skilled driver of a diesel truck.

Anton followed the truck up the hill. He hoped they could load the order quickly, getting this man on his way. The less time they spent together, the better.

Anton was taller than both Giorgio and Ricardo. His broad shoulders and muscular build allowed him to carry several cases at a time. Giorgio, however, took one, even though it was apparent he could lift more.

They hauled the cases up from the cellar in silence, except for the occasional grunt and groan. After hoisting a single crate onto the truck's bed, Giorgio nosily looked around. Anton ignored the odd behavior the first couple of times, but Giorgio's persistent snooping became annoying.

"You alright, Giorgio?" Anton barked.

"Fine, why do you ask?"

"You can't keep your eyes still. You lookin' for someone?"

"No," Giorgio replied, picking up a crate. "This is an amazing place! Guess I didn't realize how..." he paused, searching for a word. "... how majestic it is."

"Yep! Majestic," Ricardo mocked, rolling his eyes.

Anton cautioned Ricardo about his tone, even though he, himself, was struggling to remain calm. He did not want any comments made that might discourage future purchases.

"Our mother and father worked hard to rebuild this place," Anton explained. "They spent many years making this the 'majestic' place you see now."

"I see," Giorgio replied absently while he gazed around the buildings rather than at them. "You say your mother helped?"

"She and Papa worked the soil together. Heck, she was helping set stones on those walls over there until she was too far pregnant to lift anything," Anton said proudly.

"Hmm, interesting," Giorgio replied indignantly, his eyes roving around, never looking at them.

The brother's anger bubbled. This prick was really getting under their skin with his sexist comments.

Ricardo opened his mouth to defend his mother's honor, but Anton gestured for him to remain calm. Ricardo quietly snarled, releasing the pressure from his boiling temper. Anton hushed him again. In one last defiant act, Ricardo spit on the ground toward the pompous ass's heels before backing down. It wasn't the desired de-escalation. Luckily, Giorgio was too busy to notice the unprofessional gesture.

"Breakfast is ready!" Angelina yelled up the hill.

"Ahh, the sound of an angel!"

Standing behind him, Ricardo and Anton exchanged disgusted glares. Now, they understood why the seemingly curious customer was distracted. He was hunting for their sister.

With a grin, Giorgio turned around and waited for the polite invitation to join them for breakfast. Anton gulped his preferred comment. He had no desire to share another meal with this man but knew it was rude not to at least invite him.

"Have you had breakfast? You're welcome to join us," Anton forced the offer from his mouth. "If you can spare the time. We know you are terribly busy."

"Busy being an ass," Ricardo mumbled under his breath.

"No, no. I would love to join you," Giorgio grinned and promptly strolled down the hill, leaving them behind.

Anton and Ricardo simultaneously released a long, deep groan before heading down the hill. They were appalled at how the perfect stranger waltzed right into the house like he was born a member of the family.

"Pompous ass!" Anton mumbled.

"Arrogant prick!" Ricardo added.

"Ohh... Hello Giorgio!"

Angelina's heart fluttered wildly, and her stomach flipped. She would not have called her brothers for breakfast if she knew Giorgio was still at the vineyard.

"Good morning to you!" He purred, placing a tender kiss on the back of her hand.

His touch made Angelina want to vomit.

"Are you hungry, Giorgio?" Sofia interrupted, stepping between them, breaking his firm grip on Angelina's hand.

"If you can spare a plate, I would appreciate your generosity!" Giorgio gave Sofia a slight bow, but Sofia walked past him, ignoring his weak performance.

"Catalina! Breakfast." Sofia called up the stairs.

"You may have a seat, Giorgio. I will fix you a plate," Sofia stated with a half-hearted smile.

Angelina glared at her brothers. She was not pleased with having to share another meal with this creep.

"Don't give me that look! You are the one who called us!" Anton whispered, washing his hands in the large cast iron sink. "Now be the *Angel* he thinks you are!"

"*You* be the angel! I can't stand him!"

"None of us like him," Ricardo said, reaching for the soap.

"Then why is he here?" Angelina asked.

"Because he has a crush on you!"

"Yuck!" Angelina's face flushed bright red.

"The three of you quit whispering! It is embarrassing!" Sofia scolded. "Go sit by him and make friends. Turn on your Beretta charm. Make that man feel like family!"

"*Family!*" They groaned at the dreadful thought.

Catalina bounced down the stairs until she saw Giorgio seated at the table. The sight of him caused her to stumble down the steps before catching her balance and her breath.

"How was your trip?" Anton teased, watching her narrowly spare herself the embarrassment of a fall.

"I didn't trip!" Cat mumbled, flushing brighter red.

"Oh! Good morning, Catalina!" Giorgio stood from his chair to greet her. "I did not know you were here. May I say your smile brightens the day!"

Catalina flushed brighter from the sophisticated greeting. She quickly recovered with an equally sophisticated reply.

"Then we are of the same thought, Giorgio. When did you arrive?" Catalina asked with a regal air.

"Only recently, we loaded the last cases onto the truck only moments before your sister summoned us."

Giorgio pulled out the chair on his right and waved for Catalina to join him. His charming manners made her melt into a puddle of infatuation. Catalina babbled something polite and batted her eyelashes.

Angelina bit her lip to keep from laughing at the exchange. Catalina acted like a puppy begging to be adopted.

"Angelina, please sit beside me," Giorgio offered, pulling out the chair on his left.

She hesitated for a moment. A firm push from her mother made her accept. Instantly, Catalina's glow diminished until he sat between them, giving each a charming smile.

"Did I hear you say you finished loading?" Angelina asked.

"We still have four cases left to load. But that will only take a few minutes, and Giorgio can leave." Ricardo grunted.

Under the table, Sofia gave her son a swift kick.

"Ouch!"

"Oh, sorry, was that your leg?" Sofia apologized in an overly sweet tone.

Ricardo opened his mouth to complain, but her look could silence an army. His temper nipped, he returned to his food and remained quiet the rest of the meal.

Anton and Catalina filled the conversation with fewer troublesome topics, keeping Giorgio entertained. Angelina gave her brother a grateful smile after a few minutes. She did not want to talk and was relieved Anton appeared satisfied with the current conversation.

After the meal, the women cleared the plates and washed

the dishes. Giorgio was enjoying his conversation with Anton enough that he did not move. He stayed seated and continued to fuel the discussion with comments and questions.

"Wow, and they say I am a charmer!" Angelina whispered to her sister. "Looks like Giorgio has a crush on Anton."

"He looks so relaxed. I really think he likes it here," Catalina swooned. "I hope he comes around more often. He's so handsome!"

"What?" Angelina almost dropped the dish in her hands. "He is a snake in the grass waiting to bite!"

Catalina's blindness frustrated Angelina so much she dunked the dish back into the sink, causing the soapy water to splash against her white shirt.

"No, he is not!" Catalina stomped her foot. "I know what you are trying to do! You have a crush on him! I have seen the way you look at him! You think he is a catch and are just trying to keep him for yourself!"

The quiver in Catalina's voice shocked Angelina. She had never seen her sister so upset.

"No, Cat, that is not so!"

"I see the two of you always talking, exchanging glances!" Cat stamped her foot. "Well, may the best sister win!" Catalina threatened with a huff and stormed out the door.

Angelina stood frozen in shock at her sister's words. She was unsure what was more disturbing; her sister having feelings for Giorgio or the two of them battling over him. Angelina shook off the horror that held her. She removed her hands from the water and peeked out the window. Absently, she reached for the white dishtowel, but her mother stayed her hand.

"I will go. She is too upset for you to talk to her," Sofia cautioned.

"Mamma, I do not—" Angelina tried to argue, but Sofia wagged her finger.

Angelina returned to washing the dishes, her mind lost in thought over what had happened. She did not hear her brothers leave.

"Did everyone abandon us?" Giorgio asked, standing a few feet behind her. "I do appreciate the time alone with you."

Angelina jumped, causing more water to slosh onto her shirt. She could feel him moving closer. She turned around to find him a few steps away. Giorgio's gaze locked on her heaving chest. The sheer milky veil of wet fabric barely hid the scalloped lace slip. Every inhalation, the seductive nature of moist fabric against the flesh, beckoned him closer. His lust intensified. She feared he would attack like a rabid dog.

"You are magnificent."

A warm rush of blood raced to her cheeks. She was embarrassed and terrified all at once. She spun away, but he continued his pursuit; every methodical step closer increased her tension. In seconds, his breath was warm on her neck.

"I am sorry. I know I have offended you..." Giorgio whispered tenderly as he reached up to touch her. His hand hovered inches from her hair, but he did not make contact. Instead, he drew in her scent. "... many times, I am sure."

"At least."

"I do not wish to be your enemy. Forgive me! If you grant me your forgiveness, I promise to be who *you* want me to be! I can be a gentleman. Please, give me a chance."

"A chance for what?" Angry, she spun to face him but instantly regretted it.

Giorgio's muscular, broad chest was inches from her face. His crisp, musky cologne blended well with his body odor, sending a tingling sensation through her core.

"Give me a chance to prove to you who I really am." He gently moved a strand of hair from her cheek.

His seductive words, alluring scent, and muscular body made Angelina feel dizzy. She tried to pull her thoughts together, but he was tantalizing.

Giorgio caressed her cheek. A tingle rushed through her. The same excited feeling she felt when Fernando's body brushed close to hers. His presence and her feelings were confusing. She pushed his hand away. She needed space to breathe. She needed him to leave.

"Why would I need to know who you really are? You and your father do business with my father. That is all I need to know!" Angelina demanded in a harsher tone than intended.

"I am sorry. I have frightened you." Giorgio, stepping back, slipped his hands into his pockets. "I only want to foster a relationship between our families. My father tends to do more business with those he feels...well..close to."

Giorgio bowed his head almost in submission, like a child punished by a wicked schoolteacher.

"I only hoped we could be...friends? Your family is so nice! I don't have any brothers or sisters. As much as I travel, it is hard to make good friends."

He stepped further away, avoiding direct eye contact. His hand ran through his thick black hair several times as he fidgeted. At that moment, she realized he was more nervous than she was. A twinge of guilt for how she reacted to him stung her heart.

"It is a silly thought, I guess."

"What is silly," she asked.

"To think *if* we were friends, I could sway my father into purchasing *more* wine."

Angelina did not know what to make of him. He changed instantly into a humble man. Despite her well of guilt, she was leery of him, even if his words rang true.

She watched him continue to shuffle about, his hand raking through his hair for the twentieth time. He *was* charming. Perhaps, if they were friends, it could encourage more sales. It was a concept she had not really put much thought into.

"Are you trying to buy my friendship?" Angelina teased.

"No, no...I mean. Well...I guess it does sound that way," Giorgio replied with a sheepish shrug.

"That it did."

"I am sorry... again!" He continued his bashful demeanor, never once looking up from his shoes. "I understand it may be hard to believe, given how I acted the last couple of times we have met, but I am a nice guy. I only ask for a chance to prove it to you."

Angelina's gut begged her to tell him off. After all, how could someone shift from being a self-centered jerk to a gentleman in seconds? The instantaneous transformation concerned her. Nonetheless, fostering a friendship would be in the family's best interest, especially if it sold more wine.

"You are forgiven." Angelina extended her hand. "I promise to give you a chance. A *real* chance to be my friend, but only a *friend*. Okay?"

Giorgio swooped in to gently kiss her hand, but she pulled back and used her mother's classic finger wag to stop him in his tracks.

"Oh no! I said only friends!"

CHAPTER 16

"He is quite the Rottweiler, Don Salvatore!" The old man remarked, watching Antonio walk away.

"Good! Then he is earning his keep," The Don laughed, causing his belly to shake. "You would do well to get one of your own."

"My boy serves that purpose. Besides, having too many mouths to feed can become expensive."

"You speak the truth, old man!" The Don chuckled.

As he followed Don Salvatore, he looked around the elegant courtyard. He had never taken the time to enjoy the peacefulness of the space on his previous visits. He could see why the Don spent so much time out here. Several olive, lemon, and fig trees were scattered about the spacious area. Perfectly manicured grass and flowers blanketed the ground. Stone walkways spread out in a diamond pattern, giving the garden a sense of structure. Water cascaded in the large stone fountain, blending with the gently swaying trees and the cooing from the feathered choir. It was a symphony of sounds soothing to the soul.

Don Salvatore sat on the bench under the lemon tree. A flock of pigeons quickly landed at his feet, eyeing the ground for a coveted morsel.

"Come! We have much to catch up on," The Don motioned for his guest to sit in the white iron chair across from him.

The birds scurried out of the way of the old man's feet, only to return in hopes of the forthcoming feast. The Don reached into the jar and removed a handful of seeds. Slowly, he scattered them on the stones and watched his little friends excitedly peck at the ground. He retrieved another handful before returning the jar to its perch on the white table.

"It has been many months since we spoke," The Don interrupted the old man's euphoric gaze around the garden.

"I have been traveling. My apologies."

The old man had learned since his first visit that Don Salvatore was a man to be feared. Either fear him or be killed. Even in the past year, the old man had known of at least a dozen souls relieved of their human form, all because they crossed a muted, grey line. Don Salvatore's rules were never challenged by any man, at least not one who wished to live to see another season.

"No apologies needed. I am not trying to bust your balls," Don Salvatore replied calmly. "But we have much to discuss, and I grow anxious!"

"I am an open book, Godfather."

"Let's start with Signor Fiori." Don Salvatore looked the old man in the eyes, watching for a reaction. "Don't lie to me. I have my own men who keep me informed. Why is he roaming around here?"

The old man was shocked by The Don's insinuation of his lying. He had done nothing to provoke such accusations. But the old man was as wise as his age. This was merely one of the Godfather's mental games.

"He does business through much of Northern Italy but does not interfere with your territory."

"Does he pay his share with the other Don's? Do I get my share when he does business with you?" Don Salvatore's temper was on the rise.

"I am told he had arrangements with the other Don's."

He tried maintaining eye contact, but The Don's gaze was dark, almost evil. The old man spoke cautiously. One misperceived word would make the old man's life a candle to be snuffed out in the next gentle breeze.

"Don Salvatore, I always pay you correctly! I am a man of honor. I am loyal to you!"

"Hmm, very well," The Don grunted. Relaxing his tone, he added, "I hear this foreigner has similar interests?"

"Do you refer to the Beretta vineyards?"

The Don's ears perked, alerting the old man he was on the right track.

"Signor Beretta is loyal to you, Don Salvatore. I do not believe he wishes to cross you."

"It may be his wish. However, my birdies tell me he is still in contact with Signore Fiori. I understand they exchange telegrams regularly."

"I must answer honestly, Don Salvatore, I do not know."

"You should! It is your business to know!" The Don huffed and slammed his hand on the arm of his bench. The commotion caused the birds to launch into flight, only to return moments later.

"It will be my first priority," the old man replied, bowing his head in respect.

"Then don't disappoint me again!"

The Don reached into his jar of seeds and threw a handful onto the path. He watched the birds chase each other away, fighting for a single, tiny grain.

"They are more like us than we think."

"Who?" the old man asked quizzically.

"Birds." Don Salvatore pointed to the grey-feathered creatures scurrying around near his feet. "They will peck another bird's eye out just to have an infinitesimal speck of grain. Fighting over something so insignificant. They know there is more food to snatch up, yet they set their eye on one kernel and will fight to the death for it."

The old man patiently listened to the parable, careful not to move or make a sound that might interrupt the Godfather.

"To some, the Beretta vineyard is like this kernel of grain, unimportant. But to me, it is the finest, best grain! A golden grain worth more money than any other." Don Salvatore glared at the old man. "I will not allow Rosario Beretta to swoop in and take control of everything! He will not keep the bounty of this golden nugget. His vines produce magnificent grapes that make extraordinary wines. All of which can make me a lot of money! I will not have Rosario Beretta growing into a Don. He will not have what I have! My father was Don, and I earned the right to remain Don. This region is mine!" His hand closed around the grains, crushing them. "He will learn his place!"

"He fears you, like everyone, Don Salvatore. I have visited with him many times, and he knows the respect due to you!"

"He should fear me!" An evil grin curled across Don Salvatore's face. "And that fear will make my plan that much more satisfying!"

"What do you mean to do?"

"I will peck his eyes out!" His face was red with anger, "and I will kill anyone who tries to keep this prize from my beak! Do you understand?"

The Don's eyes burned like the devil, searching for souls to devour.

"Si, Don Salvatore," the old man replied in terror.

"Now," Don Salvatore said calmly, brushing the husks from his hands. "What of the young Giorgio? He has been to the Beretta home many times. I hear he spends many hours with the family, si? He has enjoyed frequent meals over the past, what six or seven months? He has become almost one of them."

"It is rumored," the old man replied sheepishly.

"Rumored? Do you not know for sure? Why do I let you live if you cannot give me useful information?"

The old man, wading too close to the fires of hell, fidgeted in his seat. He had been traveling most of the past six months and had minimal contact with Giorgio. The only word he received was things were going as planned.

"He spends many hours with the family. He has become good friends with the children of Signore Beretta. I am told he has at least one meal a week with them."

"Is he in love?"

"It appears he has desires for the daughter." The old man gulped back his nerves.

"Good, then perhaps we should encourage a more permanent relationship."

"I do not think Rosario will be supportive of this."

"No?" Don Salvatore bellow sent the flock of birds into a squawking frenzy of flight. "Here, you said he did not wish to cross me?"

"Sorry, Don Salvatore." The old man cowered down. "I will instruct Giorgio to ask, but?"

"But what? Tell Giorgio he *will* marry the Beretta girl. Tell him there better be a blushing bride on his arm by the end of summer!"

The old man, frightened by The Don's anger, tried to reply. But the fiery black orbs glaring at him instantly silenced him.

"Well?" The volcanic anger flushing The Don's face erupted. He slammed his hand against the bench, and from the bowels of hell, an unholy growl erupted from his lips.

"Have the fucking brat ask for her hand, or I will do it for him!"

CHAPTER 17

Angelina sat at a small table under the cherry tree's beautiful canopy. The crisp morning breeze tickling the leaves sent a shower of white petals into her sanctuary. Enveloped in the tree's peaceful aura, she watched the blanket of dark grey clouds across the horizon. An ominous shadow slowly grew over the distant vines, swallowing them and the lingering hazy mist around them. A loud crack unleashed a thunderous growl to rumble over the rolling hills.

"Angelina, come inside before you catch a cold!" Sofia yelled from the safety of the house.

"Give me five more minutes, Mamma. I am dressed for the cold air. I will be ok."

"Five minutes, no more!" Sofia rubbed her shoulders, grumbling as she went inside. "I hate this nasty cold. Makes my old bones ache!"

"Which of your bones are old? You work as hard as your children, and your skin has not a wrinkle. You are not old," Angelina said, mumbling to herself.

The reality of life made her sigh. It was hard to imagine her mother as an elderly woman.

"One day, Mamma will be. Time passes by quickly."

The smell of rain filled the air, foretelling the liquid purification of the earth. Tilting her head back, Angelina watched the first few delicate drops cascade down the cherry tree's satin leaves. Slowly, the droplet rolled down and landed on her temple. She did not flinch. She welcomed the holy water.

The Spring showers provided a healthy dose of moisture for the vines. On the horizon, another one promised more drops of God's growth serum. Angelina drew in a deep breath. The cool, moist air felt good as it filled her lungs. This was going to be an excellent growing year. She could feel it in her bones.

"Ah! My bones are omnipotent, too?" She chuckled.

A roll of grey steam carried the espresso's aroma, luring her into a thoughtful reverie.

When she could steal a few minutes alone, Angelina was lost in thought. Being outside provided a peaceful space to work through all that had evolved. So much had happened in the past six months.

With the war finally over in Europe, a sense of freedom melted across the continent. Each son's return home was celebrated, making the past few weeks one continual party. The festivities were not over yet and would not end for some time. Many more were due home, including her brother Marcus. She and her mother knelt in prayer each night for his safe return.

Angelina wondered if Marcus would like the new family friends. Mario and Giorgio were regular customers, buying a truckload of wine every week. With droves of soldiers returning, they doubled their wine order to accommodate the increased business.

Giorgio did not hide his attraction for Angelina, which caused Fernando tremendous frustration. It also sent her sister into a tirade of self-pity and anger. Angelina kept her actions in the realm of friendship. He, however, frequently overstepped. Words of adoration, the flash of a seductive gaze, or the wayward contact was far from that of a friend. To punish him, she lashed back with an acid tongue, earning her a few days of freedom from his advances.

During Angelina's reprieve, Giorgio shifted his attention to

Catalina. His suave flirtations sent the adoring woman into the clouds. But the constant swing of attention perpetuated a wedge between the two sisters.

"He is a young man, unsure of his true desires. Both of you are beautiful in your own ways. It *would* be a hard choice for any man!" Sofia explained, keeping the peace in her home.

Easily charmed, Catalina and her mother only expressed loving thoughts toward his nature. Frequently having whispered conversations about Giorgio.

Rosario became enamored as well, but not with Giorgio's personality. Rosario was overjoyed with the hundred and fifty cases of wine they purchased in a week. The wine flowed out, and the money flowed in. He would not place any more profound thoughts on the matter. In Rosario's mind, this was just a lucrative business arrangement.

After a stern lecture from their father, Ricardo and Anton kept their opinions to themselves. However, they continued to tease Angelina about being in love with Giorgio. Which she fervently professed against the insanity of the notion.

Her family, each tied up in their own vision of Giorgio, prevented Angelina from discussing her woes with anyone. So, when left alone, she would find a quiet sanctuary on the vineyard to release her thoughts and feelings.

A lightning bolt flashed across the sky, splintering out in five directions. A tingling swirl of electricity danced on her skin, giving her goosebumps. Two seconds later, a loud crack of thunder rumbled around her. Another flash electrified the air. The storm had reached the edge of the vineyard.

The gentle tap of droplets dancing on the cherry tree's leaves gradually crescendoed into loud plunks as the raindrops grew in size. Angelina released the negative thoughts clinging to her mind in a long exhale, allowing the rain to carry them away.

"You go inside before you worry your mother to death."

Rosario's warm hand on her shoulder and deep voice pulled her back from her reverie. She found comfort in the peaceful outdoors and the powerful storms. But her father's voice was by far the most healing of all.

"It is so pretty to watch."

"Si, but the lightning is dangerous."

"I won't get hurt, Papa."

"Because you will go inside before you have the chance."

"Oh, Papa! You are no fun."

"I am a lot of fun, but I know when to enjoy life and when to take shelter."

"It is only a storm!" Angelina argued, but Rosario's furrowed brow squelched her ambition.

"Angelina, you are bold, more so than any of my children. A trait that will take you to places out of my protection. When you do, I must know you understand there is a time to stand your ground and when to leave."

"I am not a coward, Papa!"

"Cowards run away, never to return. Leaving for the sake of gathering your wits is different! Strength comes from within," Rosario explained, tapping his hand against his chest. "Sometimes, pulling back from the chaos allows you to see the road to victory. Being injured by foolishly standing your ground can make your fight long and hard. Injury to the body or mind increases your chances of defeat."

Angelina bowed her head, acknowledging her father's insight. His ever-poignant parables always proved to contain timely wisdom.

"Our time is limited," Rosario nodded at the rapidly approaching sheet of rain. "What brought you out here in the first place?"

"To think."

"Then tell me your troubles before we are drenched."

Angelina hesitated. Her brothers received a long, bitter

scolding for voicing their concern. Adding her father's disapproval would not help calm her torrid thoughts.

"Well?" Rosario prodded.

Unable to confess the whole truth, Angelina shared a sliver of her concerns.

"I do not trust Giorgio or his father. My gut tells me they are dangerous men!"

"*All* men are dangerous."

"Not all, Papa." Angelina smiled at her father.

"*All* men, Bella. All can be dangerous. Never forget that!" Rosario cautioned. "I only contain my anger better than most. Now, let's go in before we get wet."

Angelina looked at the approaching wall of moisture. Another bolt of lightning ripped across the sky. Almost instantly, the vibration of the thunder reverberated around them. She drew a deep breath, momentarily savoring the view before following her father into the house.

Rosario held the door open for her. Just before she crossed the threshold, a loud pop echoed around them. Angelina jumped. She looked back at the tree engulfed in heavy rain. A plume of smoke drifted up from it. The large branch, gently sprinkling her with white petals, was severed by a bolt of lightning. In its fall, the limb crushed her chair.

"See, Bella. Even the places you feel the safest can be the most dangerous!"

CHAPTER 18

The morning sunlight filtering through the window cast a warm glow on Sofia's skin. Rosario had been watching her sleep for nearly an hour, waiting for her to stir. She rolled onto her back and stretched the sleep from her stiff limbs.

"Do you know what this weekend is, Bella Mia?"

"No, what is it?" She yawned and rubbed her eyes, trying to hide her playful grin.

He reached down the sheets to tickle her side.

"You know what this weekend is! You better!"

Rosario kissed her neck and rubbed his mustache across her sensitive skin. Giggling, she squirmed to free herself from his torturous tickling.

"Oh no, you don't. You aren't going anywhere!"

"I can at least make you work for it!" Sofia teased.

He crawled under the sheets, gently kissing her soft skin.

"If you love me, you will tell me what this weekend is?"

"If I tell you, will you finish what you have started?"

"Maybe I should wait." Rosario surmised, climbing out of the sheets. "Perhaps, if you desire me all day, it will jog your memory."

Her hand landed on his head before he could move too far.

"Oh no, I think *now* is good."

Rosario looked up at her.

"Well?"

"It is our anniversary." She confessed.

He placed three slow, tender kisses on her body, then poked

his head out of the gold satin sheets.

"Which one?" He asked, grinning.

"Oh, Rosario, you torture me!" She flopped against the bed in playful retaliation for his incessant teasing. "It is our twenty-fifth!"

Exchanging gazes filled with ravenous desire, the lovers savored the sensual embrace. Each kiss and gentle caress was filled with the purest love. A love deep enough to span across many lifetimes. Their hearts beat as one, and the world stopped while the two souls entwined in a sacred union. Reaching the peak of ecstasy, they released muffled moans of pleasure.

"Good morning, Bella Mia."

"Good morning, Cara Mia," Sofia said with a smile.

Rosario rolled onto his back, and Sofia snuggled under his arm, resting her head on his chest.

"I have a surprise for you," Rosario said tenderly as his fingers gently grazed her skin.

"Oh?" She asked, snuggling closer for warmth. "What is it? Or will you tease me with that, too?"

Playfully, she jabbed him with her finger.

"No, my love. I will tell you now."

He kissed her forehead and drew in the refreshing scent of her hair. The sweet smell of honeysuckle and patchouli always made him smile.

"I made arrangements for us to go away next weekend."

Rosario nuzzled deeper into her hair and filled his lungs.

"We have not taken a holiday for over a decade! Oh, Cara Mia!" Sofia gushed. "Where are we going?"

"Ah, now that part is a surprise, so you must wait." He ran his fingers through her soft black curls. "I would like for you to go to town and buy a new dress for the occasion. I intend to wine and dine you!"

His finger gently flowed down her cheek as he memorized

every beautiful inch of her face. He continued his soft touch down her neck and gently caressed the curve of her breast.

"Of course, I do hope to get lucky!" He grinned.

"Have I ever refused you?"

"No, my love, you have not!"

"I do not expect the next twenty-five years to be different." She returned his playful smile. "Unless you give me cause."

He stroked her hair, then trailed his hand down her back, settling on her butt. He gently squeezed her cheek and leaned in to kiss her soft pink lips.

"I am the luckiest man alive."

"Never forget it."

"How can I when your presence continually reminds me."

Sofia's hand flowed lightly across his skin, stirring his passion. Her hungry eyes confessed she was not satisfied either. She mounted him. Her long, dark locks glided over her shoulder. She was a goddess glistening in the golden morning sunlight.

"You are the most beautiful angel, Bella Mia."

Before she could respond, the thud-thud of footsteps and loud voices from the hallway invaded their world.

She sighed. "The family is awake."

A car horn blared several times in quick succession.

"Who could be here at this hour?" Rosario grumbled.

He looked out the window. A dark car had pulled up to deliver a telegram. He watched as the young man handed the yellow paper to Anton in exchange for a few coins.

"Who is it, Rosario?"

"A courier with a telegram." He rushed to button his pants.

"Do you think it is about Marcus?"

"I am not sure, but I will find out."

Reviewing the letter's exterior, Anton didn't see his father running down the hall.

"Who is it from?" Rosario snatched the envelope out of

Anton's grasp.

"I don't know, it says it's from Alessandria, but it—"

"I have a friend living there. It is probably a letter about nothing." Rosario mellowed his tone to hide his anxiety.

"Then why send it urgent?"

"I will find out. Get the eggs for breakfast. Your mother will be down soon."

Rosario walked to the living room, away from his son's confused gaze and any other curious eyes. He threw several logs into the fireplace. They were dry and eagerly took to the flame. He peered around to ensure he was alone, then tore open the envelope. It was a brief but direct note. Rosario read it three times to memorize every word. As a habit, he tucked the note into his shirt pocket but stopped. It was not safe to keep this letter. The content could place his family in danger. He closed his eyes and silently repeated every word until he had it clear in his memory. Satisfied, he tossed the letter into the blazing fire.

Sofia entered the room as the last remnants of the letter dissolved in the flames. She gasped at the ominous sight.

"What did it say?"

"It was not about Marcus, Bella Mia."

"Then why do you burn it like a thief in the night?"

"It was about our getaway. I do not want to spoil the surprise." Rosario enveloped her in his arms. "Nor do I want to tempt you into uncovering my plans! I told you I have something special planned. That was merely a confirmation of our arrangements."

She looked at him, her eyes scrutinizing his face.

"You do not lie well, Rosario!"

"And you are hard to plan a surprise for!" He said, leading her away from the fire. "Anton is fetching the eggs for breakfast. I am going to get ready for the day. Carlos will take you shopping after lunch. Take the girls. I think they would enjoy helping you pick something out."

"I cannot go today!"

"Why not?"

"Tonight, Giorgio and Mario are joining us for dinner."

He nodded his disappointment. "Then make time to go later this week."

****

The evening was filled with laughter, especially from the men. The fluid in their veins was more wine than blood, and their guts were stuffed with Carmella and Sofia's delicious meal. Compliments flowed from Giorgio and Mario like wine from a bottle. Each praised the women for their masterful skill in the kitchen. Mario often begged them to teach his chefs to cook delicious meals, adding it would sell more wine.

"My finest chef does not cook as well as you talented women!" Mario toasted. "To another magnificent feast!"

Sofia laughed. "You are too kind and too drunk to know the difference!"

Her remark ignited a roar of laughter by all, making her blush.

"Do you smoke cigars, Rosario?" Giorgio asked.

"I have been known to enjoy one from time to time."

"Well then, let us enjoy the summer air and a good cigar!" On their way out, Giorgio rummaged through his coat in search of a lighter. Rosario reached to open the door and noticed Mario had not moved.

"Are you coming, Mario?"

"I am too fat to move, you two enjoy! I will wait here for your return." Mario patted his belly and belched.

"Suit yourself!" Rosario replied and stumbled outside.

The evening air was warm and inviting. A gentle breeze floated through the trees, and the smell of summer flowers accented the air. A cloud occasionally drifted by, blocking flickering stars scattered across the deep blue sky.

Giorgio held the lighter while Rosario puffed the cigar, encouraging the red embers to take the flame. Rosario pulled a long drag, the tip glowing with the infusion of air. Smoke rolled from his nose and joined the night air like a ghost floating into the distance.

"A beautiful evening!" Giorgio said, lighting his cigar.

"That it is!" Rosario released a stream of smoke. "This is fine tobacco. Do you import these?"

"We sell them at our establishments. This one is my favorite. It has a hint of sweetness at the end of a full flavor. Do you notice it?"

"Si, very nice!" He released some smoke into rings and watched them briefly hover before fading into nothingness.

Rosario observed the young man beside him. He was handsome, strong, and tall. Moreover, Giorgio was wealthy. Even through the purgatory of war, he maintained significant wealth. Though, Rosario never placed much thought on how or why. In fact, he had not formed any opinion on Giorgio. In the waning moonlight, Rosario wondered if he would ever be forced to assess the man.

"Something plagues your mind, Giorgio. You did not ask me out here just to smoke a cigar, did you?"

"You are perceptive, Signor Beretta." Giorgio smiled. "I drew you away because I wish to discuss something important with you."

"Then free your thoughts, young man! I am drunk enough to agree to almost anything." Rosario chuckled and patted Giorgio's muscular shoulder.

"I hope even sober, you would be agreeable, to this request." Giorgio made eye contact with Rosario, his face filled with sincerity. "Signor Beretta, may I marry your daughter?"

Rosario's heart jumped from his chest. He knew a man

would ask him such a question one day, but like any father, no man would ever be good enough. Nor would his daughter ever be old enough.

The wine flowed heavily in Rosario's blood. He braced himself and tried to compose an answer to Giorgio's question. However, his intoxication won, and he blurted out his protest on the subject.

"Which one, young man? You seem to have a fancy for both! From one day to another, I am not sure which you prefer more!" The words flew from his lips. "My daughters are young, much younger than you. And I fear you do not know your heart enough to choose one. You can't have them both! My answer is no!"

Rosario stopped his rant and wished his mind would do the same. He had said enough, perhaps too much. If his answer ended their business together, so be it. His daughters' happiness meant more than the money.

He drew another drag from the cigar and patted Giorgio on the shoulder.

"Thank you for the cigar. I will keep it to enjoy later." Rosario crushed the cigar's end on the sole of his shoe. He returned inside without a single glance at Giorgio.

CHAPTER 19

Angelina woke from a nightmare, her clothes saturated with sweat. Her entire body shook with fear, and her heart thundered. Slow, deep breaths failed to calm her nerves and banish the unending horror of her dream. She needed fresh air, but the dim light from the waning crescent moon was not enough to light her path.

She snuggled into her blanket and chanted the rosary, waiting for the blooming rays of dawn. She recanted the prayers to the rhythm of the clock. Before she finished the first decade of the rosary, the scenes from her nightmare returned. Her anxiety strangled her throat. She had to breathe the fresh air, regardless of the looming dark veil.

Angelina's hands blindly snatched her clothes and work boots. She slowly opened her bedroom door and paused, glancing back into the dark room.

You are coming with me! She thought, grabbing a thick wool sweater.

Careful to avoid the boards that creaked with pressure, Angelina made her way out the back door. Standing on the first step, she drew in the crisp air. Anxiety's grip on her throat loosened. She could breathe again.

The sliver of moonlight barely illuminated her path through the vines. Her heartbeat slowed, and her breathing steadied with each step. Like her Papa, the vineyard was where she made sense of the senseless. Her dream was filled with absurdities.

Praying the Hail Mary, the unsettling nightmare replayed. It was a recurrent dream, one she had a dozen times. Tonight, it was more vivid than ever. She convinced herself it was intensified by the excess wine consumed the previous night.

Mario and Giorgio had stayed later than usual. Not that it mattered. Everyone was too drunk to comprehend the concept of time. Rosario's heated exchange with Giorgio while they smoked cigars was disturbing. Giorgio did not rejoin the festivities for at least thirty minutes. His head hung like a schoolboy whipped for pulling a girl's braids.

Angelina gazed up at the twinkling stars performing their dance across the sky. Usually, the heavenly display eased her troubled mind, but this morning, the usual did not happen.

She took a deep breath.

"Let go of that which haunts you," she mumbled.

She repeated her mantra several times, drawing in a breath and slowly releasing it with her worries.

A few rows away, crushing the earth, a pair of heavy feet crept toward Angelina. Her instinct told her to hide, but where? She crawled under a large cluster of vines and peered through the leaves. The sunless sky limited her vision.

Angelina planted her hand on the ground to brace her trembling body. She looked in every direction for her uninvited shadow companion but saw nothing.

A light tickle moved across her fingers. It took a moment to register the sensation. She screeched in horror and sprang to her feet. In the silvery moonlight, a long black snake slithered toward her. On her tippy-toes, she scurried backward, right into the chest of the tall stalker. She screamed again, but the man covered her mouth before a sound escaped. In a quick motion, he tossed her over his shoulder. Angelina frantically kicked and screamed until the loud pop of a gun made her go limp like a rag-doll.

****

The morning sunlight crested the horizon, illuminating the large boulder where Angelina's limp body lay. The warm summer air gently caressed her skin, pulling her from her slumber. The chirping birds and rushing river below brought her fully back to reality.

The rows of vines trailing in every direction banished her anxiety. Angelina released her tension and relaxed against the boulder, satisfied with her location.

"Finally, you're awake!"

"What happened?"

"I saved you!" Anton bragged, puffing his chest.

"I heard a gunshot and—"

"That was me. I pulled the trigger!"

Anton climbed onto the rock and draped his coat over her trembling shoulders.

"Thank you." She snuggled into the coat, soaking in the warmth.

"Always here to help my little Sis!"

Anton wrapped his arm around her and patiently waited for her tremors to subside before asking any questions.

"I heard you screaming in your dreams again. Is that why you left so early for your walk?"

She shrugged. Everyone knowing about the night terrors bothered her.

"Do you want to talk about it?"

"Not really." Angelina avoided his gaze.

"I could tell by your screams that your dream was more intense than usual. You had already gone when I went to your room. I followed you because it was too dark to wander through the vines. I am glad I did."

Confused by the comment, Angelina sat up to look at him.

"When I reached the vines, I heard footsteps. You might

have big feet, Sis." Anton teased, pinching at her toes. "But I knew you weren't the one creeping around!"

"I heard them too!" She perked up. "Who was it?"

"Don't know, it was still dark. Besides, I needed to find you before someone else did." Anton brushed a strand of black hair away from Angelina's eyes. "You were my first concern."

Angelina rested her head against his shoulder, soaking in her protective brother's love.

"How did you find me?"

"When you jumped out from under the vine, I was right behind you. You backed into me. Your kicking and screaming damn near killed me! Not exactly the thanks a rescuer wants, but hey..." Anton laughed.

"I am so sorry!"

"You should be. I won't hear out of this ear for months!"

Angelina jabbed her elbow into his ribs for his sarcasm.

"A big black snake crawled over my hand," Angelina explained. She shuddered. "All I could think of was run!"

"After I tossed you over my shoulder. The snake slithered by. I shot it. Thankfully, you went quiet! Ya know, two birds, one bullet!" Anton puffed his chest and blew the smoke from his finger pistol. "Without your deafening screams, I heard the heavy footsteps run toward the road."

"Who was it?"

"I don't know, but he was big! When there was enough sunlight, I returned to that spot. I found his shoe prints. They are bigger than anyone I know."

"Why would someone wander around our vineyard?"

"Good question!"

"Do you think they know Mamma and Papa are away?"

"Probably. That kind of news travels fast. Don't worry, Sis, I will keep you safe." He rubbed his sister's arm and gave a reassuring smile. "Once a hero, always a hero!"

"I feel better already." Angelina rolled her eyes.

The siblings continued to zing jabs at each other. It was their way of hiding their anxiety. Anton would never say something that would feed her concerns. His philosophy was, worrying over something doesn't change the outcome; it only makes the road more daunting.

"Nan is bringing us breakfast. I thought a picnic would speed your recovery. Your night terror sounded intense."

"It is becoming more vivid." She hugged her legs and rested her chin on her knees. After a long silence, she asked. "What do you think of Giorgio?"

"I try not to."

Angelina furrowed her brow. "Do you trust him?"

"Do I need to?"

"Anton!" She smacked him on his leg. "I am trying to have a sincere conversation with you!"

"No, you are interrogating me!"

"Oh, stop!" Angelina rolled her eyes. "Seriously, I need to ask you something."

"No!" He chuckled.

Angelina flashed a reproving glare. It quickly faded when she saw Anton's ornery grin. She giggled, then tried to regain her harsh gaze but failed.

"Well...ok...fine!" Anton chuckled.

The sun sparkling off the water cast a soft glow on his skin. He had not shaved in several days. The dark, thick hair accented his tan, weathered skin, making him look older. She smiled; he was good-looking, funny, and well-built. The girls in town swooned over him, yet he had not found the perfect girl, though many had tried to win his heart.

"Why haven't you picked a wife?"

"Why haven't you picked a husband?"

His words stabbed her gut, making her want to vomit.

"I probably won't get to pick for myself. Everyone wants me to marry Nan." A tear streamed down her cheek.

"What are you talking about, Lina? I want you to be happy! No one wants you to marry because you feel obligated!" Anton hooked her chin and locked gazes with her. His eyes emitted a tremendous compassion. "Everyone thinks you would make an excellent match. No one is calling the priest!"

She released a heavy sigh, and several more tears escaped.

"Lina, this is not like you. What has made you so upset?"

Angelina couldn't respond. It was too painful of a subject to speak rationally. Her chin returned to her knees. Anton wrapped his arm around her. It was his way of being supportive without prying into a sensitive subject.

In their silence, they listened to the wind caressing the leaves while the water rushed over the protruding rocks. A fat frog jumped on the opposite bank, creating a big splash as it belly-flopped into the water. Angelina and Anton released quiet chuckles in unison, which made her smile. They were both watching the same event.

"Remember how we used to play in the river?" Angelina asked, breaking the silence.

"We had so much fun. Marcus would hold your hand to make sure you didn't slip." The memory made Anton smile. "You are his favorite, you know!"

"Don't be silly!"

"No, really! He hovered over you all the time. He would never let you out of his sight!"

"He hovered over both of us. We were inseparable!" Angelina returned to her knees. "I *really* miss him."

"We all do! I wish he were here to keep Ricardo in check."

"I bet! Ricardo loves to pick fights with you and Nan." Angelina glanced back at him. "Still can't believe he made you bet on Maria's affections!"

"I don't want to remember that fiasco!" Anton tossed a rock into the water, making a loud plunk. "I heard Marcus's unit will return home in the next week or two."

"That will make Mamma's day!"

Angelina looked at her brother and expected to see a smile, but his face reflected sorrow. She returned the courtesy of silence. If he wanted to discuss his feelings, he would talk when he was ready.

"I've been having this dream," Anton mumbled. "Well, it is more of a nightmare."

She placed her hand on his. "Can you tell me about it?"

"It is not pretty."

"My brothers have made me tough enough to manage just about anything." She assured him with a wink.

"If you'll help me figure out what it means, I will tell you."

"I can try."

Anton remained quiet for a few more minutes before he began his description.

"Mother and father were dead on the kitchen floor, their clothes soaked with blood. And this eerie, dark shadow moved through the house until Marcus entered the room. Even he was covered in blood. It all seemed so real, especially *your* screams. You were crying for help, but no one came."

"Where were you?" she asked.

"I don't know. I could see everything but couldn't move. It was like I was somewhere else, yet there, watching. I felt a certain warmth, but everything around me was cold and dark," Anton spoke reverently, staring off into the sky.

The color drained from her cheeks. Apprehensively, she asked, "Was anyone else in your dream?"

"No. No one else."

He turned his head slightly, but she looked away. She did not want him to know she was upset. Any display of emotion would insinuate his dream bothered her. But something far more disturbing than his dream upset her.

"You have Nonna's gift for interpreting dreams. Tell me what it means?" Anton asked.

"I don't have Nonna's gift. I only said I would *try* to help you make sense of it!"

Their Nonna believed dreams were messages, warnings of what was to come. Angelina prayed Nonna was wrong.

"Oh, come on! Everyone knows you have her gift of interpreting dreams!" He chuckled, poking her sides.

Angelina tried to wiggle free, but the boulder was not big enough. If she moved too far, she would fall. She refused to give his ego the satisfaction of a win by torture.

"Well, they say if you dream of your parents, it is good luck!" Angelina giggled, gasping for air.

"Only if your parents are dead in life and alive in your dream. Even I know that! Try again!"

"Oh, you are impossible!" She laughed. "Look! Nan is bringing us our picnic!"

Pointing out Nan was an unsuccessful attempt to end his tickling torture.

"You better give me my reading before he arrives!"

Nearly two decades of abuse trained his fingers. He knew exactly where to attack to achieve the most impact.

"I can't!"

"You are just trying to weasel out of it! As the Oracle, you must read the dreams. It is your duty!"

She jumped, nearly falling off the rock.

"Stop! Stop! Anton!"

"Not until you tell me!"

"Fine!" Angelina caved, gasping for air. "Your dream means you are a Mamma's boy and miss your mommy!" She wiggled away, but only for a second. "And my screams are for Nan to come here and save me from my brother!"

"Oh, you are gonna get it now!" Anton laughed.

CHAPTER 20

Rosario placed a note under a rose beside her pillow.

> *S,*
>
> *I have gone to fetch my
> beautiful rose, breakfast.
> Do not dress, for I am
> not done ravishing you!*
>
> *Love,*
> *R*

They had spent most of the evening making love, something they had not had the privacy to do for years. Their love affair weekend had started better than he had imagined.

Her head resting softly against the fluffy pillow, she looked angelic. She was the most beautiful woman he had ever seen. She truly was the love of his life.

Watching her peacefully sleeping, he wondered if he had made the right decision to come to Alessandria. It was a choice that required him to lie to his wife. She did not know the trip was only a cover for him to meet someone in secret. For a moment, he regretted the whole thing; the trip, the lying and sneaking out to meet a man who could change their lives for good or possibly bad. Would he be able to pull off his dual purpose of this trip?

Rosario slipped out the door, trying not to disturb Sofia. He took a deep breath and made the sign of the cross, praying for God's protection over his family.

Only a few employees milled about the hotel's quiet lobby. Most appeared half-awake as they prepared for another busy day of guests coming and going. He walked confidently across the marble floor, trying not to look suspicious. To him, he felt like someone obviously out of place and certainly up to no good. To the rest of the world, he was just another man. It was early, and if a man wanted to leave at this hour, it was of no concern to them.

Inching higher on the horizon, the sun cast orange and red hues on the clouds. It was a beautiful morning, but Rosario was too nervous to notice.

He took a right out of the hotel door. He searched for the landmarks listed in the telegram. When he reached the end of the second block, he recognized the first building.

"Left at the bank."

He glanced over his shoulder, fearful he was being watched. A warranted paranoia since Don Salvatore had connections everywhere, even in Alessandria. Rosario's family would be in grave danger if any information about this meeting reached The Don's ear.

Acting fearful draws attention. He thought. *You are a curious tourist on a trip with your wife. Act like it!*

Rosario looked around, observing the commotions of a town yet to be fully awake. Across the road, a young woman in a white uniform sprinted down the walk. At the bank, an older man in a grey, three-piece suit fumbled with his keys. Straight ahead, a short, round police officer strolled with no ambition to be anywhere.

Black metal balconies accented the architecture. Plants

dripped from windows, and white sheets flapped in the gentle breeze. A jagged pattern of red and brown bricks formed the streets. Everything existed in a normal, peaceful state. Everything except Rosario, who was grateful he had pockets to hide his trembling hands.

He approached the piazza with an elaborate towering fountain in the center. The surrounding buildings housed various boutiques, alimentaris, panificios, and ristorantes. Rosario's destination was at the end of the block, Bella Anna Caffè. Under an awning were six empty tables. His nerves continued to fire wildly. He nervously looked in the direction of every noise or movement.

"Table for one, Signore?" A woman asked.

"Si, outside if you don't mind."

She led him a few feet away to a table by the sidewalk and gestured for him to sit.

"Over here is better." He pointed at a table by the building.

Less than thrilled, she escorted him to his desired table.

"Menu?"

He nodded.

The waitress returned a few minutes later with a menu. He picked it up but quickly laid it back on the table. His trembling hands caused it to wobble in his grip.

As each moment passed, he became less and less sure if he could pull this off. Sneaking around and lying to his wife was too stressful for his nerves.

"You would have made a terrible spy." He took a deep breath and said, "Remember why you are here."

Over the past several months, he exchanged telegrams with his old friend. Both sought the same thing, to make more money. There were a few loose ends before he could finalize a deal with the customer of his dreams! Then Rosario could afford anything he or his family could want. His decades of patience and hard work would finally pay off.

"What would you like?" The waitress asked

Unaware she had returned, he jumped.

"A...uh...espresso and a cornetto."

The waitress huffed at Rosario's odd behavior. But he was too consumed with his thoughts to notice. A young man on a bike, his basket filled with bread, zoomed past. It reminded him of his children's hard work. He couldn't have grown the business without them.

The waitress brought him his order and handed him a ticket.

"You can pay me now!" She held her hand out.

"Uh...I would like to order some to take with me, too."

"What do you want?" The waitress snapped.

"The same, for two. After I finish this."

With another disgruntled huff, she returned to her post by the front door and pretended to read the paper. Occasionally, she peered over the top to see if Rosario had finished.

"Buongiorno."

Rosario jumped and looked over his shoulder at the young man behind him. He started to get up, but the young man placed a hand on Rosario's shoulder.

"Please, do not get up on my account."

Immediately, the waitress appeared beside the handsome man, batting her eyelashes and smiling sweetly.

"May I bring you some espresso, Signore?"

"I will have what my friend is having."

"Right away, Signore!"

The young man gave her a polite smile and returned his focus to Rosario.

"I know this must be hard for you."

"Is it that obvious?" Rosario chuckled.

"You are doing fine. Do not worry. I have made sure no one is watching us. You are safe."

"It is not me I worry about. It is my family."

"I understand," Maximus said. "Perhaps, if you take a step back. Focus on the benefit of this endeavor."

The waitress arrived with the espresso and sweet roll for Maximus, leaning over so he could smell her perfume.

"May I bring you anything else?"

"No. Thank you."

Without looking at the ticket, Maximus reached into his pocket and removed a thick stack of money folded in half. He popped the gold clip and peeled away two bills.

"This is to pay for both of us," Maximus stated.

"Oh, I have another order...for my wife," Rosario interjected. "I will pay for that before I leave."

"This is on me. I insist!" Maximus handed the woman another bill, and her eyes lit up. "That covers everything, si?"

Maximus's eyes remained focused on Rosario.

"Si!" She nearly melted into a puddle at his feet. "Grazie, Signore!"

"You may bring him his other order after I leave." He waved his hand, dismissing the woman.

"Si, Signore!"

The waitress, thrilled with the tip, worth more than she could make in a month, pranced back to her station.

"Our business is a complicated one. Before we can export your wine, I must secure the proper permits. There has been a delay, but don't let that concern you. We should be able to start exporting in a month, maybe two."

"That is wonderful news...I suppose." Rosario's fear crept into his voice.

"You hesitate. Have you changed your mind?"

"I must admit, my feet are cold."

Maximus chuckled at Rosario's attempt to use an American phrase.

"The purpose of our meeting is to assure you, face to face, of my sincerity. I will always be an advocate for your family."

"You mean well, this I do know. You are your father's son. But my fears reach beyond sincerity. If word reaches Don Salvatore." Rosario gulped back his fear. "We would be dead before you even had a chance to help us. So I will tell no one about this meeting, not my wife or daughter Angelina. She is my successor in the business. Both deserve to know, but our discussions remain a secret until I am confident we are safe."

"I always have a man or two in the area, watching over my investments. I will send a few guys to live nearby, always ready to help *if* an issue arises. Remember, Don Salvatore is my problem, not yours."

"I hope you understand the reasons for my concerns."

"As my father has said, you are a very wise man!"

CHAPTER 21

"You make excellent wine," Don Salvatore complemented Rosario, plucking a cluster of grapes.

"Thank you, Godfather," He said with a respectful bow.

The surprise visit caused Rosario to become paranoid. He had returned home from his trip only a week ago. Had word traveled back so quickly? Was the Don here to punish him for doing business with Maximus?

To make things more perplexing, The Don was never seen out with only Bruno at his side. Where was his right hand, Antonio? Carlos had taken the women into town to buy new dresses for Marcus's return home party. Rosario feared The Don had sent Antonio after the women. Regret flowed through Rosario's veins, and fear trickled down his spine. Even in its infancy, his greed had put his family in danger. The Don was formidable. Today, Rosario feared he would learn the breadth of his power.

"I hear you have a good business. They say your wines are the best in the area, yet I have never received even a bottle from your vineyard. This lack of respect offends me, Rosario." The Don grumbled.

"I have tried Don Salvatore, but I was told you would not receive the gift."

Rosario drew in a deep breath to calm his fears. He needed to focus only on the man before him. For all he knew, The Don was unaware of what Rosario had done. He could not let the stigma of terror created by Don Salvatore control his mind or his actions.

"I am a generous man, Signor Rosario, an honest man. Perhaps today I shall trust a new face... Hmm? If you say you sent your wine as a gift and I refused, then I apologize," Don Salvatore hummed and bounced the bundle of grapes in his hand. "So today, I will accept your gift of wine, and we shall talk of business that is long overdue." He gripped Rosario's shoulder firmly, giving him a subtle smile. "My feet ache. Let us find a place to rest."

"Of course, Don Salvatore!"

Rosario whistled, and three young men came running from the stone building. He pulled his children to the side, instructing them quietly.

"Ricardo, run to the cellar and fetch two bottles of wine and glasses. Anton, fetch some cheese and a loaf of fresh bread your Mamma baked this morning. Quickly now!" He patted them gently on the back. "RJ, help this man to the table over there."

"Don Salvatore, please allow my youngest son to escort you. We can discuss business over some refreshments."

The Don grunted his acceptance of Rosario's invitation.

"This way, Signore." RJ smiled. "You can lean on me. I am strong. It's not far, just over there."

Don Salvatore chuckled. He found RJ's youthful vigor contagious.

"Ahh... To be so young and strong again. You must sell me your youth?"

RJ looked up at the old man, confused by the offer.

"Ha ha, I only tease." Don Salvatore laughed, tossing RJ's hair with his plump hand. "Ah! Is this our destination, boy?"

"Si, Signore. Right here. It is an amazing view. See!" RJ exclaimed, waving his hands toward the rolling hills of vines.

"Grazie! Si, the view is Molto Bella."

"Bravo, RJ." Rosario patted his namesake on the shoulder.

"Run along and finish your chores."

His son bowed to his father and guest before he scurried away. His older brothers arrived moments later with a small feast. They quietly worked, laying a cloth over the table and setting the wine, cheese, fruit, and tableware. They looked for their father's approval and hurried away after receiving it.

"Your sons are handsome. Well, behaved too. You have done well, Signor Rosario."

"Thank you. God has blessed me with so much."

"Si, it appears you have more than most! Maybe even more than me." The Don hissed with an acid-laced tongue.

"My wife and I worked hard for many years. We have what we have because of our efforts." Rosario remained calm.

"You married well. A beautiful woman who was rich, too!"

"Her family left her this vineyard. The land had been abandoned for two decades. Years of neglect had turned it into a wasteland of hard soil with patches of grub- brush, and weeds. It took all of what she inherited to make the place habitable."

Rosario would not allow this known master of manipulation to outwit him. He seldom interacted with this snake for fear of being bitten. When forced to converse, Rosario kept the conversation short.

"So, the woman provides for you?" The Don goaded.

"No, Godfather. That is not how we see our life together. If you would like me to tire you with the details of our love story, I would be happy to oblige." Rosario joked.

"Please, tell me. I do enjoy a good love story!"

Don Salvatore picked up the knife, sliced a large wedge from the brick of cheese, and tore a sizable chunk of bread from the loaf. He filled his plate while Rosario filled his glass. The Don waved for Rosario to continue to pour until the wine reached the brim. Satisfied, he sat back in his chair, one hand shoving the bread into his mouth, the other holding the wineglass, beckoning Rosario to tell his story.

"Godfather, I would not know where to begin!"

"Start from the beginning, when you became enraptured by the enchanting Sofia. Few know I am a romantic to the core and never pass up the chance to hear a tale. And there is nothing better than a well-told love story," Don Salvatore crooned with his mouth full. "It tugs the heart like a dog ripping flesh from a bone!"

Rosario gulped. He had no intention of telling his love story. He had never been a person of interest, which was how he preferred things to continue. However, today, The Don was salivating with fascination, forcing Rosario to entertain or suffer the consequences.

"Sofia and I fell in love before The Great War. However, circumstances prevented us from being able to marry."

"I heard she was already married!" The Don interrupted.

"Her Uncle had arranged a marriage to another, Si. But no vows were exchanged."

Rosario watched as the large man stuffed his mouth. Crumbs fell onto his shirt, and his cheeks grew with each bite.

"Tell me what happened to him?" Don Salvatore muttered before he slurped from his glass of wine.

"The man died in the war."

"I was told he was killed!"

"Many were killed. There is nothing as terrible as war," Rosario sighed. "I lost many friends defending our beautiful country."

Rosario made the sign of the cross and bowed his head, holding a reverent moment of silence. The Don joined him in the act. A surprise, given The Don's well-known merciless nature.

"Were you a war hero?" Don Salvatore interrupted the silence

"I was honored with the Croce al Merito di Guerra, the War

Merit Cross, Si," Rosario said humbly.

"For what?"

"I was shot while saving the life of a friend."

"How many men did you kill?"

"Taking a man's life was not something I did for sport."

"Oh, come now, you can tell me! Ten, twenty... a hundred?" The Don antagonized, his eyebrows bouncing. "All soldiers count their kills! How many lives did you take?"

"I was not that kind of soldier. Life is too precious to mock by counting souls." Rosario sighed.

"I heard you killed for your own benefit," Don Salvatore taunted as he tore off another chunk of bread.

"Then, Don Salvatore, you have been misled."

The Don's chipmunk cheeks were full, and his eyes danced with the excitement of a child on Christmas morning. The pleasure from his hunt made Don Salvatore's countenance glow. The Don would not release his prey. With a gulp of wine, he washed back his food and continued his pursuit.

"Let me see, what was his name... Vince... Vito... no, no," he paused and waved his hands to conjure a name. "Victor! Si, I believe it was Victor. He was the young man who had eyes for the woman you wanted as your wife, no?"

The Don's eyes danced as he held Rosario's gaze. The stage for the winemaker's execution was taking shape.

Rosario sighed inwardly; he had no desire to trudge through the past. Partly out of fear and a little out of courage, Rosario sat quietly, his facial expression unmoved by The Don's taunting.

"Oh, do let me fill in the blanks of this part of your tale. It is a tragic love story, and I would not want you to lose your pride by crying in front of your protector," Don Salvatore said with a wily grin.

Rosario gave a slight nod. There was no point in resisting the cat itching to pounce on his prey.

"Ah! You are a good man, yielding to your elders! I promise to do you justice!" Don Salvatore exclaimed as he rubbed his palms together. "Let's see, you met the angelic Sofia and instantly fell for her beauty. But her Uncle had already arranged her marriage. Oh, how you dreamed of the beautiful Sofia. Ah, but all healthy young men were called to duty. Tell me, am I right so far, Rosario?"

Rosario sat quietly and allowed The Don to continue spinning his version of the tale.

"Life is strange, eh Rosario? You show up to the front lines, and who is your commander? Victor, your precious love's fiancé! Si, you found yourself being ordered around by a man who would marry your love." The Don savored the wine in his mouth for a moment before continuing his account. "So, what did he do to make you kill him, besides outmatch you as a suitor? Did Victor mock you? Did he speak of Sofia's soft breasts, her smooth thighs? What drove you to murder, Signore?"

The Don leaned forward, ready to spring from his perch to devour his prey. Wickedness danced in Don Salvatore's eyes, and his nostrils flared with each breath.

Rosario's blood pressure was rising, but he refused to allow this devil to manipulate him. He knew the truth of this tale; he lived it, and the truth would forever rest in his heart, not on his conscience. It had been nearly three decades ago, a distant thought buried in his memory. Nonetheless, he knew this day would come.

With confidence, Rosario relaxed back in his chair and pretended the words did not affect him, even though he could feel the rush of blood warming his face. The birds chirping their summer song, and the vines swaying in the gentle breeze soothed his temper. He could feel The Don's beady eyes on him, his mouth salivating like a tiger that closed in on the kill. Yet, despite the pressure, Rosario remained still and allowed the peaceful surroundings to keep him calm.

"Ah! It must have been the story of losing her purity? Which would, of course, cause any man to lose his place. In fact, I saw Victor at lavish events with his paws all over her. She didn't seem to mind. But she is a woman who knows her place, something this generation does not understand." Don Salvatore waved in disgust at the insolent offspring of today. "How did you kill him? You can confess to me. I will forgive you of your sins, and your soul will rest in peace."

Rosario remained silent while his eager opponent sat on the edge of his seat. The Don wanted a confession so Rosario would oblige.

"You speak the truth, Don Salvatore!" Rosario admitted. "Victor was my commander. And you speak the truth, he was betrothed to Sofia. Her Uncle felt strongly about whom she should marry, but he cared nothing for love. He was concerned with amassing more wealth. The marriage between Sofia and Victor would provide a nice profit."

Rosario leaned forward to pour more wine into both glasses. He picked up his and slowly sipped the flavorful liquid. It was Rosario's turn to pause for the dramatic effect. To play the tête-à-tête of old men boasting about the stories of their lives required special skills; when to slow the pace of speech, the right amount of description, and the cleverness to tell a parable with two meanings.

Dignified, Rosario relaxed back into his chair, gently rocking as he mulled over the accounts given by The Don. Many stories about him and Sofia floated around over the years, but they ignored them.

Rosario wet his lips with the wine again and blotted his mouth with his napkin. Slowly, he folded the white cloth, placed it back on the table, and continued his side of the tale.

"Our union is that of two soulmates falling in love at first sight." A smile curled Rosario's lips. "She was a pure, enchanting soul with hair soft like spun silk, and her eyes sparkled like polished onyx. Without a doubt, she was, and is, an angel walking on earth."

"Si, she is still a beauty, even after all these years." The Don moved his hands through the air in the shape of a curvy body, taunting his prey even more.

"And again, you are correct; she is an obedient woman." Rosario pressed on, ignoring The Don's lewd interjection. "Sofia told me she would marry Victor against her will. She felt she must do as her Uncle commanded, but Sofia promised to love me for the rest of her life."

"A woman of wealth, in love with a poor man sounds so romantic." The Don bantered whimsically. "Beautiful hair. Silky skin. An angel! How Shakespearian of you!"

The Don continued his theatrics, placing his hand delicately on his forehead and leaning back into his chair as if he were to collapse.

The mocking, dramatic gestures were obvious attempts to enrage Rosario. Such habitual tactics were used by this manipulating machine to achieve his desired results. Rosario's awareness of the antics rendered them useless.

"I am bored with the mushy part. Get to the good part, where *you* killed Victor!" The Don barked, springing up from his feigned-weakened pose.

Rosario drew a deep breath and repositioned himself in his chair before he locked his eyes with the tyrant.

"I know this man was a relation to you, Don Salvatore. Knowing such, I cannot lie to you. Victor was my commander. I fought under his charge for fourteen months until his tragic death," Rosario confirmed.

"Oh, now! That is not a delightful story! I want details! Did you sneak up on him in the middle of the night, stabbing him while he slept?" The Don inquired, rubbing his plump hands together. "Tell me the *gory* details!"

Rosario sighed. To relive the moments before a man's death, the only man Rosario ever despised, was daunting. Nevertheless, The Don would not relent until the bloody details splattered the ground.

"Victor was forever by my side during numerous enemy attacks. I killed many men, too many to count."

Rosario hung his head low. The vision of life as it left a man's eyes was still a vivid scene in his mind.

"When all seemed calm, we sat in the darkness quietly listening to screams of men dying in the distance. Victor lit a cigarette and spoke of Sofia. Her soft skin, sweet pomegranate lips, smooth thighs, and how she moaned in pleasure as he took her virtue. Victor bragged that Sofia begged him to stay and make love to her each night. He described her supple breast, how he made her back arch in pleasure. Night after night, he would sneak into her room to have her. With pleasure in his voice, Victor taunted me, saying *the wanton bitch melted easily*. But I knew the truth. Sofia had told me of his indiscretions. She told Victor she hated him and would only love one man for the rest of her life, no matter who her uncle made her marry."

Rosario raised his gaze to see his opponent enjoying the confession like a picture show. The Don's beady eyes danced wildly. His hand absently stuffed his round face with bread between noisy slurps of wine.

Though it entertained The Don, Rosario was trudging through the worst days of his life. The memories wrapped tightly around his throat, limiting the air into his lungs. Each word, a massive weight in the chain, slowly strangling him.

"Some said the war made him evil, but I knew he was evil before. His excessive drinking only inflamed his temper. The constant stench of death loomed everywhere. The war in Victor's mind made him forever lost in his cup. He was ill beyond the help of man or God. It was his choice, bottle by bottle, to live in a hell of his making."

Rosario sipped his wine. The Don refilled his glass and cut another chunk of cheese from the half-eaten wheel.

"I listened each night and each day to the accounts of this man's demonic deeds. Victor kept me within arm's length. Constantly reminding me he had stolen my flower and trampled it to nothingness."

"One night, we crossed a field to advance on the Germans. He grabbed my shirt, pulling me close. The stench of liquor and stale cigarettes loomed like a dark cloud around him. He growled his threat, a threat he said before every battle. 'If *I* die, *you* die. That bitch will *not* have a happy moment for the rest of her life. I promise you that, Beretta!'" Rosario took a sip of wine and sighed. "That was our last battle together."

Rosario placed the cup on the table, hoping the tale had satisfied The Don's lust for a love story. Even if it fulfilled his glutenous desire for chaos, Don Salvatore had not chosen to visit today to hear a tale three decades old.

"Don Salvatore, please forgive me. I rattle on and waste your time with trifle stories of so long ago. You wished to discuss business, Si?"

The Don could not clear his mouth fast enough to answer. Don Salvatore waved and nodded to encourage Rosario to continue his gripping tale.

"Very well, if it pleases you, Signore," Rosario replied.

"Si, si!" Don Salvatore mumbled with his mouth full.

"As we approached the trench, we came under fire. Victor was hit in his right shoulder. Two more inches to the right, it would have been me who was shot. I dragged him to the medic tent and returned to the battle, fighting and killing every enemy I could. Every German soldier had Victor's face. I took pleasure in seeing blood spill from their guts. I slit throats and cut open bellies. I shot them between the eyes. Everyone I killed, I felt as though I had killed a little more of Victor. I wanted his evil gone from this earth. I wanted revenge for my Sofia. I wanted him dead with all my heart!"

Rosario paused. Partly for effect but more so to settle the bubbling anger for Victor that grew in his gut.

"After we had seized the trench, I visited Victor. He was in surgery, so I waited, and I prayed he would die the worst death, a painful, slow death. Victor was in a hospital for two months because his wounds would not heal. The infection was rooted deep in his body. By the time they amputated his right arm, it was too late. The infection was coursing through his veins. The wickedness he thrust on the world came full circle; his evil blood was killing him. He caused others pain, and his last days were spent in utter agony. I shall not lie; I relished hearing him moan and scream in misery. I sat outside his room, savoring his cries for mercy. He deserved his death, Don Salvatore. But it was *not* by my hands."

Rosario stopped, waiting for The Don's response. He knew the end was not as The Don wanted, but it was the truth.

"Si, Si, a good winemaker and an excellent storyteller, too." The Don raised his glass, toasting Rosario, before taking a hearty swig. "Si, and a good family man!" Again, hailing his glass in salute to Rosario's many fine qualities. "You take pride in your work, your family, and your lovely bride."

"Si, I am immensely grateful for all of God's blessings!"

Rosario could tell the time for storytelling was over, and true business was about to be revealed. He steadied his breathing and willed his body to remain calm.

"Delightful story, delightful indeed," The Don gushed after clearing his mouth of food. He brushed a few crumbs from his shirt. "I, too, tell an intriguing story!"

The Don finished the wine in his glass and handed it to Rosario to refill. Don Salvatore nodded in gratitude for the generous pour, then told his tale, animating it with his hands.

"There is a man who owns a winery. He makes excellent

wine! The best it is said." Don Salvatore raised his glass to salute. "He fell in love with a woman betrothed to another man. Oh, the agony of never tasting her sweet lips or savoring her body. But fate was merciful and freed her from her promise. Happily, the love birds wed and now live in a world filled with beauty, joy, bountiful harvests, lustful passion, and eternal love. In short, they lived a perfect life!" The Don continued shifting his tone from playful to pure evil. "Now, the rich winemaker has two beautiful daughters, a good business, and a lot of land. A happy life, free of troubles. *Too free!*"

"I pay my tax to you, even in lean times."

The Don ignored Rosario's plea and continued his story.

"But the winemaker has forgotten who protects him from evil people like the man he killed so long ago. You see, this happy man must share his happiness with others. *With me!* The happy winemaker *will* share in his bounty."

Don Salvatore sat on the edge of his chair, his dark eyes burning a hole of blackness into Rosario, only pausing to refresh his tongue. The wine sloshed out of the cup, missing The Don's mouth, and splashed on his shirt. He ignored the mishap and continued to paint the scene of Rosario's future.

"But since I am a generous man, I will not seek restitution for murdering Victor. Instead, I pose a choice to the happy winemaker. His daughter's hand in marriage to the man of *my* choosing, or he pays *three times* his usual tax."

"Don Salvatore, I could not possibly keep the winery going if I paid such a high price!" Rosario protested, running his hand through his thick black hair.

"Then your daughter will *marry!*" Don Salvatore gloated.

The wolf's eyes lapped up his prey's fear.

"I...I cannot."

"You have no choice!" The Don's deep voice boomed. After he slurped more wine, his tone became jubilant. "Come, what is wrong with a wedding? There has not been a big wedding in

Brusnengo in years! Your daughter's wedding shall be the grandest celebration our little town has ever known! Such glorious news, and you still frown. Are you worried about the cost? Blah!" A devilish grin curled Don Salvatore's lip. "I am sure you can afford a wedding of the century!"

"I cannot arrange my daughter's marriage. Sofia and I—"

"This is how you save your vines. You said it yourself; you cannot sustain the vineyard with my tax. So, tell that beautiful rose, the darling Sofia, a wedding or the vineyard!"

Rosario sighed and slouched into his chair. He raked his hand through his hair as the vision of Sofia's wrath washed over him. His heart pounded like it would explode.

"Well? I do not have all day!" Don Salvatore stood.

"Godfather, which daughter? Who is she to marry?"

"Eh, I do not care which one! Whoever my nephew wants!" Don Salvatore smiled as his final blow was delivered to his prey. Rosario's face drained of all color. The pressure across his chest was so intense he could barely breathe.

"He is a good boy and will make a good husband," Don Salvatore grunted and tipped his hat at Rosario. He paused for a moment to relish the fear in Rosario's eyes. "No worry, he is no Victor. She will be happy."

"Please, Don Salvatore, wait! How will I know which daughter to pick? Who will be the better bride?"

"Pick well! Or you will have another tragedy to tell!"

Don Salvatore made his way to his car while Rosario's brain bobbed in the sea of tumultuous thoughts. The most prominent is that he never knew The Don had a nephew.

"Don Salvatore, wait! What is your nephew's name, and when may we meet him?"

"You have already met him." Don Salvatore looked back with a devilish grin. "His name is *Giorgio*!"

CHAPTER 22

"Angelina, are you coming?" Rosario yelled from the bottom of the staircase. "Hurry up. Carlos is waiting!"

"I am almost ready, Papa!"

"She is always running late, isn't she?" He asked Sofia

Light filtered into the kitchen, illuminating Sofia. A dirty apron covered the stains on her old dress. The strip of white flour on her cheek and her hair in a messy bun completed the disheveled appearance.

"Like her father," Sofia replied with a wink.

"Very funny, Bella Mia! And you are a clock, eh?"

"Of course! Someone has to keep this place on schedule," Sofia razzed, preparing the fava beans for their evening meal.

"Si! Lucky for us, we have you!"

Rosario wrapped his arms around her and kissed her neck. His hands traveled down her torso. But he did not snatch the usual loving grab of her breast. Before Sofia had time to react, his fingers found the tickle spot that always made her jump. The bowl of fava beans wobbled and nearly spilled.

"Now, now stop! That is not nice! Carmella is ill today. I have much to do with no help, and you are *not* helping me!"

"Oh, *I* will help you!"

He nibbled on her neck again. This time, he tickled her skin with his mustache. She giggled and squirmed.

"Rosario! Stop, stop!"

She tried to wiggle away, but he embraced her firmly.

"I thought you liked me kissing your neck?"

"Si, but I have things to do, and Angelina will be down any second!"

"She knows we kiss!"

"That is not the point."

Sofia tried again to free herself. He maintained his hold and allowed her to spin around to face him.

"Then kiss me goodbye, and I will leave you to your work."

"I will kiss you goodbye, and you may return later to finish what you started!"

Sofia gazed up at him with a seductive smile, her twinkling eyes begging him to kiss her. Rosario savored her beauty.

"You are the sun and the moon that lights my soul!"

"I love you, Cara Mia." She kissed him. "Now, go so I may finish my cooking!"

Rosario smiled and patted her behind. "I love us."

"As do I," she said, snuggling into his chest.

Angelina scurried down the stairs, interrupting their hug.

"Ah, finally! She graces us with her presence!" Rosario grabbed their hats from the table. "Carlos is waiting in the car. We must hurry. Your mother needs your help when we return."

Standing with the rear car door open, Carlos waited patiently for them. His perfectly ironed shirt accentuated his broad shoulders and solid form. Carlos was a few years younger than Rosario, but looked ten years his senior. When she was young, Angelina asked Carlos how he came to know the family. His response was quiet and simple.

"Signor Beretta is a good man. All I can tell you is he saved me from evil. For this, I give him my eternal loyalty."

"Where *are* we going?" Angelina asked.

"We have several errands to attend to today," Rosario replied.

Carlos opened the door for Angelina before repeating the gesture for Rosario.

"Carlos, I wish to see the vines first, please. "I want to see how the new crop grows with the limited moisture. We may need to have the men bring more water."

"Si, Signore." Carlos turned left on the meandering road that surrounded the vineyard.

"You cannot resist a chance to examine every angle of the picturesque view." Angelina smiled.

"I have spent my life working hard to make this a beautiful place. I will enjoy it every chance I get," he said emphatically. "How is my Principessa this morning?"

"Good, Papa."

"Did you sleep well, or are you still having night terrors?"

"No, I slept well." She stared out the window, avoiding any further questions on the matter. "Is Carmella ok?"

"She suffers from a headache and will be back tomorrow."

Rosario picked up her hand. Holding it, he remembered when she was a little girl, and her hand looked so tiny in his. Rosario's heart sank. He missed his little Principessa, the toddler who would greet him at the door every evening with a smile. Her long curls bounced with every step as she excitedly screamed, "Papa's home, Papa's home." He would pick her up, touch her head to the ceiling, and gently tickle her belly with his mustache. Angelina would giggle wildly, wiggling her small frame. Aside from a kiss from Sofia, it was the best part of his day. But those days were long gone. Now, she was a beautiful woman, and her tiny fingers had grown long and elegant.

Time never seems to go at the pace we desire. He thought.

"You have grown so much." A lump formed in his throat. "So beautiful and smart."

Angelina smiled. She leaned against his shoulder and said, "It is the same dream as before."

"Will you tell me what you see in your dream?"

"I only remember running barefoot up the hill from the stream, and I am scared."

"What at the river makes you run?"

Angelina looked out the window, pondering the question.

"My fear comes from behind me, at the river, and before me...by the house. I do not understand why I run from one terror toward another.

"Your fear is understandable. If you dream this again, and I hope you do not, write what you remember. Allow the pen to transfer the monsters onto the paper. Burn the paper after to purge your mind of them forever."

Rosario rested his head onto hers. Her hair was still damp, and the sweet smell of roses filled his nose. He smiled.

Quietly, he watched the rows of vines, each branch heavy with fruit. It was a beautiful sea of green flowing over hills and down through the valleys.

"We are almost to your favorite spot, Signore," Carlos interrupted the silence.

At the hilltop, a single tree, as old as time, stood in a patch of grass. From the grand view, endless rows of healthy vines rolled over the hills in every direction. The roadside patch, under the magnificent tree, was Rosario's throne.

"Ah, very good. Stop here, Carlos. I would like to get out."

Carlos held the door for Rosario. As nimble as a cat, he moved around the car and opened Angelina's.

"Thank you, Carlos." She smiled, accepting his hand.

"Carlos, have the men carry water to the new vines every other day until we have rain."

"Si, Signore. I will inform them when we return."

Rosario extended his hand to help Angelina traverse the uneven ground.

"Had I known we were stopping here, I would not have worn my best shoes," She said, wobbling with each step.

"Look how healthy the vines are!" Rosario waved at the valley below. "It will be another good year of wine."

"Do you feel it in your bones, or is Mamma the only one with a wise skeleton?" Angelina chuckled.

He wrapped his arm around her and laughed.

"Beautiful and charming, plus Mamma's wisdom and Papa's humor. I fear for the world." He moved farther away from the car than usual. "I need to share something with you. But it is words only for your ears." He whispered, glancing back.

"I thought you trusted Carlos."

"I do. However, even the most trusted people should not hear everything." Rosario glanced back again, confirming the distance. "We must discuss...a difficult...a delicate topic. Will you just listen to make it easy on your Papa?"

Angelina nodded.

With a broken-hearted smile, he gazed at her beautiful skin. He cupped her chin and stroked his thumb across her cheek. Her dark eyes, looking up at him in adoration, made his task more daunting.

"Where to begin?" He looked back over the vines, hiding the tears that filled his eyes.

"I dreamed big for you. Well, for all of my children, but especially you. I try not to show it, but you are my favorite. You remind me of myself when I was your age. Ambitious! Clever! Able to move people like pieces on a chessboard. You will go far, my child!" His chest swelled with pride.

"I look over this land, the vines I...*we* planted. I see you, my beautiful Angelina, taking my place as master of this business. You will, one day, sell our wine in far-off places. I know this, in here!" He poked his chest, emphasizing his passionate belief.

Rosario's emotions tremored within, and he feared he could not finish without them erupting. He steadied himself and softened his tone.

"I had always hoped you would fall in love like I did with your Mother. I prayed God would place before you a man you instantly knew was the love of your life. But sometimes we must make sacrifices to become what God intended us to be."

Tears streamed down his cheeks when she slipped her hand into his. A simple gesture to strengthen him and ease his pain.

"Bella, would you do anything to save all of this?" Rosario motioned toward the vines. "To save all of us?"

"Of course, Papa! I would do anything you ask of me!"

"I have worked many years, some harder than others, to create this legacy. Laboring over the land is one of many sacrifices." Rosario stared at a rock he moved with the tip of his shoe. "Bella, bonds are sacrifices to strengthen our hold on what we wish to preserve. That is why, for the sake of the family, you must take Giorgio's hand in marriage."

The rose color drained from Angelina's cheeks, leaving an expression of shock and horror. Unconsciously, she dropped her father's hand and took several steps back.

"But Papa! I have no desire to marry Giorgio. None!" Angelina's hand clutched her chest. "I... I...do not love him!"

Tears of rage flowed down her cheeks. She shook her head in disbelief, and her heart thundered her refusal. After a few minutes, she finally met Rosario's mournful gaze. Her eyes conveyed the understanding that Papa *needed* her to marry. Love did not matter.

"Forgive me, Bella."

"Does Mamma know?"

"I wanted to discuss it with you first," Rosario said, his head hanging low.

"Why do you need *me* to marry him, Papa?"

"What I tell you now, you must not mention to anyone. Do you understand?" Rosario looked her in the eye, a silent plea issuing out, begging her not to fight him. "The Don has ordered my daughter...you...to marry his nephew, Giorgio."

"*Giorgio* is his nephew!" Of a thousand questions, she could only speak one word. "Why?"

"Sometimes in life, we must unite families for the sake of business. We have done well over the years, and The Don insists his nephew marry into a family of wealth. According to The Don, we are the only wealthy family with daughters."

He hoped his explanation would suffice. Telling her the threats made by Don Salvatore would only intensify her dislike for Giorgio.

"We must do whatever Don Salvatore desires."

His foot found the rock again, and he rolled it around. Giving his favorite child to a man she did not love to save his vineyard made him feel like a coward.

"Maybe I should take our wine to another country...to America. I can speak their language." Angelina looked up at him, her eyes pleading for mercy. "You said yourself I could sell it anywhere!"

Rosario's eyes remained transfixed on the ground. Her mention of America added to his guilt. He had not told her of his dealings with Maximus. Admitting he kept that from her now would only add to her anger. Or fuel the mad desire to go to a country far beyond his protection.

"It is not that easy."

"Why not? Why can't it be that easy?"

"It is an order from The Don!" Rosario snapped. "He is a powerful and dangerous man! A man you *never* say no to!"

"We are to just give up?"

"Si," Rosario replied, defeated.

CHAPTER 23

Rosario stood outside, waiting for Mario to arrive to pay his bill. It would be the only good part of today's visit. Rosario had no desire to extend hospitality to anyone, especially Mario. What choice did Rosario have? He was a cornered mouse with no escape from the hungry cat's paws.

Twenty-four hours ago, Rosario broke Angelina's heart, saddling her with an unimaginable weight. She was like him more than any of his other children. She understood the situation and would dutifully play the part.

He feared Angelina's future and his own. As expected, Sofia was adamant Angelina had the right to reject the marriage proposal. They argued for hours, but Sofia refused to change her mind. His spirit broken, he finally agreed to her demands. Both conversations took their toll, and sleep evaded him. Adding exhaustion to his woes made this day a sequel to the nightmare.

He tried to focus on more pleasant thoughts. The sun was warm and sparkled in the clear blue sky. A perfect day, like the day of his meeting with Maximus. He and Sofia had returned only ten days ago, yet the trip's memories were as vivid as the present moment.

When Rosario returned from his secret meeting, Sofia was awake. She stood naked, hiding behind the curtain to peek at the beautiful landscape. Next to the velvet drape, her olive skin was a vision of perfection, one Rosario would never forget. They spent the rest of the day in the room, wrapped in each other's arms.

When it was time for dinner, Sofia adorned her new dress. The red silk material clung to her soft curves. Rosario's heart thumped in his chest. She was the most radiant creature on earth. It was tempting to keep her locked inside for only his eyes to admire, but he promised her an evening to remember.

They strolled along the streets of the lively city. A stark contrast to his morning outing. Their path was a meandering one, taking the next beckoning street. The town was a continuous stretch of beautiful statues, savory smells, and music floating in the air. Lively chatter from happy patrons filled the streets. Many lovers strolled arm in arm and enjoyed the fresh evening air. Rosario did not want the trip to end. He had all he ever wanted right next to him. It was a refreshing getaway.

The bang of a door slamming pulled him from his reverie.

"How was your trip?" Mario asked joyfully.

"It was wonderful. We hardly left the hotel room!"

"Good for you! You work too hard and should sneak away more often. Your children are old enough. No need for you to hover over them!"

"Si, but this vineyard is my life. My mind is always filled with what must be done, making it difficult to leave."

Rosario patted Mario's back like they were still old friends.

"Walk with me for a few minutes, Mario. There is something I wish to discuss with you."

The two men strolled between the vines, the vibrant green leaves brushing against their shoulders. Rosario leaned over to pull a weed and discarded it. He was stalling. The subject made his stomach turn, yet he knew he must follow the old traditions of an arranged marriage.

"I understand Giorgio wishes to marry my daughter."

"Si, he does, but I thought you told him no!"

Rosario spent the early morning hours practicing his

carefully chosen words for this moment.

"Well, in my haste *and* intoxication, I did not give the young man a chance."

"I see," Mario replied, scratching his chin.

Rosario held his tongue while his companion pondered the situation. Mario had Rosario's balls in his hands. He could gently caress them or clamp down with the grip of an eagle's talons. Rosario was forced to wait patiently to let the fate of his balls play out. Mario held his tongue for several minutes, obviously enjoying having the upper hand.

"Giorgio will be by later today. Perhaps you could have a *sober* conversation!" Mario grinned with satisfaction.

"And your thoughts on the matter?"

"Si, si! Of course, I have no objection to the union! Let me know when we should have the celebration dinner!"

Mario extended his hand, and Rosario accepted. The negotiation completed, they had an obligatory brotherly hug.

"I must go, but I am eager to hear the details of your chat when Giorgio returns home!" Mario gloated, waltzing away.

Rosario stood by the kitchen door to gather his thoughts. Once he passed through the threshold, he would be transported into a dimension of emotional instability. Each day was different. Either a catfight or giggle-fest awaited him in the realm beyond the door. He was in no mood to deal with irrational minds. It was difficult to survive in that world during times of peace. He was about to start a war.

"Ciao, Papa!" Catalina nearly ran her father over on her way out the door to fetch some eggs.

"Ciao Bella, how are you this morning?"

"Better than you! You look like someone stole your dog? What is wrong, Papa?"

Rosario shrugged, not willing to burden his daughter.

She slipped her arm into his and walked toward the chicken coop. "What bothers you so much?"

She leaned her head on his shoulder, and he smiled.

"May I help you gather the eggs?"

"That would make my day even more beautiful, Papa!"

Walking arm in arm, Catalina chattered away. Her happiness was contagious. Soon, Rosario felt strong enough to endure the onslaught of emotions inside.

"Well, what did *he* want?" Sofia stamped her foot.

"He came to pay his bill."

"Why did you not invite him in for breakfast?"

Inviting Mario into Sofia's layer was begging for disaster. She wanted to scream her rejection directly to Mario. Of course, that tirade would be preceded by a sizzling plate of food in his face.

"He was busy and had to go." Rosario's tone hardened.

He began to second-guess his resolve to manage the emotional abyss. Had his stomach been full, he would return to vines or invent a task needing immediate attention.

"Well, he could have said hello."

"He said to give you his greetings."

"Coffee, Signore?" Carmella asked sweetly.

The short, round woman gave Rosario a motherly smile. He was grateful for her timely compassion.

"That would be great, thank you!"

For the next hour, Rosario listened to the women talk about the weather, clothes, love, and more. More than his pounding head wanted to hear. He was tired, and this looming marriage weighed heavily on his heart. Needing a reprieve, he allowed his thoughts to drift while he ate.

"Rosario? Rosario?" Sofia shouted to get his attention.

Deep in thought, he blinked several times to regain his grip on the present. "Huh? Si, Bella Mia!"

"Carmella left with the wash. We must discuss this now?" She motioned for Angelina and Catalina to sit beside her.

He did not wish to discuss this *now*. He did not wish to

discuss it at all. The look on the faces of the three most precious women in his life made his task more daunting. Sofia wore an evil glare that would send the devil himself running in fear. Catalina had the usual joyful morning demeanor. Dejected and lifeless, Angelina was greener than a sick frog.

"Rosario?" Sofia snapped.

His face had turned pale as if he was near death.

"Are you ok?" Sofia asked with an arched brow.

"I am fine!" He lied. "Can a man not finish his meal!"

He swallowed his last bite of food and wiped his face. Out of habit, he assessed the eyes of his beautiful Italian Roses. Blending the three women's volatile emotions would cause far more problems. He decided to address it in a way that suited him, one woman at a time.

"I have made my decision! All of you will abide by it." He held up his hand to silence the revolt. "No more!"

"What!" Sofia fumed.

"Temper your anger, Sofia."

"I am not angry. I am furious!"

"Precisely why we cannot discuss this now."

"*No, now*! They must know how quick you are to cast their lives aside!" Her glare hardened. "You made this horror! You shall bear their outrage and mine!"

"Catalina. Angelina. Outside, now!" He waved them away.

Rosario scowled at his wife, waiting for the door to close.

"You promised me! You promised to never arrange their marriage! Tell them their perfect Papa broke his promise!"

"Enough! Contain your emotions and sit! I will tolerate no more of your tirade! Delicate things must be handled delicately." He held up his hand to silence her. "We must unify and show joy. To do otherwise will fester more issues. Listen and listen well, Sofia Rose! You *will* be the happy mother of the bride!"

CHAPTER 24

"What is going on?" Catalina asked in confusion.

"It was not my decision! Papa said I have to marry him!"

"Who?"

Angelina braced for her sister's outrage. "Giorgio."

A stone of guilt landed in Angelina's gut with a thud. Accepting Giorgio's marriage proposal was the single worst thing she had ever done to her sister, worse than all the teasing, hair-pulling, insults, and dirty tricks combined.

"You can't! You wouldn't?" Catalina's face filled with rage, and a fountain of tears spilled from her eyes. "I hate you! I *hate* you with *all* my heart!"

"What is this chaos about?" Sofia shouted, racing down the steps. "We do not *hate* in this family! *Ever!*

"Papa did not tell her about Giorgio and I marrying. So, I had to tell her."

Angelina reached out to comfort her sister. Catalina, beyond consoling, pushed her away.

"Papa, why?" Catalina sobbed. "Why would you hurt me? Do you despise me so much that you freely torture me?"

Sofia placed her hand on her daughter's shoulder, but Catalina pulled away. She refused to be comforted by anyone in the traitorous family.

"I hate *all* of you! I will never forgive you for this. *NEVER!*" Distraught, she ran up the hill.

"Are you happy now?" Sofia scolded Rosario. "See what happens when you play puppetmaster with people's lives?"

She turned and scolded Angelina. "You knew how she felt about him, yet you torment her with this...this...! You are as monstrous as your father and deserve her wrath."

She gave both a reproving glare, then left to find Catalina.

"Papa! Why? Why didn't you tell her? Why did you make me do it? She will never forgive me! *Never!*"

"Bella," Rosario reached out to comfort her.

"How could you, Papa? I am only doing as *you* commanded. You sacrifice my happiness...my life. Have I not lost enough? No, now I have lost my sister. She will never forgive me, Papa! Cat hates more fiercely than anyone. She will stop at nothing to destroy my happiness if I ever find any. I thought you loved me."

Fernando and Carlos emerged from the building at the top of the hill. Telling Fernando the unhappy news made Angelina's stomach turn. She could not obliterate the heart of another loved one. She wiped away her tears and did something she had never done. Spit at her father's feet.

"*You* have to fix this, Papa!" Angelina stormed toward her only sanctuary, the vines.

"Bella! Wait!"

Rosario continued to holler, but she ignored him. In seconds, she was enveloped by a curtain of green leaves.

"What has happened?" Carlos asked, but Rosario raised his hand.

"They shall be the death of me." Rosario groaned, rubbing his forehead. "Nan, get Angelina. Carlos, fetch Sofia and Catalina. They went up the hill. Bring them back, no matter how much it infuriates them! I, too, have a temper."

A truck roaring up the drive blared its horn in long blurts between short toots, adding to Rosario's frustrating day.

"Great, Giorgio! This day just gets better and better."

****

"Angelina, wait!" Fernando hollered, running to catch up.

"Go away, Nan! I want to be alone!"

"Lina! Wait, please!"

Fernando's long legs quickly made up the distance between them. He fell in step with her, but she kept her head down, pretending he was not there.

Her engagement had caused enough pain and suffering to those she loved, including herself. Discussing it further, especially with the person it would hurt the most, was inconceivable. She would prefer to keep her head in the sand and suffocate than cause more pain to someone she loved.

"Lina, why are you crying?"Fernando gently placed his hand on her shoulder, stopping her.

"It is complicated."

"Tell me! Let me in. Please, let me do something for you."

For the first time, he spoke as if he no longer was afraid of her. He lovingly stood at her side, ready to hear anything, even if it would hurt him.

She would not have faced this horrible destiny if she had accepted Fernando's love. She was an ungrateful fool. God supplied her with a good man, and she rejected him. Now, a life with Giorgio would be her penance. Her purgatory would begin with breaking Fernando's heart.

"Papa ordered me to marry Giorgio. It is not what I want. I have no love for him!" Sobbing, she collapsed into Fernando's chest.

"Tell him you refuse the marriage." Fernando lovingly wrapped his arms around her.

"I have no choice. Papa ordered it."

"You can marry me!" He pulled her from his chest and cupped her chin.

Before she could answer, he leaned in and kissed her passionately. Angelina melted into his arms, his tender lips pressed against hers. The world slowed to a peaceful lull. For a moment, she felt safe and loved.

The sound of a horn broke their tender embrace.

"We better go. Your father asked me to bring you back to the house. He is worried." Before he stepped away, Fernando brushed her cheek with his thumb. "Thank you."

"For what?"

"For kissing me back." Fernando beamed with happiness.

Hand in hand, they walked together toward the house in silence. Being Fernando's wife was much more appealing than Giorgio's bride. Her heart melted, and a calmness settled over her. Her peace, however, did not last long.

At the end of the row of vines, the reality of life rushed back. It was Giorgio blaring the horn as he always did when he arrived at the vineyard. Once they emerged from the vines, their momentary joy would dissipate in the face of her betrothed. It was her *duty* to marry Giorgio. A nun takes her vow to serve God, and so must Angelina vow to serve her family. She would play her part with false enthusiasm and pretend to be a loving, devoted bride.

They exited the vines, stepping into the blazing sunshine. Angelina blinked to regain her vision. Recovered from the blinding glow, her father, hands flying passionately, conversed with a tall man. Her heart pounding, she dropped Fernando's hand.

"Look who I found!" Anton boasted to Angelina as he climbed out of the rig.

"Marcus!" She squealed. "Oh, thank God you are home!"

"And none too soon!" Marcus picked Angelina up and spun her around. "Must I be St. George and slay the dragon before he consumes the princepessa and the kingdom where she lives?" He chuckled, placing her on the ground.

"How I have missed you," she said, hugging him again.

Sofia's loud scream echoed from the top of the hill. She ran as fast as her legs could carry her, screaming Marcus's name with every step.

"Marcus! Ohh, my Marcus!" She blubbered as tears of joy rushed down her cheeks.

"Mamma!" Marcus gave her the embrace she longed to receive. Holding her tight, he twirled her.

Sofia kissed his hands and hugged him several more times, praising God for his safe return. She placed her hands on his waist and scoffed.

"You are too thin! Come inside! You must eat!"

Sofia babbled on, praising God and lovingly scolding Marcus. Frequently, she stopped to hug and kiss his hand as she walked him to the house.

"Ohh, Blessed God! Marcus, why didn't you send word you were coming home? I would have prepared a feast of your favorites! Thank you, God! Thank you!"

The morning's catastrophe was completely erased from her mind. Her son was home, and her heart was whole again!

"Sofia!" Rosario repeated, his voice growing louder.

"What?"

"We must mend our daughters' hearts before we welcome Marcus home." Rosario huffed and pulled his daughters close. "Let us try this again. All three of you will hold your tongues until I have—"

"Papa, I—" Angelina started.

Rosario silenced her with a wave of his hand.

"*Angelina*, just *listen*. You...both of you, have cause to be upset with me. It is true; I have made a mess of things. If you can contain yourselves for a moment, I shall set things right."

Rosario puffed his chest, more out of self-preservation for impending calamity than a show of strength.

"Though I wish Ricardo were here, he will surely understand the need to dispatch with this...news. Giorgio extended his hand in marriage to my daughter. Devoted to her family, she has agreed to marry him."

Sofia, Catalina, and Angelina erupted in shouts of condemnation for Rosario's actions. The trio's tirade was a thundering avalanche of chaos, building in strength with each second. Rosario held up his hand. Like Sofia's magic finger, it instantly made the women stop bickering.

"I have agreed with the match. There shall be no more arguing on the matter. My word is final! Since Marcus is home, I think a summer wedding will be perfect." Rosario looked at Angelina. "Bella, you will accept this marriage as a joyous occasion."

Rosario paused, jetted out his jaw, and watched his daughters' reaction. Both remained contrite with their chins tucked.

"Cat, you, too, must accept this marriage with grace and dignity. I expect you to forgive your sister...*immediately.*"

Both girls opened their mouths to protest, but Rosario held up his hand.

"You must find a truce. I will not have a man divide my family. Nothing is more important than family. Si?"

Dutifully, they nodded.

"That is settled. Catalina, you must extend the first olive branch to your sister. It is only fitting."

Catalina scoffed, and Sofia stomped her foot.

"How can you ask that of your daughter! She is heartbroken!"

Rosario silenced both of them.

"Catalina, I am certain Angelina will extend the same courtesy when she weds. You must set a precedent, as the *first* blushing bride, by asking her to stand with you. Capito?"

The words took a moment to register in all their minds.

"First?" Catalina stuttered.

"Rosario! You cannot force her to forgive..." Sofia began but paused. "What are you saying. Cease your games and speak plainly!"

"This morning, while Catalina and I gathered eggs, she confessed her feelings for Giorgio. When I shared his desire to marry, she accepted with elation!" Rosario said proudly.

Fernando slipped his hand back into Angelina's and gave her a loving smile.

"Now. Let us celebrate Marcus's return and Catalina's nuptials!" Rosario exclaimed, hugging his daughters. "Sofia, have Carmella prepare a feast for us! Fernando, bring us a case of the *1925 Nebbiolo*. We have much to celebrate. I, for one, plan to drink until the sun rises tomorrow!"

CHAPTER 25

"You look lovely, Cat!" Angelina said, forcing a smile.

"It is a perfect day, not a cloud in the sky! Did you see the decorations? Everything is covered in flowers! Papa bought hundreds of them! It smells like Nonna's rose garden!"

Catalina continued babbling as she twirled in her gown. Her long chestnut brown hair and olive skin gave the white silk fabric an angelic radiance. She was gorgeous, but not because of the dress. It was her happiness that made her glow like an angel.

"Have you seen the cake? Signora Vittiano makes the best. Because everyone in Brusnengo and hundreds of Mario's business associates are attending, the cake had to be nine tiers high! They needed four men to carry it! It is a strawberry cake with buttercream icing and a Lemoncello custard filling. It will be the sweetest summer melting in your mouth!

Mamma and Carmella baked cookies for two weeks, and Papa hired the best chef in town to prepare dinner. Of course, it won't be as good as Mamma's cooking, but she couldn't do *everything!*"

Catalina stopped twirling long enough to admire her hair in the mirror.

"Lina, I am so happy! Giorgio is better than a storybook prince! His love letters are works of poetry! Of course, all the jewelry he has given me certainly adds to his charm. The latest addition is a pair of ruby earrings.

He is simply perfect, as is his taste in jewelry! He promised

I shall never want for anything. Our children shall always have the best. A woman could not ask for more!"

"I am sure he will treat you well, Cat."

Angelina wanted to be elated for Catalina. She would be if her sister were marrying someone...*anyone* else. She stared out the window to hide her emotions. As her sister, she was forced to accept the situation but could not raise her mood above gloomy despair.

Two months ago, Angelina stood beside her father as they looked over the vineyard and discussed her marriage to the man who would now be her brother-in-law. She did not understand why the situation changed. Her conversation with her father after the announcement only added to the confusion.

"Why did you give Cat to Giorgio?"

"Bella, you did not want to be saddled with a loveless marriage. Catalina was eager to marry. My decision was a logical one. You are happy. Cat is happy. I am happy." Rosario explained nonchalantly.

"Papa, you begged me to marry him. No, you ordered me, *'for the good of the family!'* Now, I am overlooked as if I was never an option? Even more perplexing, no one is concerned! Why am I the only one to smell a dead fish?"

Angelina posed the same question to the rest of her family. No one acknowledged the need for concern. Catalina believed she had won his hand and never doubted Giorgio's intent to wed her. The family's blindness meant they did not know about Don Salvatore's involvement in the marriage. Everyone, including her father, sloughed off her gut feelings as jealousy, especially after all of Giorgio's lavish gifts.

Giorgio never showed up empty-handed. After the giant diamond engagement ring, he showered Catalina with expensive jewelry, fresh flowers, and fine clothing. On every visit, he had a new gift for Catalina and one for Sofia.

Angelina had to admit it was hard to watch. Occasionally, she felt a sting of jealousy. However, she clearly recognized his generosity was a way of manipulating them. All the blind love made it painful *and* nauseating to watch.

One good thing about the engagement was that Giorgio stopped flirting with Angelina. He hardly spoke two words in her direction. If he intended to slight her, it did the opposite. The frequent family dinners were more enjoyable for her.

"Are you going to get dressed, Lina?"

"After you are ready."

"My apologies for my vanity. I suppose I have used the mirror for at least an hour longer than needed! My gown is so beautiful, I cannot stop admiring it!" Catalina replied, catching one last glimpse of her radiance.

Angelina watched her sister dancing as if she were practicing for a formal performance before royalty.

That could have been me lavished with an unending river of gifts. I could be the one twirling in a sea of endless joy. Angelina thought.

Absently, Angelina brushed the same section of hair until Catalina's question pulled her back to the present moment.

"You don't still love him, do you?"

"What? Who?" Angelina replied, startled.

"Giorgio!"

"No! No! Cat, I *never* loved him!"

"Then what is bothering you? You are supposed to be happy for me, but you act as if this is my funeral!"

Her words hit her hard. More than once, Angelina had thought this marriage was her sister's funeral. To be a heavy cloud hanging over her sister's wedding day was unfair. Catalina was the beautiful bride. Today was *her* joyous day. To honor that, Angelina made up a reason.

"Cat, you are leaving, and I already miss you. But this is *your* day. How I feel is unimportant."

"That is so sweet! My new home is not far away. You can visit, or even stay the night, anytime you like. The villa is enormous!" Catalina hugged Angelina.

"That...would be nice." Angelina faked a smile.

She would miss her sister, but the idea of sleeping under the same roof as Giorgio made her skin crawl.

"Let me do your hair," Catalina said, snatching the brush.

Catalina prattled on about her new life for what seemed like an eternity. She stressed the size of her new home and surrounding land well exceeded the requirements to be considered a villa. She gushed with details about their honeymoon, her personal maid, and her station in society. Angelina sat quietly, nodding and smiling, pretending to be happy for her.

"How are you and Fernando doing?" Catalina asked. "I saw him kiss you. Has he spoken of marriage?"

Angelina rolled her eyes. A moment before, she wanted her sister to talk about anything but her fairybook life. Her relationship with Fernando was not a preferred topic, and she wished they would return to discussing Catalina's perfect life.

"Let Papa recover from yours before we plan mine!"

"Very funny! You *do* love him, right?"

"I guess so."

"What does that mean?"

"I don't think I will ever prance around the house like you do about Giorgio."

"I do not prance!" Catalina failed to contain her grin.

Angelina arched her brow.

"Ok, I prance a little, but Giorgio is different. He is handsome, rich, and exciting. He has traveled the world and is filled with adventure. A man like that makes you... I don't know...excited to think about! Most of all, he is so passionate when we kiss. I melt every time!"

The description made Angelina's stomach turn.

"Cat, I don't need to know details. You are happy; that is enough!" Angelina shook away the image of the mushy lovebirds. "Are you saying Nan is not handsome?"

"Well, not exactly." Catalina flushed in embarrassment. "He is just...different from Giorgio, that's all."

Angelina was grateful when a gentle rap on the door interrupted their conversation.

"Carlos has arrived with the car. Are you ready?" Anton asked.

"We need ten more minutes," Catalina replied.

"Wow! Only four hours of primping. A record!" He teased.

Catalina threw a shoe at the door.

"Easy!" Anton laughed. "I will let him know. We will take Mamma to the church. Papa will ride with you."

Angelina was eager for her imprisonment with Catalina to end. She repeated the exact phrase in her head. *This day, too, shall pass.*

Catalina finished the last braid and pinned it into place.

"There. Beautiful!"

"As are you!" Angelina hugged her. "You greet Papa on your own. He will need a minute after seeing his gorgeous daughter dressed in white."

Angelina gathered the dress's train and draped it over Catalina's arms.

"You okay to walk down by yourself?"

"I think so."

Catalina walked out the door, her fluffy lace and silk gown swishing with each step. She was a beautiful vision of white flowing fabric, beaming with eternal happiness.

"Dear God." Angelina shut the door. "Please, bless this marriage! Keep Cat safe. And help me be happy for her!"

The bells announced the bride's arrival. With his hand extended, Carlos helped Catalina climb out of the car.

"You look beautiful, Cat," Carlos choked back his tears. He

had watched her grow up, and today, he felt as if his own daughter was saying, '*I do.*'

"Thank you, Carlos," Catalina kissed him on the cheek.

Rosario extended his arm to his daughter and escorted her up the stone steps to the chapel doors.

"You look like your mother, an angel in white," Rosario smiled and discreetly wiped away his tears.

"Thank you, Papa. I am so happy! Thank you for making sure my wedding day was perfect."

Rosario patted her on the hand and smiled. The wedding cost a small fortune. However, the money spent was only a fraction of Don Salvatore's tax. The only comfort against his guilt was Catalina loved Giorgio.

"Your happiness is worth it, my little rose."

CHAPTER 26

"Do you know how to make the wine yet?" Don Salvatore asked, watching Rosario and Sofia dance.

"It is wine. How hard can it be? Do not worry so much." Giorgio replied nonchalantly.

"Beretta wines are known to be the best! That is not by accident! You are just like Victor! Your arrogance will get you killed!"

"We all die eventually. The question is how many lives we destroy on the way out!"

"We are not barbarians on a raid! Your ignorance is appalling! To be the future Don, you must be cunning!"

Most of Giorgio's life was spent in poverty. He stole food and huddled in the darkness with the rats at night. When Mario found him, he was emaciated, dirty, and wearing torn clothes that were too big for his frame. Under Mario's care, he fostered the boy into a strong young man who could read and write. He enjoyed a rich man's life of decadence. Now, as the nephew of Don Salvatore, he lives as a king.

His poverty was well behind him, but Giorgio still acted like an ungrateful, entitled brat. His lack of gratitude irritated Don Salvatore, but the assumed right to the wealth and power of a Don infuriated him.

"Have you learned enough to outsmart your enemy? Can you manipulate the man standing in your way to greatness?"

"I only await the right moment to seize what is mine!" Giorgio mused, reclining back into his chair.

Though he was not convinced of Giorgio's assertion, The Don grunted in acknowledgment. He, too, was ready... more than ready. His enemy was allowed to roam free for too many years. It was time to slaughter the fatted calf.

"Rosario is known for his piety. But I know his secret and shall make him atone for it and his glutenous ambition. He shall die like a sacrificial beast."

Don Salvatore grumbled his frustrations into his wine. The pious Rosario was known to make the best wines. Tasting the truth of it only aggravated him more.

"How long have you been married. Is it what, about four months?"

Giorgio nodded.

Rosario's business flourished since Giorgio and Catalina wed. Tonight, The Don was forced to watch another flagrant display of wealth by the Beretta family. It nauseated him to see Rosario and Sofia in their loving happiness, celebrating Rosario's fiftieth birthday. The lavish event only added to The Don's indignation toward the *perfect* family.

"Nearly three decades of *blessings*. Despite your sins, God, in his perversion, continues to bless you with good fortune and happiness. God may reward your remorseful piety. I shall punish you for your sins. You will rot in hell for what you have done. For what you have taken from my family!" Don Salvatore grumbled.

"It's easy to run this place. I know enough. The rest we can figure out in time," Giorgio said, refilling The Don's glass.

"I despise the man!"

"He will fall like any other."

"Does she have any idea?"

"Catalina? She is easily entertained with gifts. She pays no attention to my actions."

"She has been seen with bruises? From you? Why?"

"Let's just say she is still in training."

"Then hit her where others won't notice. It will not due if the town knows you enjoy beating women. Another thing. Keep your extracurricular activities with the local whores discrete. I have heard too many tales of your conquests. It is a disgrace! Moreover, it is reprehensible that I must even tell you to do these things! You are a grown man, well-stationed in society. Act it!"

Giorgio rolled his eyes, unmoved by The Don's tirade.

Reprimanding the boy for his lecherous activities was a distraction from The Don's plan. If the whores did not prevent Giorgio from doing what was told, then what did it matter. It was a nasty habit that could be dealt with later.

"Have they completed the harvest?"

"Everything should be finished by midweek."

"Waiting is torture but a necessity. Removing good help at such a laborious time would not be prudent." His upper lip twitched. His desires outmatched his patience ten to one.

Don Salvatore looked at Catalina. She was intoxicated and could barely stand. Every eruption of laughter made her wobble in her stilettoes.

"Is she pregnant yet?"

Giorgio did not respond until The Don glared at him.

He shook his head.

"Perhaps, if you spent as much time in *her* bed as you do with the whores, she would be with child!"

Don Salvatore watched his nephew pout. Giorgio acted tough and easily sluffed off some of The Don's displeasure. But he had a breaking point. Usually, after being caught doing something wrong. The short walk from tough guy to pouting baby frustrated Don Salvatore. How could this weak boy be heir to The Don's power?

"Look at him, smiling, enjoying his party. A life without a care. Is he always like that?"

"Pretty much."

"Do you at least know when the help comes and goes?"

"Carlos and Carmella arrive after sunrise. Anton is usually gone by eight."

"What of the young boy fawning all over Angelina?"

"Fernando? He arrives with his parents."

"She is much prettier than Catalina," Don Salvatore said, watching Angelina elegantly maneuver around the room. Her smile and mannerisms exuded an enchanting charm that could easily tame a fierce lion.

"She is the prize filly in more ways than beauty and charm. She is intelligent enough to run the vineyard on her own!"

"Why not her?"

"She was my preference, but Catalina is a better choice."

"Why so?"

"Angelina is headstrong and ambitious. She is not easily appeased or manipulated. Shiney things do not erase her memory as they do with her sister. "

"Sounds like a worthy challenge." The Don licked his lips.

"Like fine wine, we must wait until she is ready."

"Hmm, perhaps. What of her lap puppy? Will he need to be removed? Will he come to his lover's aid?"

"He is weak but is a good worker. Heroism is not in his blood." Giorgio chuckled, adding, "Angelina may take care of him for us."

"Ohh?"

"In a few months, she already shows signs of disinterest."

"Why?"

"According to Catalina, her sister prefers a strong, intelligent man. Fernando is a hard worker, but only a worker. He is happy with a simple life and will make nothing more of himself."

"Ah! Then she wants to be controlled by a man of power!" The Don grinned.

Angelina walked past him, smiled politely, then continued

her conversation with her friend, Maria. The smell of her perfume gently settled around Don Salvatore. He inhaled deeply and savored the sweet scent.

"Mmm...delicious!" Don Salvatore whispered.

Her long, lean muscles in her calves, flexing with each step, and the sway of her hips were an enticing show. A show he intended to watch when she was wearing less clothing.

"She is confident and likes to manipulate others to her advantage. She is someone we must keep close, preferably under lock and key. Her independent nature could cause us many issues," Giorgio said.

The Don pondered the value of the alluring creature. Was she worth the risk?

"Then remove her from the situation."

"Not yet. Angelina knows the business inside and out. In the beginning, her skills will be useful."

The Don gave his nephew an approving nod for his valuable information; it was a refreshing change.

"Will she do as she is told?"

"With the proper motivation."

"Very well. If she gets out of line, you know what must happen," he said. It was a reminder for himself as much as it was for Giorgio.

Carlos escorted Angelina to the dance floor. Her fluid gait and skirt rippling with every step made her appear as if she were floating.

"Getting rid of her would be a waste." Giorgio licked his lips. "She is such a beauty."

"Si! That she is!" Don Salvatore's greedy eyes danced with delight. "We shall enjoy our fun, but we must never underestimate her. She has a charm and ability far better than anyone I have ever met."

"If she poses a threat, we will eliminate her!"

"Oh, my boy!" Don Salvatore patted Giorgio's knee. "It is

not if. It is *when*!"

The Don and his nephew, enraptured, watched the prize filly. Her spine was straight, chin level, and her flowing curls gently swayed as she gracefully floated across the dance floor.

"She is an excellent dancer." The Don commented, sipping his wine. "You desire her, don't you?"

"She makes my cock hard."

"Ha! She would make an impotent man's cock hard!"

"I *will* have her!" Giorgio licked his lips. His desire for her was intense.

"That will be decided later!" Don Salvatore grabbed Giorgio's wrist. His mighty grip was stronger than expected from a man his age. "By *me* and not before!"

Giorgio winced and ripped his hand from The Don's clutches.

The Don glared into his eyes. "Not before! *Capito?*"

Giorgio inaudibly grumbled, then nodded his acceptance.

"When does Marcus return to his military base?"

"Tomorrow afternoon."

"And the other three brothers?"

"Ricardo leaves Thursday night. On Fridays, Anton and Fernando leave by eight. RJ is too young to matter."

"The young grow old, and their memory never fades!"

Giorgio grunted his understanding of the order.

"Friday morning. Pick me up before sunrise."

"You are coming?" Giorgio asked.

"Oh, my boy! I have waited *many* years to see the happiness drain from Rosario Beretta's eyes. I shall savor every second of his demise!"

CHAPTER 27

Angelina jolted awake, sweat dripping from her brow. Her nightmare was more vivid than ever. Her heart racing, she stared into the darkness. She remained still, listening for footsteps, praying her screams did not disturb Anton's sleep, as they had so many times before.

She tip-toed to her window, peering at the heavy blackness in the night air. A glance at her clock confirmed her intuition. The sun's slumber would last another hour. With no moon to light her way, her therapeutic morning stroll through the vines was delayed. Until then, she would try her father's suggestion. She removed her book from the nightstand. Through the ink, her horrid visions would transfer from her mind to the paper, thus ridding them from her sleep forever. Well...she hoped.

Holding the pen, her trembling hands attempted to scratch out the words.

"The quality of penmanship is not important. Only the details matter," Angelina whispered into the cool air.

Each sentence she wrote increased her anxiety. Her third sentence resurrected a traumatic scene from the nightmare that shook her. The pen fell to the floor.

"I can't do it, Papa," She whispered toward her father's room.

Slipping off her bed, she kneeled. Angelina, her head bowed, begged God to remove the nightmare from her mind.

The clock chimed six a.m., pulling her from her prayers. Angelina dressed and quietly snuck out of the house. A dense fog lingered around the vines, and the chilly air pulled goosebumps from her flesh. The buildings loomed tall over her, casting menacing shadows in every direction. Steadying her resolve, she pressed up the hill. A cat bolted out of the darkness, racing across her path. Its spine-chilling hiss echoed off the buildings. She reflexively clapped her hand over her mouth, muffling her scream.

She composed herself, then offered the cat her hand in sympathy. "Elmer, did you have a bad dream, too?" The cat flashed a reproving glare before trotting away. "I don't like talking about mine either."

Every step further up the hill, the haunting shadows pressed in, defeating her confidence. She shuddered and turned back. She would take a different route than usual.

The sun was breaking through the horizon, casting faint streaks of pink and yellow across the sky as she headed toward the river. The soft chirp-chirp of birds warming their voices in preparation for their morning floated through the air. She climbed to the top of the rock and embraced her knees. A shudder quaked in her bones. She told herself the cool morning mist clinging to her jacket caused the shiver, not the premonition looming in her soul.

"Our Father," she whispered. "Who art in heaven."

She recited several prayers as she watched the rushing water below. The heavy curtain of fog slowly unveiled the other bank, where a frog croaked loudly. The soothing memory of the picnic with Anton and Fernando made her smile. It was the first positive thought of her day.

"Hail Mary, full of grace..."

Her prayer was interrupted by a car racing up the drive. It abruptly stopped at the bridge, about a hundred yards away. The dense fog and dim lighting made it impossible to make out any details. A loud splash was followed by two car doors slamming shut. The tires spun on the gravel road, spitting rocks and dust into the air as it raced toward the house.

A dark hue mixed with the water as it cascaded around the rocks. Curious, she climbed down for a closer look. A dark mass tumbling over and over in the current held her gaze. Her hand covered her mouth, and she stumbled backward.

"Oh, My God!" Angelina froze in terror. "That is a...body!"

The horror intensified with each flip of the body. Soon, it would reach the bank by Angelina's feet. She prayed for the body to float past, taking with it the chaos it pulled in tow. But that was not her fate. The body crashed into the bank three feet away. She leaned over and tugged. It was too heavy, and her footing was poor. Angelina removed her shoes, returned to the chilly water, and tried again. This time, she managed to pull the torso onto the bank. Water crashed against the legs, launching droplets into the air. Angelina used her arm to smear the water from her eyes before rolling the corpse on its back.

"Ohhh no! No!" She wailed, collapsing next to the body. "No...Dear God, It...can't...be!"

Angelina pulled the body onto her lap and gently rocked it. The ache of grief reverberated through her bones. She stroked his cheek and kissed his forehead. The lifeless, dark eyes staring into nothingness became a haunting image permanently etched into her mind.

"*Ricardo*..." She sobbed into his chest.

Time stood still while her mind played a reel of her favorite moments with him. The smile that curled his lips when he was teasing her, his witty humor, and the joy radiating from his heart. He was ornery and enjoyed a good fight but was a cheerful soul full of life.

"*Ricardo*..." Angelina hugged him tightly and sobbed.

A scream ripped Angelina from the abyss of memories muddled by grief. Her mind, hurdling back to the present, shifted to survival mode, executing every movement without thought.

She wrapped her arms under his and pulled as hard as possible. It took three tugs to remove him from the water. Choking back the flood of tears, she closed his eyes and kissed his forehead.

"I don't want to leave you, but I must go," Angelina said between sobs. "I am sorry, Ricardo!"

Her mother's repeated cries for help drew Angelina toward the house. Every second felt habitual, an action performed a thousand times. The familiarity was disturbing. She pushed away the sense of deja vu, concentrating on getting to the house in time. Her focus did not last.

Everything abruptly stopped when she lifted her shirt to wipe her nose. She gagged. The cotton fabric was soaked with water and blood...her *brother's* blood...her *dead* brother's blood. She looked back toward the river. Though the blood and the guilt for leaving him yanked at her gut, it did not cause the nausea.

"Dear God!"

A sharpness pierced her heart, and her body quaked. Her blood stained hands and shirt were an unmistakable Deja Vu. She had lived this before, many times.

"Dear God, No, not my nightmare!"

Panic seized her lungs, and she collapsed to the ground, sobbing. She wanted to wake up. She needed this nightmare to be over. Another scream came from the house, but it was not her mother this time.

"Papa!"

Angelina snapped from her emotional paralysis. Her father's screams were never part of her night terror. She swallowed hard; this was *not* a dream.

Parked in front of the house was a car with three doors open. Cautiously, Angelina snuck around the vehicle to make sure no one was still inside.

"Thank God!"

Angelina gasped for air, not realizing she was holding her breath. The stupidity in her actions rang loudly. What would she have done if there was someone in there?

Another scream came, followed by dishes crashing against the floor. Angelina crept to the window. A man dressed in black shoved Sofia into a chair and tied her hands behind her back.

A tall, haunting figure held Anton by his hair on the other side of the room. Repeatedly, he hit him until his body went limp. With a vindictive chuckle, he released Anton's thick, dark locks, allowing the injured form to collapse into a heap on the floor.

"Anton!"

Angelina muttered too loud. One of the attackers glanced toward the window. She ducked under the small shrub, praying he did not see her. Huddled in fear, her body trembled uncontrollably. The morning breeze shifted to gusts of chilly wind, intensifying her shudders. Cold, terrified, and helpless, her emotions threatened to emerge.

Don't just sit here! Do something!" Angelina thought.

Peeping through the window was dangerous and foolish. The movement from darting out of sight could draw the attacker's attention if they had not already noticed two eyes peering through the window pane.

Another eruption of shouting kept Angelina by the window. There were three voices. Ignoring her better judgment, she peered through the window again but only saw two men. After several minutes of listening to the abuse, she still could not identify them. Conceding to her gut's wisdom, she sought another place to continue the surveillance. Crouched low, Angelina crept around to the other side of the house, carefully avoiding the dry twigs and piles of leaves.

A chair shattered against a wall in the entry room as Rosario shouted a run of cuss words. Seconds later, a body crashed against the kitchen door. Angelina peeked through the small panes of glass and watched a burly man, his broad shoulders hunched forward, approach the door. She ducked.

"We ain't done yet," The burly man growled.

If the burly man glanced out the window, he would see her. She pressed her body against the wall, her thundering heart the only thing moving. Another bang from a body slamming against the kitchen door. The vibration from the impact reverberated through Angelina's spine. Tears streamed down her cheeks as the attacker's verbal assault grew louder. Only a thin wall between them, the attacker was inches away.

The wind ran its fingers through Angelina's long hair, the black strands whipping about like Medusa's snakes. If her hair didn't get his attention, the dancing whirlwind of leaves would. Mother Nature continued to toy with the surroundings. Ten feet to Angelina's left was the cellar. Little bursts of wind tickled the cellar's wooden door, making it screech and clap.

She was trapped. Her back firm against the house, she inched back to the car. There was no way she could stop the assault, and knowing the assailants meant nothing if she were dead. Her only hope was to get help.

The driver's door was open, but Angelina feared she could be seen darting from the house. Huddled beside a thick bush, she waited for her moment to sprint to the car. Her patience paid off. The attacker hovering over her mother moved to another room. Hunched over, she dashed to the car. In a swift turn, she whipped around the door, her feet sliding in the loose gravel. She peeked to see if anyone noticed her.

"Thank God!" Angelina leaned against the car, winded, but relieved.

Crawling into the driver's seat, her hand fumbled around the steering wheel for the ignition.

"Come on, please be there." Her hand found the ignition,

but the keys were gone. Frantic, she searched the seat, dashboard, and glove compartment.

"Damn it!" The increasing sunlight illuminated the area, reducing her ability to hide. "I gotta get out of sight!"

The buildings were too far away, and she would easily be seen running up the hill. She looked at the vines; they would provide cover, but getting to them would be risky.

"Well, you only have one option," Angelina whispered. "And you better get there fast!"

She waited until she had a clear shot to run back to the side of the house. Slinking against the brick wall, she headed toward the cellar. The wind continued to whip her hair and play with the cellar door. At first, she worried that the creak and slap from the door would catch their attention, but then she realized it could play in her favor.

Angelina drew a deep breath to steady her nerves. This time, she would use Mother Nature to her advantage.

"You got this. Just run!"

When she heard a big gush of wind rustle the leaves, she darted past the steps, sliding under the cellar door as the wind lifted it.

Into the darkness, she plunged, stumbling down the small wooden steps. Before she hit the bottom step, she caught her balance. The clink of glass jars reminded her of the landmine of noises she would make if she bumped a rack. In the pitch blackness, Angelina sat motionless for a few minutes to allow her eyes to adjust. To sit was torture, but nothing as painful as hearing her mother cry for help.

"What do you want?" Rosario roared. "I will give you anything!"

"Shut up!"

Impatient, Angelina moved across the dirt floor with one hand on the cold stone wall. It would be her guide to the wooden stairs that led to the kitchen. When she reached the steps, she paused to consider her next move. She needed to look through the crack in the door, but the wooden steps usually creaked with any pressure.

Her body shook in horror when a shrill came from her mother's lungs. Angelina abandoned her fear and crawled up the dirty steps. They were damp and cold, like the air around her. The smell of rotting wood only added to her eerie confines. One hand over the other, finally, she reached her perch at the top. She hunched down and peered through a space between the door and its frame.

Anton's body was slumped in a heap next to the chair where her mother was bound. Angelina willed her brother to rise from his slumber and fight. If he did, she would rush into the room.

"Come on, Anton. Get up!" Angelina whispered. "Get up!"

Anton's face was bludgeoned. His right eye was swollen shut, and his jaw was broken, but his chest still moved. He was alive, but barely.

A tear landed on the back of Angelina's hand. She sat back away from her tiny window to dry her eyes.

"No!" Rosario screamed.

Her father's cry pulled her back to the small portal. With a warrior cry, RJ lept from the stairs onto the large masked man's back. Her little brother's hands pummeled his opponent's head. The ominous giant plucked the small-framed body off his back and threw him across the room.

Sofia screamed again.

"Quiet, bitch!" the brutal man said in a deep voice as he bludgeoned her face with the butt of his knife.

"No! Leave her alone!" Rosario screamed in horror.

He tried to reach his wife, but the man he had been fighting tackled him. Rosario's face collided with the hard floor. The impact knocked the wind out of him, and he lay motionless. Angelina's heart willed her father to get up. He was the only one who could save RJ. If she entered the room, it would only provide another body to punish. RJ was a small boy -he needed help. RJ needed their father to fight.

Sofia cried out again when the large beast plucked her youngest son up like an empty sack and threw him onto the table in front of her. His body made a loud thump as his head hit the table first.

The brutal man stood behind her and pulled her hair. "Look at the clock on the wall bitch!" He laughed. "Pick him up. He needs to watch his bride die."

Angelina gasped. Rosario heard the sound and saw her eyes behind the door.

He whispered to her, "Run, Bella, Run! Please Run!"

"What is that, old man?" the large beast asked, lifting Rosario off the floor.

"Leave my family alone!" Rosario growled. He looked the man in the face and launched a mouthful of blood at him.

"You are going to regret that!" the large masked man roared and pulled his gun from his jacket.

"No! Wait! He must watch this," the brutal man behind Sofia shouted. "Tie him to that chair."

A large, round man stepped into view, and Angelina could see the backs of all three men hovering over her family.

"Put that gun away," the round-framed man commanded.

Angelina listened carefully to the voices. The one who stood behind her mother seemed familiar, but she struggled to place the other voices.

The tall man yanked Sofia's hair again, and she screamed.

"Watch the clock, bitch. It is almost seven," The tall man laughed.

Following orders, the large guy tied Rosario to the chair and moved him so he could see his wife's bloody and bruised face. Rosario struggled against the rope, and the man hit him with his gun.

"Look at your bitch!"

"Look precious, Sofia. At seven, your son will die!"

"No!" she wailed.

"Ohh, it is true! Your perfect son, your *bastard* son, Marcus, will drift from this world."

Sofia struggled, but the man held her hair too tight. Every movement caused her tremendous pain.

"You can't hurt him, not at the military base," she argued.

The man laughed. "You think we don't have friends in the military. You would be surprised at how little it costs to have a man killed. But then, Rosario here would know. He killed his own commander while he was in the military."

"I did not kill him!" Rosario shouted.

"Really!" The round man waltzed over to him. "We have had this discussion before, Rosario. Have we not?"

"I told you, Don Salvatore, I did not kill him. Victor died of his own wounds!"

"Rosario, what does he mean? What is going on?" Sofia asked.

The man behind Sofia yanked her long black locks again when the clock sounded the seventh hour. "He can explain it to you in hell! Right now, you need to say goodbye to your bastard!" He pulled off the mask and released an evil laugh that echoed off the walls.

Angelina covered her mouth to silence her gasp. Bile rose up Angelina's throat as the villain's name formed in her mind, *Giorgio!*

"Dear God, Noo!" Sofia sobbed. "Please don't hurt him!"

"It will be a quick death. A sharp knife across his throat while he sleeps, just like this," Giorgio said and slowly pulled the blade across her neck. The sharp edge brushed her skin, and blood oozed down to her chest.

Rosario struggled against the ropes that bound him to his chair, but his guard punched him in the gut to subdue him.

"He will not kill her yet!" the large, beastly man growled.

"I wouldn't hurt dear Mamma!" Giorgio leaned down close to Sofia's ear and whispered. "But Ricardo, I killed an hour ago... with this same knife. Want to taste his blood?"

Giorgio brandished the blade covered in red in front of Sofia's face, making her wail uncontrollably. Her agony pulled Anton back to consciousness. Giorgio noticed the movement and turned his attention away from Sofia.

"I have despised you from the first night I sat at this table. When you and your cunt sister tried to make a fool of me," Giorgio kicked Anton in the stomach.

Weak from the abuse, Anton could barely stand. Giorgio continued to reign down his cruel abuse. A final powerful blow squarely against Anton's jaw sent teeth scattering across the floor. He collapsed to his knees, his face obliterated. Anton tried to beg for mercy, but his swollen mouth made his words unclear.

"Now you are not so full of yourself!" Giorgio kicked Anton again. "Bruno, pick him up."

"Finish your business!" Don Salvatore's command echoed around the room.

"They will suffer first!" Giorgio glared at The Don. "Watch, old man, as your beloved son dies!" Giorgio grabbed Anton's hair in one hand and gripped the knife handle in the other. "Can both of you see? I wouldn't want either of you to miss this!"

Sofia cried uncontrollably from the loss of two children. She begged between sobs to release Anton, but Giorgio ignored her pleas.

Rosario struggled against the tightly bound rope as he helplessly watched the atrocity. His fury pulsed the blood vessel on his temple, and froth filled his mouth.

"Say goodbye, little brother!"

Giorgio cackled as he stabbed Anton in the gut. An eruption

of blood spewed from Anton's side, and he cried out in pain.

"Vengeance is so sweet!"

Giorgio rejoiced as he continued to stab Anton. A sickening sound filled the air as the blade pierced Anton's flesh over and over. Watching the horrific act made Angelina ill. Hearing it was soul-crushing. Tears and shock blurred her vision. She struggled against the internal and external assault. Under no circumstance could she pass out. She could not allow them to hurt her any more than this massacre already had.

"*NO!*" Rosario pleaded with each thrust of the blade into Anton's body.

Entranced, Giorgio enjoyed each moment until, finally, Anton's soul left his body. The thrill on Giorgio's face as he murdered Anton was beyond maniacal.

Angelina's body trembled violently from the horror. She cradled her knees and buried her head. Anton's agonizing pain and Giorgio's grin of satisfaction haunted her vision. A wave of desperation crashed against her chest, making her gasp for air and her head pound. The deafening whoosh-whoosh from the blood rushing to her brain bulged her eardrums. She needed to scream, to release the pressure from her overwhelming anguish, but the fear of being discovered strangled her. A quiet whimper could disclose her location, hurdling her into the chaos. There was no doubt, they would happily provide her with the same fate or worse.

"Dear God, please no!" Rosario screamed repeatedly. "No! Please, No!"

Straining against his bondage, Rosario's red face was now a deep purple. Every fiery breath released a new gush of tears, snot, and saliva.

Bruno released his grip on Anton, allowing the lifeless body to slam against the stone floor. The loud thump provoked Sofia into another round of wailing.

"I said to keep your sniveling to yourself, bitch!" Giorgio

scolded, hitting her cheek with the handle of his knife.

The impact knocked out her teeth, sending them across the room. They hit the floor, and a soft click-click echoed around the room. Her crying stopped. The blow was powerful enough to end Sofia's agony; her head fell limp and lifeless.

"Sofia!" Rosario howled, lunging toward her. But his restraints did not budge.

"Gag him!" Giorgio ordered Bruno. "I have had enough of his mouth as well. Now, let me see. How should we end *this* little boy's life?" Giorgio asked, turning his attention to the unconscious body on the table.

Fighting against the gag, Rosario mumbled words against harming his son. Giorgio flashed Rosario an evil grin.

"Save your breath, Papa. He is going to die too!"

Giorgio slowly dragged his blade across the table. The sharp tip emitted an unnerving sound that echoed around the room.

"Wake up, little brother!" Giorgio whispered into RJ's ear, but the boy did not move.

Her eyes transfixed on her little brother's chest, Angelina prayed he was already dead. RJ was a sweet, loving soul who had never hurt anyone or anything. Even the ugliest, creepy-crawly bug was safe in RJ's proximity. Tears raced down her cheeks, remembering his logic.

"It is alive, just like me," RJ explained to Angelina one sunny afternoon. *"It would be cruel to destroy something just because it is ugly and I am bigger."*

In her dark dungeon, Angelina's heart collapsed. RJ's lungs slowly filled with air. He was still alive, barely. She hoped he was far enough gone that he would not experience the pain like Anton.

Giorgio slid his blade under RJ's shirt. The sharp edge sliced through the thin material with ease. With the tip of his knife, Giorgio moved the cut fabric to expose the small chest. RJ, so young, had not sprouted any hair, nor had he lived enough years to grow muscles. His form was still that of a little boy, a skinny, harmless boy.

"I remember being twelve," Giorgio's tongue slithered as he hissed into RJ's ear. "I was alone. Homeless, eating garbage out of a can and wishing I could die to end *my* miserable life."

Evil exuded from Giorgio's eyes. The devil had a firm hold on him. His voice, deep and satanic, added to his monstrous persona. Giorgio smiled and licked his lips as he slowly dragged the sharp tip across the boy's wrists. A crimson fluid pulsed out in spurts, creating a growing pool that drained over the edge, spattering on the floor by his parents' feet.

"He is already dead; finish his parents. We must go!" The Don ordered.

Giorgio looked up at The Don with a sadistic grin. In a swift movement, Giorgio drove the knife into the boy's heart. RJ's small frame lurched with the impact, his lungs gasped for air, and he released a short, high-pitched squeak. His body convulsed for a moment before collapsing against the wooden table.

Her son's last noise pulled Sofia back, her eyes darting in every direction in search of RJ. When she saw the blood flowing from his lifeless body, she began convulsing; her eyes rolled back, and her mouth foamed. The cruelty she had witnessed removed all the desire to live. She gasped for air one last time, and her body went limp.

Rosario saw his wife's body crumble into a heap, and he cried out for her. His purple face lost all color when Sofia drew her last breath. He sobbed and struggled against his bondage. Rosario tried to stand, but his injuries and the chair's weight were too much. Unable to be beside her, in intense sorrow, he stared at his battered wife.

"She is dead. Kill Rosario, and let's be gone."

"With pleasure!"

With a wicked grin, Giorgio grabbed a handful of Rosario's

hair and brandished the blood-covered knife.

"Where is Angelina?" Giorgio demanded.

Rosario shook his head and mumbled his ignorance.

"Bruno, search the house," Giorgio ordered.

"We do not have time. The help will arrive soon," The Don thundered, holding up his hand to halt Bruno.

"I will rape that bitch here and now!" Giorgio argued.

"I think you have done enough!" The Don roared. "Violence is not the only way to achieve a desired outcome."

"She rejected me! She will learn her place!"

"You ignorant fuck! Play your cards right, and you will have control of both of his daughters!"

Giorgio gave him an inquisitive look.

"The little bitch will need someone to protect her from the horrible people who killed her family. She will need a savior and protector to come to her aid. In repayment, she will gratefully do as she is told!"

Giorgio smiled at the prospect of controlling Angelina.

"Did you hear that, Papa? All those nights worrying about which daughter to pick? Did you ever imagine I would have both?" Giorgio cackled and stabbed Rosario in the gut.

"Leave the blade in him. He will die slowly," The Don commanded.

Giorgio leaned down and lifted Rosario's chin to see the life slowly drain from his eyes.

"You killed my father and ruined my life! Did you really think my family would let you go free?" Giorgio roared. "Your death is not the end of my revenge. Let your final thought be of me fucking your daughters and torturing them for decades to come!"

Rosario gasped for air. He tried to argue, but it was too late. The damage was done. Nothing, not even words, would bring his perfect life back. Nothing could make his world whole again.

CHAPTER 28

Smoke from the celebratory cigars filtered into Angelina's dank prison, adding to her hell. Not only had they taken her family, but their presence also forced her to weep in complete silence. They had won; they had murdered everyone, and all was lost for her. Huddled in the darkness with a river of tears rolling down her face, Angelina agonized over the brutality and blood. A black velvet curtain waved in her vision as she struggled to remain conscious.

"I have waited for this day," Giorgio boasted, puffing his cigar.

"Revenge is sweet, my boy!" Don Salvatore patted his nephew's back. "But you can celebrate later. Right now, we must go."

The floor creaked as they walked past the door to the cellar. The sound slapped Angelina back from her fading consciousness hard. She knew that spot; it was inches from her only barrier between her dark purgatory and hell. The shoes stop at the door. Her heart insisted she scurry away like a mouse, but her mind questioned, to where? Any movement would cause a sound and break her veil of protection. Even her breathing had to be silent. Shrouded in darkness, her heart thundering, she prayed St. Michael would protect her from the demons beyond the door.

The scrape of the lock turning pierced the silence. Terrified, Angelina watched the handle slowly turn. She made the sign of the cross and braced for the evil beyond the door to take her life.

"Giorgio! Let's go! Now!" Don Salvatore yelled.

"You can wait a minute!"

"No, Giorgio. Now!"

Two car doors slammed shut, and the engine revved. Ignoring the commotion outside, Giorgio pushed the cellar door open, the hinges screeching in protest.

A beam of light illuminated the left side of Angelina's face. Her pale skin was a stark contrast to the black chasm in which she huddled. She stared at her brother-in-law while her mind rapidly repeated prayer after prayer in silence. Fear held her lungs hostage. It was her turn to suffer from Giorgio's wrath.

Outside, the car engine revved and the horn blared.

"Old fuck!" Giorgio's lip curled with hate. "Five minutes ain't going to change anything."

The horn blared again, and the car started to pull away. Angelina did not move a muscle, not even to blink, for fear the movement would catch his attention. If he turned his head to investigate the cellar, he would find her kneeling three steps below the threshold.

"God damn it!"

Giorgio's hand released the cellar's door handle. Grumbling his displeasure, he marched out to the car.

The cellar door remained slightly ajar, allowing the morning sunshine to continue its penetration into the darkness. The slam of the third car door jolted Angelina, but she was still afraid to move. She remained on her knees, her body trembling until the shower of gravel pelted the side of the house.

They were gone, but her fear still held her lungs hostage. The lack of oxygen blurred Angelina's vision and she collapsed. Reflexively, her right arm snapped forward, planting her hand on the next step. She forced her lungs to expand. Slowly, her head stopped spinning, and she regained her balance.

Angelina counted to fifty before she dared leave her dank prison. She opened the door just enough to crawl into the kitchen. A river of cold air flowed in from the partially opened back door.

"Please be gone," Angelina whispered, crawling toward the doorway.

She peeked outside at the grey cloud hanging over the drive. Her shoulders relaxed a little; they were gone.

Blood dripped from the table, feeding the growing scarlet pools. The small, soulless body made Angelina tremble in horror as she caressed RJ's lifeless, bare feet. She swooned. It was the first time she touched a corpse. Struggling to keep her balance, she clamped her hand on the wooden chair. The rapidly whirling world slowed to a dizzying twirl.

Angelina kneeled by her brother Anton and checked for life, even though she knew he had drawn his last breath. Her fingers brushed his hair away from his temple, and her tears cascaded onto his bludgeoned cheek.

"I will miss you, my dearest brother. You didn't deserve this." She sobbed as she closed his eyes. "I love you."

The smell of death permeated the air, making her nauseated. She stood to untie her mother, but her weak knees buckled, and she collapsed, sobbing. Her body thumped against the floor, wishing she had fled her cave to help. It would have saved her from this agony because she would have been dead, too.

"Why? Why?" She screamed. "Oh dear God..."

A low moan from across the room silenced her. Adrenalin filled her blood, propelling her to her father's side. Blood leaked from around the blade, saturating his shirt. She lifted his limp head to examine his face. His jaw was broken, as was his nose, and his left eye was swollen shut.

"Papa! Papa, please! Papa, don't die!"

Frantic to save her father, Angelina grabbed a couple of kitchen towels. Gently, she removed the knife and placed a towel on the wound. With the other towel, she tenderly wiped away the blood and tears.

"Papa! Please, Papa, come back to me!" Angelina pleaded.

She cleaned his face as best as possible, then held the towel against a two-inch gash across his forehead.

"Papa! Papa!"

Another low moan came from his throat.

"Papa! You can do it! Fight off the dark angel! Stay here! I need you! Please, Papa, you must live!"

Slowly, Rosario's groans became stronger as he returned to consciousness. He blinked his eyes and grabbed Angelina's wrist. He was weak and could barely speak, but he forced out a single word. His voice was barely audible, but Angelina understood him.

"She is here, Papa."

A sharp pain pierced Angelina's chest. Watching Sofia and Rosario slowly die was witnessing the most beautiful love affair drift into darkness. For Angelina, how they loved each other was what she hoped for in a marriage. It was genuine love, deeper than the ocean and as radiant as the sun setting over the sea.

Rosario moaned in pain when he stood, his arm reaching out toward his bride. Angelina slipped under his arm to support him. They walked past the table, and Rosario reached toward his son. He ran his fingers through his namesake's hair, but RJ lay unresponsive to the gentle touch. Grief convulsed through Rosario's body, and a flood of tears raced down his cheeks. In a ramble of blubbering words, he kissed RJ's face and hugged the lifeless form. Angelina sobbed with him. Her heart shattered from the loss of life and her father's tremendous grief.

Rosario's grief transformed into a fiery rage when he looked at his battered and bruised wife. As he mumbled curses into the air, spit flew from his mouth. He lunged to reach her side and fell to his knees, kissing her limp hands.

"Bella Mia," Rosario wailed, burying his face in her hands. "Bella Mia!"

"Mamma! Mamma, please say something!" Angelina pleaded. "Mamma, it's me, Angelina!"

Rosario cradled Sofia's face, his thumb stroking her cheek.

"Bella Mia! I am sorry, Bella Mia!"

He kissed her blue lips several times. Distraught, Rosario pulled her to his chest and rocked her back and forth.

"Bella Mia! I am sorry, Bella Mia! Please come back to me, my beautiful songbird."

Angelina tried to comfort her father, but he pulled away, tightening his hug around Sofia. In a manic tirade, his face beet red, Rosario screamed and cursed.

"You will pay for this, Giorgio! I promise! You *will* pay!"

CHAPTER 29

A frightened child running from a masked villain, Angelina feared her next step. How could she explain what happened? What could she say? The wolf was too close and would continue its bloodletting if he felt threatened.

Angelina staggered down the cobblestone path, her legs weak and heavy. Her chest heaved as life seemed to flee her body with every exhalation. Her mind continually replayed the morning's events, leaving her more exhausted than an entire week of harvest.

Lost in her own world, she nearly passed by the grand, rod-iron gate. Angelina looked around at the elegance and beauty on the other side of the black bars. Colorful roses climbed the stone walls, perfectly manicured grass accented the cobblestone drive, and, in the center, water cascaded down a large gold and stone fountain. It was a lavish display of wealth, and for the first time, Angelina wondered if everything before her was bought with blood money.

"Who died for all of this?" Angelina mumbled.

A vision of her family's brutal deaths flashed before her eyes, sucking more of her energy. She rested her pounding head against the cold metal. She wanted to vomit. The nauseating smell of cologne muddled with cigars, the stench of blood, and death was a lingering cloud around her. An invisible rag saturated with the intolerable odor was permanently sewn over her nose. She forced the tragedy from her mind; living it once was more than enough. She willed her body to stand, mentally pushing herself further and further away from the morning's events.

She was grateful when Fernando and his parents arrived. They were a life raft in the sea of blood and haze. Somehow, she uttered words and explanations. It was surprising how the directions flowed from her lips. The ability to work well under pressure was a gift, one she cherished. She never wanted to know her limits. It helped her survive the previous hours, but her day was far from over.

After a conversation with the police, she knew there would be no accounting for the murders. It was apparent The Don held them in his pocket. But she could not think about restitution; there were other tasks to attend to.

She walked up the grand marble stairs to the large double doors. The mahogany wood glistened, and the sunlight danced off the golden doorknocker. It was *his* house. The last place she wanted to be, but it was also her sister's home.

She gulped back her fear and banged the heavy metal knocker. A deep bam-bam echoed around the portico. A few agonizing moments passed before the sound of feet grew louder.

Angelina prayed, "Please God, let it be Catalina. Don't make me face him!"

The latches slowly unlocked. A loud creak from the rusty hinges protesting sent a chill across Angelina's skin. Tension held her rigid. The fear of seeing him again was suffocating. When the door finally opened, she nearly collapsed.

"Signorina, what has happened?" Constance, Catalina's maid, gasped at Angelina's haggard appearance.

The maid's warm arm wrapped around Angelina's waist, helping her into the grand entry. In every direction, lavish decor dripped from the walls and furniture. Fine art, marble floors, and an elaborate crystal chandelier looming overhead made Angelina dizzy. Whose life had paid for all of this? The weight of that thought pulled on Angelina, making her stumble.

"We are almost there, Signorina. Stay with me."

Constance adjusted her grip around Angelina's waist and ushered her into the hearth room. She gently positioned Angelina on the sofa near the roaring fire. Deftly, the maid removed Angelina's shoes, rested her feet on an ottoman, and covered her with a soft blanket.

The cozy room tempted Angelina with a much-needed slumber. She resisted the urge, knowing Constance had left the room to fetch Catalina. She had to tell her sister everything before Giorgio arrived.

Soon, the pitter-patter of hurried footsteps racing down the stairwell filtered into the hearth room.

"In here, Signora! We are in here, by the fire!"

Catalina entered the room, and the blood drained from her usually rosy cheeks. Angelina looked deathly ill.

"Come sit with her, Signora. I shall make something warm for both of you. Please, please sit, Signora." Constance placed her dazed mistress on the sofa and scurried from the room.

"Angelina?" Catalina's voice cracked. She cleared her throat and inched closer, gently wrapping her warm hand around her sister's. "Lina, what is wrong? Lina?"

The gentleness of Catalina's touch was comforting. But her blank stare reminded Angelina of each pair of eyes she had closed that day, starting with Ricardo's. Her wall of defense crumbled, releasing the flood of tears she held back all day.

When Constance returned, Catalina was rocking her sister as she wept uncontrollably. Constance poured two cups of coffee and placed them on the dark mahogany table. Catalina gave a nod of gratitude, followed by a gentle brush of her hand to dismiss the maid.

The warmth from the fire and the weight of the thick, soft blanket was a loving hug, beckoning Angelina to give in to her exhaustion. Angelina's sobbing finally stopped, and her body became limp in her sister's arms. It was a peaceful moment, and she was grateful for it, even if it only lasted a few minutes.

When Angelina broke the loving embrace, Catalina urged her to drink the coffee. "This will calm your nerves."

As she picked up a cup, Catalina's hands trembled, paying false testament to the calm tone in her voice. She placed the cup in front of Angelina and gave an encouraging gesture.

"That's better," Catalina said in a motherly tone.

Angelina's mind felt like a machine that needed to be oiled. Each sip of coffee lubricated the cogs of her mental wheels, and her sharpness returned at a steady pace. She dried the tears from her face and took another sip from the delicate porcelain cup. She allowed the warmth to fuse with her body as she broke free of her cocoon of grief.

The clock's deep chime of the hour provoked an urgency in Angelina. It would be hard enough to tell her sister; waiting would not make it any easier.

"Catalina, I must tell you something more tragic than anything a person can imagine." The words spilled off Angelina's tongue. She could feel her voice strengthen, her mind sharpened with every chime from the clock. "But first, are you the only one home? Besides Constance?"

"We are alone. Giorgio left last night," Catalina mumbled and looked away.

"You should feel no shame for his actions." Angelina's harsh comment made her sister wince. "Look at me."

Catalina's gaze remained on the floor, and her body stiffened in anticipation. Angelina tempered her voice. What she was about to say would prove far more painful than the woes of marriage.

"I fear for our lives."

Angelina scanned the room to ensure they were alone. She trusted no one, not anymore. How could she? Catalina was the only person Angelina could turn to. She needed her sister. Together, they would deliver revenge.

"Cat, I am so sorry, but..." Angelina choked back her tears.

"Tell me, Lina. Whatever you have to say, I am tough enough to hear."

Lovingly, Angelina rubbed her sister's arm. Catalina always said she was tough enough, but she never could stand the weight of stress.

"Oh, Catalina, this will be hard for you to hear and even harder for me to explain," Angelina admitted with a sigh. "This morning..."

Three car doors slammed outside the window. Angelina wanted to hide. Her heart thundered, and the pounding in her ears was deafening. She was back in the cellar, huddled in fear of being discovered. This time, Giorgio *would* see her terrified face and know she watched him. Now, she would have to relive it, only this time *he* would kill *her*.

"Lina?"

The three muffled voices approached the door. Angelina grabbed her sister's hand, her eyes pleading for help.

"Lina! What is wrong with you?"

"Catalina, listen to me and remember these words," Angelina shuddered as the heavy wooden door creaked loudly. "There is a wolf in our family den!"

CHAPTER 30

Angelina jumped when Giorgio slammed the front door. The loud stomps from heavy boots and the jubilant voices filtering into the hearth room immobilized her.

"Are you ok?" Catalina asked, brushing back a wayward strand of Angelina's hair. "You look terrified!"

Angelina's eyes darted from her sister to the doorway. In seconds, Giorgio would waltz into the room. Was she brave enough to look at him?

"Lina, you are shivering. Are you cold?"

As if cued, a gust of the evening's frigid air rushed in like a ghost, sucking the warmth from the room.

"Lina?" Catalina shoved a napkin in her sister's lap. "Look, you spilled it. It will stain if you don't hurry. You blot, I will get some soda water."

Angelina grabbed her sister's arm, yanking her back down. "No, don't leave..."

"Well, well! Look who is here!" Giorgio bellowed across the room. "To what do we owe the honor of your presence?"

"She is upset," Catalina explained.

Giorgio leaned over and gave his bride a loving kiss. The display made Angelina ill. If her sister only knew the truth, would she still receive her husband so warmly?

Giorgio looked Angelina over with his dark eyes and a wild grin. "What? Strong Angelina? I didn't think anyone could upset you."

He pulled up a chair close to the two women. Angelina

struggled not to vomit when a strong waft of alcohol and cigar smoke enveloped her.

"Tell me, who has offended you? I will be your champion and beat him to death!" Giorgio roared with laughter.

Angelina flinched. The word death so easily spilled from his mouth. He was the vilest of all creatures, a leach sucking the life out of its prey.

Haven't you killed enough people today? Angelina thought, barely preventing the words from escaping her lips.

"What's the matter, cat got your tongue?"

Giorgio's friends erupted into another round of laughter.

Oh, how she wished she could scream at the top of her lungs. She hated this man, this pretender. He lied to his wife, beat her, was unfaithful, and murdered her entire family. But that would play into his hand, and she had no intention of doing *anything* Giorgio wanted.

"No," Angelina replied softly. She bowed her head to hide the anger in her eyes. *I will play you like you have played my family. You fake, evil liar!* Angelina thought to herself.

Thinking quickly, she set her intentions. *She* would be the cat, *he* the mouse.

"I am glad you are here, Giorgio. What I have to say will affect *all* of us."

She tucked away her actual feelings, replacing them with insecurity. Angelina's every move was a controlled part of a scripted play. She was merely an actress playing the role of a needy girl searching for a hero to save and comfort her. Giorgio, being the arrogant, self-centered, controlling asshole, would play right into her hands. Her eyes filled with tears, and her voice trembled as she told them the horrible news.

"Catalina, I went for my walk this morning. As usual, I left the house just before sunrise."

Angelina watched Giorgio's face out of the corner of her eye as he squirmed in his chair. His companions, posted like centurions in the entryway, exchanged worried glances.

"I walked up the hill to the cliff to watch the sunrise," Angelina described. "It was so peaceful. The fog was so thick... as if I was above the clouds. You couldn't even see the grapevines below. I was all alone, floating in heaven."

As she told her story, Angelina felt the tension melt from Giorgio and his men. Giorgio's breathing slowed to a relaxed rhythm. He believed her tale.

"I must have fallen into a deep sleep because when I woke, the sun was up, and the fog was gone. It was well past breakfast, and Papa," her voice cracked. "He would be displeased if I had not collected the eggs. So, I wandered back down through the vines. I stopped at the chicken coop, fed them, and gathered the eggs. When I walked into the kitchen to help Mamma with breakfast..."

Angelina, weeping, paused while the tears, *real* tears, welled in her eyes. The pressure in her heart was immense. How could she describe what happened? It was a delicate subject requiring every word to be carefully chosen, so she did not expose her knowledge.

"Trust no one," she silently reminded herself.

Angelina wiped her tears and squeezed Catalina's hand.

"Catalina... when I walked into the kitchen, I found..."

Angelina struggled to speak; it was too horrific to say. She questioned her ability to complete the account. Her sobs frequently interrupted her story.

"Mamma and Papa were... tied in chairs... they were badly beaten... and..." Angelina choked on her tears. "They were... They were... dead."

Catalina collapsed into Giorgio's arms, bawling.

"I am afraid it is worse! When I checked for life... our beloved brothers, Anton and RJ... were dead... laying lifeless, in a sea of red."

Angelina, her anger bubbling, glanced at Giorgio. She

wanted to tell the truth, but her gut urged her to finish her theatrical performance.

"Who could have done such a thing to our family?" Angelina pleaded between sobs. "Such a terrible tragedy. A horror! I thought we were safe, living in our own small world. Giorgio, *you* must help us find who did this, please? Giorgio! We have no one but you to protect us now!"

The words left a horrible taste in Angelina's mouth. She would rather him be dead than be anywhere near her or her sister. Her fate was unstable regardless of his proximity. He would either act as their protector or kill them.

"What about Ricardo?" Giorgio asked.

"My love, you are right!" Catalina perked up. "Thank you for remaining clear-minded. Where is Ricardo? We should send for Marcus as well. Constance? Constance?"

"Cat, the police found Ricardo's body, too." Angelina chose her next words carefully. "Thank God I was on the hillside, or surely I would have been killed as well. Who would attack our family?"

"The police found him already?" Giorgio snapped.

"It was horrible!"

"How did they know to look in the river?" Giorgio huffed but quickly rephrased his question. "I mean...*where* did they find him?"

Angelina glared at him, her body rigid with anger. She heard him the first time. Every fiber of her being wanted to scream, "*Murderer!*" But these men would slit her throat if they knew what her eyes had seen that day.

"The river?" Catalina asked in a daze. "What makes you think he was in the river?"

"Angelina said they found him by the river," Giorgio replied quickly. "Isn't that right, Angelina?"

Angelina willed herself to only look at her sister.

"Oh, Cat! It was so awful!"

CHAPTER 31

Angelina struggled to speak while Giorgio was present, even though he remained silent and relatively uninterested after the slip of his tongue. He was drunk, and drunk men talk more than they should.

How much of the day would he remember anyway? The sun will rise tomorrow, and Giorgio will hardly recall all his cruelty. Only his head will hurt, and his mind will be free of guilt, Angelina thought.

In shock, Catalina babbled. She asked questions but frequently lost focus and asked the same one again. After the fourth recount of the morning's events, the men tired of the tale and left to find more booze.

"What's done is done. There is not much we can do about it now, is there? You two can cry all you want, but it won't bring back the dead," Giorgio droned and kissed Catalina's forehead. He waved for his companions to follow him. "We will be in here, drinking away our sorrow. Constance, fix us something to eat and bring us the *best* wine."

Catalina flinched at his insensitivity.

The men waltzed into the dining area and never looked back. They dismissed the horror story as if it were a tale from a book. The fictional characters had nothing to do with them.

Their laughter, digging at Angelina's emotions, was torture. She wanted to leave the house, but going home was not an option. She had no place to stay. At least here, she could grieve with her sister.

"Cat," Angelina whispered, "Cat, look at me!" She held her finger to her mouth to keep her sister quiet. "There is more I must tell you. But not here. We must go somewhere where no one can hear."

"We can go to my room. It will be quieter, and I am sure you could use a hot bath." Cat glanced over her shoulder at the men. Giorgio's apathetic and unsupportive attitude was an embarrassment. "I will tell him we need our rest."

Catalina's wedding ring captured the firelight as she nervously rubbed her hands against her thighs. The engraved filigree pattern around the smaller stones accented the large, oval diamond in the center. The radiant work of art scattered sparkles around the room.

In her new life, Catalina had not washed any clothes, cooked any meals, or labored outside in the garden. She had no chores because the hired staff kept the enormous villa and expansive estate in immaculate condition. In just a few months, Catalina's hands turned into supple canvases to display expensive jewelry. In this regard, Giorgio was true to his word; he made sure Catalina wanted for nothing.

The women in town were jealous. Catalina lived the life of royalty with a handsome prince who frequently lavished her with expensive gifts. But they didn't know the entire story. The cover of a book never displays the whole truth of its inner secrets.

The marriage was not as perfect as it appeared. A month after their wedding, Catalina had several bruises from Giorgio hitting her. Catalina tried to pass it off because he was drunk and didn't know what he was doing. Two days later, he presented her with a diamond bracelet and begged for forgiveness. Catalina accepted the gift and quickly exonerated him.

When Catalina came to the vineyard the next month, she averted her eyes, refusing to look at anyone, especially

Angelina. When Angelina confronted Cat, she confessed Giorgio had hit her again. Her eye was swollen with a minor cut across the lid. Because his strikes left no permanent damage, Catalina claimed Giorgio was only expelling pent-up aggression spawned by a fight with his uncle.

"You are not his punching bag!" Angelina insisted.

"Lina, you don't understand. Don Salvatore is not like our Papa. He isn't loving or compassionate."

"That doesn't give Giorgio the right to hit you!"

"Giorgio has lived his entire life without the love of family. He is merely lashing out because he doesn't understand that love heals, not hurts," Catalina explained.

"Where did you hear that pile of..."

"Lina, you have never been in love! Therefore, I don't expect *you* to understand!"

A few days later, Catalina arrived wearing a beautiful sapphire and diamond necklace. Her bruises were easily concealed with makeup. Even if a bruise showed, the necklace was stunning enough to keep an onlooker's focus away from the fading injury.

"Isn't it beautiful, Mamma!" Catalina exclaimed. "He said there is a sapphire for each day we have been married. He handpicked each stone and designed the necklace himself! Isn't that romantic?"

Angelina didn't understand her sister's marriage, but not by the reason Cat gave. True, she hadn't been in love like Catalina, and she never wanted to be.

"I have heard of 'blind love' and Cat, you are blind!" Angelina grumbled after her sister paraded around, showing everyone the sapphire necklace. "Papa didn't shower Mamma with lavish gifts, and they are in love. Papa had a tough childhood, but he never beat Mamma like a filthy ox! Sixty-five sapphires to mark every day of wedded bliss. Blah! More like tombstones for every barbarous act you must endure!"

Catalina wasn't the only one in her family to be blindly in love. Because the vineyard's profit soared, the rest of her family ignored the occasional bruise.

"He is a passionate man," Sofia reasoned. "He is not an evil man. Cat will train him to temper his emotions; just give her time."

"Not all men are perfect like your father," Rosario joked.

"Lina, I never thought you would be jealous of our sister," Ricardo stated. "Do you still have feelings for him?"

Anton and Fernando held their tongues, neither wanting to push Angelina away or cause waves in Catalina's marriage.

Angelina did not want to create waves either, and she didn't like being called jealous. Therefore, she had to pretend to see no evil, much less speak of it. Now, Angelina was forced to expose Giorgio for who he really is... a monster.

Catalina's exhausted form, free of its usual bubbly nature, slowly moved toward the stone-edged archway by the dining room. Angelina sighed. Cat's grief tugged at her heart, intensifying her own heavy sadness.

How can I tell her the truth? Angelina thought.

"Giorgio, I think Lina should stay with us. Don't you?"

"Of course!" he slurred.

"Good night then," Catalina murmured with a slight bow.

Angelina's eyes widened. To watch her sister pay respect to a man who deserved a slow, painful death for destroying their perfect world was infuriating.

Her eyes cast down, Angelina followed her sister up the never-ending staircase. The dried mud on her boots and bloodstains on the hem of her dress stirred her hatred for Giorgio. She wished she had a gun to kill him, to end his evil existence, for the hell he created.

"Constance will bring us wine and draw you a bath. You will feel better after a warm soak," Catalina opened the doors to the tall, dark armoire and pulled out a nightdress for Angelina.

"Here, you can wear this to bed."

Catalina looked away to hide her grief and the tears rolling down her face. But nothing could conceal the agonizing sorrow seeping from every pore.

"I know this is difficult, but I must tell you the rest of this nightmare."

Angelina led her sister to the settee by the crackling fire. The heat embodied Sofia's loving hugs. It steadied Angelina enough to finish her story.

"This will be difficult to say, so please just listen."

Catalina nodded.

"I must apologize for two things. First, for not telling you Mamma and Papa are alive!"

"Ohh, thank God!"

"I have kept this a secret for *their* protection... and ours. I hope you understand."

Catalina nodded again.

Angelina continued with her account. Only holding back the gruesome details. Those images were her burden to carry. Besides, knowing the truth about Giorgio's part in the massacre would be enough of a hardship.

"The other thing is... I know who murdered our brothers. I saw everything and heard every word they spoke."

Angelina's mind transported her back to the dark cellar. The fire's warmth faded as the memory pulled her into the abyss of hell. She saw the light glinting off Giorgio's blade, his fiery eyes dancing, and his smile. His smile was frightening. He didn't enjoy taking a life; he *loved* it.

Living it once was enough, Angelina quietly berated herself. *Stop. Stop reliving it!*

"The man sitting at your kitchen table...The man drinking the wine from *our* father's grapes. The man *you love... He* killed our brothers!"

Catalina pulled her hands back, breaking the contact

between them. In disbelief, she shook her head to deny the possibility of such accusations.

"Please, Cat. Please believe me. Why would I lie about something this horrible!"

All the color faded from Catalina's face as she stared blankly at Angelina.

"I... No... It..." Catalina mumbled.

"I know it is hard to comprehend. But Cat, *we* are in danger! If he finds out we know the truth, he will kill us too. That is why we must be careful. We cannot trust anyone!"

Angelina waited for a response, an acknowledgment of the peril they faced. However, Catalina remained quiet, her eyes staring off into the distance until a knock on the door broke the silence.

"Come," Catalina said.

"It is only me, Signora," Constance replied as she gently pushed open the door. "I have brought you something to eat and a carafe of wine."

Though her sister sat less than a foot away, a vast cavern separated them. The emotional distance between them made it difficult to believe she had done the right thing.

Was it wise to tell Catalina about Giorgio? Angelina questioned herself.

"Please, Signora, eat. I know you are in a deep state of grieving, but you will need your strength if you are to avenge your family's name!" Constance placed a small plate of fruit, cheese, and bread before the sisters. "I am very sorry for your loss." Her eyes raised to meet the woman she worked for. "If there is anything you need me to do, I am here for you. Please accept my pledge of loyalty."

Prior to her current employment, Constance worked as a maid for an elderly woman in Bergamo. When the old woman passed, the maid was recommended to Giorgio as a good 'gift' to his future bride. Taking her role seriously, Constance worked diligently to make Catalina's life that of a princess. Her cheerful personality, positive spirit, and devotion to Catalina forged a close friendship in a brief period.

Constance's hand trembled as she filled two glasses with red wine. Through her eyelashes, her bright blue eyes occasionally flashed their concern for Catalina. It was heartwarming to know her sister had someone watching over her. Nonetheless, Giorgio hired Constance. Therefore, the maid was untrustworthy, regardless of her emphatic pledge of loyalty.

When Catalina opened her mouth to speak, a pit formed in Angelina's gut.

What is done is done, Angelina thought. *I can only hope Cat has the common sense to keep the details a secret.*

"Thank you, Constance. You *are* a loyal friend. We will need your help now more than ever."

"It is no problem, Signora. I will do whatever you ask."

"Thank you, Constance. We will do our best with some food." Catalina placed her hand on Constance's arm. "Please use caution in all that you say and all you do. Keep your eyes open, for they may seek to take our lives as well. It is more troublesome because we do not know *who* did this. But rest assured, we will find out! For now, I believe the best thing would be a hot bath for both of us. Please draw one for Angelina? I shall take my bath after her."

"I have already started preparing the water, Signora. It will be ready in a few minutes."

Catalina gave her maid a warm smile. Constance bowed slightly and left the room.

"I know you trust her, but thank you for not telling her."

"I trust *her!*" Catalina's body stiffened. "Right now, I must decide if I trust *you!*"

CHAPTER 32

Angelina slid into the white claw-foot tub, the warm water engulfing her. Gradually, the heat steeped every ache from her body. Though she had suffered no blows from a fist, no broken bones, no loss of blood, nor wounds from an evil man's blade. Every part of her cried out in misery. But a vision of her father's battered face filled her heart with guilt.

"How can I feel abused? I was not beaten to death!" She sobbed. "Oh, Papa. I am sorry I did not save them... I didn't even try!"

She forced herself to push past her emotions by scrubbing away the grime, but every moment of her day flashed before her. Hypnotized by the vivid images, Angelina stopped fighting against the scenes and watched the motion picture play on an endless loop. Her visions started with Ricardo's lifeless eyes and ended with her father's unbearable grief.

The mountain of frothy white bubbles dwindled with every slosh of the rag into the water. Angelina's hand worked as fervently as her mind. Finally, she sighed. Her body was as clean as it would get, and her parents were safe. No amount of soap would remove the rest of the stress her day had thrust upon her.

Angelina relaxed back, soaking in the last few minutes of warmth from the water. Longing for something positive to focus on, she recalled being with her best friend Maria at the hospital.

"Mamma is safe, Papa." Angelina tried to sound strong, but

she intermittently broke down in sobs. Maria squeezed Angelina's hand, giving her strength. "You were worried she had died, but she is alive! Be strong for her, Papa. Please!"

"Do not fear for them, Angelina. My husband and I will guard them as if they were our own. After everything you have done for my family, it is the least we can do."

Angelina gave her best friend a faint smile. It was comforting to know Maria and Dr. Leonardo would watch over them. Yet, she still found it difficult to leave her father's side.

"God is not done with him, Lina." Maria placed her hand on Angelina's arm. "Rosario is a good man and has helped many! My mother thinks he deserves a sainthood for his generosity. When there was no work to be found, your father gave mine work for many years!"

"Your father is a good worker. That is why Papa kept him," Angelina sniffled, her tears abating. "Not out of generosity."

"You are humble, just like your father," Maria marveled as she tucked a wayward hair behind Angelina's ear. "Your family is my family! I love them, and I love you."

Angelina patted Maria's hand in gratitude for her supportive comments.

"I love you, too."

Rosario's hospital room was a bright white canvas, amplifying the bluish-purple bruise on his face. It was a heart-wrenching splash of color in a sterile, depressing space, and it made Angelina weep.

"Look at me, Lina. It is an honor to care for them. Besides, you would do the same for me."

With a sigh, Angelina nodded, "You are right, I would."

Maria wrapped her arm around Angelina, giving her a comforting hug. "They will be fine."

"What about tomorrow?" Angelina asked. "The doctor doesn't think they can be moved for several days!"

"My cousin, Anna, will be his nurse tomorrow. I trust her to help me keep them safe. That will give you time to tell Cat and get some rest."

"Thank you, Maria! Thank you!"

"You can thank me by taking a long hot bath," Maria smiled. "You don't just deserve it... you *need* it!"

Angelina, relaxing deeper into the water, chuckled at her friend. Maria's comment was confirmation that she smelled as rotten as she felt. Her time with Maria was the only reprieve from the day's chaos. She clung to the loving memory of her friend's comforting hug. Soon, one by one, all the day's events began melting away, and her eyes closed.

A rap on the door snapped Angelina from her dream.

"Signorina?" Constance hollered through the door. "Signorina, are you okay?"

Abruptly, Angelina sat up and gasped for air. Her rapid motion sent bathwater sloshing over the edge of the tub.

"I am fine! I am almost finished."

Angelina tried to get up, but the water was a heavy anchor, pulling her back into the tub.

The bubbles were gone, leaving a placid surface that reflected her face. A few droplets fell from her pruned hands, rippling the water. In the distorted surface, she saw a vision of Ricardo's bloated body and his lifeless eyes gazing up at her. With a pang of deep sadness in tow, the sight sent a shiver down her spine.

"Cry, damn it! Cry," a voice in her head begged. "Let the tears wash it all away."

As if she needed permission to break the dam of emotions, a flood of tears unleashed, and her body convulsed with every sob. The day's events loomed heavy, but her sister's lack of trust was the most soul-crushing. Without Catalina, she had no one to confide in and no one to comfort her. She was totally alone.

When the bath became unbearably cold, Angelina pulled

herself from the tub. She dried her body and wrapped herself in the plush blue robe Constance had laid out for her. The soft fabric captured her warmth, allowing the goosebumps on her skin to retreat. She rubbed her arms to enjoy the luxurious material. It felt good against her skin. She wondered if it was really that posh or if her exhaustion exaggerated the lavishness. One glance at her pale, drawn face in the mirror made her believe the latter was the truth.

"You look like shit!" she said to her reflection.

Angelina smoothed her hair and pinched her cheeks, but nothing helped her appearance. The day had drained her. She had nothing left to give, much less to supply energy for a beautiful complexion.

The words of her Mother echoed through her head.

"When someone takes all your power, look deep inside your soul. Your energy is more abundant than the water in the sea. Will you allow others to weaken and drain you, or Will you be stronger than they believed? Remember, God gives you opportunities to realize the magnitude of your strength. Choose daughter, are you the victim or the victor?"

Angelina heard her mother's voice so clearly that she turned to see if Sofia was standing in the room. But no one was in the bathroom. Angelina was all alone.

"Close your eyes and choose my daughter," Sofia's voice repeated. Eyelids relaxed, she slowly inhaled, filling her lungs, before similarly releasing as her mother taught her.

"I choose to be the victor! I am strong, I am strong!" Angelina repeated the mantra with growing conviction. "I am victorious, I am victorious!" Widening her eyes, she looked at the mirror and sighed, "...and I am exhausted!"

Angelina's fatigue overruled the decant robe. She needed sleep, more than a fuzzy hug, so she removed it and slid into the nightdress. The soft, pink silk felt like cream pouring over her skin. Angelina never felt a heavenly fabric caress her body, making her feel beautiful inside and out.

She donned the robe again and slid her feet into the soft cotton slippers. The degree of decadence surpassed a hot bath on a chilly day or a refreshing plunge in the river on a scorching summer afternoon. It was hard to not enjoy such luxuries. With compassion, she understood how her sister could become a slave to such finery. When you feel battered and bruised, the exquisiteness of luxury effortlessly draws you into its folds.

"Where would you like for me to sleep tonight, Cat?" Angelina asked gently.

"You can sleep in my bed with me," Catalina responded, her voice still cold. "I have locked the door so no one can enter. We will be safe here."

"Thank you, Cat."

"I think a good night's sleep will do us both good," Catalina interjected before Angelina could say anything further.

"Si." Angelina tenderly touched her sister's arm. "Cat?"

Catalina turned, her eyebrow cocked. The fiery blaze in Catalina's eyes was the same as Sofia's. Without question, it was a warning of the wrath to come if pressed any further. It was a look Angelina knew all too well. Now was not the time to argue with her sister. Tomorrow was another day. Tomorrow, Angelina would prove what she knew all along, Catalina's husband was an evil wolf.

"The robe and slippers are so soft! And your silk nightdress..."

Catalina coldly cut her off. "I will remember that when it is your birthday."

Before Angelina could say anything further, Catalina had disappeared. It would be unreasonable to expect her sister's temper to soften in two hours, so Angelina released the idea of a peaceful truce. For now, she must rest and regain her strength. Tomorrow, the horror of reality would return.

Angelina rubbed her hand across the comforter's beautiful gold and burgundy brocade. The colors blended well with the deep-red cherry wood of the poster bed. Elegant hand-carved swirling patterns climbed the posts that held the sheer, golden silk drape. The floating fabric provided a veil between her and the fresco on the ceiling.

Angelina marveled at the hues of color in the painting. The sunbeams illuminated the puffy white clouds floating across the light blue sky. Doves glided through the air while four cherubs sprinkled petals from the heavens onto a beautiful goddess relaxing on a bed of roses. It was an enchanting scene that mimicked Catalina's life. The goddess, like Catalina, lounged in beauty while the heavens served her more decadence. Angelina felt a wave of jealousy wash over her. It would be nice to be submerged in constant luxuriousness.

She crawled into the cloud of white, her body instantly enveloped by the comfortable mattress. Her hair still damp, she flipped it up off her neck and rested her head on the oversized, fluffy pillow. Cuddled in the loving embrace of the bedding, Angelina's eyes instantly became heavy. She blinked to keep awake, but the silky sheets and the heavy comforter added to the lure of slumber.

As she melted into a deep sleep, Angelina took in the details of the room one last time. Everything from the furniture to the plush drapes, beautiful paintings, and delicate figurines was evidence of the magnitude of wealth and comfort her sister enjoyed. Experiencing the extravagance first-hand provided a purpose for her sister's reservations. Catalina would lose all of these luxuries if she believed Giorgio murdered their family.

CHAPTER 33

The cold pulled Angelina from her dreams. With a shiver, she rolled to her side and snuggled under the thick bedcover while her eyes panned the room. The chilly air made the space feel haunted, intensifying the eeriness of every shadow. Angelina brushed away her childish imagination. The large villa was old, but that gave no credence to the notion of it being haunted. The sound of her sister's steady breathing reinforced her more practical mental process.

"You are safe," Angelina reminded herself. "You are cold because the fire has dwindled. Don't be a ninny. Get up and fix the problem. God knows we have enough already. No need to create more issues from nothing!"

Angelina had not heard her sister come to bed. By the minimal glow from the fire and pitch-black sky, Angelina assumed they both had been asleep for a while. It would be several hours before the sun appeared on the horizon or Constance's entrance to freshen the fire.

She gazed at Catalina's soft features. Her little sister had grown into a beautiful woman, living a life full of every pleasure anyone could ever desire. She watched Catalina's slow, steady breathing and smiled. When they were young, Angelina would tuck Catalina in bed and kiss her forehead before snuggling into her own bed. Angelina wanted to kiss Cat's forehead but feared it might startle her. Instead, Angelina lay still and enjoyed her sister's peaceful slumber. Being with Catalina gave Angelina a thread of happiness in a sea of despair.

As children, their relationship was strong. Yet, as teenagers, Angelina felt her sister pull away. It was natural for her to want to become a unique person. Angelina had often heard Cat say, *"I am not Angelina!"* Out of maturity and respect, Angelina allowed the space between them to widen. She expected the phase would pass and they would resume a close friendship. Giorgio's presence, however, widened the gap into a canyon. Angelina needed her sister, and she prayed Catalina would need her too.

As quietly as possible, Angelina slipped out of bed. The cold marble added to her chills. She made her way to the fireplace and added a piece of wood to the dancing embers.

Yesterday's events were tragic, and Angelina felt terrible. She placed an enormous amount of stress on Catalina when she accused Giorgio of murder. Angelina hoped her sister could find forgiveness and, in time, understand her words were the truth, not just another attack based on jealousy.

After another shudder trickled across her spine, Angelina placed two more logs on the red embers. Poorly seated, one rolled toward her. Angelina hopped back to avoid being burned by the tagalong hot coals. With a loud thud, the log landed inches from her toes. Less concerned for her own well-being, Angelina looked to see if the noise had disturbed her sister's slumber. Catalina rolled over, snuggled back into her pillow, and quickly fell back to sleep.

Convinced her sister was undisturbed, Angelina carefully placed the log back on the coals. She stirred the embers and gently blew to encourage the flames. With a bit of effort and a lot of blowing, the yellow and red tongues licked at the fresh log. Angelina rubbed her hands together in eager anticipation of the warmth. After a few minutes, Angelina's trembling form was rewarded. The heat slowly made its way up her body, and her goosebumps diminished.

The glow entranced Angelina, and her mind returned to her conversation with her sister. She chided herself for not being more sensitive to Catalina's position. Why didn't she think of how that would make her sister feel? After all, Catalina genuinely loved him.

Angelina sighed. "What else did you screw up?"

She reviewed her conversations from the moment Carlos pulled into the drive. Her exchanges with Carlos, Carmella, Maria, and the police were managed professionally. A moment of relief trickled in but instantly rushed out, leaving an intense pang of guilt.

"Nan!" Angelina whispered.

Fernando arrived with his parents. He helped mop up his best friend's blood without a single complaint. A vision of Fernando on his knees, a stream of tears flowing down his cheeks as he rang out the cloth, stabbed Angelina's heart. Fernando hurt, too, but she didn't offer him comfort.

"Oh, Angelina, you are so cruel!"

Her loving actions toward Fernando since they started dating were nearly nonexistent. He was the one to initiate a kiss, a hug, or even the most common display of affection; holding hands. Though he expressed his love, he did not press her to reciprocate with action or words. He was patient and compassionate. And she hated to admit Fernando was a damn good kisser.

"How can one be so ruthless to someone who loves you more than any man could. Yet, you repay him with a chill that would freeze earth's core!"

A flash of the flame made her step back from the fire. As she stepped back, her thoughts did, too. Not once had she questioned why her family was targeted. Nothing could explain Giorgio's motives, much less his wildly excited joy when carrying out the act. There was no money to gain by killing her brothers or her parents. Giorgio swam in a sea of wealth. He would inherit more than he could ever want as heir to Mario's and Don Salvatore's fortunes. Angelina combed through the memory of the massacre, however, this time with no emotion. This was a review for context, words, and clues to help her understand the crime, not a stroll through memories to gather flowers of misery.

Giorgio had two odd comments that made Angelina sit back in puzzlement. His claim against Rosario. *"You killed my father!"* And the accusation of Sofia's infidelity. *"Sofia's bastard son, Marcus!"* Neither made sense. Mario was Giorgio's father. Her parents lying about Marcus's parentage was nearly as ludicrous as Giorgio's despicable actions.

The warmth of the roaring fire freed her mind to focus on gathering pieces to the puzzle. Angelina reached for the fireside chair, and a chill engulfed her. But this time, the chill was not from the frigid air. She felt the prying eyes of someone lurking behind her. Frozen by fear, she dared not turn around to investigate what might be hiding in the shadows. Keeping her gaze on the tile in front of the fireplace, Angelina began to pray. A mental exercise her mother taught her to use when the monster under the bed visited.

It is merely your exhaustion putting your imagination in overdrive. Angelina thought. *At most, it was Constance keeping watch.*

Both seemed reasonable explanations, especially after Catalina said she locked the door. Her reasoning brought her comfort until a movement in the darkness caught her attention. Even with the less frightening explanations in her mind, Angelina steeled her nerves and slowly turned around.

"That is a lovely shade of pink," a deep voice said.

The air in her lungs rushed out, and her heart thundered in her chest. The shadow wasn't a figment; it was real! Blinded by staring endlessly into the firelight, Angelina blinked wildly to clear away her impaired vision.

"Who's in here?"

"Ha, ha, are you frightened little girl?" The voice spoke in a vile, devilish tone.

"You can't be in here!"

"*Can't?* I will be where *I* want!" The shadow taunted, moving into the light. "It is *my* house!"

Angelina retreated in horror.

"How... how did you get in here? Cat locked the door!"

"I can open every door in *my* house? I have all the keys."

Angelina's vision returned. Before her stood a man, his powerful muscles chiseled from stone. Without his shirt, Giorgio's broad shoulders, washboard abs, and deeply etched arms were proof that his significant strength far overpowered Anton and Fernando.

Giorgio stepped out from the sofa, moving within an arm's length of her. He was completely naked. Angelina averted her eyes and stepped away.

"I know you want me. You could have had me." Giorgio crept closer and closer. The firelight dancing in his eyes added to his wickedness. "I asked for your hand first, but your father refused. He didn't like me, did he? I was not good enough for his favorite. No, he wouldn't share the steak on the table. He threw me his scraps. He couldn't wait to rid himself of Cat. She meant nothing to him!"

"That is not true!"

"He thought he would keep me from getting you. But, like you, I know how to get what I want! You have desired me and this life of luxury!" Giorgio flourished his hands, emphasizing the surrounding wealth. "All this around you could have been yours. You and me. We could have ruled this town...*We will* rule this town. All of Northern Italy will bow like slaves at our feet!"

He gently caressed her arm, but she shoved his hand away.

"Do not be repulsed by that which you are! You manipulate

people with your looks, as do I. You are willful, as am I. All your cherished talents, I, too, possess. My plan was for you to be my bride. For us to wield our powers together. But...your sister is good enough entertainment... *for now!*"

He grabbed her shoulders and pulled her back into him. Angelina felt his erection against her back. Reflexively, she pulled away from his grip and moved behind the armchair.

"Stay away from me!"

"Now, now! You are in *my* house! I am the *only* man in the family. I control you *and* your little brat sister." His escalating tone conveyed his growing aggression. "*Both* of you will do *what* I say! *When* I say! *How* I say! You *will* make *me* happy..." He lunged toward her. "...and *rich!*"

She dodged his attack and shouted loud enough to wake her sister. "You're already rich!"

Angelina needed Catalina to wake up. She needed her to hear Giorgio's 'plan.' To see him standing naked, making advances. But Catalina's breathing remained constant.

"The sleeping pill in her wine will prevent her from interrupting us for several more hours. Consider it a honeymoon for us to consummate our love."

"How could you?" Angelina replied in disgust.

"It is for *your* benefit as much as hers. Women can be so possessive. This will allow both of you to get used to your new arrangements." Giorgio cackled. "I know how much to give her...now. It took some trial and error, but I am confident I know the amount that would kill her."

"Does she even know you put drugs into her wine?"

"What is the fun in that!"

"You are *Evil!* I wish you never married my sister!"

"See, I knew you were jealous. Papa should have allowed the love birds to unite."

"I do not love you! I want nothing to do with you!"

"Ah, now, now. That is not what you said earlier. What was

it? I think...something about helping you find the murderer? Protect you? I do believe you were almost *begging* for me!" Salivating, he added, "And I *will* help you. For a *price*!" His tone elevated. "Everything comes at a price!"

"What do you want?"

"To start, you will submit to me!"

Angelina's face filled with horror.

"Oh, it won't be so bad. You will learn to enjoy *this!*" Giorgio began pleasuring himself. "Then, since you have no man to run the family business. I will take the vineyard and all the wine!"

"You know nothing of how to make wine!"

"Precisely why I left you alive!"

"What do you mean, *left* me alive?"

"Your intelligence is an alluring part of your charm. Don't play an ugly, stupid girl with me!" Giorgio scowled. "I killed your brothers and your parents. It was the only way to take control of the vineyard."

"What?" Angelina looked at him incredulously. "Have you been planning this for years?"

"I told you, I *always* get what I want! Some things, like you, are worth waiting for!"

He stared at Angelina's chest and licked his lips. She looked down. The firelight turned the pink nightdress into a sheer veil. Giorgio saw her visible curves and erect nipples as a sign of her arousal.

"You like what you see, don't you?" Giorgio bragged.

"No! You disgust me!"

Angelina moved further away from the fire. His eyes still focused on the curves of her body; he moved with her, maintaining the distance between them.

"Why *my* family?"

She needed to understand her enemy and buy her mind time to get out of this rat trap.

"History repeats itself!"

"What history?"

"Your father destroyed my life!" Giorgio looked into her eyes and smiled with delight. "Ohhh! Of course, they kept their corruption a secret!"

"Secret? What secret?"

"The secret about *your* father murdering *my* father?"

"You are delusional!"

"Do you know *who* my father was? What he would have been if it weren't for Rosario Beretta?"

In puzzlement, Angelina stood frozen, her mind reeling from the idea of her father killing anyone. It was impossible. Her father was kind and compassionate. A man full of love and wisdom. Not a murderer.

"Where did your parents make their bond?"

"They married at St. Agatha's!"

"That is not what I asked! Their sins began long before wedded bliss!"

Giorgio took a step closer to her. The movement pulled her from her frozen gridlock of thoughts. More alert, Angelina moved around the room.

"Did you know Marcus was not your father's child?" Giorgio, matching her every move, gloated, enjoying the game. "It is true! Marcus was the bastard son of a whore!"

"My mother was not a whore!"

"See, my love, your family has many secrets. But I will not keep you in the dark. We shall have an honest, open relationship." Giorgio uttered the words like a romantic tale. "I shall tell you about your *not-so-saintly* parents. I have seen the pictures of your mother at your age. You are an exact replica of the radiant Sofia. The lovely goddess who seduced your father into killing mine! The whore mother of the bastard, Marcus. You see, your parents are liars, *not* saints!"

The words hypnotized her. Her mother wasn't a whore. Marcus wasn't a bastard. Her father was not a murderer!

In her dazed state, Giorgio cut across the room. He reached over the chair between them and caressed Angelina's face. His touch ripped her back to reality.

"What? No! No! My father didn't kill your father! You are sick, so *sick*! Your mind is beyond warped!"

She slapped his hand away and darted behind the sofa, watching for which direction he would go. He was a skilled hunter, forcing her to be focused and cognizant of his proximity. She could not allow him any more advantage than nature had already given him.

He moved to the right, and she reacted, not allowing the space to diminish. The fireplace was about five steps away. If she timed it right, she could grab the half-burned log from the flames. Mentally, she prepared for the searing pain that would accompany the red-hot embers. Her hand reflexively opened and closed. It would be worth it...if it worked.

"Someone has filled your head with lies!"

Angelina darted across the room. Her back against the fireplace, the fire's glow illuminated Giorgio's face. Her heart raced. He was a rabid wolf, ready to devour her.

"Your ignorance is appalling. But I will make you see the truth! I will *show* you the proof! Then you will understand it is *your* head that was filled with lies!"

Giorgio moved across the room so quickly that Angelina had no time to react. In a split second, he was standing beside her, his hand firmly clamped on her throat. He squeezed, and she gasped for air.

"Your father killed my father," Giorgio growled. "It's revenge, Angelina! Sweet revenge! An eye for a fucking eye!"

In one furious movement, he tossed her onto the sofa. The force of her body colliding against the furniture made the sofa bump into the table behind it. The lamp and porcelain figurines jostled, threatening to crash to their demise on the hard floor. Angelina's body bounced on impact. She used the momentum to roll onto the floor and avoid another assault.

With a scream, she jumped to her feet. "You took more than an eye!"

"And I intend to take more!" Giorgio boasted. "The best part about revenge is being in control."

"Control of what?"

"The ugly stupid girl returns!" Giorgio's temper flared. "I want... No! I *will* control you!"

Giorgio lunged for Angelina, but she maneuvered out of the way. With a loud thump, Giorgio's body collided with the floor. The impact knocked the wind out of him, allowing Angelina time to move again.

When Giorgio regained his breath, a fire coursed through his veins. He stood with a wicked scowl and growled while he scanned the room for his prey. Their eyes met, and he lunged toward her, pushing an antique armchair out of his way. Angelina, prepared for the attack, moved further back.

"If Mario is not your father, who is he?"

"He pulled me from the streets, raised me, taught me how to make money."

"You mean how to murder and steal!"

"No, that vein of evil is from my Salvatore lineage!" Giorgio grinned proudly, tracking his prey, matching her step for step. "When I was old enough, Mario revealed my true identity and my birthright. When the time was right, we called on Don Salvatore, my Uncle. Mario, the astute businessman, knew exactly what Don Salvatore craved most. The truth of his brother's demise. Mario just so happened to witness my father's death. It is marvelous when everything comes full circle, is it not?"

Angelina tried to follow his story. Some words she heard, others were drowned out while she focused on her freedom. She noticed he was stroking himself again and was closing the gap between them. Her heart thundered in her chest, terrified of what he planned to do next?

"What is your plan?"

"And the beautiful, charming Angelina returns! A good question deserves the truth." Giorgio licked his lips again, his eyes watching for which direction Angelina might run. "I get all the money from Papa's business. And best of all, I get *you!*"

Giorgio lunged at Angelina, but she shoved the chair into his path. He vaulted over it, grabbed her nightdress, and pulled her toward him. Angelina resisted but lost her footing and fell to the floor. Without hesitation, Giorgio pounced on her. His hand fumbled around to raise her nightdress while Angelina struggled against his weight. Her fists futilely beat against his muscular chest. Annoyed, he grabbed her arms and pinned them to the floor above her head.

"Finally, I get to mount the prize filly!" Giorgio grinned, relishing his victory.

A ravenous dog enjoying a fresh bone, he attacked her neck. His free hand fumbled with her nightdress, excitedly searching for an opening. Angelina struggled to break free, but Giorgio's grip on her wrists tightened, intensifying the pain. She whimpered in agony. The noise drew his attention to her lips. He leaned in to kiss her. His foul breath, a mixture of wine and cigars, reminded her of the lingering stench in her family's kitchen. She turned away, nauseated by the pungent odor. Her disinterest redirected his attention to other enticing places.

"I have wanted these since that day in the kitchen. You teasingly splashed your white shirt so the wet fabric could tempt me even more. That is the day I knew you desired me as much as I did you!" Giorgio effortlessly ripped her nightdress, exposing her breasts. "They are more beautiful than I dreamed!"

"Get off me! You sick fuck!"

Her legs forcefully kicked his muscular thighs. She wiggled and twisted, but her inferior power did little to deter him. He had his prey, and he would enjoy his victory.

"You are mine, Angelina! *Mine*! Think of it like this..." With an evil smile, he cackled. "I inherited you!"

She closed her eyes and turned away when he tried to kiss her again.

"Open your eyes! Bat those lashes as you did the first day we met! You wanted me then, and now you get all of me!"

"No! No! Please, no!"

Angelina tightened her eyelids and shook her head. She wished she were dead. She wished she had run out to save her brothers, and he killed her too. It would have been better than this... *anything* would be better than this! She wanted no more terrible memories, no more horror. She had enough for a lifetime.

"Catalina!" Angelina screamed. "Please, wake up!"

Tears escaping from her tightly closed eyes, Angelina continued screaming, but her sister did not respond. She was alone in the room with a monster. She tried to think of anything... anything, but what was happening to her. Visions of her happy family floated through her mind: her father's smile, her mother's warm embrace, her jovial brothers enjoying life. But nothing minimized the damage he inflicted.

The roaring fire and his enthusiasm for her flesh burned hot. Perspiration beaded his brow and drenched his hair. Angelina opened her mouth to scream, and a drop of his sweat fell into her mouth. Revolted, she spat it at his face. She wanted nothing of *his* in her. She tried to roll over, to squirm away, but his grip threatened to break her wrists.

"Constance! Please help me!" Angelina screamed. "Help! Someone help me! Please!"

He paused his carnal pursuit and used his heavy, muscular form to imprison her against the floor. He reached up and gently wiped the matted hair from her brow. She turned her only unrestrained body part. He grabbed her chin, holding her face hostage while he drank in her beauty. Lovingly holding her gaze, he gave her a tender smile.

"You need no help! Not with me, your shining night, protecting you." A maniacal grin curled his lips. "Actually, I *own* you, now and forever. Until death do us part, my love!"

He forced his tongue into her mouth, and she bit it. Disgusted by the taste of his blood, she launched it at him.

"You bitch!"

Giorgio smacked her. A fiery pain surged across her cheek. She had never been struck before. The searing sting made her body go limp in shock. Like a predator realizing his cue to attack, Giorgio positioned himself between her legs.

Angelina searched her surroundings, hoping for a lifeline, anything that could save her from reality. The warmth of the fire reached her skin, and the glow of orange and yellow filled the room. She could hear the wood crackle, like bones, popping. Her squirming resistance caused the carpet's thick braided trim to rub a raw line across the middle of her back. Warm blood oozed from her flesh as the fabric ground deeper and deeper.

His weight and toxic odor were stifling. Angelina felt like she could lose consciousness. She prayed she would. In her last attempt to free herself, she raised up and bit his chest.

"*Ouch!*" Giorgio screamed.

When he released her hand to feel the blood, Angelina used her freedom to pummel his chest. But she was a feeble woman in the shadow of his strength.

"Hold still, bitch!"

His anger surging, Giorgio growled and firmly gripped Angelina's throat. The limited oxygen weakened her senses. Everything shifted into slow motion. She opened her eyes, but the room was blurry and dark despite the glowing flames.

Her life slipping away, Angelina's only thought was of her sister alone, in a world filled with evil. Tears streamed down her cheeks. She prayed God would protect Catalina.

"You will submit every night!" Giorgio's focus on his prize loosened his grip. Angelina sucked in enough oxygen to speak her final wish with conviction.

"I curse you and your entire family, *forever*!"

The sound of her voice reinvigorated his grip, and her breathing slowed. She tried to turn her head toward the fire to watch the colorful glow, but her vision faded behind the closing velvet curtain. A loud noise echoed in the darkening world. A log on the fire exploded, or perhaps her hips gave way to the weight of his body. Whatever it was, it did not matter. Angelina's lungs could not expand. She ceased the fight for air as she faded into the dark abyss.

CHAPTER 34

In the sweltering heat, a heavy blanket of smoke loomed above their heads, diminishing the oxygen. Their bare feet slapped against the cold floor, scurrying to contain the fire.

"Open the window. Quickly, before we both pass out!" Catalina yelled at her maid.

Constance's vision was impaired by the billowing smoke. She toppled over a table, landing with a thud against the floor. She yelped in pain. Refusing to stop, she clambered back to her feet. Her outstretched hands became her eyes as she pressed through the darkness.

An ember lept from the fireplace to a chair tossed too close to the fire. The smoldering fabric produced the acrid smoke. A second spit from the fire rapidly dissolved the material, giving birth to another tendril of blackness. Like a rabbit on the run, a flame jumped from the fiery ring. Catalina grabbed her water pitcher and doused it. The flame sizzled a goodbye, but the damaged fabric continued to pollute the air.

"Constance," Catalina yelled between coughing fits. "Open that damn window!"

In a rush, the plume of smoke raced out the window, improving visibility and oxygenating the room.

Catalina kneeled beside her sister. Gently, she moved a chunk of hair, matted with blood and sweat, from Angelina's lifeless face. A river of sorrow flowed down Catalina's cheeks, dripping onto the torn, pink nightdress.

"Bring me a bowl of water and a washcloth."

"Si, Signora," Constance stepped over Giorgio's limp body.

"I am sorry," Catalina said to her sister's battered body.

"Here, Signora. Here is the water and a cloth."

Catalina began washing her sister's face with a soft white washcloth. With each plunge of the rag into the water, the bright red blood swirled into a pink hue.

Constance straightened Angelina's legs and covered her body with a blanket.

Trembling, Constance asked, "Do you think he is alive?"

"I wish he was dead, but I know he still breathes. He will probably be out for a little while. I hit him pretty hard."

"*Should* we kill him while we can? I will gladly end his life if that is what you wish!"

"Constance! How can you say such a thing? Murder is a sin!" Catalina snapped, reflexively scolding her maid. In truth, she, too, had contemplated killing the man only moments before her maid suggested it.

Catalina's gut warned her of Giorgio's roving eye, especially around her sister. Yet, her husband's professions of love and her luxurious lifestyle lulled her into a state of denial. She enjoyed her fancy parties, the jewelry, the expensive clothing, and the elevated social standing. They were hard to step away from. Like the sweetest chocolate, once you have savored the richness, you want more.

"We cannot kill him. Unfortunately, we need him."

Constance, eyes wide with fear, stared back. "Signora, I will always do as you say, but can we not find a way! He...after all he has done..."

"We will only need another man to take his place. I know this man's faults and will use them to my advantage."

"How, Signora?"

"We will outsmart him. For now, however, we need him alive."

Catalina looked at his body, and for the first time, she did not desire him. She knew she married a womanizer; therefore, she easily overlooked his proclivities. However, catching Giorgio and Angelina together, she felt betrayed.

"How could I have been so blind?" Catalina muttered, holding the cloth stained pink with her sister's blood.

"He has always been good at acting the part of a gentleman." Constance placed her hand gently on Catalina's shoulder. "You have come so far, Signora. Do not let the past weigh so heavily."

Catalina nodded. "Thank you for your wisdom. We must focus our energy on the task at hand."

She returned to washing Angelina's face. The red swirled to pink again and again. After a long, quiet spell, Catalina dropped the rag into the water.

"Let's drag him to his bed and place a carafe of wine laced with his infamous sleeping pills. I shall even soak some fruit in the wine. When he wakes, he will eat and drink as usual. He will barely be able to piss before he falls back to sleep."

"For how long?"

"For as long as it takes to establish a plan."

"What of the funerals?" Constance asked.

"We have one week."

Catalina stood to walk to the dresser but hesitated. Could she trust Constance with her secret? Tears filled her eyes, the pain of loneliness crushed her heart.

"Constance, look me in the eye." Catalina stared deep into her maid's soul. "Can I trust you?"

"Si, Signora! Have I not proven myself worthy? Please tell me what I have done so I may prove my loyalty to you."

Catalina waved away her maid's plea. "No, you have done nothing wrong." She sighed, mustering the courage to trust...anyone. "I need to tell you a secret. I warn you, to share it could cost you your life." Constance's eyes widened. "Not by my hands. Do you not know me better than that?" Catalina held her maid's hand and sincerely gave her the freedom to choose. "Given the danger, if you wish not to hear it, I..."

"Signora, you are so brave. I wish to be brave like you! I will hold your secret and protect you with my life. Ti prometto!"

"Very well." Catalina motioned for Constance to sit beside her. "Mamma and Papa are still alive. They suffered terrible injuries. Though they survived surgery..."

"Signora, they are alive!" Constance made a sign of the cross and sent a kiss to heaven in gratitude. "They are strong..."

Catalina held up her hand. "Their fight is long from being over. I shall inquire more at the hospital. For now, this must remain a secret. You understand why, si?"

Constance nodded.

"When they are healthy enough, I shall move them. I fear it will be many months before they can return. Even then, their lives may be in danger. Only time will tell."

Catalina looked down at her sister, her heart torn by betrayal. Giorgio had crossed a line. An unforgivable line. In one day, her family was destroyed. Her heart grieved the expansive loss of her siblings and the luxury of trust.

"Help me move Angelina to the bed."

All the filth, blood, and tears washed away; they dressed her in a green nightdress. Catalina softly kissed her sister's forehead, then tucked her hair behind her ear.

"There, just like you like it," Catalina whispered.

"She looks so peaceful, Signora."

"She is, finally, she is," Catalina replied as the tears of regret rolled down her cheeks.

CHAPTER 35

"Help me carry him to his room."

"Si, Signora."

Constance moved to his feet. The two women tried to hoist his heavy, limp body, but his weight was too great. They tried various positions, and none proved successful. Frustrated, they stood there staring at his naked body.

With his perfect lines delineating every muscle, Giorgio could have modeled for a sculpture or a class of aspiring doctors who wished to draw and label each muscle. His rippled flesh was an aphrodisiac for women. Even fully dressed in a tailored suit, his stature aroused lustful desires. However, at that moment, for Catalina and Constance, his body was more akin to a mangy wolf.

Catalina took a step closer to him. His lungs filled with air before releasing his poisonous exhaust into the room.

"You bastard!" She kicked his ribs with all her might again and again. "I hate you!" Her cries of revulsion echoed the sorrow of a wolf howling at the full moon. "Why her? Why?"

Her assault on Giorgio's limp form continued until she collapsed onto her knees and wept into her hands.

"Signora." Constance's arms enveloped Catalina as a mother would hold her grieving child. "Cry every tear you need to shed for your brothers, your parents, and your sister. But do not shed one tear for this disgusting pig! He deserves not one ounce of your love. He deserves to live in hell, and we shall make sure he does!"

Catalina sobbed into Constance's shoulder. The horror and madness of the past twenty-four hours gnawed at her. At that moment, the tender memories of her brothers' love and laughter were as cold as the table on which they lay.

Rosario and Sofia's survival brought her minimal comfort. Their bodies still drew breath, but their idyllic life was over. Even if they lived, they would never be who they were.

Every aspect of Giorgio and Angelina tortured Catalina. Seeing the tragedy unfold made sanity an elusive ideal afforded to only the lucky. In one day, the entire Beretta family's luck ran out.

Catalina clung to Constance's comforting presence. She was a friend, a devoted friend, and now the only one she could trust.

"Thank you, Constance. You are a loyal friend."

"As are you for me, Signora."

Constance continued to rock Catalina and gently stroke her hair. The soothing kindness helped dry Catalina's tears.

"Constance," Catalina said, sitting up suddenly. "Get a blanket from the wooden chest in the guest room!"

Constance flashed a quizzical look, then quickly did as she was asked. When she returned, Catalina had moved several pieces of furniture.

"Here, Signora. What do we do now?"

"You will see."

Together, they moved the sofa and end table, then spread the blanket beside Giorgio's body.

"Oh, Signora! You are so smart!" Constance said, understanding her mistress's plan.

"Papa taught me to be clever," Catalina said with a grin. "Now, help me roll him onto the blanket."

"We will drag him to his room, si? But how will we lift him into bed?"

"We shall worry about *if* we can get him to his room."

She picked up her corner of the blanket and motioned for Constance to do the same. Working together, they drug him across the cold marble floor. Their arms were burning, and their lungs begging for oxygen when they finally reached the grand staircase. In unison, they let go of the blanket, and Giorgio's head hit the floor, making a loud thump.

"Oops!"

Catalina's lack of compassion for the wallop to his head ignited a roar of laughter. The early morning hour, lack of sleep, and pure exhaustion had shifted their mood from somber to the giggles.

"I have got it!" Catalina shouted spontaneously, making Constance jump. "We will roll him down the stairs. It will appear as an accident in the morning."

"It is morning, Signora," Constance said with a giggle.

"Ok, Ms. Precise! The sun shall rise, and the rooster shall crow his morning tune, but *neither* has happened, *yet!*"

After several minutes, their laughter faded, and Catalina revealed the next phase of her plan.

"When you come in to fix the morning coffee," Catalina began. "You will scream at the sight of Giorgio at the bottom of the stairs. I will come running, and we will call the doctor immediately. We will let the doctor put the pig in bed!" Catalina said triumphantly.

"Perfect, Signora, see, I knew you would figure something out!" Re-energized, Constance stood ready to dump the lifeless creature down the steps. "The doctor will think his injuries are from the fall, and no one will question us!"

"Exactly! If we create enough force, gravity can do the rest of the work," Catalina explained, pointing down the sweeping staircase. "On three. One, two... three!"

They shoved the body as hard as they could, but their effort only awarded them two steps. They looked at each other with a defeated expression.

"Let's try again," Catalina said, "but with our legs."

From the top step, they positioned their feet on his torso.

"Ready?" Catalina asked.

Constance nodded.

"One, two…"

A deep moan came from the body at their feet. They exchange terror-filled glances. Both knew the consequences if Giorgio remembered *they* shoved him down the steps.

"Now what?" Constance whispered.

"Three!" Catalina exclaimed.

Abruptly, they pushed with all their might. The torso took flight, with arms and legs flopping about. Giorgio tumbled down the stairs. His head banged against every other step. They grimaced at each painful thud until he stopped. Worried the tumble might wake the beast, Catalina and Constance watched in timid silence. Much to their relief, Giorgio remained motionless.

"Do you think that killed him? I have heard people can die from a fall like that," Constance whispered.

"*Now* you mention that bit of information! That would have been helpful *before* we pushed him to his death!"

"Sorry!" Constance said, shrugging her shoulders.

"Go see if he is still breathing!"

"You go! I will fetch his robe!" Constance replied and left before Catalina could protest.

"Fine! I will go…when you get back with his robe." Catalina stared at the motionless body. "What next?"

"Life is like a chess match. Always know your next three moves," Rosario taught her when they played chess.

"I hear you, Papa. But what *should* my next move be?"

"Think, Princepessa."

"Step one, I will call the doctor *if* he is alive. Next, keep him sedated long enough to discover the status of Mamma and Papa." Catalina quietly strategized. "Three steps," she repeated softly. "What is the third step?"

Catalina surveyed the future, looking for the most important tasks to keep her ahead of the train.

"I need to figure out what to do about the vineyard," Catalina whispered. "With my siblings gone, *who* will run it?"

The idea of being alone, running the business, and worrying about what would happen if her father could never return twisted a blade in her gut.

"Ok, Papa. Before the vineyard, I must get past the funerals." Catalina sighed. "That makes three."

"Here is his robe!" Constance dropped it by her mistress.

The movement startled Catalina, and she stumbled from the top step. She reached for Constance's hand but missed it, tumbling down several steps. When she caught hold of the railing, she remained still....very, very, still.

"I am sorry, Signora! Are you ok?"

"Just a little shaken. I will manage."

Constance hurried down the steps to help Catalina.

"I am so sorry, Signora!" She brushed off her mistress's nightdress and thoroughly inspected her for injury.

"I said, I am fine!"

"Si, Signora." Constance tucked her chin. "I am sorry!"

"Just don't sneak up on me again." Catalina sighed and added, "Please."

"Si, Signora."

"Let's finish this. Both of us need some sleep."

By the time they reached the last step, Catalina and Constance were holding hands. Catalina glanced at her companion for encouragement, but the maid trembled more.

With a deep breath, Cat composed herself and begged God for courage. Her hand quivering, Catalina placed it on his chest but only felt the tremors in her hand. She growled quietly and moved a little closer to try again.

"Well?" Constance whispered.

Catalina glared at her maid. "Do I look like I am squatting here for fun? If I knew, I wouldn't be hovering over him!"

With a huff, Catalina lowered her hand to his chest. This time, she watched with her eyes as well. Though it seemed like an eternity, she finally felt the rise and fall of his chest.

"He is still alive."

"That is good...si?"

Catalina scowled at her maid. "Help me with his robe."

They struggled to get his arms into the robe. Both were huffing and groaning as they fumbled with his heavy, limp body. It was a daunting task, but they worked as a team. With sweat dripping from their brows, they stood above the mass of cotton and flesh and admired their teamwork.

"That should do it. Now, we shall get everything cleaned up, including ourselves!"

"Si, Signora."

The cleanup finished, Catalina soaked her aching body. It was tempting to remain in the warm water, but her mind needed a few hours of rest. There was much to be done, and exhaustion was not a luxury she could afford.

Constance helped Catalina into her nightdress and braided her wet hair. The maid's exhausted features tugged at Catalina's sympathy. Giorgio's sinfulness robbed the woman, who worked hard every day, of her precious time to rest. Catalina vowed to allow the woman time to recoup once the funerals were planned.

"Thank you," Catalina said, breaking the silence.

The maid had something she wished to say but fearfully kept it hidden behind a wain smile. Catalina looked away to give Constance the time needed to find her courage.

"Signora, what will you tell him when he wakes?"

Without hesitation, Catalina said, "A lie!"

CHAPTER 36

"Excuse me, is Maria here?" Catalina asked the dirty-grey-haired woman at the reception desk.

The old woman pretended not to hear the question. The scowl on her face reflected her level of distaste for her job. She no longer cared about anyone or anything.

"Excuse me, is Maria here?" Catalina asked, speaking louder.

"I heard you the first time! I will be with you in a moment!" The old woman snapped.

The old woman's rudeness perked Catalina's eyebrow, but she held her tongue. A snarky remark would not get the grumpy bag of bones to cooperate.

Catalina took two steps back, giving the old woman space, and looked around the empty waiting room. The drab space was decorated with two paintings and a small lamp on a rickety table in the corner.

"Blah!" Catalina thought. *"No wonder this woman hates her job. I would hate staring at this every day, too. After the funeral, I will transform this into a suitable space."*

Down the long white hallway, eight gurneys with perfectly tucked, white sheets sat ready for an onslaught of wounded people. Twenty-four hours ago, her parents would have been placed on them. The color drained from Catalina's cheeks as her mind flashed the chilling image of her parents' battered bodies. Frantically, doctors and nurses fought off the Grim Reaper's bony fingers, eagerly tickling the white linen stained by her parent's blood.

The air saturated with fumes from iodine and cleaning solution burned Catalina's nasal passages. She held her stomach, fighting back her nausea.

"Are you ok, Signora? You do not look well?" Asked the tall, thin nurse, who was carrying a metal tray.

The four small glasses of water and dark brown bottles clanked together as the nurse placed the silver tray on the countertop.

"Go fetch Dr. Vetula quickly!" the nurse instructed the old woman. "Now!"

The old woman grumbled a few inaudible words in protest. With a huff, she stormed down the hallway, slamming her feet against the tile floor in retaliation for being disturbed.

"Come, sit over here," the nurse said.

Her white cap pinned to her silky hair like a coronet, leveled chin, striking red lipstick, and immaculate white dress looked picture-perfect. The woman looked like a model in a nurse's uniform rather than an attendant for the sick.

Lovingly, the nurse wrapped her arm around Catalina and guided her to a chair. In a daze, Catalina flashed a weak smile in gratitude for the kindness.

"Sit right here while I get you a drink of water. It will help you feel better."

Her new patient settled in the chair, the nurse went to the counter. She glanced around to see if anyone was nearby. The fall of footsteps rapidly approaching made the nurse move quickly. She grabbed a glass and added two spoonfuls of medicine from the jar, stirring until the powder disappeared. The nurse inspected the concoction and grinned. It looked like clean, clear water.

"Here, my dear, drink this. It will help calm your nerves."

"Thank you," Catalina mumbled.

Catalina brought the glass to her mouth but stopped. "Is

Maria here? It is imperative I see her."

"You are in shock, my dear, and are asking too many questions. First, we will take care of you. Then we can find your friend, Maria. Ok?" The nurse placed her hand under the glass and encouraged Catalina to take a drink. "You will feel much better after you drink some water."

Catalina grimaced and brought the glass to her mouth. But the ominous boom-boom of heavy footsteps echoing down the hall made her pause.

"Drink!" The nurse said again, a little too forcefully. Her gentleness melted away as her fiery anger emerged.

"What is your name?" Catalina asked.

The nurse's anxious movements and accelerated breathing snapped Catalina back to reality. Cat looked down at the glass of water, then looked up at the woman who had seemed so pleasant only moments before.

"Over there, doctor. She asked for Maria, then just about fainted."

The old woman, obviously not hired for her caring and compassionate attributes, oozed hatefulness.

"Thank you, Brunilda. You may return to your duties. I can take over from here." The doctor's dismissive tone tamped down the old woman's temper.

Brunilda went back to her drab desk and plopped into her chair. Intermittent huffs and mumbled words of agitation spilled from her lips as she shuffled her papers. The errand had destroyed the progress of her task, and now she needed to start over.

"Quietly, Brunilda, patients are resting," Dr. Vetula scolded the old woman.

To capture the last word, the aid gave a final huff before she quieted down. Dr. Vetula, ignoring the old woman's childish behavior, bent his knees to be eye to eye with his lovely new patient.

"I am Dr. Vetula, Signora. Is there something ailing you?"

Catalina examined the compassionate, middle-aged man. His neatly pressed, white jacket brought out the grey strands peppered through his perfectly combed, dark hair. Thin age lines along his puffy dark eyes spoke of the long hours caring for the sick.

"I am ok, Doctor," Catalina replied. "I need to speak with Maria. Please."

"You look very pale," he replied, noticing the water in her hand. "Let's get you to my exam room, and we will give you a look over to make sure."

"I am fine, really!" Catalina emphatically assured the doctor.

"What is your name?" Dr. Vetula asked.

"Catalina Giovannese! My husband is Giorgio Giovannese, a name you must recognize!" A pain of guilt rose from her stomach. Though she despised his actions, it was necessary to use the protection his name provided. "I *must* see Maria!"

"I believe she has gone home for the day," Dr. Vetula stated. "Vanna, help me take her down to my exam room."

They worked together to raise Catalina to her feet.

"I can walk! Really, I am *fine*!" Catalina snapped as she pulled away.

"Signora Giovannese, I am very familiar with your husband! He is not the type of man you wish to upset, and I believe not taking good care of his lovely wife would be... well... unwise. It is my observation that you appear very pallid. It would go against my oath to not do my due diligence with you," Dr. Vetula explained. "Please, drink this glass of water. If your color returns in a few minutes, I will leave you be. Ok?"

"My husband would be angered to know you tried to treat me *unnecessarily*! Especially since I am a *visitor*, not a *patient*!" Catalina's temper escalated. "Now, direct me to my parent's room!"

The smell, the people, and the purpose of her visit made Catalina want to run. She hated hospitals. Even when her grandmother was dying, she squirmed all the way to the room. Her mother smacked her butt and told her to hold still and be a young lady.

"Who are your parents, Catalina?" Dr. Vetula asked.

"Rosario and Sofia Beretta. They were brought in yesterday with severe wounds. Maria was their nurse last night. She was to meet me here this afternoon!"

"Ahh, si! The couple who were attacked. Dr. Andriano was their surgeon. Excellent Doctor! He informed me this morning they were stable, and their surgery went well," Dr. Vetula slipped his hands into the front pockets of his lab coat. "Unfortunately, your father is in the critical care unit. For his well-being, he can receive no visitors. Your mother is in a delicate state as well. Psychiatric patients may not have visitors for the first seventy-two hours."

"Where is Dr. Andriano? I shall speak with him," Catalina insisted.

The more Dr. Vetula talked, the stronger her gut warned her to be cautious. His white jacket and eloquent speech made him appear like a skilled doctor but did not make him one.

"He is gone for the day as well," Dr. Vetula replied, puffing his chest. "Would it make you feel better if I escorted you to their wards? Perhaps you can see them through the window. But I warn you, I will not let you in to see them, no matter how charming you are! Understood?"

Catalina's eyes flashed with hope, and her temper softened with the proposal. She wanted to see them, to make sure they were still alive.

The trio walked down the long hallway, passing the gurneys. Catalina kept her gaze forward and tried to ignore the eerie silence. To her, the silence meant all the patients died. And the creepy gurneys were waiting to usher a fresh batch of souls into the bowels of purgatory.

"Focus on something else!" Catalina chided herself.

She raised her chin a bit more and scanned the walls for something besides a blank canvas of white. Above each set of large doors was a crucifix. To the left was a small plaque with the ward's name. She read each sign, hoping it was the unit her parents were in. Her heart sank with disappointment as they walked by each set of doors.

The sterile white seemed to go on forever with no end in sight. They had made several turns, either to the left or the right, and Catalina wondered if she could find her way out of the maze.

They turned again, and just as they cleared the corner, the doctor grabbed Cat's arm and yanked her into a room. Before Catalina could scream, a cloth was placed over her mouth. Vanna ensured the doors closed behind them before helping Dr. Vetula put Catalina on a bed.

"Quick, tie her legs too," Dr. Vetula ordered Vanna.

"I told you she would come to see them!" Vanna replied triumphantly. "What will we do with her?"

"For now, we keep her sedated."

Catalina's eyes were heavy, and she struggled to stay coherent, but the chloroform had weakened her senses.

Dr. Vetula carried a syringe filled with a clear liquid toward Catalina. Her mind raced as she struggled against the restraints, but it was useless; they were too tight. She flinched from the prick of the needle. Within seconds, she could feel every muscle in her body relax as the medicine flowed into her system. Catalina struggled to keep awake, but her eyelids were too heavy. Even though her assailants stood beside her, their words seemed far off in the distance and almost inaudible. Before the medicine took complete control, she understood a few words and hoped to remember them...*if* she ever woke up.

"Do you think he will let us kill her?" Vanna marveled at the prospect.

"I'm not sure. But I must inform him the parents are here and *alive*!"

Dr. Vetula slipped his arm around Vanna's thin waist and kissed her neck.

"Do you have to kill the parents too?"

"Most likely!" He replied, unbuttoning her dress.

"Will he pay us well for disposing of them?"

Dr. Vetula, less interested in the Beretta's mortality, raised Vanna's skirt and caressed her thighs.

"Maybe," he replied between kisses.

"*Maybe?*" Vanna pushed him away.

"I get what *I* want, and you will get what *you* want!" Dr. Vetula replied sadistically.

Vanna flashed him an evil smile, her eyes dancing to a lustful tune. "The idea of killing them turns me on, my love!"

Dr. Vetula unbuttoned her blouse and plunged into her deep cleavage.

"What will it be like to kill them," Vanna demanded. "And tell me how rich we will be."

"As rich as you want," Dr. Vetula replied, enjoying her ample breasts.

Vanna ran her fingers through his hair and arched her back in ecstasy. "Just remember the deal." she moaned. "Remember what you promised me!"

CHAPTER 37

"Brunilda, has a young woman been here asking for me?" Maria asked in a panic.

Brunilda looked up, ready to give her usual rude response, but stopped when she saw Maria's worried face.

Brunilda had been an aide at the hospital for over two decades. Given her lowly state in the employee pecking order, she was subject to various insults and condescending attitudes. In the beginning, the rudeness didn't bother her. After two years, Brunilda lashed back at everyone. Everyone except the pleasant and kind Maria, who never spoke down to Brunilda. Maria always helped get the job done, regardless of whom the duty was assigned. Since Maria was nice to her, Brunilda was kind in return.

"You just missed her."

"Shoot!"

"She is still in the hospital."

"Where did she go?" Maria looked around the empty waiting area. Hopeful, she asked, "The wash closet?"

"Dr. Vetula and his slut girlfriend, Vanna, took her to see her parents," Brunilda replied, rolling her eyes. "Vanna should be back soon to administer medications. Although, I'm sure she will just give the task to me...*again*!"

Maria looked at the open jar and the spoon next to it. She turned the bottle to read its label.

"Phenobarbital!" Maria's heart pounded in fear. "I know you are busy, Brunilda, but I need your help! Please! Please find Dr. Andriano! I must speak with him at once!" Maria's pleading eyes told the urgency of her request.

"Dr. Vetula told your friend he went home already."

"Then ring his home for me, and quickly. This is a matter of life and death!"

"Are you ok?"

"No!" Maria gave an apologetic glance for her abruptness.

Brunilda patted Maria's hand, acknowledging the unintentional rudeness.

"My friend is in great danger. I think someone is going to try to kill them!" Maria whispered to the aide. "You must find Dr. Andriano!"

"Do not worry, I will."

From an adjacent hallway, a warble of words floated in the air. Maria watched intently to see who was coming. She prayed her anxiety was unfounded. Brunilda reached for the phone and dialed the operator. The hurried words floated past Maria, whose sole focus was on the approaching voices.

In the sea of white, two black gowns rounded the corner, their strides in synch. The length of the frocks and the soft shoes made them appear to be gliding across the floor.

"Good morning, Mother Concetta. Sister Carmela," Maria greeted the two nuns with a slight bow of respect.

"Good *afternoon*, Maria," Mother Concetta corrected sharply.

"My apologies. I meant good afternoon," Maria responded with a nervous laugh.

"Maria, you do not look well," Sister Carmela commented.

"Thank you for your concern, Sister. I am merely worried."

The sister was correct; in a way, she was not well. Her friend was in danger, if not already dead. Maria needed help now, and the blockage of two pious nuns only added another obstacle in her path.

"Do you remember the husband and wife who were brought

in yesterday?" Maria asked.

Both women nodded, their black and white habits moving in unison. Their synchronized movements were a reminder the reverent women served together for many years. If she were to enlist their help, Maria needed to convince *both* women.

"I appreciate your prayers, for they came through their surgeries and are recovering."

"The power of God's miracles, is it not, Sister Carmela?" Mother Concetta boasted.

In eerily precise synchronicity, both nuns made the sign of the cross with the wooden crucifix adorned around their necks.

"Indeed." Maria agreed, making the sign of the cross. "I do have some unfortunate news, which I fear must be handled only by the most qualified and skilled hands."

The nuns exchanged quizzical glances.

"You may already know the tragedy that brought them to our care," Maria continued reverently.

The nuns nodded in sync.

"We are well aware of the horrific events. It is a scandal already and has caused much gossip," Mother Concetta said with a harrumph.

"Indeed. A most appalling situation," Sister Carmela added.

"Precisely my thoughts as well. Unfortunately, I fear more sins will be committed. The killer believed this lovely couple died in the massacre. Now that he is aware of their state and location, he..."

Maria bowed her head and exaggerated her despair. Her hand stretched out, begging for comfort.

"Oh, Mother Concetta! Please pray God will place his hand of protection over this loving and devoted family. They have seen too much pain already! If only God could reach down, pluck this beautiful couple from this place, and put them somewhere... somewhere no one could reach them. A safe place where they could heal, inside and out! Heal with the love of God surrounding them!"

Maria forced a tear from her eye for effect, then gently brushed it away.

"Now, now, my child. God is good and loving," Mother Concetta consoled.

"Did you know these two saved my parents? Signor Beretta gave my father a job, even when another laborer was not needed! He made sure my family was fed in a time of great strife," Maria said with a sniffle.

Maria dug in her purse for a handkerchief, though she did not need one. Rummaging in her bag was a stall tactic to allow Rosario's saintly image time to permeate the nuns' minds.

"Beretta, hmm?" Mother Concetta looked at her sister. "Is this the winemaker who brings us wine for our convent?"

"*Si!* He is a charitable man and a faithful servant of God. You may have seen him and his wife, Sofia, at St. Agatha's every Sunday?"

"We see many of God's flock on Sunday." Sister Carmela dismissively waved away Maria's comment.

The nuns exchanged knowing stares for a long moment as if reading the other's minds. Maria watched the silent movie and prayed the seed she planted would take root.

"Maria, I have Dr. Andriano on the line," Brunilda said.

"Thank you! I owe you!" Maria whispered with a grateful smile. She took the phone and covered the receiver. "Excuse me, Mother Concetta, do you mind if I speak with the Doctor? I want to ask about the care of Signor Rosario and Signora Sofia?"

"Of course, my child." Mother Concetta gave an authoritative wave of approval.

The nuns took two steps back and turned for a private discussion. Maria was amused by the redundant precaution of turning away. Even standing close, no one could decipher their muffled whispers. She doubted *they* could hear each other. Frequently, the pair of nuns appeared to read each other's minds. Communicating with words was a crutch for the unanointed. Occasionally, the nuns *chose* to use them.

"Dr. Andriano, this is Maria Sarducci. I am the nurse caring for the Berettas."

In a professional, succinct fashion, Maria informed the doctor of her concerns, omitting her suspicions of Dr. Vetula. She did not want to insinuate he was the assassin until she had more proof.

Maria's telephone call continued longer than Mother Concetta really desired to wait. Especially since she and her fellow sister had finished their conversation. The impatient nuns rocked back and forth from heel to toe. Two black-cloaked rocking chairs, intent on crushing a long tail. The motion agitated Maria. She felt the need to shorten her answers and rush through the conversation with the doctor. After a couple quick exchanges, she hung up the phone and turned to the two women swaying in metric unison.

Instantly, they stopped and walked back closer to Maria.

"We have a suggestion *if*, of course, the doctor feels it is appropriate." Mother Concetta's commanding tone echoed around them. "We feel God has spoken to *our* hearts, as he does so frequently."

"That he does, My Sister-In-Christ," Sister Carmela added.

The nuns rocked heel to toe several times while they exchanged an all-knowing nod. After basking in their blessed exclusivity, Mother Concetta finished sharing her epiphany.

"As you know, the convent has several sisters trained as nurses. It is their calling to help the sick. As such, they volunteer at local hospitals to heal God's flock. Like these unselfish sisters who share their God-given gifts, we, too, are called to care for those in most need. We believe the Berettas are worthy of God's love and protection. If the doctor feels the patients are in a capable condition, we would like to offer them care at the convent."

Mother Concetta finished her offer with a glance at Sister Carmela. With rigid spines, both nuns held their chins up high and puffed their chests. Two hens proudly strutting around the barnyard, showing off their supreme enlightenment.

Maria smiled gratefully and pretended to be surprised by the divinely given idea, which could only be bestowed upon the holy women before her. It was a typical display of superiority by the nuns at her school. The soldiers for God's Army were less intimidating to Maria now that she was a grown woman.

"That would be most generous of you!" Maria replied. "I am sure their daughter, Catalina Giovannese, will be most pleased with this news."

She paused long enough for the nuns to exchange the wordless acknowledgment of Catalina's wealth.

"In fact, she is here now, visiting her parents. If you follow me, I wager she would like to thank you personally."

"Well, we do have a *few* minutes before evening Mass, Mother Concetta. A brief visit would be acceptable, don't you think?"

"It is indeed a sign of God's affirmation of our duty to this pious family. Lead the way, my child." Mother Concetta commanded with a wave of her hand.

Maria guided the women through the maze of hallways, pausing at each turn for the sisters to catch up. A new wing was added every few years to accommodate the growing population. Maria had walked these halls many times without thinking about the floor plan. Today, however, a brew of frustration for the architect's creativeness simmered in her gut.

Why did the architect need to extend the next wing in a different direction than the previous one? Maria thought.

"You walk too fast for my old bone's child. Do slow down," Mother Concetta demanded.

"Very sorry, Mother Concetta. I do not want to make you late for evening Mass."

Though Mass was the least of her concerns, Maria hoped it would encourage them to walk with a bit more speed.

"We have plenty of time," Sister Carmela huffed between gasps for air.

Frustrated, Maria slowed her pace. At the next turn, she looked back at the nuns. Much to her dismay, she was still several leg lengths in front of them. Maria released a low, nearly inaudible growl and tapped her foot. As the sisters approached, she realized she was parroting the standard actions of an impatient nun. Mortified, she immediately stopped.

Dear God! How often do I tap my foot like them?

A flirtatious giggle from a room halfway down the hall pulled Maria from her concerns. It was definitely Vanna's giggle, which meant Dr. Vetula was the person causing the lustful chord.

Around the hospital, Dr. Vetula seduced all the pretty women. He had a history of engaging in sordid affairs with the nurses, usually more than one at a time. Mother Concetta severely frowned upon his activities yet could never catch him in the act. Since the nun had not personally seen the adultery, the Bishop disregarded the allegations as shameful gossip. Thus, no punishment was ever delivered. Having been a victim of Dr. Vetula's advances, Maria hoped she might kill two birds with one stone. If Mother Concetta found the doctor and Vanna in the lascivious act, Maria could look for Catalina *and* prevent any future groping from the doctor!

"We are almost there, just down this hallway," Maria coaxed, offering to be a crutch for Mother Concetta.

"Thank you, my child, but I can manage. I may be old, but I

am not dead!"

The nun put more effort into each step to prove her youthful abilities.

If that was all it took to make her move faster, I would have offered earlier! Maria thought.

A few steps into the next hallway, Mother Concetta perked up. Surprisingly uncompromised by age, her ears heard part of her flock in the midst of sin. The nun's pace quickened, eager to catch the sinners. Maria smiled for a brief second. Maybe the sister did have some youth left in her.

"Where is that noise coming from?" Sister Carmella's eyes darted. The desire to catch the devils empowered her senses.

"It sounds like it is coming from that door over there," Maria said with a fake gasp.

Stealthier than ninjas, the nuns scurried to the door. Their eyes widened with excitement as they listened for a moment. In silence, they rejoiced. They finally caught the mouse stealing the cheese!

"How dare you defile this hospital with such wanton behavior?" Mother Concetta said, springing the door open.

The loud bang made the naughty couple jump to their feet and cover their exposed skin as quickly as possible.

Maria stayed out of sight; there was no need for her to assist in the raid. Besides, she had no desire to see either of the two criminals undressed.

Mother Concetta and Sister Carmela took turns preaching the evils of unwed souls fornicating. Aside from imposing extreme guilt on the sinners, Mother Concetta commanded them to confess to the Bishop himself, do penance, attend Mass daily, and so on. The list of punishments for their sins was growing longer than Santa's.

Maria relished the moment. There was nothing like the acid tongue of a nun, provided it was not flicking the scarring venom at one's self. The nun's tyrannical lecture was entertaining. Maria would gladly watch the show for hours but needed to find Catalina.

She peeked into the room, but the round nuns' full black skirts blocked the entire entrance. On her tippy-toes, Maria looked over the nun's shoulders.

This was the newest wing in the hospital. During the war, it was used to house wounded soldiers from nearby battlefields. The hospital was a busy beehive of nurses, doctors, aides, and patients milling about. Every day, a group dressed in white would rush a patient on the edge of life to the operating room and pray for the best. It was a place filled with blood-stained bandages, screams of agony, and the foul smell of rotting flesh.

The war over, this wing was no longer used, nurses moved at a slower pace, doctors were less stressed, and the ailments treated were significantly different. Instead of men wounded in mind or body, patients were mothers in labor, children sick with a fever, or a man in a bar fight needing stitches after a bottle gashed his head.

Maria's eyes bounced down the left side for a body piled in a heap, but every bed was made to perfection. Her gaze followed up the right until it landed on a lifeless body.

"Dear God!" Maria exclaimed, oblivious to the use of the Lord's name in vain.

The nuns ceased fire on the wide-eyed sinners, huddled against a bed with their hands firmly clasped on their unbuttoned clothes.

"What have you done to Catalina?" Maria screamed, pushing past the nuns.

Quickly forgetting Maria's transgression, the ladies of God made the sign of the cross in unison and pressed forward to inspect the motionless form bound like a savage dog.

"What did you give the poor child?" Mother Concetta demanded, but she turned a moment too late. The lovers wisely used the distraction to flee their captures.

Genuinely concerned, Sister Carmela asked, "Is she alive?"

"Si, she is still breathing," Maria replied.

Her eyes panned the room, looking for signs of what medication the doctor used. A few feet from the door was a rag that Maria had overlooked as she raced into the room.

She took a whiff and gagged. "Blah! Chloroform!"

"Then why did they need this?" Mother Concetta asked, picking up a syringe under a bed.

"Good question! They used it on Cat. See the sheet and the injection site." Maria pointed to the blood trickling down Catalina's arm. "Look for a small glass bottle."

"Is that it?" Sister Carmella asked, pointing at the bed.

"Good eye! Now, what did they use," Maria mumbled. "Ohh, thank God! They only sedated her. Dr. Vetula is guilty of carnal sin and incompetence, given how much anesthetic remains!"

"Meaning?" Sister Carmella asked.

"He could have administered the whole bottle!" The sisters remained confused, so Maria added, "Your prayers worked! She should wake in a few hours."

The nuns made the sign of the cross and bowed their heads for a quick prayer of gratitude. Maria happily joined them.

"It appears your suspicions are correct, my child." Mother Concetta said, blessing Catalina's forehead. "We must move them *all* to God's safety *tonight*!"

CHAPTER 38

The cool fall air, laced with the scent of the early morning rain and sweet gardenias, filtered into the room. A gentle rustle of leaves and the chirp-chirp of gleeful birds added to nature's good-morning call.

"How do you feel?" A soft voice asked.

From the shadowed corner came the rhythmic creak of a rocking chair and the click-click of a pair of knitting needles.

"My head is pounding," she groaned, blinded by the golden rays streaming in through the arched window. "Everything is so bright!"

She held up her hand to block the blinding light. Blinking fervently, she looked around the room.

Four golden cherubs sat atop the dark posts at each corner of her bed. The heavenly, winged babes stretched their arms to hold the gauze canopy swooshing over the bed. Tucked in the corner, opposite the woman knitting, was a tall armoire made of the same wood as the bed. Her eyes more accustomed to the light, she glanced to her left. Between a pair of arched windows was a short dresser with a white pitcher and bowl on. On the wall above hung a gold crucifix.

"What happened?"

"A lot, but all is safe now. You must rest," the short, round woman stated, placing her needles on the small table beside her. "I will bring you something to eat and drink. We can talk after."

The natural light glinted off the woman's crisp, white attire as she walked to the door.

"Wait! Who are you?"

Her words were too late. The angelic voice had already left the room.

The birds on the windowsill chirped in protest at the bang from the heavy wooden door shutting. Miffed by the rude interruption of their morning serenade, the feathered musicians departed as quickly as the woman in white. In their hasty departure to find a peaceful venue, they left behind a single blue feather that floated into the room. Slowly, the feather glided through the darkness, landing in an illuminated patch on the wooden floor.

A cloud passed in front of the sun, dimming the blinding light. Out the window, her view of the rolling hillside was dappled with the beauty of the fall colors. The yellow, red, and orange hues tempted her to come for a closer look. Cautiously, she pulled her legs out from under the heavy blanket. She tried to stand, but her weak legs gave way. Her hand caught the edge of the night table. Exhausted, she collapsed back onto the plush mattress.

Staring at the happy cherubs hovering above her, she drew a deep breath and slowly released it.

"You survived, Angelina. But *how?*"

CHAPTER 39

"Good morning, my love," Catalina said sweetly, though her heart was filled with the black blood of hatred.

She placed a serving tray on the small table between the fireplace and his smoking chair. She spread the curtains wide open with a flourish, allowing the bright morning sun to illuminate the room.

Giorgio groaned in protest at the piercing light.

"Does it still hurt?" Catalina tried to hide her malicious smile, but his pain gave her too much satisfaction.

"Like an ax."

He tried to shift his weight, but a searing pain pierced his side, and he wailed in agony.

"No, no! You must not move. The doctor said you have three broken ribs and a concussion!" Catalina grinned with delight. "Here is some water. I am sure you are thirsty."

"Not water, pour me wine! It will kill the pain!"

"If you wish to perpetuate your misery, I will not stop you!" Catalina said curtly as she poured him a glass of wine. "Lord knows, you deserve it tenfold!"

"What the hell happened?"

"You do not remember?" Catalina searched Giorgio's face for any clues of what he recalled. His swollen eye and puffy, busted lip obscured his usual tell-tell signs. "Do you remember *anything*?" Catalina asked incredulously. *Have a care with your words, Signore! I will happily leave you to rot in this room!*

Giorgio opened his mouth to speak, but one look at his wife's scowl curtailed his response to a shake of his head. The movement was enough to flare another stab of pain.

"Why am I not surprised?"

"With this headache, who could remember anything?"

Catalina gave a harrumph and walked over to the window. The view was not as majestic as hers, but this view from the fourth floor made one feel superior.

In the distance, stretched high above all the other buildings in the town of Brusnengo, was St. Agatha's Steeple. On a beautiful sunny day, the happiest day of Catalina's life, they exchanged vows. Giorgio loved her and fulfilled her every desire. But his romantic ways and lavish gifts were not the only precious things that won her heart.

Leading up to the wedding, Giorgio told her about his childhood struggles and what Mario had done for him. He sincerely professed his desire to be a good father and to have a happy family. He wanted to have all these things with her, his *"beautiful bride."*

After last night, the contradiction between his pledge and his actions tore at her heart. She wanted her happiness back and the memories of the night before erased. And she wanted to stab his eyeballs out!

The bell tolled the hour, pulling her back to the present moment. The low bong had once been a reminder of joy, but today, the tone was mournful. To add to the depressiveness, a cloud blocked the sun, casting a shadow over the church. She sighed. The church *was* a shining reminder of jubilation. In a few days, a shadow would diminish its radiance forever. She would say goodbye to her brothers at the altar that blessed her elation. From now on, what was the sunshine of happiness would be veiled by an unremovable stain of grief.

"Argh!" Giorgio wailed in pain when he tried to free his legs from the blankets.

With a sigh, Catalina wiped away her tears and returned to her unworthy patient. "Tisk-tisk!" She jammed the blankets around his legs. "You broke your ankle as well! You will not do any more sleepwalking!"

"Sleep... walking?" He grunted between bouts of pain.

Catalina deliberately jabbed him with her hand as she tucked the blanket. Giorgio's penance for his sins was far from over, and her hands maniacally stabbing his legs only marked the beginning of his suffering.

"Si! You had too much to drink and must have gone sleepwalking. After Angelina and I went to bed, Constance said you and your friends drank for several hours. She said it was about three a.m. when she heard them finally leave."

"Yes... *Ouch!* That is... *ouch*... about right!"

"Did you go to your room after they left?"

"I am not sure?"

His eyes darted back and forth, searching for an answer, but remained stranded in a sea of unknowing. The harder he thought, the stronger the vein across his temple throbbed.

"You must have because you had your robe on and *nothing else*!" Catalina glared at him. "You do not remember because you were drunk!"

"I don't remember that—"

"I am not sure what made you leave your room, *especially* dressed as you were! Or, really, not dressed is more precise!" Catalina's hands flew wildly as she ranted. "We found you lying, exposed to the world, at the foot of the staircase. For Christ's sake, I had to throw a blanket over you! The doctor said such a fall could have ended your life! After all the loss my family has experienced, and you are so careless!" Her voice teetered on grief and rage. "You promised to protect us! How can you keep us safe if you are gone?"

She smacked his arm with her left hand, hoping the enormous diamond would inflict more pain than her weak hand could achieve.

"*Ouch!* Easy!"

"Is that all you have to say? My family is *dead!*"

The word caused an eruption of tears. Sobbing, Catalina sank back on the edge of the bed with her face in her hands.

"It will be ok. I will be better soon. I *will* protect you." Giorgio promised. He lifted his arm to comfort her, but the pain was too intense, and he yelped again.

Catalina was glad he couldn't reach her. She didn't want his comfort. Not now! Maybe not ever!

She choked back her sobs and returned to the window. Leaning her head against the cold glass, she fought to regain control of her emotions. Catalina made a pact with herself that she would tuck her feelings deep inside and not allow them to show. However, speaking of her family's demise crushed her composure.

Giorgio was not the only one who suffered growing up. Her abandonment was not physical like Giorgio's. It was emotional. No one loved her like they loved Angelina. Though her father tried to hide his favoritism, she felt the coldness of being in last place behind all her siblings, especially in Rosario's eyes. Catalina felt her mother's love, but Marcus was Sofia's favorite, then Angelina. Her unimportance created Catalina's wounded inner child, a lack of self-confidence, and the inability to nurture herself.

A ring from Giorgio pulled Catalina out of the shadows. With a prominent husband, she became a star in the region and with her family. If she needed love and attention, she could go shopping, even hours away from her hometown, and be treated like royalty. As Giorgio's wife, Catalina had a place in the world. A place that was leagues above Angelina.

Tormented by her thoughts, Catalina went into his private

bathroom to recompose. She splashed her face, cleared her nose, and took a drink of water. With an exhausted sigh, she returned to face her monster.

"You are in no condition to help me now, are you? Thanks to you, I have funerals to plan, people to notify, and a business to run without any help!"

Before she realized her slip, Catalina had firmly smacked his arm. This time, she felt a burning sting on the back of her hand from her violent hit.

"My love, please!" he begged.

"The worst is, you cannot attend the funeral! What will everyone think?"

"Who said I will not be there?"

"Dr. Mariano said you must stay in bed or lose your leg!" He attempted to move again, but the pain was too intense. "Hold still! Do you want to be a cripple? Do you want to add more to my overflowing plate!"

"Please, don't shout, my love. My head is pounding!"

"Ha! Be glad it is from your hangover and not my hand!"

"Cat!"

"I have errands to attend to. These funerals will not plan themselves! Thank God for Constance! Oh! And no visitors. It will not do for the city to know of your state. It would bring complete embarrassment to our house! I am sure your uncle would not appreciate the town gossiping about his drunken nephew who nearly fell to his death! It would be a disgrace! For that matter, I am already mortified by your actions!"

"I am sorry, my love! I promise to be better."

"That is doubtful!" Catalina interrupted. "You probably want more wine now!"

"Only to help kill the pain."

"Fine! One more glass and no more until dinner. *You* are going to sober up!"

CHAPTER 40

"Where am I?"

"You are at St. Theresa's convent," Catalina replied.

"Where?" Angelina gave her sister a quizzical look.

"It is an old castle that has been turned into a convent. Sister Carmella was kind enough to make the arrangements. You are safe here."

"Who is Sister Carmella?"

"Someone your friend, Maria, works with at St. Jude Hospital. Maria and the nun arranged everything."

"Where are Mamma and Papa? Are they ok?"

"They are here as well!" Catalina sighed. "There is much we need to discuss, Angelina. I know you have many questions, but I am too exhausted to placate you." Catalina tried to shift her attitude, but her emotions raged like a stormy sea. "Let me tell you what has transpired while you were unconscious."

Catalina sat at the edge of the bed. She held Angelina's hand and gently stroked it.

"First, I must apologize for not believing everything you said the other night. It was wrong of me not to trust you. You are family and had no reason to lie to me. I must admit, from time to time, I believed you were jealous of my marriage, my luxurious life, and my position in society. Since Papa announced my engagement, you have appeared envious of all the love Giorgio showed me." A tear escaped and trickled down her cheek. "To be honest, the first time Giorgio came around, I thought he was seeking your hand. But after Papa gave him his blessing, Giorgio showed me how much he loved me. Not just with gifts. He shared with me... well, some very personal things that he had told no one!"

Angelina listened patiently, mindful of her breathing and the tension within her folded hands. This was not the time to lash out. Catalina deserved a chance to explain her hesitation.

"I remember dreaming how wonderful it would be to have such a handsome, wealthy man as my husband. I would go for walks through the vineyard daydreaming about the extravagance a man like Giorgio could provide." Catalina sniffled. "One time, I cut a grape, with the small vine still attached, wrapped it around my finger, and pretended it was a giant diamond engagement ring."

Catalina looked at her wedding ring. With a little twist, a shower of light danced around the room. She chuckled.

"I guess I got what I wished for." Her smile twinkled for a moment, then quickly faded away. "Anyway, I was shocked when Papa told me Giorgio wanted *my* hand. To say the least, I could barely contain myself! My deepest fear was your disappointment. I could never tell how you truly felt. One minute, you would be supportive; the next, you pointed out his flaws. As the wedding approached, your agitation with the whole situation seemed to escalate. You always seemed to be searching for a reason why I should not marry Giorgio. Mamma assured me you did not have eyes for him and that you were only a protective sister. I guess I never really believed it."

Catalina wiped away her tears and looked directly into Angelina's eyes.

"The night you came to my house and told me he was the murderer, all those old feelings...I worried..." Catalina steadied her voice and choked back her tears. "I worried you were trying to break up my marriage! I felt as if you stabbed my gut with a blade and twisted it over and over!"

The analogy sent a flood of anger to Angelina's heart. *No! It was your husband who drove a blade into our Papa's gut!* Angelina's mind screamed.

"Oh, Lina! It was overwhelming to lose our brothers and then you. I felt... all alone."

It was a moving and sincere revelation. However, it was not the entirety of Cat's confession. Angelina had seen her sister's current state many times. She had something else to admit.

"That was not all I was afraid of..." Catalina released a heavy sigh. "I was afraid to lose the comforts I am so accustomed to. It is shameful to say the material things around me seemed too precious to sacrifice. I am so sorry, Lina! I know now that you were only trying to protect me."

"It's okay, Cat." Angelina squeezed her sister's hand. "We are safe! Mamma and Papa are safe."

"Not exactly."

"What do you mean? We are all here, far away from him. Besides, who would dare attack us in such a holy place?"

"You, Mamma, and Papa are safe here. I cannot stay."

Angelina opened her mouth to protest.

"Wait, let me explain... Oh, there is so much to explain!"

Catalina dried her eyes with a handkerchief that matched her mocha dress. Her composure returned; she tucked it away and scanned the room.

"What are you looking for?"

"Something to drink. My tongue is drier than an old cork!" Catalina noticed a pitcher on the small dresser. She frowned. "It's empty. I will be right back."

Before Angelina could protest, Cat slipped out the door. Though the prospect of something to drink was appealing, Angelina grew impatient. What she had shared, except the apology, was nothing new.

"I found a Sister close by. She will bring us some water. And I asked for some fruit and cheese." To calm her tensions, she smoothed the sheets. "You look like you could use something to eat."

"You are acting nervous. *Why*?"

"I am not!"

Angelina cocked her brow.

"I am exhausted, not nervous!" Catalina argued and plopped on the bed. "I have not had a bite to eat since breakfast. So perhaps I said you were hungry so we both could eat!"

"Nice try. You are stalling. I know my sister. Tell me what is bothering you."

Avoiding direct eye contact, Catalina rubbed her hands across the top of her thighs and nervously rocked her torso. It was unnerving. But it was Catalina's way of figuring out the best approach to a painful subject.

"Do you remember what happened..." She hesitated. "*After* we went to bed?"

"Until I passed out. Honestly, I thought I had died."

"Do you remember what *he* said to you?"

"Perfectly! How much did *you* hear?"

"Enough." Catalina stood and paced the floor.

"He will never lay a hand on us. I will kill him first!"

"We are in a house of God. You must not say such things!"

The door opened before Angelina could argue the notion of what to say and where. A young woman in a white dress entered with a carafe of wine and a plate of fruit, cheese, meats, and bread.

"It is good to see you awake, Signorina." The young lady rejoiced.

Though the petite lady smiled and spoke with a sense of happiness, her eyes appeared dull. Her skin was an unhealthy pale, and her shoulders slumped with a heavy sadness.

Angelina wondered if the woman's grief was sympathy for the Beretta family or a burden of her own? If it were the latter, what could have caused so much sorrow?

"It is good to be awake, Sister." Angelina moved to get out of bed.

"Oh, no! Do not move. The doctor said you must rest. For now, enjoy eating in bed. It is a luxury in this place."

Catalina bowed her head in shame. The women at the convent lived in stark contrast to her decadent lifestyle.

The fair-haired woman filled two plates and poured two glasses of wine. Though patterned like a nurse's uniform, her garb stretched to the floor like a nun's dress. The young lady's golden hair was combed flat against the top of her head. However, the ringlets refused to maintain such a harsh, straight line. Her blue eyes were the most telling, with a chasm of dull pain that robbed the gems of the sparkle of happiness. This woman's suffering would be invisible unless you peered deep into her eyes. In them, a story of heartache hid under a superficial veil of peace.

"Here you are," The young lady gave them a glass of wine. "I think you will enjoy this. I believe you had a hand in making it! Is there anything else I can do for you?"

"No, I think this is perfect. Thank you for the wonderful food. It looks delicious," Angelina said.

"The wine is a very welcomed surprise, Sister! I was not sure if it would be allowed," Catalina added sweetly.

"Oh! I am not a Sister, only a young woman blessed with the safety of God's goodness. As for the wine, I was told your father has been sending it to the convent for years. More than they can drink, in fact. So, Mother told us to make sure you and your family are treated as special guests!"

"You are too kind, but we are just the daughters of a winemaker," Catalina said, bowing her head.

"If you are not a sister, may I ask how you came to be here?" Angelina asked.

Something about this woman piqued Angelina's interest.

She did not look Italian, and her accent was unfamiliar as well. So, why would a woman who is not a nun be here of all places?

Before the lady could respond, the church bell rang.

"It is a long, tragic story. Perhaps I will come by after evening Mass." The lady pointed toward the bong, summoning all to the chapel. "We can become more acquainted. I am sure some company would help soothe your mind, especially after all you have endured."

"That would be nice," Angelina replied.

CHAPTER 41

"Your reprieve is over," Angelina said when the door closed. "What have you not told me?"

"You have been unconscious for several days, Lina. A simple sentence or two will not explain everything."

"Alright. Then what happened after I passed out?"

Over the next two hours, Catalina told her sister about the incident at the hospital, Maria's aide, and how they all came to be under the same holy roof together.

"I awoke a few hours after they had found me." Catalina sipped from her glass of wine. "Maria was like an angel standing above me. Luckily, I could return home before Giorgio noticed I was gone."

Angelina winced at his name.

"I am very sorry for not—"

"He will die for what he has done! To you! To our family! And to me!" Angelina vowed, beating her fist against her heart. "I will not allow that monster to walk the earth!"

Catalina held up her hand to stop her sister's tirade.

Angelina's eyes burned with rage. "No! He is a dead man. Mark my words either by my hand or by someone else's! I will see the last breath squelched from his lungs. He will die a slow, painful death, and his soul will rot in hell!"

"I do not want your hands to bear the stains of evil!" Shaking away her admonishment, Catalina padded her hands to calm her sister. "Listen, Angelina, please listen to me! He has wronged me too! But he is surrounded by men of power and greed. If we kill him, another will take his place. I know these men, Lina. I have dined with them, hosted them at home, and spoken with their wives. They will not slither away. To rid one only invites more to the carnage."

"Then they all will die!"

"If you will not speak sensibly, I *will* leave!" Catalina's disapproval darkened her eyes. "Papa taught us to respond, *not* react, remember? Violence is never a response! Besides, The Don is powerful. As are Mario and Giorgio by their association with him. Each will use whatever means to take the vineyard and ruin our lives if we press in the wrong direction."

Angelina's core thundered with anger. She did not care about her sister's warning. If they converged on them, she would gladly fight back.

"I will kill—"

"Lina! Enough!" Catalina held up her hand. "Not now. Not ever! I will not become a monster! And I won't let you either."

Angelina slowly exhaled a low growl.

"I am warning you, Angelina. If you stain your hands with blood, I will never speak to you again!"

"But you will sleep under a murderer's roof?"

Catalina's temper flared. "You want to know why I was stalling? Because of this! Because you *always* jump to the extreme! For a week, I have done everything! *Everything*!"

"Because of him!" Angelina's roar echoed off the walls.

"No! Stop!" Catalina shouted in frustration. "Stop it!" Her emotions were too great; she sunk into the chair and cried.

The exhaustion and sorrow overpowering her sister's composure stung Angelina's soul. She slipped out of bed and gently embraced Catalina's trembling form.

"Shhh. I am sorry, Cat. You are right." She nearly choked on the words, but it was what her sister needed to hear.

"We can't argue," Catalina said between sobs. "We can't..."

"It's ok."

Angelina gently stroked Catalina's hair while she repeated the two reassuring words. After a few minutes, Catalina calmed. Sitting back, she released a heavy sigh.

"Carlos will pick you up tomorrow for the funerals. Our brothers will be buried together near Papa's favorite spot overlooking the vineyard. Carlos has made the arrangements for the ground. Constance and Carmella have worked diligently to prepare a feast and clean the house."

Angelina's face went pale, and she sat back on her feet. In her blinding rage, she forgot about the disaster in the kitchen. She left with her parents for the hospital, leaving Carmella, Carlos, and Fernando to erase the horror. It would be impossible for them to remove the stench and stains on the wood. A flash of Fernando silently cleaning the floor while tears streamed down his face stabbed Angelina's heart. It was not just the sisters who suffocated under the weight of this tragedy.

Remaining composed, Catalina solemnly continued. "We will use the tents outside, as we do during our annual festival. We do not have to go into the house. Dr. Mariano warned it might be overwhelming and recommended we wait a few days before we go inside."

Angelina nodded. She had no desire to enter that hell.

"I know this is difficult. I have had several days to process my thoughts and grieve. You were robbed of that."

"Will *he* be at the funerals?"

"No. *He* fell down the stairs," Catalina glared at her sister's continued aggression. "Giorgio has several broken ribs, a broken ankle, and a concussion. He is to remain in bed for several weeks. He is to put no pressure on his leg for fear of losing it."

"Is he in a lot of pain?"

Ignoring Angelina's question, Catalina walked over to the bag she brought with her.

"You need to cover up all of your bruises. If The Don suspects you know anything, he will try to have you killed."

Angelina's rage was directed at Giorgio and not his uncle. It was Giorgio's hand that murdered her brothers, tortured her mother, and stabbed her father. Giorgio performed the heinous acts, not Don Salvatore. However, Catalina's warning connected the dots. Don Salvatore ordered the massacre. His hands were as stained as his nephew's. Though Giorgio was psychotic, Don Salvatore was far more ruthless. A fact that made Catalina's words more powerful.

"I have kept all the details very quiet. Maria and Carlos are the only ones who know where Mamma and Papa are staying. For now, that is more than I want. But they were needed to bring them to the convent. We told everyone else they are recovering quickly."

"You have done well."

She meant it too. All the effort Catalina put forth after having so much stripped from her was an inspiration.

"There is more to do. I can plan a funeral and a reception, but I need your help to plan your escape."

"We cannot leave Mamma and Papa!"

"No, *we* cannot! It is too risky for you to be near Giorgio. Eventually, he will remember details and share them with his uncle. If Don Salvatore even suspects you know anything, he will call for your life!" Catalina squeezed Angelina's hand. "I cannot lose you! Mamma and Papa may not survive their injuries. Both suffered deep wounds, emotionally and physically. It will take them time to recover. Until then, you and I are all that is left of our family."

"I will not abandon you!"

Catalina turned away, unwilling to argue. She was fixed on the notion, and understandably so. Giorgio was unpredictable, and landing on Don Salvatore's vendetta list was terrifying. However, the potential for Giorgio to continue his pursuit of

Angelina was far more distressing.

Angelina slumped against the bed and exhaled. "Where do you want me to go?"

"I do not know. I am exhausted, mentally and physically."

A chilling howl of the wind and the distant rumble of thunder pulled Angelina to the window. Miles away, lightning illuminated the puffy clouds that stretched across the horizon. The sun would set in a few hours, making the trek back to Brusnengo through the rain and blackness a dangerous journey.

"I should probably head back."

"You could stay."

Catalina ignored the comment and returned to the bag. "Carmella spent two hours packing. You should have seen how frantic she was. She didn't want to forget anything you *might* need." She gave a wimpy chuckle before continuing. "Be sure you cover the bruises." Catalina pulled a bottle of foundation out of the bag. "She packed a high-collared dress, and here is your hat."

Catalina hung the dress up and smoothed out the wrinkles. Of all their differences, the sisters shared the desire for neatness. Both despised wrinkles in clothing and linen and were adamant everything must be folded to perfection.

Catalina's shoulders drooped, and her head tipped forward. Before the first tear fell, her crumbling form was cradled in Angelina's arms.

"It will all be ok. You will see, Cat." Angelina, her emotions composed, remained an unwavering force holding her sister.

"How do you do it?" Catalina sniffled into Angelina's embrace.

"Do what?"

"Hide your emotions. Even now, when most would cry, you stand resilient. Emotionless."

Angelina pulled back and smiled with compassion. She

gently wiped the stream of tears from Catalina's cheek.

"Because it is what you need from me. Even if that is leaving everything and everyone I love." Angelina's gaze hardened. "But I would rather free you...*us*...from him."

Catalina sighed and stepped away.

"I know you mean well, Lina. But there are far more pressing issues than *my* marriage."

CHAPTER 42

Carlos removed his black hat and slightly bowed to Angelina before opening the passenger door. "You look lovely this morning."

"Thank you, Carlos."

Angelina tugged at the high collar of her dress. The scratchy lace trim combined with the thick makeup was suffocating. She was unused to either. The tenderness of her bruised neck intensified her discomfort.

It will be a miracle to get through this day without ripping this dress to shreds, Angelina thought.

"Today is a grueling day for all of us, but we will face it together," Carlos said.

The comment, though not its purpose, made Angelina aware of her facial expressions. Her frustration and agony were details no one needed to know. There was already enough gossip.

"Thank you, Carlos. It is comforting to have you with us."

Carlos drove away from the convent, frequently checking on Angelina through the rearview mirror. His watchful stare was a comfort to her. He was doing as her father would want.

"Angelina, may I tell you something?" Carlos asked.

She nodded, meeting his gaze in the mirror.

Carlos's pupils were dark spheres floating in a sea of red. In her entire childhood, she had never seen him so upset.

"I must apologize for not being there the morning of—"

Angelina stopped him. "It was early, Carlos. Even I was not

home from my morning walk when it happened. Thank God I left earlier than usual, or I would have perished, too!"

"I am sorry, I should have seen this coming—"

"You had nothing to do with this, Carlos. Please do not blame yourself!"

"No. I should have known. It is my job to foresee trouble. Now, my heart is broken. Your father is a brother to me. And...I loved his sons as my own..." His grief stole his voice.

Such parental love could only come from a lifetime of bonding. Carlos spent many hours playing ball, taking all the Beretta children for rides in the car, plus he helped teach them how to bottle the wine.

More composed, Carlos said, "It's as if Fernando himself will rest in those graves."

Angelina's stomach flipped. Fernando could have easily been a part of the madness. Many nights, Fernando stayed over so he and Anton could make an early run.

She swallowed the rising bile. "Will...Nan be there this morning?"

"He is there now helping Carmella prepare."

"Then we are well cared for. Your family's service is invaluable!" Angelina mustered a small smile.

"I hope it will always be so."

"Carlos! We need you now, probably more than ever!" Angelina gently patted his shoulder.

"But times will be rough. We understand—"

"Papa taught me well. I will see us through," she replied with confidence.

Angelina leaned back into her seat with an immense weight on her heart. Providing for Carlos's family would be difficult, but they needed them! They were loyal.

Even the most loyal can turn against you. Angelina heard her father say.

Don Salvatore, by money or torture, could force Carlos's

family to part with what little information they had.

You are right, Papa. It would only take one little birdie tweeting the right information to cause more bloodshed. Dear God, I love a challenge, but please, I can only handle so much! Angelina thought.

Carlos continued to monitor Angelina through the rearview mirror, though neither spoke another word during the long drive. When they pulled into the church's lot, Angelina clutched her chest and broke into a quiet sob.

"We are early, Signorina. I shall drive around the block until you are ready."

Angelina nodded in appreciation. The car's purring engine and gentle sway as it drove over the uneven road, soothed her spirit. It was a mother's soothing hum while gently rocking her newborn baby. Angelina bathed in it.

When she regained her composure, she met Carlos's gaze in the mirror.

He nodded. "I shall park in the back to avoid the crowd."

"Thank you."

Pulling into the lot, Carlos cleared his throat and glanced into the mirror for one last peek at Angelina.

"If you need anything, Signorina. I am here for."

"Thank you."

Carlos's dark eyes evaluated Angelina with a similar parental gaze as her father. Rosario's words, *'Do you need me to talk or listen,'* echoed in her mind. At that moment, Angelina did not want to express her anxiety and grief. The idea of receiving any words of wisdom made her muscles tense in agitation. She was broken beyond repair, and more advice could not mend her or make this day any less stressful.

If he says anything, it is out of love.

Carlos dropped his gaze, giving Angelina precisely what she needed, silence.

Angelina accepted Carlos's hand to exit the car. Every

movement sent a quake of pain to her core, and she winced. When her eyes opened, she met the sorrowful look in Fernando's eyes.

"How are you feeling, Lina?"

"I am trying not to. How are you?"

Angelina genuinely took in Fernando's countenance for the first time in what seemed like months. A shadow of sorrow blocked the usual dancing sparkle in his eyes when she was near him. His drawn, pale face told her he hadn't eaten in days.

"It has been tough. But seeing you are ok makes today less difficult," Fernando said tenderly as he placed his hand on hers.

Angelina jumped, making what little color left in Fernando's face drain away. Carlos stepped between them and mumbled something to his son.

"I am sorry, Nan!" Angelina pleaded, but her words fell on deaf ears. She sighed as Fernando stormed away.

"He will be ok." Carlos escorted Angelina to the church door, holding his arm close but not touching her. "He does not know *everything*. We have kept many details from him."

Her throat swelled with tears. Carlos protected her, just as her Papa would have wanted him to.

Carlos pulled out two chairs from the priest's room and gently guided Angelina into one.

"We still have ten minutes before the service will start. If you are comfortable here, I will find your sister."

"You, Carmella, and Nan should walk in with us."

Carlos nodded his appreciation. "If you wish."

"We are a family, now and forever."

He nodded. "Fernando. Stay with Angelina. She is not to be left alone."

"Si, Papa." Fernando, his back turned, kept his distance.

His shoulders slumped, he leaned heavily against the wall. Even though he was many yards away, his quiet sobs filtered down the hall.

Angelina wanted to run over to him, snuggle into his chest, and feel the warmth of his arms around her. His tender love would be a healing salve for her deep wounds, and she for his. But the thought of being touched by any man, even one she loved, was unbearable.

"I am sorry for earlier."

"It's ok." His body stiffened, refusing to look back.

"Nan, a lot has happened."

Angelina stood to move toward him, but he stepped further away.

"I know you do not love me."

"Nan, that is not true! Please, this is not the time to discuss this. Can't you see I am suffocating!"

"My love for you has always been suffocating."

"That is not true either! Please, Nan. My world has caved in around me. Can you not see—?"

"I see you." Fernando turned to face her. "But you never see me!"

His words plunged a sharp dagger into her heart.

"Nan, please!" Angelina rushed toward him, but he walked away, passing Catalina and Carmella. He nodded at them before ducking down the adjoining hallway.

Tears welled in Angelina's eyes, and her lungs nearly caved from the pressure. She took three steps forward, and her legs buckled.

"Angelina!" Catalina yelled, rushing to her.

She heard her sister's cry and felt an arm wrapping around her like the tender touch of a loving mother. The pleas of her sister pulled Angelina back from the darkness.

"Sit, my child. You have been through too much to be moving about like such," Carmella said. She tidied Angelina's hair and fluffed her dress. "There, there. Just rest."

Angelina's vision returned to normal. She looked down the

hall, but Carmella and Catalina blocked the view.

"Do not worry about him, Lina. He has lost his family, too. Fernando grieves as you do." Carmella gently patted her shoulder. "These things are harder on men than women. They must fix things... always fixing, fixing." Carmella's hands emphasized her every word. "If they are not, they feel lost and helpless. Fernando wishes to 'fix' your pain, my dear. He loves you so much. But you know that."

Tears streaming down Angelina's cheeks, she nodded.

"He needs to feel helpful. Do not worry. I will find a task for him. He will be okay, but it will take time. It will take time for *all* of us." Carmella slipped her left hand into Catalina's and her right into Angelina's. "Both of you must remember that every person grieves differently and at a different pace."

Angelina dried her tear-stained cheeks before resting her face against the back of Carmella's hand.

"Thank you," Angelina said with a warm smile.

She wished to say more for all the kindness, yet her mind could not conjure anything more than two simple words.

"If you are well, I shall see to my son," Carmella asked more than stated.

Catalina nodded her approval and appreciation.

"All will be fine," Carmella said, kissing each girl's head.

Catalina sat in the chair next to Angelina. Only an occasional forced smile was shared as silence filled the expanding cavern between them.

Tired of the awkward silence, Angelina wrapped her hand around Catalina's, prompting a truce.

"How are you feeling today, Lina?"

"Weak, tired, overwhelmed...!" Angelina admitted. "You?"

Catalina shrugged her shoulders.

Angelina looked at Catalina's tired eyes and felt guilty for expressing the truth. Her sister had spent a week preparing for this day and suppressed a horrible secret. Though they each had a heavy cross to bear, Angelina had spent most of the week in bed resting. Catalina, however, had no sleep and a thousand decisions to make. Yet, even with the weight, today, Catalina looked calm.

"I guess today you are able to suppress your feelings. Care to teach me?" Angelina teased.

"I learned from the best." Catalina forced a smile. "You are the one who remains fearless in the face of others."

"Today has not started off that way." Angelina glanced in the direction of Fernando's departure.

"Nan does not know everything."

"I don't want him to know!"

"Besides us, only three other people know. It is my wish we keep it that way."

Angelina nodded.

Catalina placed her hand over Angelina's and squeezed.

"I mean *forever*, Lina. Never speak of it to anyone. Even the man you marry! It will go to my grave. Out of love for me, it must go to your grave, too."

Angelina's eyes widened. Keeping such a stalwart vow of silence was unconscionable. Given the already overwhelming hardship of the day, Angelina decided it was not the time to argue. Catalina needed to believe, so she lied.

"Out of love." Angelina agreed.

Catalina released her grip, and their silent misery returned.

Though they did not see eye to eye, and Catalina's delusional aspirations irritated Angelina, they didn't need to be enemies. Their mother would want them to be understanding and consoling but, most of all, compassionate with the other.

You are different in many ways, but by blood, you are bound, which is sacred! Sofia often preached to them.

"*I am not the only one in pain.*" Angelina thought."*Be a leader. Be the big sister she needs so we can move forward.*"

"Cat, I am grateful we have each other."

Catalina gave a small smile of appreciation. "Me too."

Angelina lovingly embraced her. In their sisterly hug, they released tears of sorrow.

Breaking the prolonged hug, Catalina pulled away and dried her tears. It was time to reveal another painful secret.

"Lina, please do not be upset with me." She rubbed her hands over her thighs. "Please, do not get angry! This day is long from being over, and I...*We* need to stand together."

Angelina nodded

Catalina willed her words to emerge, but they refused. A well of tears filled her eyes. She blinked, releasing the damn, and forced the words to leave her lips.

"Don Salvatore is here."

Anger and fear compressed into a tremendous weight on Angelina's chest. She refused to make eye contact. Her emotions were volatile, and meeting Catalina's dark eyes could ignite an explosion of damaging words. At least, that is the excuse, Angelina told herself.

"There is something else you must prepare for—."

"You said *he* wouldn't be here!" Angelina's cheeks flushed, her anger rapidly escalating.

"I cannot control him! Though appreciated, your confidence in my abilities is untimely and aggravating."

Angelina growled and unleashed her rage. "Giorgio cannot be here!"

"What? No, Lina, stop! Your uncontrolled anger is tiresome!"

It was Catalina's turn to growl. She clenched her fists and pounded her thighs, trying to contain her composure, but it shattered. The delicate words needed to be delivered with compassion were hurled in anger.

"I had them cremated!"

Angelina's eyes widened, and her jaw gaped open. She was

beyond stunned. She was speechless. Her lips formed the single word, *why*, but her voice could not utter it.

"Why must you always push me into anger! That information was a delicate subject and should have been handled with care. Enjoy your stew of jumbled emotions; you made it!" Catalina said and stormed away.

Devastation consumed Angelina. Anger, sadness, hatred, and surprise all twirled in her gut. Every hour of the day seemed to be more challenging than the hour before. She wondered how much worse the day could become?

Catalina returned a few minutes later. Her composure had calmed. She sat beside Angelina and reached for her hand.

"I am sorry! I am sorry you could not see them one last time, but... The condition of the bodies... You do understand?

It pained Angelina to admit cremation was necessary. Yet, her anger did not settle on Catalina. It fell on Giorgio. Because of him, her brothers died. Because of him, she was sent to convalesce so far away. Because of him, the small crevasse between the sisters was an expanding canyon.

Angelina closed her eyes and drew in a few deep breaths. This anger was a distraction from what was most important. Catalina did the best she could with no support. It was a tough decision and was not made with malicious intent, a fact Angelina needed to accept, no matter how painful.

"You had a lot to command on your own, Cat. I trust you did what was best." Angelina's words were dry and forced. But deep down inside, they were sincere.

Their eyes cast down, the sisters returned to their mournful silence. Each lost in their own perils of sorrow while the emotional chasm between them widened. In the expanding space, one small link remained; they continued to hold hands.

"Are you ready?" A gentle voice asked.

The sisters jumped.

"My apologies for startling you, but we must begin Mass,"

the Priest said.

As if God commanded them to rise and go forth, they stood and replied in unison. "Si, Padre."

When they reached the end of the hall, Carlos flashed a compassionate smile and joined the procession. Catalina nudged Angelina, curious about Carlos.

"I asked them to walk in with us," Angelina whispered. "They *are* family."

Catalina smiled her approval.

"You tell him." Catalina mouthed, nodding at the priest.

Angelina gently touched the priest's shoulder. "Padre, if you do not mind, we seem to be missing a couple of people. If you would give us a minute?" Angelina smiled sweetly and thanked him before he could respond. "Go ahead, Carlos, we will wait here until you return."

Impatient like the Priest, Angelina fussed with her hat. The band rubbed her moist brow and intensified her pounding head. Oh, how she longed to rip the stuffy contraption from her scalp. She tugged at the scratchy lace collar that seemed to tighten with each breath. Both compounded the discomfort of her mental prison.

The movement caught the Priest and Catalina's attention. His first glance immediately turned into a wide-eyed stare at the dark purple bruise on Angelina's neck.

"Lina, your collar is crooked. Again!" Catalina reached to straighten it and huffed. "What is this? How embarrassing! The color has marked your neck. I knew I should have taken you shopping. I do not understand why you purchase anything at that cheap dress shop!"

"I like the owner." Angelina shrugged, trying to sell the lie.

The priest arched his eyebrow at the bickering sisters.

"You *will* throw out this dress. Pray I can get that dye off your neck!" Catalina stamped her foot, adding to her theatrics. "But we will have to tend to that later." She fluffed Angelina's hair, bringing a few long black strands in front to hide the bruise. "There, that will help hide it."

The Priest released a disapproving harrumph, making his disdain for the vanity and theatrics evident.

"Thank you!"

Catalina smiled, knowing the duality of Angelina's gratitude.

The Priest glanced at his watch. His patience was at its end. Before he could insist they proceed, Carlos appeared with his family close behind.

"Very sorry for the wait," Carlos said, a little winded.

The sisters gave him a comforting smile, then pulled their black lace veils down from their hats. They slipped on black satin and lace gloves and removed a matching handkerchief from their purses.

Catalina forced a smile. "Thank you for your patience, Padre. We are ready now."

Butterflies took flight in Angelina's stomach, and a lump lodged in her throat. "And so it all begins," Angelina whispered to her sister.

Catalina linked arms and gave her a loving pat. "Indeed."

The last few attendees scurried to join the congregation when they saw the grieving family entering the vestibule. Two alter boys closed the heavy wooden doors behind the last guests and waited for the Priest's nod to reopen them. The organ's first notes and the nod happened simultaneously. As the doors opened, angelic voices from the grand balcony graced the ears of all below with "Ave Maria." The beautiful bellow of the organ's big pipes resonated loudly in the church, setting the procession's slow pace.

Four young men dressed in black with white gloves carried an urn, followed by another four similarly dressed men carrying a beautiful portrait of the Beretta sons. Angelina whimpered, and an endless stream of tears flowed as the faces' of her handsome brothers passed before her.

Two young altar boys dressed in white followed the portraits. One held the gently swaying silver urn as it released the incense into the air. The other carried a staff with a beautiful jeweled crucifix. The priest followed in a slow, reverent gait.

Angelina stepped into the church and was in awe of the cathedral packed with women in black dresses with stylish matching hats, men in dark suits, and children huddled close to their parents. The pews were packed and every inch of space along the walls and down each walkway was crammed with more sorrowful faces. A thousand eyes intently watched the mourning procession slowly walk down the center aisle; it was as unnerving as it was endearing.

"It is a short walk." Catalina gently squeezed her sister's arm. "Remember to breathe."

Angelina forced her lungs to inhale. Regardless of the distance, reaching their seats would take an eternity at this pace. To numb her senses, she kept her eyes forward and focused on the altar.

The sunlight dappled across the altar and illuminated the four urns. The young men carrying the portraits took turns bowing to the altar before climbing the steps and placing the image behind the corresponding urn. A perfect depiction of each Beretta son, their vibrance for life radiating from their smiling faces, stared back at the congregation.

In an array of colors, flowers filled every available space in the church. The tall, towering arrangements consumed the altar. The smaller but equally beautiful bouquets filled any available space, including the end of each pew. It was as if the congregation was transported into a world made of flora.

The women sobbed into their handkerchiefs, and the occasional wail of grief echoed off the tall stone walls. Every man clutched his hat, their cheeks stained by tears. Some bit at their lip to refrain from an eruption of emotions. The whimpering children buried their sad faces into their mother's skirts or clung to their father's arm.

A hand reached out to touch Angelina, and she flinched, fearful of whom it belonged. A wave of relief washed over her; it was Maria with her usual compassionate gaze.

Carlos and his family filed into the first pew, followed by Catalina, leaving Angelina by the center aisle.

The priest started the Mass when the organ's last vibrating note ascended to the heavens. His words were elegant, meaningful, and filled with love. Each person's soul was prayed for, their ashes anointed, and a heartfelt eulogy was given.

The excess of reverent words and the overpowering floral perfume consumed all the oxygen in the chapel. Angelina had an unquenchable desire to fill her lungs with untainted air. She searched for the nearest exit. Catalina patted her thigh just as Sofia did when her children became fidgety. From years of programming, Angelina transformed into a seated statue with slumped shoulders and a bowed head.

When the priest made his final sign of the cross over the congregation, Angelina sighed in relief. The service was finally over. Now, they could flee the abundantly fragrant prison. Picking up her purse to leave the pew, Catalina's hand halted her.

"Can this day be any more painful?" Angelina grumbled as Fernando took the podium.

"Today, I say goodbye to my best friends, to four men who were brothers to me," Fernando began his touching eulogy.

The grief in Fernando's voice, the memories he shared, and the tears that fell as he spoke were more than Angelina could bear. Every word was a dagger to her heart, a trigger that made her mind relive the massacre. The flowers, moving eulogies, her collar, the pain when she swallowed, and the loud thud of her headache made the present moment, in the space of piety, a living hell.

Out of her peripheral vision, a flash of light grabbed Angelina's attention. She turned her head slightly and found the source of the twinkling light was an ostentatious diamond pinky ring. The owner was Don Salvatore. He wore a mournful expression as he focused solely on Fernando. The reverent Godfather's performance was perfect, too perfect for Angelina.

She glared at Don Salvatore and whispered, "The devil in my hell."

The growl of a rabid dog rumbled in her gut. To see this man, wearing a pious expression, mourning the souls *he* commanded to death was infuriating. All her emotions urged her to lunge across the pews, spit in his face, and scream, *murderer!* But the pain cracking Fernando's voice as he spoke his last goodbye snatched her attention.

"I thank God..." Fernando sniffled. "for the fellowship he gave me in my dearly departed... brothers. May you rest in peace for all eternity." He sucked in a breath and bit back the flood of tears. "Until we meet again."

His shoulders slumped by the weight of sorrow, Fernando returned to the pew, and his eyes met Angelina's. Hoping her scowl of hatred for The Don had receded, Angelina gave Fernando a smile of appreciation. But Fernando's pale face remained motionless in response. The lack of reciprocation added to Angelina's internal pain. She had wronged him one too many times.

As the priest came to the bottom of the altar, the organist began playing "Amazing Grace," and the young men dressed in black picked up the urns and the portraits.

Moments ago, Angelina was ready to race out of the church, but now she found it difficult to leave. Forcing her body to move, Angelina stepped out of the pew. With a gasp, all the air rushed out of her lungs, and her knees became weak. An arms-length away was the image that crippled her was Anton's face.

During the mass, Angelina deliberately avoided looking at the four framed faces. Though the photos were perfect reflections, it was not how Angelina wanted to remember them. In her solitude at the convent, she picked unforgettable memories to stitch together a montage of each sibling. It was a living remembrance, not a depressing, one-dimensional picture.

Angelina cast down her gaze, and her right hand slipped into Catalina's arm. Locked together in grief and love, the sisters followed the procession, frequently wiping away the trail of tears.

A gust of fresh air rushed down the aisle when the front doors opened. Angelina stretched her neck like a kitten dying for air in the suffocating grip of a toddler. She ravenously inhaled the chilly, damp breeze.

"We have to stand at the door and thank the guests," Catalina whispered, pulling Angelina from her oxygenated reverie.

The thought made Angelina want to vomit. In her mind, allowing everyone to leave the abundantly fragrant air seemed thanks enough. Besides, an hour plus of grieving and the torture from the oxygen deprivation should have made the guest eager to return to the comforts of home.

Angelina's shoulders slumped as the word 'home' echoed in her mind. Her home wasn't a place of refuge, not anymore.

Catalina gave Angelina a comforting pat. "It will be ok."

Every fiber of Angelina's body protested, but she nodded and stepped into her position. It would be rude to do otherwise. A wisp of a smile briefly flickered in Angelina's mind. Catalina, for once, was the one in charge, charming everyone with her beauty and social grace.

Face after face passed by to give hugs and kisses laced with condolences. The number of people in attendance was staggering. Catalina, given her higher station in society, knew everyone's name. However, Angelina had never met most of them. Occasionally, a man would pass a thick envelope in a heartfelt handshake followed by glowing words of respect for the Beretta family. Many asked about their parents' health, to which the sisters answered with the exact same phrase, "They are mending."

Catalina's ability to engage each person was astounding. Angelina felt like a broken record repeating two words, "Thank you," to hundreds of people. It was another reminder of Catalina's tremendous growth since marrying Giorgio.

Little by little, the crowd dwindled to one last individual, Don Salvatore. Oozing compassion, he gave each a hug before showering them with kisses and words of sympathy.

"If you, my beautiful flowers, need *anything*, please allow me to assist. After all, your family is my family," The Don said, cupping Catalina's chin, "and this tragedy affects *all* of us."

Acidic bile stung Angelina's throat, her hands clenched, and her face flushed with anger. The only palatable assistance from The Don was for him to die a slow, painful death, preferably at her feet so she could relish it. Expressing her genuine feelings would not bring about anything positive. So, as her father taught her, Angelina played her part with the skill of a famed actress.

"Your kindness is much appreciated, Signor Salvatore. We will keep your offer in mind." Angelina lied. "The coming weeks may be trying. But knowing we have your blessing is truly a comfort."

The words effortlessly spilled off her tongue, leaving an acrid residue she wished to scrub off. Unfortunately, the deep cleaning would have to wait for the end of the play.

"Signor Salvatore, we are grateful," Catalina added.

"Ah, my little Kitty-Cat, I have told you before, I am your Zio. Please address me as such!"

"Thank you, Zio," Catalina said and grimaced.

"Do give my condolences to my nephew. I am sure this tragedy is difficult for him as well. But I must ask, is it true?"

Angelina felt an icy chill trickle down her spine. The memory of Giorgio's hand firmly clamped on her throat made her hands sweaty and her heart thump loud enough for the world to hear. To remain calm with such an accusation lingering in the air was difficult. Angelina resisted the urge to tug at her collar, fearing she would expose the bruise, thus answering his question. Before Angelina could gather the words to respond, Catalina spoke up.

"Si, Zio. But we are keeping the details to ourselves. It will not due to have such accusations breeding into never-ending tall tales," Catalina replied.

"You are a bright lady, Kitty-Cat. And your discretion will be rewarded!"

Angelina's head felt light as the words passed between her sister and her enemy. As their lips moved, the air became thin, their mouths consuming all the oxygen. It was hard to comprehend Catalina's traitorous words and unrestricted loyalty to The Don.

"He is grieving as well. This tragedy has taken its toll on all of us. Perhaps you could call him. He brightens after he speaks with you."

"That is an excellent idea! Call me old-fashioned, but I prefer to visit face-to-face. In fact, I shall swing by on my way to the vineyard. I am sure you lovely ladies can delay the start of the reception for me. Besides, it sounds as though the young man needs to be instructed on how much wine is too much! He will not disgrace either of us, my Kitty-Cat!"

Angelina was relieved that she had not made a fool of herself. However, the drop of relief was overpowered by the fear of Giorgio sharing every detail with his uncle. Even though Catalina had continued to have Giorgio sedated, the risk of him providing too much or any information was astronomical. The sisters had hoped his current condition would keep visitors away and allow time to make decisions for their safety. The instability of it all created a wave of soul-crushing fear that washed over Angelina, causing her mind to revert to her two simple words.

"Thank you." Angelina's involuntary response of gratitude infuriated her, but she had nothing else to say. Besides, she definitively wanted the man out of her sight.

"Ohh, no need to thank me *yet*," Don Salvatore insisted as he placed his chubby hand on her face, gently stroking her cheek with his thumb. "I intend to be... Shall we say, a *powerful* influence over your future."

CHAPTER 43

"Carlos, please park the car around the back," Angelina said, nodding toward the house.

The tires crunched the gravel along the winding, tree-lined drive. In the distance loomed the building she once called home. Though only a week had passed since she last laid eyes on this place, her heart ached as if it had been years. Angelina wondered if this was how Marcus felt when he returned from his military duties.

The car crossed over the roaring river, making the wooden planks needing repair slap against the bridge's structure. The whomp-whomp hurled Angelina back in time to the beginning of this tragedy. Her body stiffened as the memory of the dark mass tumbling in the water stole her vision.

A warm hand embraced Angelina's, pulling her back to the present. The dead body's image faded from her eyes, leaving only the clear water crashing against the protruding rocks.

Carmella patted Angelina's hand and gave her a compassionate smile. It was a familiar endearing countenance given in times of physical pain, careless behavior, her brothers' harsh words, or the unfavorable outcome of a boy crush.

Carmella was always present in good times and bad. She urged Angelina from her mother's womb and presented her to Sofia. From Angelina's first cries, Carmella was the first to hold her. The first to wrap her in a bundle. The first to shower her with kisses and utter the calming shh-shh in her ears. There was not an age without memories of Carmella's love.

"Thank you for your assistance this past week. Cat said you were a tremendous help."

"We did our best. Nan was an immense help with all the cooking and cleaning," Carmella replied.

Angelina's lungs ceased to expand as the memory of the pungent room filled her nose. When she left to get help, the kitchen was a massive puddle of blood and excrement. To remove the smell alone had to be an insurmountable task.

"That could not have been easy."

"We did, and will do, what we must." Carmella gave another gentle squeeze.

"Thank you."

Carmella bit her lip and shifted her gaze out the window. The sun, breaking through a cluster of trees, illuminated a tear rolling down the matronly woman's wet cheek. She, too, was emersed in overwhelming sadness.

Angelina searched for words of appreciation and comfort. *Thank you* did not express the vast amount of love and gratitude she had for Carmella. The woman deserved more than two simple words falling mechanically from Angelina's mouth. Unable to move her tongue, Angelina gave Carmella's hand a loving pat, hoping the return of the nurturing gesture would convey more than any word.

Carmella wiped away her tears before turning to acknowledge the tenderness. They briefly exchanged grateful smiles and returned their sorrowful gaze out the window.

Two enormous white tents were placed side by side next to the barn. The towering flower arrangements and smaller displays from the church created a grand entrance of cascading colors. More undulating displays graced the corners and serving tables. Many worker bees buzzed about the flora, preparing the space for guests.

"Who are all these people?" Angelina blinked in confusion.

"Cat hired a crew to serve the food and drinks. She wants all of us to relax and enjoy, as best we can, a celebration of your brothers' life."

It was a busy hive of waiters dressed in black tuxedoes with bright white gloves. Final adjustments were made to the silverware while bartenders examined wine glasses for water spots. Four sharply dressed men climbed in and out of a black box truck parked beside the far tent. Two additional men, similarly dressed, carried a drum set toward a woman practicing her vocals on a raised platform.

"She hired a band?" Angelina asked incredulously.

"It is a nice touch."

"Shouldn't this be more of a somber event?"

"It has been many years since you attended a funeral, my dear. This is a party to honor your brothers."

Angelina rolled her eyes. "I think it is in poor taste!"

"Your brothers were fun-loving, happy men who would detest a boring meal and down-turned faces. This event expresses their charming qualities so all can enjoy the happiness these lives brought into our hearts one last time." The explanation unleashed Carmella's tears.

Angelina was not in the mood for an elaborate party. However, the woman beside her, whose love and devotion were unmeasurable, would find closure in such an event.

"A beautiful gesture." Angelina patted Carmella's hand.

Carlos pulled the car around the back of the house. Habitually, he parked the vehicle precisely as her father had always requested. As a child, it seemed silly to Angelina that the car would be backed into its space, and as her father described it, "Ready for a quick departure." Today, however, it gave her peace of mind that if she *needed* to escape, the car could quickly whisk her away.

"I want to go into the house... *alone*," Angelina said.

"Are you sure?" Carlos asked, shocked at the notion.

"Take your time, Dear. The guests should not arrive for a

little while yet." Carmella, ignoring her husband's exasperated look, patted Angelina's hand. "We will be right outside if you need anything."

"Thank you."

Instantly, she chided herself. Her automatic response infuriated her. The two words were meaningless, an empty response that neither implied a level of gratitude nor a heartfelt connection repaying kindness.

Fernando opened her door and offered her his hand. The first thing she noticed about him was the twinkle in his eyes and the soft pinkness in his cheeks. Angelina, entranced by the significant change in his appearance, did not move until a breeze danced through his dark locks, breaking the spell. Fearful Fernando would take her lack of movement as a rejection, Angelina removed her glove and placed her hand in his. The skin-to-skin connection ignited a rush of warmth up her arm. She felt the same tingle when their hands would accidentally touch. Inwardly, Angelina sighed. She wondered if Fernando's touch would rekindle memories she wished to forget or stimulate the desire to be held in a loving embrace.

Fernando tried to hide his expression of surprise, but Angelina could read him better than he could ever imagine. It was unfair to expect him to be as intuitive as her, but deep down, Angelina wished Fernando understood it was never her intention to hurt him.

"Thank you, Nan."

"I will go with you if you want," Fernando said.

"Thank you, but I need to face this demon alone."

She squeezed his hand and hoped he would find no injury in her words.

"I'm here if you need me," he replied with a tender smile.

She gave him a grateful smile and walked up the steps to the kitchen. Angelina paused for a moment to look at the cellar door. Her heart thundered as she remembered the portal dancing with the wind, threatening to reveal her presence. Today, the rotted wood lay silent against the ground. Even though the cellar protected her, she would forever see those wooden planks as the doorway into hell.

When Angelina's hand turned the handle to the kitchen door, a gust of wind whipped the cellar door open and, in defiance, slammed it shut. The loud bang sent a jolt to Angelina's soul. She stood frozen while the horrible nightmare replayed. She drew in three slow, deep breaths to calm her frazzled nerves.

Carlos stepped on the door and struggled with the latch. "Son, fetch my tools."

Angelina held up her hand to stop both of them.

"Leave it, Carlos. You need not do any work today. It will be just the same tomorrow."

Giving a command in a controlled tone, and Carlos's look of awe empowered her. A wave of calm flowed over her as resilience and strength returned to her spirit.

"Are you sure?" he asked.

Angelina's long, black hair floated effortlessly in the wind. Her level chin and straight spine added to her confident appearance. For the first time in a week, she was definitively sure of something.

"You and your family should be given time to grieve. Whatever repair or chore that arises can be done another day. Today, we honor my brothers. Go enjoy the festivities as best you can. I will be along soon."

With a steady hand, Angelina opened the door to a world she hoped never to return to. She crossed the threshold into the hollowed space, allowing the door to close quietly behind her. The kitchen had been cleansed. But the smell of death lingered in the air, and the bloodstains would never wash from her mind.

Her hand touched the table and gently stroked the smooth

wooden surface where RJ's little body lay limp, and the vibrant red fluid flowed over the edge. Angelina could still hear his lungs yearning for air as his young soul desperately fought to remain in this dimension.

Two chairs were moved into a shadowed space against the wall where Rosario and Sofia's blood seeped deep into the wood. Carmella was a masterful cleaner. However, some stains can't be removed.

At the end of the table, Angelina fell to her knees. Her hand trembled over the space where her dearest brother's soul departed from his body. The sucking sound from the stab wounds to his chest and his throat gurgling as blood filled his airway echoed in her ears.

"Anton, I am so sorry!" Angelina sobbed as the full weight of his loss crushed her chest. "How could they? How could they be so cruel!"

She laid her head on the cold floor and longed for the warmth of Anton's hug. As much as he was her brother, he was her friend. Angelina wept, wishing her tears could fill the emptiness left in her heart. But nothing could fill that void.

"Now what, Lina?" Anton's voice echoed around her. "Will you be weak or strong?"

She sat up on her knees.

"Who is on my grave? Certainly not my sis!"

"Anton?"

"Silly Lina. You are better than this! You are smarter than *them*. You know how to beat him!"

"No, I don't! How? How can I?" Angelina begged.

She wanted to stand and chase after the voice, but her body felt frozen to the cold floor.

"No one is a match for *my*, Sis." The voice laughed.

Angelina saw Anton's figure leaning against the door frame, playfully tossing a red apple.

"Anton! Please help me. I need your help!"

"You need no one! *You* can trick a wolf with its own game!"

"But, I am afraid."

"Ha! Not *my* Sis!" Anton stood upright and looked out the window. "Better hurry, though. Time is running out! Think fast!" Anton chuckled as he threw the apple at her.

"Anton! Wait!" Angelina pleaded, but the vision was gone.

His laughter faded into the distance as the apple careened toward her face. She flinched. Her senses returned, and she felt the cold tile floor against her moist cheek. She gasped for air while her mind wavered between a dream and reality. She pushed herself to her knees and noticed the lighting had shifted. It was almost sunset. In the distance, the band and happy voices filled the air, beckoning her back to earth.

How long have I been in here? Angelina wondered, wiping her cheek dry with her hand.

As her eyes refocused to the changing light, a twinkle under the bench caught her eye.

"What are you?" She grunted, stretching her arm. "Come on, don't be difficult!"

She repositioned her body flat against the cold tile and tried again. This time, her fingertips pinched a cold piece of metal. Holding her prize, Angelina dusted the dirt from her dress and sat on the edge of the bench.

"Where did you come from?" She held the trinket up to the waning light. "A cufflink?"

A neatly engraved monogram surrounded by diamonds and an elaborate filigree was on the face. Her finger traced the two letters.

"Lina, are you ok?" Fernando peeked through the door.

Angelina jumped, and her hands fumbled to keep the prize as she bolted onto her feet. "Huh? Umm, I...I am fine."

"I know you said you needed time—"

"It is okay, Nan."

"The guests have arrived and are asking questions. Are you

ready to greet them?" Fernando slowly approached her.

Still lost in her dream, Angelina's fingers nervously fidgeted with the cufflink. It took a moment, but she finally regained her wits.

"Cleaning up this mess must have been difficult."

"Mamma and I cried the whole time."

"Do you know what happened?"

"No, they removed the bodies before I came in." Fernando stepped a little closer. "Did you see—?"

"I saw...too much."

Angelina choked back her emotions. Her hand gripped the cuff link tightly; the corners threatened to puncture her skin, but she didn't care. Her palm hurt less than her heart.

"I'm sorry, I wish I could have been here. Perhaps—"

"No!" Angelina's tears streamed down her cheeks. "No! They would have killed you too!"

The thought of him being slaughtered overwhelmed her, and she crumbled into a sobbing heap on the bench. Fernando rushed to her side and gently wrapped his arm around her. His chest flexed against her cheek as he slowly caressed her back. To her surprise, his embrace made her feel safe. It was the comforting touch she longed for but feared no man could ever provide, not after Giorgio's assault.

"Do you know who killed them?" Fernando asked when her crying faded.

"Si!" Angelina sat up to clean her face.

Her abrupt response made Fernando flinch.

"Are you sure?"

"It is best if you do not know, Nan. I do not want them coming for you! I cannot bear another loss..." Her eyes welled with tears. "Nor can your parents!"

"But, Lina, I want to help."

"I know you do, and you will. I promise."

"How, if I don't know—?"

"For now, we have a party to attend. We can discuss later what needs to be done."

"I'm not afraid to kill them." Fernando's brow furrowed.

His defiance made Angelina's body shudder with fear. She had never seen a fiery revenge and determination dance in his eyes. In a different situation, it would have made her heart flutter with infatuation. But at this moment, it stirred an immense fear.

"I know, Nan. I know you would, but you must promise me you *won't* seek revenge for their deaths!"

Fernando's gaze remained intense until Angelina wrapped her hand around his.

"Please?" Angelina's eyes pleaded with him.

He dropped his gaze and gave a reluctant nod.

She appreciated his heroic desire to defend her family and seek retribution. Though she wanted to thank him for it, she feared any further discussion would ignite his vengeful rage. Instead of words, she chose a nonverbal show of appreciation, stroking his hand with her thumb.

Angelina's thoughts drifted off as she stared at the marbling in the floor. She did not hear his question the first time, so he repeated it.

"Are you bleeding?"

Angelina looked confused. He pointed to her other hand. Breaking her tight grip, Angelina revealed the gold treasure. In her anxiety, she unknowingly punctured her skin with the back of the cufflink.

Fernando grabbed a wet cloth and returned to wash Angelina's wound. His warm hand gently held hers, and Angelina could feel his love for her.

In the waning sunlight, Angelina traced his features with her eyes. She couldn't remember the last time she relaxed and soaked in every line of his profile, his dark eyes, wavy black hair, and eyebrows that could use a good taming.

Angelina searched her heart: could she love this man? He met her gaze. For a long moment, they stared into each other's souls. The world faded away. Fernando's love was an oasis in a sea of disaster. She stroked his cheek, then twirled a ringlet of his soft hair.

"Can we try again?" Fernando asked.

Angelina's heart urged her to tell him the truth about her feelings and about the past week. She wanted to trust him as Anton did. She opened her lips to respond, but her mouth became dry. Only seconds passed, but her silence seemed to last for eternity.

Tell him! Angelina's heart pleaded.

She picked up Fernando's hand, kissed his palm, then rested her cheek against it. The smell of his cologne and the warmth of his hand entranced her. Angelina drew in every ounce of the moment as if it would be her last. She didn't want to lose the love, peace, and happiness he effortlessly... *faithfully* gave her.

The door flung open, breaking the tender moment. Fernando lept to his feet. Angelina, dazed by the interruption, dropped the cufflink. With a high-pitched ting, it scurried out of sight.

"Lina, you must come now!" Carlos pleaded.

Angelina glanced at Fernando, but the moment for a response was gone.

Snarling, Fernando snatched up the gold cufflink and inspected the monogram. Bouncing it in his hand, he narrowed his eyes and slammed it on the table. Angelina reached for him, but he stormed away.

CHAPTER 44

"Sorry, Nan," Carlos whispered as his son rushed by.

Fernando ignored the apology and slammed the door behind him.

"What is wrong?" Angelina tried to hide her anger but knew she had failed when Carlos flenched at her sharp tone.

"Don Salvatore is here. He is looking for you."

"He can wait like the rest of the guests!"

Carlos's unusual behavior and Fernando feeling injured *again* agitated Angelina. She knew everyone's emotions swelled uncontrollably, and she should be more patient. But she was at her max, and her rage flared.

"He is very agitated...and..." Carlos stammered.

"And what?"

"Catalina has not returned."

Angelina rushed to the window. More than a hundred people milled about the tent, and the drive was lined on both sides with cars, but Catalina's reserved spot was empty.

"How long ago did Don Salvatore arrive?"

"About an hour."

"An hour?" Angelina stumbled backward. "I have been in here that long?" She waved off Carlos's answer. Her dallying did not matter; she needed to find her sister. "I will be out directly. Let him know I am on my way."

A golden ray of light glinted off the cufflink, catching Angelina's attention.

"Carlos, wait! Who has the initials 'MF'?"

"Why do you ask?" Carlos stopped at the door.

His curt reply surprised Angelina. She inspected his countenance and understood he was more concerned about Don Salvatore than solving a riddle. Looking down at the trinket again, Angelina decided it could wait.

"Perhaps it is nothing." She slipped it into her pocket.

After Carlos left to deliver the message, Angelina took a moment to adjust her clothing and her mind.

Where could Cat be? Angelina wondered.

To prevent Don Salvatore from learning the truth about Giorgio's injuries, Catalina was to rush home and hover over The Don's visit with Giorgio. If The Don was at the vineyard for over an hour, where was Cat?

A bellowing voice arguing with Carlos vibrated through the door. Don Salvatore's tirade of words whipping Carlos infuriated Angelina.

"You will not bully us!" Angelina adjusted her hat and stormed out the door, fury raging in her eyes. She glared at the man whose head she wanted on a pike!

"What is the meaning of this fighting?" Angelina's eyes narrowed.

"There you are, My Little Dove!" Don Salvatore gushed. "We have much business to discuss, but this man refuses to allow us time together. I do not have all day! You have kept me waiting too long." Smiling, The Don wagged his finger at Angelina. "Tisk-Tisk!"

"He is following *my* orders!" Angelina slowly descended the stairs, her eyes locked on her prey.

"Perhaps I am mistaken, then. Maybe you cannot conduct business on your father's behalf." The Don's wavering smile emphasized his dislike for people who wasted his time.

"Oh, you are *not* mistaken, Signor Salvatore. *I am* in complete control! However, business shall be addressed in order of importance!"

"*Importance!*" Don Salvatore laughed.

"Si!" Angelina stopped two steps above the fat man. "First, come with me." She waited for The Don to accept her order, but he did not move. "Well?"

"Where are we going?"

"Inside!"

Her chest filled with confidence, Angelina glowed with an unmistakable authority. This was her domain. In her father's absence, *she* ruled. Don Salvatore had stepped over the line with his pompous attitude and, for that matter, his presence. He was a trespasser at the mercy of her temper.

"Carlos, please bring us some wine." Angelina barked the command and led The Don into the kitchen.

Before she allowed the door to close behind her, Angelina noticed Carlos looking at her in awe for the second time that day. It bolstered her confidence. With her chin raised a little higher, she smiled at Carlos in gratitude.

"Signore, this is a special place," Angelina explained as she paraded him around the room. "It is the place my family communed every day to share meals, laugh, and enjoy the pleasures of each other's company."

Angelina motioned for The Don to sit at the table on which he witnessed her baby brother's execution.

"Si, very nice." Don Salvatore whispered, his beady eyes bouncing around the room.

"You do not need to be quiet in here, Signore. Please, speak up!"

"I do not think it wise we are alone. It might seem..."

"If you wish to discuss business, then we do it *here*," Angelina pointed at the table. "Where my Father *always* does business!"

"Now, now." Don Salvatore patted his hands to calm her.

"Does this room make you uneasy?"

"No. It is not proper to be alone..."

"Signor Salvatore." Angelina's voice continued to rise with her growing confidence. "Do you know what happened in this room a week ago?"

"Is this where..." A sorrowful gaze matched his sympathetic tone. "Where they found your brothers?"

Ignoring his pseudo-grief, she locked eyes with him. "Si! The men who slaughtered them did it right here!"

Angelina slammed her hand on the table. The swift movement and loud percussion made The Don jump.

"My Little Dove, I can see you are very upset over the loss of your family. Rightfully so, but..." He opened his hands and shrugged. "What business is that of mine?"

"Well, here I thought *you* wanted to do business. But perhaps you do not have the *authority*." Angelina mocked. "Especially since you seek no restitution for the dead!"

Angelina's hands pressed against the table as she loomed above the devil's face. His blasé attitude was expected. A man who created the sin cannot seek restitution from himself.

"I cannot start a battle over these deaths. You want restitution, yet we do not know who did it or even why!"

"Do you even inquire?"

"Now, now, My Little Dove. To lose a family member is difficult." Don Salvatore confessed sympathetically. "I, too, know the pain from the loss of a loved one."

"I did not lose *a* family member; I lost *several*!"

"Ehh! These things...they happen. For a woman, it seems like the end of the world. But do not worry, My Little Dove, I will find you a husband." He waved his hands to conjure an idea from the ethers. "Ehh...you can sooth your heart as all women do. You make babies and name them after the lost." Don Salvatore met her gaze and grinned.

"Signor Salvatore, you insult me!"

"You are not insulted. You are just a wounded woman."

He brushed away Angelina's inferior femininity with his left hand. With his right, he consolingly patted her hand.

"Do not touch me!" She snatched her hand out from under his. "You step into *my* house! Into *my* family's home! And you insult me! Do not place your chauvinistic ideals on me! I am not a fragile woman in need of rescue. I am the daughter of a wise man who raised me to be strong and resilient!"

The blood in Angelina's veins bubbled, and dark hatred oozed from every pore. She despised him. An eye for an eye was not enough. He must suffer a slow, agonizing death. Her eyes narrowed, and she unconsciously licked her lips as The Don's demise played in her mind.

"Giorgio is right. You *are* a fiery one!" A wicked grin curled his lips. His finger danced in delight on the table. "He told me a lot about you, but his description did not do you justice! You will do nicely for our plan."

Plan? What plan? Angelina's confidence deflated in a heartbeat. *I am the one with a plan!* But she did not have one. The revelation was paralyzing. *To think a ruthless man like him could be tortured by the place he commanded the innocent to die? You fool! This place is only sacred to me!*

To Don Salvatore, this was just another location that held no place of value in his heart, or mind for that matter. Her blind arrogance allowed The Don to flip the table of control and extinguish her perceived power.

"Now listen closely, My Little Dove." The Don snatched her hair and dragged her to his side of the table. "I will touch you *when* I like and *how* I like." Inhaling her sweet scent, he licked his lips. "Mmm, sweet like honey."

The stench of his breath, sour from wine and cigars, smelled like Giorgio's. Angelina struggled to free herself, but the movement only made him pull her hair harder.

"Easy! My Little Dove. You have a beautiful head of hair. It would be a shame to lose a chunk, wouldn't it?"

The Don yanked her head, reinforcing his words. A painful

prick from each hair screaming in revolt against his grip held her motionless. She swallowed and braced for his assault.

"You see, My Little Dove. You have not been a good girl."

The Don's eyes danced with lust as he drank in her beautiful form. Eager to enjoy his prize, he released her hair and grabbed her hips. With surprising strength, he whipped her around like a rag doll, pulling her waist flush with his.

"But good girls are not near as fun as bad girls, are they?"

"Get away from me!"

"You see, My Little Dove, I know your secret!" He fumbled with the buttons on Angelina's dress. "You are a clever girl, but you still have much to learn!"

Angelina slapped him. "Let me go, you disgusting pig!"

He grabbed her face with his stubby hands.

"Not yet! We have business to finish! Since this table is special to your family... *to you*!" The Don shifted his efforts to lifting her skirt. "I think taking the wise man's daughter on his sacred table is fitting. What do you say, My Little Dove, shall we commune and share the pleasures of each other's company?" Don Salvatore laughed maniacally. "I think it is time I enjoy the fruits of this vineyard!"

Angelina prayed for Carlos to burst in and stop this monster. Tears streamed down her cheeks. Every agonizing second crushing her soul a little more.

"Will you confess?"

Angelina whimpered. "I didn't do anything!"

"It was you!" He grabbed her face again. "You are the clever one. Catalina is not that smart! You sent your sister to prevent my conversation with Giorgio. *Didn't you?*"

Her heart thundered in her chest, and tears steadily streamed down her cheeks. Terrified of what he would do next, she shook her head.

"Oh, what? Not so strong? Where is the controlling little bitch you *think* you are?" He squeezed her cheeks harder.

"Maybe Papa didn't raise you to be as strong and resilient as you thought. Perhaps now you understand you are only a *cunt!* Nothing more! Capisci?"

Angelina, frozen in fear, couldn't answer.

"And Good little cunts *obey!*"

His left hand greedily crawled up her thigh.

"No*! Please. No!*"

"You will submit to me!" He pulled her close to kiss her.

Outside, the thud-thud of feet running up the steps stopped The Don's pursuit. He growled and released his grip.

Free from the devil's clutches, Angelina lept to the other side of the table. She tried to wipe his foul drool off, but the evil stench only seemed to spread.

She hated herself. Taunting the devil from his den was arrogant and stupid. Her years of training to be cunning and resilient only led into his grasp. The consequence was an eternity of suffering at the whim of his unfathomable power.

"We will continue our conversation later, My Little Dove," Don Salvatore said as the door handle turned. "Do not let my age fool you. I have an excellent memory. I will happily remember *precisely* where we left off."

"You are a sick bastard!" Angelina spit at his feet.

"You still think you are something." The Don chuckled, his belly jiggling from the exuberance. With a malevolent grin, he whispered. "It is a sexy attribute, No?" His face instantly hardened. "But, be a good cunt and play your part!"

Fernando rushed into the house and gasped. "Angelina?"

Carlos, on his son's heels, entered the kitchen, his left hand clamped on a wine bottle, his right, wisely grabbed Fernando's shoulder. Angelina's disheveled appearance and Don Salvatore looming over the table like a silverback gorilla protecting his conquest terrified them. The roar of The Don's boisterous laugh still lingered in the air, adding to the nonverbal control his presence had over all of them.

When Fernando's gaze met Angelina's, she winced and turned away in shame. She didn't want to see the disgust in his eyes. Her tangled hair, bright red face, and unbuttoned dress were evidence of the liberties Don Salvatore took. She was a woman tainted by a villainous man, and Fernando had every right to reject her for it.

Angelina tried to fasten her dress, but her trembling hands could not hold the buttons. She quietly growled in frustration, more for her feebleminded actions than the lack of her fine motor skills.

"Come in, come in!" The Don waved cheerfully. "Ahh! Bring the wine! We should toast! Come, come, don't be shy!" Don Salvatore puffed his chest and gloated over his three puppets. "Boy, find us some glasses. This is a kitchen, no?"

Though he spoke to Fernando, Don Salvatore's eyes never left Angelina. She squirmed inside and out, resisting the strings of control his plump hands stitched into her skin.

"Good boy!"

Don Salvatore rubbed Fernando's head as a reward for playing fetch like an obedient puppy. He waved for Carlos to bring the wine, sewing a string into flesh with every gesture.

"Good man!" The obnoxiousness of his pseudo-praise was deliberate. "Pour the wine...Carlos. That is your name, Si?"

His ability to effortlessly pull the strings of his puppets made Angelina ill. Because of her, he owned *all* of them.

"Si, Signor Salvatore." Trembling, Carlos poured the wine.

"What causes you to shake, my friend? You are spilling the wine everywhere!" The Don audibly clucked, his hands shooing Carlos away. "Angelina, My Little Dove, you pour the wine. After all, it is *your* home!"

Angelina hesitated. The implications of doing what he commanded were extraordinary. The simple act of filling his glass would confirm his victory over her. She was afraid of him, of being within his grasp, but conceding to be his eternal slave terrified her.

"My Little Dove, come. Come, pour me some wine." Don Salvatore begged, but his eyes demanded her to obey. When she hesitated, he growled. "Do not test my temper... *again*!"

Angelina willed her body to move, to accept her fate. He had proven his power was far greater than hers. She lost the battle. She had no other choice than to comply with his commands. With a nod, The Don smiled and offered a toast.

Dejected, she joined him.

Satisfied the strings sewn into his prize puppet were working correctly, The Don turned his attention to Fernando.

"What is your name, boy?"

"Fernando," he mumbled.

"Boy, I am old. Speak up! What is your name?"

"Fernando," he replied a little louder.

"A good name. Who are you to this family?"

"He is my son," Carlos interjected.

The Don glared. "The boy has his own tongue. Let him speak for himself!"

A whipped mutt, Carlos bowed and stepped backward.

"I...work for the...Beretta family, Signore."

"What *did* you do for them?"

"We delivered wine."

"We? We? Do you have a mouse in your pocket?"

Fernando raised his head and spoke as if he possessed his brothers' confidence as well.

"Anton, Ricardo, and I delivered the wine."

"Ahh! So you were friends?" The Don nodded with compassion. "Do you miss them?"

"Si."

"I imagine you would. Losing a loved one is difficult.

Don Salvatore drained his glass and held it up. Angelina obeyed his silent command. A devilish grin pressed his cheek as he reveled in his victory.

"You gave a lovely eulogy today. Very touching, indeed. It brought a tear to my eye. Did it make you cry, Carlos?"

Carlos nodded.

"What about you, Angelina?" Don Salvatore asked rhetorically. "Ahh, no. You didn't cry, did you, My Little Dove? No, you were too busy looking at me. Though I am flattered, this young man deserves your attention far more!" The Don took a swig of wine. "It seems, Fernando, that Angelina needs a champion, someone who will exact revenge for the deaths of her family. I, being an old man, am feeble and tired. I no longer have the..." Don Salvatore's hands gesticulated, struggling to find his words.

"Balls?" Fernando blurted out.

"Hahaha! No, my boy. I have been told mine are a sizeable pair. No, I don't have the desire nor gumption to achieve such lofty goals for such a beautiful dove. No, my abilities would be better suited in business." Don Salvatore emptied his glass and held it out for Angelina to refill. "And perhaps arrange a good marriage for this lovely dove."

Don Salvatore enjoyed a few more sips of his wine before continuing his manipulation game.

"You, my boy, are young and have the *balls,* as you say. Perhaps *you* would be willing to find the person who committed this heinous act."

Fernando swallowed hard and leveled his shoulders, ready for the next verbal punch.

"Tell me, Fernando, would you kill the man who murdered your friends?" Don Salvatore asked.

The Don had spun a trap, and Angelina had foolishly aided him by luring him inside. He would never heartlessly wield his power in public. He had men to do his dirty work. Behind doors, however, The Don was free to torture anyone without losing the stigma of being the generous man who throws lavish parties and cares for the sick and the poor.

Silently, Angelina screamed, say no, please say no. If Fernando admitted his hatred and vengeance, it would only add to The Don's growing list of reasons to kill him.

"No, Signore. It is not for me to exact revenge," Fernando replied with conviction.

"No. Hmm. You would not avenge your friends? I find that hard to believe. I thought you were close. Brothers, I believe you said in your touching eulogy. What has happened in four hours that makes you abandon the ones you love?"

Angelina watched in horror as Don Salvatore's chubby hand bounced the strings of his puppet, Fernando.

"Signore, I cleaned up the mess that was there under your feet. The smell of the slimy blood made me vomit. So I say no, Signor Salvatore, because I could not stomach creating such a depressing scene. It is not in me to take the soul of a man. Even if I hated them, I could not make him bleed and cry in pain." Fernando looked at Angelina. "I am sorry, Lina, but I cannot be someone I am not."

Tears streamed down her cheeks. "I am not asking you to."

"Ah, now, isn't that sweet!" Don Salvatore chuckled. "Carlos, I think we have two young lovers in our midst."

"We are only friends," Angelina stated harshly.

Seeing Fernando stagger, she knew her words had shredded his heart. She wished she could tell him how it pained her as well, but would he believe her? Could he believe her? She sighed. Everything felt pointless.

The Don waggled his empty cup. Obediently, Angelina refilled his glass and then her own.

"This is an excellent wine!" He smacked his lips.

"I am glad you like it."

"To new beginnings!" Don Salvatore toasted.

Her spirit broken, Angelina drained her glass, too.

CHAPTER 45

"Good wine needs good food. Si?" The Don suggested.

"Si, I am sure many guests are waiting," Angelina agreed.

Carlos opened the door for Angelina. Though she saw his apologetic eyes, she kept her gaze forward. To express love or compassion for anyone placed a mark on their head. Out of fear, she shoved her feelings into a concrete vault.

On their way to the tent, Angelina noticed Catalina's empty parking spot. On the long list of mistakes, sending her sister to oversee The Don's visit was stamped with a big, red *wrong*. The Don was right; Angelina had much to learn, and his tutelage began today. The first lesson was not to underestimate a man's power and the inherent weakness of being a woman. A complete contradiction to her father and mother's guidance.

Don Salvatore was the son of a Don, but his legacy did not start with his father. The money and title of Don were handed down from father to son for five generations. This man was raised by a Don to be a Don. Like a blacksmith teaches his heir the art of shaping metal, the Salvatore family taught the art of manipulating people.

As a child, Angelina heard the lore of brutality. The myths and legends about the Salvatore family were as vast as the grapes on a thousand vines. But Angelina also witnessed this man's sincere generosity. Years of fostering love and fear created a town full of mindful servants devoted to one family. Now, Angelina knew the stories were real. His public displays of compassion were the marionette's strings effortlessly sewn into the people of Brusnengo.

The Don's right hand slid to the small of Angelina's back. She shuddered.

"She will be here soon, My Little Dove." Don Salvatore gave her an assuring patt. "Don't worry, I won't hurt her *if* you are a good girl."

Acting as a compassionate man, Don Salvatore smiled lovingly at Angelina. Outwardly for others to hear, he sang words of respect for her family. He appeared as the caring shepherd for an abandoned sheep. But his right hand at the base of her spine was the unspoken words of dominance.

After a brief stint of congeniality, Don Salvatore shifted back to his quietly spoken brutality.

"Now, let us conclude our business."

Angelina tensed. "I have guests to attend."

"You do. But in order of importance!" He adjusted his suit coat with his left hand while his right communicated who was most important, *Me*. "Now, My Little Dove, I am not a cruel man. I will not subject you to certain things on such a somber day." His hand bounced playfully on her firm butt. "Those deeds can be dealt with later. Tomorrow, maybe. But we shall see. Personally, I enjoy a good chase. I find it to be the most exhilarating part of the hunt. The element of surprise adds a certain... Hmm...thrill to the kill. You may not know it yet, but I have been known to stalk my prey for years, planting traps along the way just to spice it up a bit. Recently, I set my longest record. Nearly thirty years!" Don Salvatore's grin widened.

Two guests walked by and smiled their condolences to Angelina. If they only knew the truth, their heartfelt sympathies would not be for losing her brothers.

"A sad occasion, but like her father, she bares it well, no?" Don Salvatore proclaimed to the sympathizers.

"Si, Signore Salvatore," the guest replied in unison.

The band struck up a loud, lively song, and The Don shifted his tone to a deep growl.

"You and your sister will ensure the wine continues with production as usual. No outward changes will be made. We do not need to make this a public affair. *Yet!*"

He smiled at another guest who walked close by. Once out of earshot, Don Salvatore continued.

"Giorgio and I will oversee the payment for all deliveries. Your boy Fernando and his family can stay on the payroll *if* they earn their way. No free rides! I run a tight ship. And, of course, we shall also ensure you and Catalina are cared for. Do keep in mind the nicer you are, the nicer you will be provided for. Your sister understands this concept well. I am sure she will happily teach you what *nicer* means."

He paused for his message to sink in. Angelina swallowed hard, and he grinned with satisfaction.

"You will have your duties *to me* for now. Consider yourself lucky. You have piqued my interest and my cock. Do feel pleased, My Little Dove. Only one other woman has ever stirred my hunger like you."

He allowed the music to fill the air for a moment while he savored the memory of a conquest from days gone by.

Surprised, Angelina asked, "Who was she?"

Her voice pulled him back from his pleasant stroll through the past, and his tender smile vanished.

"My nephew has eyes for you, but you know that already. So, as a reward for your good behavior, I will keep his grubby hands off you. If you keep me happy, that is. If you can't..." The Don's hand waved away the concept of protection. "My nephew will enjoy you as he wishes."

Numbness was her refuge, but the unexpected movement made Angelina flinch and return to reality. The Don laughed. Pretending she asked a question. He nodded and glanced at her, amused. His act was merely a ruse for onlookers.

"Hmm." The Don fabricated a question to answer. "What excites me more, taming you or plucking your flower? A good question, My Little Dove. There is something about taking a young woman's virtue. I have had many. Ah! But that is rude of me. There is no room for the green-eyed monster in our relationship!" He chuckled and patted her butt again. "Nonetheless, I will enjoy both equally. Perhaps we can name our first child after your father or maybe...a brother?"

Angelina ground her jaw, and her lip twitched with the desire to strangle at him. But an outward display of rejection would earn her a heaping dose of his cruelty.

"You are right, My Little Dove. We *must* stick with tradition, or such rules shall fade from our children's memories. I wholeheartedly agree. If it is a boy, we will name him after me. You can pick the name of our second child! After all, our relationship will be one of give and take. You will give, or *I will take!*"

He motioned to a server carrying a tray of wine. With a slight bow, the young man presented the tray.

"Thank you, young man. I have been chatting away, and my tongue desperately needs a delightful libation." Don Salvatore plucked two glasses from the tray.

After handing Angelina her glass, he raised his for a toast. Had she the courage, she would have thrown the wine in his face, smashed the glass over his head, and stabbed his gut with the jagged edge.

"To a lovely party. I believe it is the best I have been to in years. Well, aside from your sister's wedding, of course. But she planned that event as well. Do remind me to compliment her on the lovely job. I believe it is important to foster the skills of women; it keeps them... well... happy."

At the base of her spine, The Don's hand tightly gripped her dress. A nonverbal noose intended to imply he held her life *and death* in his hands.

"Now, let's see, anything I left out?" He paused while the sting from his ominous blow sizzled.

In his silence, the soul-crushing sound of Angelina's dreams imploding into a pile of rubble echoed in her ears. Don Salvatore squelched her dreams of traveling. Under his rule, she could not fill her father's shoes at the vineyard, either. But most devastating of all, she would never experience the joy of falling in love. All life's desires dissolved like a snowflake floating too close to a flame. Her brothers' deaths were part of The Don's strategic plan. *Why* no longer mattered. He deliberately removed her brothers and her father, her only natural barriers of protection. Now, Angelina would forever be at the mercy of a man's fierce desire.

"Oh, one last thing. You *will* tell me where your parents are convalescing."

Why was the only word that formed, but it was firmly lodged in her throat. The answer was terrifying. The Don had to finish what he started, not just out of revenge. Giorgio could not formally own the vineyard as long as Rosario still drew breath.

She looked into her glass of wine and sighed. Her crimson reflection only added to her distress.

Now what? Angelina thought.

No one could help her. Even though she was surrounded by hundreds of people, Angelina was alone. Every guest was either afraid of or adored the man standing beside her. Angelina was disgusted with herself and her new future. Internally, she released a ferocious growl, then downed her wine.

If I have to stay shackled to this man for eternity, then I will do it drunk! Angelina thought as she waved for the waiter to bring her more wine. *I shall start now. I will drink enough to erase the memory of this dreadful day!*

The waiter delivered the glasses and departed quickly.

Angelina huffed, even he was afraid to be close to the devil.

"Where are your parents, My Little Dove?"

"It was a lovely funeral," Angelina said dryly.

He glared at her for the insolent response. She did not care if it angered him.

"Don't test my patience!"

"I am not. I merely stated a fact."

"Si, it was a nice funeral."

"A lovely party, too," Angelina added calmly.

"It is." Don Salvatore's jaw tightened.

Even before Angelina's eyes could see his face flushing red, the heat from his rage radiated with the fury of an untamed fire. Instinct told her to stop provoking him, but she no longer cared about her life. At this point, death by his hands would be the better alternative.

"Do you prefer red or white?"

"Both," Don Salvatore huffed. "You try my patience, cunt!"

"It is not my intention. The guests are becoming nervous. Many of them have been staring at us for some time now," Angelina explained.

Angelina looked at the red liquid in her glass and mumbled the name and year before exhaling a soft huff. She fought back the tears, begging to be freed. With a gulp of wine, she washed them down, along with the memories of making the wine.

"You said to keep things looking normal on the outside. I am merely doing as told," Angelina stated.

Appraising the guests' mood, The Don chuckled; Angelina was right.

"You are very clever."

"Not as clever as you, Signor Salvatore."

Across the room, Angelina's friend Maria sat nervously at a table with Carmella. Angelina refused to let her gaze sit long on anyone, especially people she loved. Protecting Maria and Carmella, Angelina looked at another family two tables over.

"Who is that family?" The Don nodded toward the table Angelina's eyes landed on.

"I do not know, to be honest. Many of these faces I do not recognize," Angelina replied truthfully.

Some guests were friends of Angelina's brothers from school. A few dozen were local business owners Angelina had met once or twice over the years. However, most of the faces were total strangers, and Angelina wondered how Catalina knew to invite them.

"Sorry I am late," a sweet voice whispered.

"Cat!" Angelina cried and tightly embraced her sister. Before breaking the hug, she asked, "Cat, are *you* all right?"

"I think so," Catalina replied quietly.

"He knows," Angelina whispered.

"He can't know? Giorgio slept the whole time he was there. They never spoke!"

Angelina felt lightheaded. Once again, the master of deception played her.

"How is my nephew?" Don Salvatore interrupted their embrace.

"He is resting. I rang the doctor as you suggested. The drowsiness is part of the concussion. All we can do is wake him every two hours. Constance will take good care of him in my absence," Catalina gently patted The Don's arm. "You worry too much, Don Salvatore. Giorgio is strong and will be back at your side soon enough."

Angelina waived for more wine. As before, the young man bowed his head slightly and scurried away as soon as the glasses were removed.

"Now, if you don't mind, I believe we should thank our guests for coming," Catalina said as she wrapped her arm through Angelina's.

"Of course!" Don Salvatore replied with a slight bow. "It is a lovely party, Catalina. I shall call on you the next time I wish to have a celebration. Be ready; it could be sooner than one might expect!"

With a devilish grin, Don Salvatore raised his glass to Angelina. It was not a toast but a reminder of his plan.

"It would be my honor to assist you, Don Salvatore," Catalina smiled. "And thank you for coming."

Adjusting her collar, Angelina's lungs drew in the precious oxygen she desperately needed. Grateful to be free, Angelina hugged Catalina's arm.

"He is awful! The vilest creature to breathe air." Angelina sighed as they made their way to the first table. "Thank you!"

"It is not over yet. Let's hope he leaves soon."

Angelina, suppressing her nausea, nodded.

Burning a hole into her back, Angelina felt The Don's fiery glare watching her every move. No wish or magic spell could remove his eyes, so Angelina accepted the fact her every step would forever be recorded by her new master.

"Keep close. We should remain together," Catalina said.

They spent the next three hours making their way around the tent, stopping at every table. Guests gushed with praise for the moving celebration, gratitude for the generosity, and the unmatched Beretta hospitality.

The sisters remained side by side and extended heartfelt thanks on behalf of their parents and the lost souls. Catalina, once again, performed the speeches of gratitude with eloquence. Angelina, however, still ill from her encounter with Don Salvatore, could only muster two meaningless words. "Thank you."

"He is gone," Fernando said when they reached his table.

"Are you sure?" Angelina asked, her tone and expression revealed far more terror than she desired.

"Si," Fernando replied. He looked into her eyes. "I am sorry, Lina."

Angelina shook her head and caressed his hair.

"Nan, you did..." Angelina stammered but couldn't finish. She bowed her head for a moment to hide her tears.

Fernando stood and pulled a chair out for Angelina.

"Not yet, Nan. We have one more table, then we can sit," Catalina said, grabbing Angelina's hand. "Come on, I am exhausted too, but we must."

Drained of all energy, the sisters walked arm in arm toward the last table. As they approached, the three men abruptly ended their conversation and stood to greet them.

"This is a sad string of events. On behalf of my boss and his family, I bring his sincerest condolences," the man said as he removed his hat and bowed slightly.

Angelina and Catalina exchanged inquisitive looks.

"May I express my personal condolences?" The man asked with his hand extended.

Entranced by his regal manners, Angelina accepted. Suavely, the man wrapped his hands around hers and placed a small, gentle kiss on the back of Angelina's hand.

"My employer asked me to deliver this to *you*, Signorina."

Her exhaustion was too great; Angelina missed the small missive between their hands. Her smile of gratitude was laced with surprise and confusion. She had never met someone with such regal professionalism.

"My employer grieves heavily for your loss and is greatly concerned on your behalf. If there is anything we can do for you, I am a phone call away. My number is listed on my card."

"Who is your employer?" Angelina asked.

"It was a moving funeral and a beautiful reception. We are honored to have shared this sacred day with you," the man extended his condolences to Catalina.

"Which family did you say?" Angelina pressed.

"That is not a question I can answer," the man whispered, his eyes scanning the entire area.

"Has he done business with my Father before?"

"My boss would be happy to discuss this with you personally. However, he is not located around here."

The sisters stared, not understanding the man's meaning.

He leaned in closer, still keeping his voice low, and said, "Please know you have friends out of the reach of local men."

Angelina looked at the note. Though eager to ask a million questions, the man's nonverbal cues said he could not reveal any further information.

"We thank you for your troubles," Angelina replied graciously. "Please come by anytime. You will always be an honored guest in my father's house."

"Meaning no disrespect, the man who kept you chained to his side most of the evening—"

"He has left," Angelina interrupted him.

"*He* has. But his men *haven't*."

"What?" Catalina gasped. "How do you know?"

"It is my job, Signora Giovannese."

Angelina barely registered the exchange the man had with her sister. Her mind was frozen by the notion Don Salvatore would have her watched.

"Signorina Beretta, *you* are in great danger. Your sister is protected, to a degree, because of her marriage," The man warned. "Do not misunderstand me, Signora Giovannese. If you do as you are told, you should be safe... at least for now."

Gallantly, he bent down and kissed their hands again. Donning his hat, the man straightened his tie and coat before uttering one last message to Angelina.

"Signorina, I beg you to read the note where the walls have no eyes."

CHAPTER 46

"Thank God this day is over!" Catalina said, slumping onto the rod-iron bench.

Angelina collapsed next to her sister, echoing her exhaustion. They gazèd at the night sky, listening to the cricket's mournful melody and the leaves fluttering in the breeze. In the distance, a rumble of thunder trumpeting the approaching storm echoed across the rolling hills. The ominous boom made the sisters shiver and unconsciously huddle closer together.

"Thank God. Today was exhausting," Angelina agreed, staring at her childhood home.

All the love and nurturing from their parents became overshadowed by death. A heavy shroud of sorrow lingered over the house, making it uncomfortable.

Angelina and Catalina watched Carlos and Carmella move into the house. It was a unanimous decision for them to live with Angelina. A loving family dwelling within would prevent the house from being a tomb.

"It is nice to know they will be here with you."

"Thank you for thinking of it."

Angelina gave her sister a grateful smile, then fell back into her thoughts. Her primary concern was finding a way out of The Don's prison. After numerous mental gymnastics on the subject, she only concluded two options. However, both were merely bandaids on a severed limb. By staying, she was accepting the role of being The Don's play toy. Though

Fernando's proposal was still an option, marrying him would increase Don Salvatore's motivation to kill him. A pit formed in Angelina's gut. She wouldn't be able to overcome Fernando's death, especially at the hands of the devil.

"What happens next?" Angelina sighed, tired of the mental turmoil.

"Do we really have any options? This is a man's world; we were made to suffer at their hands."

"Who brainwashed you to think that defeated thought?" Angelina popped up. "We will *not* be governed by anyone!"

"I wish I were as strong as you," Catalina said, weeping.

"You are! Look what you accomplished this week by yourself! I know you are exhausted. All that has happened has been overwhelming, but we must stay strong. We must choose our next step *together*."

"*I* don't have a choice."

"*We* have a choice!" Angelina argued. "We can leave! It is the only way to survive!"

"I will not leave Mamma and Papa!" Catalina glared.

"They are safe for now. When we return—"

"How long would we be gone, Lina? Until The Don dies? What about the vineyard? Are you willing to let go of everything Papa and Mamma built?"

"What about *our* lives?" Angelina asked. "Mamma and Papa wouldn't want us to suffer at the hands of tyrants!"

"You surprise me! Of all of us, I thought *you* would never let go of this land! Beretta Vineyards is their essence in life and death. It *is* and always will be Mamma and Papa's legacy!"

Catalina was right; the vineyard and their parents should be the priority. However, fear of The Don's dominance overwhelmed Angelina's common sense.

"I am more afraid of leaving than staying, Lina."

"How can you say that after all that has happened?"

"Because I am not ready to die!"

"Then we will kill him first!" Angelina pounded her thighs.

"Dammit! No more death!" Catalina erupted in rage. "Stop it! Stop this compulsive desire to commit murder! I cannot stomach any more of it. Please, for your sanity and mine!"

"I didn't start this war!"

Exhausted, Catalina crumbled into a heap, sobbing.

"That night, the night... Giorgio... I wanted to kill him. Part of me wished he would have died in the fall." Catalina admitted between sniffles.

"Why didn't you kill him. You had every right?"

"Because the stain of blood on my hands would haunt me. I would never be free of that sin."

"You would not have committed a sin, Cat. You would have served justice for our family!" Angelina's temper rose. "An eye for an eye! He deserves to die!"

"It is still murder!" Catalina wiped away her tears. "Angelina, knowing how strongly I wished for his death, haunts me. I will confess my sin and repent. I never want to know this feeling of self-disgust again." Catalina held up her hand to stop Angelina from arguing. "I am not you...I am not strong like you!

I am also not the first woman to be married to a man who is like Giorgio. I am confident in that fact!" She gently embraced Angelina's hand. "I love you, Lina. But my path is clear, as soul-crushing as it may be. God will protect me as long as I remain a dutiful wife. I must turn the other cheek, forgive myself for my sins, and do the same for Giorgio. It is the only way to continue the legacy of Beretta Vineyards."

"You can't be serious, Catalina!" Angelina retracted her hands. "There must be another way we can save the family legacy and not be subjected to torture! I can not... will not subject myself to the whims of a predator!" She began to pace, her mind churning through possibilities. "What about the man who gave us the note? Perhaps he will help us, or maybe his boss?"

"They are men, the same as Giorgio and Don Salvatore. Besides, what good is he to us right now? He is not in Brusnengo." Catalina stood to face her sister. "Lina, I do not wish to fight with Giorgio, his uncle, or you. At least with Giorgio, I have learned how to manage him. Plus, he needs me to help run the vineyard. He has no clue what he is doing. As long as I have value to him, he will be nice to me. Do what you must, Angelina. I will stay here and continue our family's legacy as best I can. Constance and I will protect each other."

The finality in her tone and abrupt retreat shocked Angelina.

"Cat, wait! *Wait, please!*"

Catalina did not turn around. Her shoulders slumped, she walked to the kitchen door. She had conceded her fate, and no one could save her.

"Carlos, would you or Nan take me home, please," Catalina asked from the doorstep.

"Nan, bring Cat's car around," Carlos hollered into the house.

Watching her defeated sister stare through the open door into the kitchen made Angelina cry. Once again, the void between them expanded.

Carlos kissed Catalina good night and helped her into the car. After the plume of dust settled, he joined Angelina under the tree and waited patiently while she wept. When her sobs dissipated, Carlos did as Rosario would want; he helped her see the truth of nature.

"I imagine you are wondering why The Don has struck such a heavy blow to your family?"

Angelina, drying her face, nodded.

"This land has been desired by the Salvatore family since before your oldest brother was born. Its position to the sun and rich soil make it perfect for growing big, hardy grapes.

Some say it is a 'golden land,' but they know nothing of making wine." Carlos explained. "Your father has refused Don Salvatore's propositions many times over the years. Though some believe the tension between the two came from your father's refusals, it is not where the feud began."

Angelina sat up and listened to a story she never heard.

"It started over the death of Don Salvatore's brother, Victor. The Salvatores grieved not only for losing their oldest son but also for losing this property and the money that came with your mother's hand. To the Salvatore family, this vineyard should be part of their fortune." Carlos shook his head and sighed. "They fail to acknowledge that the land was abandoned for over two decades before your parents owned it. Rosario and Sofia spent many years and a lot of work to make it a *golden* land. It takes more than good soil to make good wine."

Angelina smiled. "Papa said that all the time."

"Si, he did." Carlos's face relaxed for a moment; the fond memory of Rosario obviously consumed his thoughts. But the flash faded quickly. Carlos sighed. "In Don Salvatore's mind, your father murdered his brother, but this is not true. Rosario is innocent, and it can be proven."

"How?" Angelina asked.

He ran his hand through his graying locks.

"Those are old ghosts, Lina."

Carlos bowed his head for a few minutes, wrestling the ghosts back into a box. The pain of the past tucked away, he met Angelina's gaze.

"The truth you need to know is your father would never commit murder, even for love. It is not in his nature. Angelina, I tell you this so you can understand your sister is not capable of murder either."

"But..."

Carlos waved off her rebuttal.

"I heard your conversation with her before she left. You

expect too much of her. She is not you, and you are not her."

"She will not be safe living with him!"

"He needs Catalina, so he will spend many months making this up to her. She will have a season or two of happiness. It is hard to comprehend, but even after all that has happened, part of her still loves him."

"She can't, not after *everything* he has done!"

"Catalina married her true love, and you have never known love... *true* love. I know you love my son, but you are not *in* love with him. There is a difference."

"Giorgio does not love Cat. She is not *his* true love!"

"Perhaps she is, but that is not for you to judge. Love can change a man; it changed me," Carlos replied. "Don't worry too much about your sister. She may seem weak to you, but one day, she will discover her strengths. And I promise to do my best to help whenever I can."

"Am I supposed to stay here? Become a mistress to the Don and aid him in his glorious victory over my family?"

"I did not say that."

"Then what? What am I to do? Become Don Salvatore's true love?"

"What are your options?" Carlos asked, ignoring her questions.

His soothing tone reminded Angelina of her father. Calmer, she approached her situation more rationally.

"Don Salvatore is far more astute in the art of manipulation that he made clear. Even if I accepted my fate as his..." Angelina gagged on the thought. "His bride, I risk becoming disposable."

"Or?"

"I join the convent?"

Carlos chuckled. "You are *no* Nun!"

"Don't laugh! I could be a nun," Angelina tried to suppress her smile, but Carlos's laughter was contagious. "Fine! You are right. I am too strong-willed to be a nun."

"Among *many* other traits." Carlos smiled. He pointed to the note Angelina unconsciously flipped between her fingers. "Have you thought of allowing him to help?"

"What do you know about him?"

"More than I should and surely enough to get me killed."

"Did my father have dealings with him?"

Carlos stretched his neck and loosened his constricting tie. With a sigh, he nodded.

"Does anyone else know?"

"It is possible The Don's attack was provoked when his spies told him."

"Then why didn't he kill all of us?"

"Because he believes women are easy to control. He will use you in more than one way, as you have discovered." Carlos cautioned. "Don Salvatore is a clever man, but he has no clue how to make the quality of wine we make here. To that point, your sister is correct; she will be safe. You, though... are headstrong." Carlos ran his hands through his hair. His next words would be difficult to say. "Though it is an attractive attribute, a man like Don Salvatore could quickly tire of the challenge of taming you. When that happens, he will dispose of you."

Holding her hand, Carlos looked Angelina in the eyes. "Your father had big dreams for you. He believed in your abilities. And yes, he favored you more than any of his children. Rosario would look to you and only you to save his legacy, for that I am certain!"

"Save it how?"

"That is for you to choose. I cannot tell you what to do with your life. You are at a crossroads and have little time to decide your direction. Whatever you choose, keep your plans to yourself. Tell no one, not even Cat or Nan."

Angelina looked down at the note. She drew the crease

through her fingers several times as she contemplated her next step.

"I don't know what to do?" Angelina admitted. "What would Papa want me to do?"

"Your father was... is a wise man. But, even for this, I doubt Rosario would know what is best."

Angelina swallowed her sadness and nodded.

"If you choose to leave, know The Don will not let you go easily. My worst fear is he will send his devil, Antonio, after you. He is a wicked man, evil to the core. They say he enjoys watching his victims die by burning them alive."

"A young woman at the convent told me about him. She had taken refuge with the nuns because Antonio burned her husband alive in his cobbler shop." Angelina shuttered at the thought. "She has been in hiding ever since."

"I remember Roberto. He was a good man. May he rest in peace." Carlos bowed his head and said a brief prayer for the lost soul before continuing. "One way or another, Lina, you will meet this man someday. Never be alone with him, and always remember he is the devil in the flesh."

"Is there no way to avoid him and the wrath of The Don?"

"Angelina, I cannot protect you. I am sorry. I am only as valuable as the knowledge I have to make Beretta wine. Maybe he can." Carlos pointed at the letter.

"What about the rest of you? Who will protect you?"

"We will stay here and do as we have always done, work for your mother and father," Carlos professed, lovingly squeezing her hand. "Know our loyalty is and will forever be with you and your family!"

"I thank you for that. It means more to me than you could ever know. Especially after all I have seen this week."

"Never speak of what you saw. That alone will place a price on your head."

In silence, Angelina contemplated her options; though they

were few, she had to choose. If she ran, it would be a complete leap of faith. One of her strongest qualities was never running from a challenge.

Being a subservient woman is not a quality I wish to acquire. She thought.

"Carlos, tell me—"

He placed his hand on hers. Angelina followed his gaze to the vines, but the darkness made shadows out of nothing.

"What is it?"

"We are being watched!" He whispered. "Unfortunately, we must get used to a pair of eyes observing our every move."

Carlos's hand urged her to stay put as the shadow moved deeper into the sea of darkness.

"Let's go inside. Mother nature is trying to tuck us into bed." Angelina pointed to the large raindrops sporadically crashing around them.

At the door, Carlos enveloped her in a fatherly embrace.

"Carmella does not know everything about your father's history with Don Salvatore. Keep what I told you and that note a secret."

"I will take that under advisement," Angelina replied with a grateful smile. "Thank you for filling in for my father. I hope you will not hesitate if you have any other insights."

"If you choose to leave, under your father's night table is a box. In it is everything you will need for your journey," Carlos whispered into her ear as he hugged her goodnight. He released her and spoke in a normal tone. "I will be here if you need anything."

"Thank you, Carlos... for *everything!*"

CHAPTER 47

"Don Salvatore, a man is demanding to see you," Antonio said, bowing his head.

Humming an Old Italian tune, Don Salvatore was enjoying his wistful daydream while meandering around his garden. He glanced toward Antonio but remained in his mental paradise, humming his song. Visions of his new prey floated through his thoughts, and he had no room for any of Antonio's nonsense. The Don had more pressing issues, like his Little Dove's supple breasts, tight ass, and long legs. Turning his back to Antonio, Don Salvatore continued his stroll along the path, gently touching every leaf within reach.

"Do you like red or white?" Don Salvatore asked a pigeon in search of food.

The pigeon cocked its head to examine the towering giant.

"She is a vixen, and I will enjoy taming her!" Don Salvatore explained to his inquisitive feathered friend. "An angelic voice and a venomous tongue...and her curves!"

He swooshed his hands to convey the pleasing appearance of Angelina's body. The grey creature hopped back twice before resuming its one-eyed observation.

"But my friend, I tell you, it is her fiery spirit that ignites my desires." The Don glanced down at the bobbing head of his friend as it clucked. "Ah! True. The full force of my ferocity might squelch her arousing temper. Tame her and keep her fiery side burning like wildfire. It may be challenging, but that only adds to the excitement, no? Si. Si. I will enjoy her resistance, mentally and physically!"

"Signore?" Antonio asked again.

"What? Dammit! Can you not see I am busy?" The Don said, his booming voice echoing about the serene space.

"There is a man here. He says he has valuable information for you!"

"Damn it, Antonio, what do I pay you for? See him gone! I wish to be alone with my thoughts!"

Antonio knew such a dismissal was followed by a delayed order. He stood motionless for a moment longer.

"Begone, *now*! I wish to speak to no one!" Don Salvatore gave a dismissive wave. "And while you earn your pay, have someone bring me more wine... and my dinner!"

"Si, Don Salvatore."

"You are hungry too?" The Don asked, returning his attention to the bird. "How delightful! We will eat together. What do you say?"

The pigeon cooed with his head tilted for its left eye to examine The Don.

"No, no." Don Salvatore replied to the pigeon. "He is aggravating but still useful. So, I will keep him until I choose what day he is to die."

****

Closing the doors, Antonio heard the tap-tap of small feet walking down the adjoining hallway. Confident it was the new maid, he sprinted to intercept her.

The Don's constant irritation and Giorgio's instant ascension inflamed Antonio's temper. However, losing the cobbler's wife significantly affected his demotion. The timing of Giorgio's surprise appearance only made the situation worse. The wayward nephew slipped into Antonio's role. Now, he and Bruno were the 'old dogs' rarely used. The culmination of irritants and his idle hands brewed a bitter stout. He needed a place to blow off his steam. The maid's timely appearance made her his next victim.

"You! Come here!"

"Si, Signore," the maid replied.

The light illuminated the maid's pretty face and shapely form. Antonio grinned, she was a perfect distraction for his idle hands.

"You are new?"

Keeping her eyes down, the maid nodded.

"What is your name?"

"I am Isabella, Signore."

"What a beautiful name for a beautiful lady."

"Thank you, Signore," she replied, peeking through her long eyelashes.

"Bella, Isabella." Antonio grinned. "Don Salvatore requested some wine and food. Be a darling and fix him something nice. He has had a long day."

The maid nodded.

"I expect he will desire a hot bath after his meal."

Isabella curtsied. "I will see to it right away."

She dutifully waited for Antonio to dismiss her, but he said nothing. He gently lifted her chin and smiled. The maid's cheeks flushed bright red under his silent gaze.

"Is there anything else you wish of me, Signore?"

"Perhaps..." His smile shifted to a lecherous grin. "*Later.*"

He slowly pulled her closer until she was inches away from his face. He allowed his gaze to dance between her supple lips and twinkling dark eyes. The slow, sensual breathing intensified the sexual tension between them.

"Bella, Bella," Antonio whispered.

He leaned in closer, their lips nearly touching. He savored the moment; the anticipation of the kiss was arousing. Without cause, he abruptly dropped Isabella's chin and walked away, chuckling inside. He did not glance back at the maid. He, too, had a new prey.

"Signore, The Don is taking no more visitors this evening. Give me your message, and I will pass it along."

The messenger was too winded to respond, forcing Antonio to wait for a reply.

"He told me... to deliver this information... only to him."

"Well, perhaps you should return at a more convenient hour. It is well past dark and too late for guests!"

"No, wait! It is important! I ran through the rain as fast as I could." The man visibly trembled in his wet, ratty clothes.

"I can see. You are making a puddle on The Don's floor! Would you like to dry yourself by the fire and have a cup of hot tea?"

The compassionate offer brightened the man's countenance, and he accepted with an eager nod. The man took two steps forward, excited for a warmer setting, but Antonio did not move. The offer was made to mock him. Understanding his foolishness, the man dropped his chin.

"I..." The man mumbled and fidgeted nervously. "I hesitate because."

"Ol' man, you are not the first to cross over the road of piety to aid The Don, and you are certainly not the first to expect to be paid for your time." Antonio heckled the man. "Tell me, who pays Don Salvatore for *his* wasted time and assistance?"

"I mean no disrespect. I'm following orders from The Don's lips!"

"I see. Well, as I said, it is late. You can either tell me or return when the news is no longer relevant!"

The messenger gripped his hat and shifted his weight from foot to foot.

"Ah! The cat still has your tongue." Antonio sighed and lit a cigarette. "It is an honorable trait to keep secrets."

The compliment sparked a smile from the man, but his

exuberance was met with an arched brow.

"Tell me, what if this important news you carry for The Don never reaches his ears? Hmm? It is late. Dangerous things happen in the dark of night, especially on a long walk home in the rain."

Antonio slipped his half-empty cigarette package into his chest pocket, deliberately exposing the gun strapped to his side. He puffed on his cigarette and released several smoke rings into the man's face.

"Oh, excuse me! How rude. Would you like a smoke?"

"No... no, thank you."

"Ah, good for you, these things will kill you! Well, maybe not a fearless man like you! You wear the muddy shoes of someone unshaken by the dangers of walking at night. And you have a tightly latched mouth." Antonio nodded in respect before exhaling a cloud of smoke into the man's face.

Being beaten down by life and the lack of material things were only two reasons men like this one became the prey of the powerful. The desperation for money was, by far, the musk that attracted the predator. A pittance for the rich was the fruit of survival for the poor. The stench of lack made batting a poor man in tattered clothing amusing for the thug of a wealthy man.

"You are The Don's right hand?" the man asked timidly.

"That is correct."

"If I tell you, you will tell no one but The Don?"

"Of course! From your lips to my ears and my lips to The Don's." Antonio added a reassuring smile to sweeten the bait.

"Don Salvatore..." The man fervently gripped his hat, his eyes bouncing around the room. "He...promised me money for the information."

"How much money?"

Increasing the speed at which he shifted his weight from one foot to the other, the man licked his lips, and his beady eyes darted back and forth.

"He... He did not say... exactly." The man glanced up at Antonio and immediately averted his gaze. "He said... He said he would pay me well for my troubles."

"Ah! Now, we are getting somewhere." Antonio removed a large wad of bills from his pant pocket. "I will gladly pay the debt."

The messenger's eyes widened at the large sum of money. Antonio, aware of the man's awe, took his time. After all, it was the largest sum of money the man would ever see. Antonio, a cigarette hanging from the corner of his grin, peeled off several bills.

The man blurted out. "She knows..."

Pausing his count, Antonio glanced at the wide-eyed man.

"Tell Don Salvatore she knows..." The man swallowed hard. "She knows who killed them."

Antonio nodded his sincere appreciation. He added five more bills to the payment and stuffed the thick stack of money into the man's wet shirt pocket.

"Did she say the names?"

"No."

"Your services to The Don are appreciated." Antonio patted the messenger's shoulder. "Bruno?"

Ten seconds later, the thud-thud of Bruno's feet approached the circular foyer.

"Bruno, this man is The Don's new informant. Take him home. Keep him safe. We don't want such a valuable asset to have an unfortunate accident walking home in the dark."

With a grunt, Bruno nodded.

"Rest peacefully knowing your message will be delivered to The Don *immediately!*" Antonio patted the man's shoulder again.

"Thank you, Signore. Thank you!"

Ready for his playtime, Antonio quickly forgot the

messenger and looked for Isabella. Turning the corner, a mischievous smile curled across Antonio's face.

"Perfect timing," Antonio mumbled as the maid backed out of The Don's room.

"Oh! Excuse me, Signore, I did not see you there!"

"As I intended. How is the Don?"

"He is well. I am going to draw his bath now."

"Very good." Antonio turned the door handle.

"Anything else, Signore?"

He allowed his devious smile to melt away before glancing back at the maid.

"Si. Draw a bath for me."

The maid bowed her head and scurried off. Antonio watched her for a moment. He licked his lips and purred, savoring the delicacy as it trotted away.

"A delicious treat she shall be!"

Antonio quietly stepped into The Don's sanctuary and bowed his head.

"Don Salvatore, if I may?"

The Don chomped on a large bite of roasted chicken. His mustache glistened, and grease dripped from his chin. He nodded and waved for Antonio to take a seat.

"My apologies for interrupting your dinner, but I have news that should not wait until morning,"

"Si! What did he want?" The Don said, smacking his food like a cow chewing its cud. "Money, no doubt. They all want money."

"True, but this information was worth buying."

The Don started to take another bite but paused when the words registered in his head. He placed the chicken bone on the plate and wiped his chin before tucking it into his shirt.

"Well, spill the beans! I don't have all night! I have a hot bath waiting!"

"*She* knows!"

"Hmm... I suspected that was why she pulled me into the kitchen." Don Salvatore laughed heartily. "She hoped it would cause me guilt."

"Shall I pay her a visit?"

"No, no. She is harmless...for now. I will visit her in the morning. I can see she will be useful." Don Salvatore's eyes danced. "Si, very useful!"

"Will she reach out for help?"

"I have her where I want her." Don Salvatore grinned and took another big bite from the piece of chicken, savoring it and his fantasy. "Did you see how she was chained to me at the reception?"

"I did," Antonio replied, reaching for a cigarette.

"Don't smoke those blasted things in my presence! Go out front for that!"

"My apologies." Antonio bowed his head and tucked his cigarettes away.

The Don grunted his acceptance of the apology. He swigged his wine before wiping his chin and moving on to other pressing matters.

"Did you find out who the guests were at the far table?"

"Si."

"Are they who we expected?"

"Si."

"Well, you know what to do," Don Salvatore commanded.

"There is a problem."

The Don arched his eyebrow in annoyance.

"They are staying at Mario Giovannese's Hotel Bella."

"Well, well! A smart move on their part. It would not do to have a scene there. Follow him. See where he goes. You can tell me tomorrow when I return."

"Do you want Bruno to drive you?"

"No, not this time," Don Salvatore replied as he picked up another chicken leg. "Keep out of sight. Your time will come soon."

"Si, Signore."

Antonio stood to leave, but The Don stopped him.

"Did you take care of our informant?"

"Bruno is delivering him home as we speak," Antonio replied with a devilish grin.

"Very good. Tell that little maid I am ready for my bath."

"She is preparing it now."

The Don, slipping back into his fantasy, grunted his dismissal. He sunk his teeth into the chicken, releasing a trail of juice down his chin. The sloppiness didn't concern him. He was a happy man.

Antonio struck a match and held it to his cigarette. The flame danced excitedly as it licked the tobacco. His mischievous thoughts danced to the same tune. Don Salvatore wasn't the only one ready to play with his new toy!

I think mine shall give me a sponge bath. Antonio mused.

He stood in the doorway to the water closet and watched the maid on her knees as she mopped up the excess water. Her curves tempted him to attack her. Taking a woman from behind was nice, but surprising her in this position was even more arousing. Staring a hole into her clothes, he imagined hiking up her tight black skirt and firmly holding on while she resisted.

"A slight problem?" He asked, flicking his cigarette into the puddle.

Isabella jumped and quickly hopped to her feet. Dripping wet, her white blouse clung to her breasts.

"My apologies, Signore. The water ran over while I was in the other room."

"Your clothes are wet."

Looking down, Isabella's face flushed. The thin material of her blouse no longer hid her cleavage; it enhanced them.

"Are both baths ready?"

"Si."

"Inform The Don, then come back to mop this up."

Isabella ran like a wild rabbit toward The Don's room. Antonio chuckled; her fear was delicious.

A fiery ring of heat from the scalding water singed Antonio's skin as he sat in the tub. Enjoying the pain, Antonio moaned with pleasure. He lit another cigarette and leaned back. As the smoke rolled up, he imagined the fun the maid would soon provide.

Isabella returned a few minutes later. Her face flushed, seeing Antonio naked in the tub.

"My apologies, Signore. I thought I was to clean this up."

"You are."

"But..."

"Close the door. You are letting in a draft," Antonio commanded. "and lock it."

The maid hesitated. He repeated her instructions more forcefully. She jumped and obeyed his orders.

"Now remove your clothing." When she didn't move, he added. "If you want to keep your job."

Her back to him, Isabella unzipped her skirt.

"Turn around."

Her chin tucked, Isabella turned to face him. She released her skirt, exposing her white garter belt and soft pink panties.

"Now, the blouse." Antonio sat up to watch the sumptuous lines of her body become exposed. A wicked grin curled his lips. "Slowly, Mia Bella. Slowly."

CHAPTER 48

Angelina fanned her damp hair across the pillow and stared at the ceiling. Pushing through her exhaustion, she mulled over the day's conversations. Her interactions with four people that day weighed heavy on her mind. The common thread in each begged her to answer one question; *stay or go?*

"I tried to outsmart the wolf, dear brother!" Angelina whispered into the cool night air. "See how well it worked? It didn't! I only paved a path for his manipulation and endangered the people I love."

Rolling onto her stomach, she buried her face into her pillow and screamed. The boiling rage and frustration shifted from defiance to sobs of defeat.

The thought of leaving her sister, parents, and Fernando ripped her heart into pieces. They were the most important people, the *only* people left in her life. Her small world was shrinking, and the confinement was suffocating.

Don Salvatore's effortless manipulation drained every ounce of her confidence. She would desire the same talent if she did not despise him so much. Suffering his mind games each day was almost as daunting as his physical demands. His fantasy of her giving birth to his children was more horrific than the previous week's atrocities. Her stomach turned sour. Could she love her child from *him*?

In an act of self-preservation, her mind played the horrid scenes of her forecasted future if she stayed. After an hour of enduring the impending doom, she rolled over and pushed away the images. Yet, the visions remained.

"Living it will be hard enough! Agonizing over what *may* happen changes nothing!" She punched the mattress. "Damn it, I cannot stay. But I cannot leave my family, my home!"

Another flood of tears rushed down her cheeks. She felt as dejected as Catalina looked. She allowed herself to wallow in self-pity. It was a state she rarely gave into. She witnessed too many people slip into it and never climb out.

Her conscience eventually urged her back to sanity.

"You done being a bawling baby who lost her bottle?"

She screamed into her pillow one more time.

"Now I am," Angelina stated, drying her cheeks.

"Good, perhaps you can make a decision!"

Angelina wrapped her arms around her knees. With a long sigh, she relaxed against the headboard and stared at the crack stretching across the ceiling. Over the past ten years, she watched the thin, jagged line slowly progress from the corner toward the center. Her father painted over rings from roof leaks and patched the areas where chunks of plaster had fallen. Rosario fixed any issue without consternation or complaint since, as he said, *"fixing things was his job."*

"Oh, Papa, I wish you could fix the crack in our family."

Angelina envisioned Giorgio and The Don dangling Cat off the edge of a cliff, out of her reach. She felt the chasm between them widen and a chilly loneliness in her heart.

She was not confident Catalina believed Giorgio was a killer. Anytime she broached the topic, Catalina pushed back because of Angelina's *"compulsive desire to be a murderer."*

Carlos's point was well-founded; part of Catalina still loved Giorgio. His attacking her, though heinous, was not murder. Thus, with no visible blood on his hands, Catalina could turn her cheek and forgive. She did not witness Giorgio brutally slaughter the Beretta sons. She did not hear the reasons for revenge or the *plan*. The only undeniable thing was seeing Giorgio naked on top of Angelina. Aside from true love, believing the truth would force Catalina to give up the comforts her marriage provided and face Giorgio's wrath.

Giorgio would eventually heal, though it could take weeks or months. As Carlos pointed out, Catalina's true love would spend time and money atoning for his sins. But for how long? Regardless of her sister's *belief*, Giorgio's temper was a ticking time bomb. Each day, the risk of retribution elevated.

Angelina leaving would disrupt the *plan*. Then what? Abuse and possibly murder Catalina in retribution? Or would Catalina become more valuable?

"If I leave, where do I go? Into the arms of a total stranger? That is ludicrous, and you know it!"

The sting of Catalina's point still burned.

"They are men, the same as Giorgio and Don Salvatore. Besides, he is not in Brusnengo."

There was no doubt about Angelina's fate; she would suffer if she stayed. Carlos warned her that Don Salvatore would hunt her; nowhere was safe from his clutches. These were hard facts to accept but pointless to refute. In short, the Beretta daughters were sentenced to a life of misery. At least they would have each other to lean on. Therefore, her choice seemed obvious. She must stay to protect her family.

Angelina slid under the sheets and snuggled her pillow while a fresh batch of tears crashed against the white fabric.

Her next thought, though, crushed her soul.

"If I stay, will they learn they don't need both of us?" Her stomach twisted. "Ugh! Stay or go; either way, Cat suffers!"

Another terrifying detail entered Angelina's mind. One that could determine her fate, regardless of Cat's situation.

"What happens when Don Salvatore discovers Giorgio's transgressions?"

The Don was from a generation where a man and a woman merely caught alone in a room tarnished her reputation.

"Giorgio was caught naked atop me. Will he take his rage

out on Giorgio or cast me aside as tainted goods? No man wants the trampled leftovers! Nan, who loves me, could not accept a damaged woman! Despite Cat's desire to keep this a secret, I cannot lie to Fernando...I cannot hurt him again!"

Angelina slumped into the chair by the writing desk, and her tears resumed their migration. Through her watery vision, she lit a candle and flipped the gentleman's note over. Her finger traced the features of the elaborate seal. The dark red, shiny material molded perfectly around the signet used to impress the high-quality wax. Even the paper felt expensive. Given the messenger's regal manners, she presumed his 'boss' was wealthy. Regardless of finances, Angelina wondered how the boss, or his messenger for that matter, was connected to her family.

"Who are you?" She asked, unfolding the thick paper.

> *Dear Signorina Beretta,*
>
> *It is with my deepest sympathy that I write you. I have been informed of the tragic loss your family suffered. Even though we are half a world apart, know I join you in your anguish, which must be beyond all mental constitution.*
>
> *Though we have not met, please know your father is very dear to my family. I will utilize all my resources to aid you with any issue you are facing. By the time you read this letter, measures for your well-being are already in motion. Soon, we will meet face to face and discuss what you desire of me.*
>
> *I am at your will and service.*
>
> > *Very Truly Yours,*
> > *Maximilianus Fiori.*

Turning over the letter again, Angelina inspected the impression in the red wax. She did not recognize the name, but the seal seemed familiar. A jolt of curiosity struck her. Angelina ran to remove her dress from the waste bucket. She wanted to burn it after everyone went to sleep but feared the acrid smell would alarm them. Throwing it away had to suffice. She could burn it tomorrow.

"Where did you go?" Angelina checked both pockets, but they were empty. She hunted through the crumpled paper in the basket. "Oh, come on! You have to be here!"

On her hands and knees, she searched around the floor, under the bed and nightstand.

"Damn it! Think!" Pacing, she mentally retraced her steps. "I came upstairs, into my room, grabbed my robe, and went to the bathroom," Angelina recited. "After I brushed my teeth, I undressed in..." She scurried to the bathroom!"

In the hallway, Angelina's barefoot stepped on something sharp. She covered her mouth and silently screamed from the throbbing pain. She picked up the stealthy aggressor.

"There you are!"

At her desk, Angelina held the treasure near the candle. The shiny cufflink twinkled in the light as she twirled it between her finger and thumb. She slowly traced the gold letters on the trinket. She looked at the red seal and repeated the action. She compared the two sets of letters, shaking her head in shock.

"Signor Fiori, when were you in my family's home?" Angelina asked, amazed both items matched exactly.

This stranger's words were compassionate. However, unmasking The Don's true nature made her question the validity of Signor Fiori's proclamations. Until the day she witnessed her brother's murder, Angelina believed The Don was a kind and well-respected man. The scary tales about him were myths to frighten kids sitting around a campfire on a spooky night. Why would Maximilianus, another wealthy man, be any different?

On paper, Mr. Fiori presented as a sincere man of integrity. Still, his elegant script did not prove his character. If he knew Rosario, she would have met him or his family. Combing the list of clients, Angelina tried to recall someone named Fiori, but no faces appeared on the roster. She started second-guessing herself. Did the name sound familiar because she wanted it to?

"One thing in your favor, Signor Fiori; we agree my father is a *very dear man.*"

Angelina sighed. The pledge and mutual feelings of a stranger, even if delivered heroically, were not...should not be enough to lure Angelina away from home.

Angelina rested her head on the desk and stared at the cufflink and the note. Neither could give her advice, yet her heart yearned for it. Looking past the objects, she searched deep in her soul for an inspiring parable from her father.

"Sometimes it is better to leave so you can regain your wits and live to fight another day," Rosario said.

"Papa, I don't want to leave!" A wave of nausea washed over her. "I don't want to be The Don's whore either!"

The struggle between her determination and heart pulled her in different directions until one overpowered the other. Broken, she picked up a piece of parchment and began writing. Angelina removed her grandmother's signet ring and folded the paper neatly. The candle licked the bottom of the spoon of crimson wax, drawing Angelina back to the day her grandmother gave her the ring.

"Do you know the story of *'The Italian Rose,'* Lina?"

Wide-eyed in anticipation, Angelina shook her head.

"Ah! It is a good lesson," Nonna said. "Sit with me, and I will tell you."

They sat side by side on the ornately carved wooden bench

in the middle of Nonna's rose garden. Nonna slipped the gold ring off her finger. Holding it in the sunlight, she reverently said a prayer. Her prayer finished, she met Angelina's gaze.

"Our family's tradition is to pass this ring to the first-born granddaughter on her ninth birthday. Nine, as in a Novena," Nonna explained with an adoring smile. "You say a novena of Hail Mary's every night?"

Entranced by her grandmother's voice and the scintillation of the ring, Angelina nodded.

"And you say a prayer for St. Theresa, The Little Flower, to ask for God's blessing upon you?"

Angelina nodded again.

"Very good," Nonna gushed and cupped Angelina's face. "Now, I shall tell you the tale of *The Italian Rose*."

"The rose is a sign of beauty and strength. The silky petals form such captivating beauty, even from a distance, begs one to come closer. With an onlooker's eyes transfixed on her attractive bloom, The Rose's fragrance captures another sense. The aroma, filling the nose, touches the soul in a way no other flower can. The Rose, a radiant creature, will easily bewitch one's heart, erase a transgression, illicit powerful love, or bring a healing smile to the face of a friend in need. The Rose's beauty possesses the power to charm the soul, Si. But she can be deceptive. Some men believe such beauty is a sign of weakness or fragility. No, she is far from weak or fragile. Aside from the strong stem and firmly attached petals, The Rose can exact revenge! With her iron thorns, The Rose will draw the blood of any man who squeezes too tightly. If she is abused and her silky petals fall, The Rose will retreat for a time. However, she will return with another beautiful bloom that is more attractive, fragrant, and stronger than before. You see, The Italian Rose is as strong and resilient as she is captivating and beautiful."

Nonna's tears welled. She smiled and stroked Angelina's

cheek. "The Italian Rose is like *you*, my beautiful and resilient Angelina Rose."

Nonna placed the heavy gold ring in Angelina's palm and folded her tiny fingers around the treasure. Nonna wrapped her warm hands around Angelina's little fist.

"Buona cosa sempré," Nonna professed. "May you have good things *always*, for you are a strong...beautiful...rose. Someday, you will captivate the hearts of men. If they are not kind to you..." Nonna paused as a tear rolled down her cheek. She lifted her granddaughter's chin and gazed deep into her eyes at her soul.

"Promise Nonna you will remember to always be strong, fear no man, and remember to use your thorns!"

"Si, Nonna! I promise!"

Angelina slowly opened her hands to inspect the ring. She had admired it on her Nonna's finger but never examined it closely. Holding it now, she was entranced by the intricate details. The band was a braid of rose stems. The face was the perfect likeness of a rose, fully bloomed, with a protective ring of thorns surrounding precious petals. Every detail of the fine craftsmanship portrayed the essence of Nonna's story of *The Italian Rose*.

"It is beautiful!"

"As are you." Nonna picked up the ring and kissed it before sliding it onto Angelina's finger. "My beautiful Italian Rose!"

"Thank you, Nonna!"

A sorrowful pain compressed Angelina's chest. She missed her grandmother's love and unwavering perseverance. In times of such grief, Angelina always heard Nonna whispering comforting words.

"Do not be sad. I am always with you. All the ancestors are. With your invitation, we will send love and guide you."

"I ask all my ancestors to help me in any way they can,"

Angelina said with conviction. "With all my heart, I willingly receive your love and care. Today, tomorrow, and always."

It was comforting to know she was not truly alone. She dried her tears and tucked away her memories with her handkerchief. Her decision was made.

She poured the red wax onto the folded paper and pressed it with Nonna's ring. Like the envelope containing her letter, Angelina sealed her fate. Her life was now in God's hands.

CHAPTER 49

Leaning back in her chair, Angelina considered the timing of her next step. Her plan was dangerous, and she would need to be clever to survive.

"I am resilient." She chanted the mantra several times to stir a matching inner strength.

Angelina slinked down the hall to her parent's room, carefully avoiding the creaky boards. She opened the door slowly and stepped across the threshold into a hallowed space. Somehow, this room felt different from the sadness and fear looming in the rest of the house. Yet inside this room, a drastic shift to a realm of love and peace seized Angelina. The sweet fragrance of her mother's perfume filled her heart with happy memories. She sat on the bed. Stroking the space her mother slept, Angelina smiled and drew in every ounce of love. She hugged a pillow and remembered sharing it while being cradled in her mother's arms.

Nostalgia pulled her in as she walked around her parents' room. Capturing memories was not her purpose for entering the hallowed space, but she soaked them in. From her mother's trinkets and jewels to her father's shirts, Angelina filled her soul with their essence.

She picked up her father's watch and noticed the time.

"Oh, no! I need to hurry!"

She crouched before her father's nightstand and looked for the box. In the darkness, her hand blindly searched the floor under the bedside table. She found nothing.

"Where did you put it, Papa?"

She searched her mother's nightstand but found nothing.

"Papa, help me find it!"

An idea popped into her head. Reaching under the nightstand, Angelina felt the underside. She smiled. A small metal box was taped to the bottom. Her first attempt to peel the securely taped box away from the wood failed. She blindly searched with her fingers to find a loose edge of tape.

"Ah, maybe you..." Angelina dug under the edge and pulled. The tape slowly separated from the wood. In the quiet night, the defiant scraping sound echoed around the room, as did her grunts of exertion. The tape made a loud rip as its final protest before giving way. The box toppled out of her hand, landing in a thud. She gasped and waited, but no hurried footsteps raced toward the door.

"I am not very good at this," she mumbled. "Thank God, they are heavy sleepers."

Huddled against the bed, Angelina eagerly removed the tape and lifted the lid.

"Oh, dear God!" Angelina's hands trembled. "Why, Papa?"

On the right was a stack of official papers, one for each family member and one for Carlos, Carmella, and Fernando. On the left was a compact, steel-blue handgun. She hesitated to pick it up.

"How different would life be if I had this gun when they attacked us?"

Her hands trembling, she picked it up and aimed it at a vision of the three attackers, but their faces were quickly replaced with Cat's, pleading not to shoot. Angelina placed the dangerous weapon to the side. The gun could not change the outcome because her hand, trembling in terror, could not pull the trigger.

Angelina continued to inventory the items in the box; a brick of bullets, several heavy gold coins, a necklace her grandmother wore, and five thick stacks of cash.

"I am not sure what you thought would happen, but I am grateful you were prepared."

She removed three stacks of cash and her travel papers before eyeing the gun.

"And what about you?"

A wave of nausea washed over her as she held the gun. Even though she *said* she wanted to kill her brother's murderers, she couldn't end a life. She repacked the box and slid it under the nightstand, well out of sight.

"Carlos will hide you again."

Angelina packed everything she needed in a large, soft bag and a small, hardcover suitcase. With one last look around, she quietly closed the door to her bedroom and slipped out the kitchen door.

Her heart begged for one last stroll through the vines and a brief visit to her brothers' graves, but she was already behind schedule. Angelina took a deep breath and memorized her home's beauty in a mental keepsake. She whispered goodbye to the vines as she slowly drove down the winding road. With every turn of the tires, Angelina felt her body being ripped away from her home like the tape securing the metal box. It was a necessary separation, but it would leave a permanent scar on her heart.

It was nearly dawn when Angelina arrived at the convent. As usual, the sister holding vigil at the entrance greeted her with a compassionate smile.

"You are here early," Sister Maria said, opening the gate.

"I am sorry to disturb you."

"Seeing you is always a pleasure, even in the early hours."

With a slight bow and a smile, Angelina thanked the nun and quickly walked the halls leading to her parents' rooms.

In the dimly lit room, Sofia lay motionless on a sea of white cotton. Though it was a sad sight, she was pleased her mother's eyes were closed. During Angelina's stay at the convent, she visited Sofia several times every day. No matter what the hour, Sofia's eyes remained open, lost in the abyss of nothingness. Angelina understood why her mother did not want to see anything in her dreams or while awake. She witnessed something no mother should and lost even more.

Sitting on the bed, she gently stroked her mother's hand. Sofia's sallow skin was more pronounced against Angelina's darker olive color. The contrast was a reminder her mother was fragile. This could be the last time Angelina saw her alive.

"I know you have suffered, Mamma, but your daughters are suffering, too. We need you! Please, Mamma! Please fight your way back to us!"

A pond of tears gathered as she watched for movement in her mother's bruised face. She prayed for a response or twitch of acknowledgment. But Sofia remained still.

Angelina longed to wrap herself in Sofia's arms and cry until she had no more tears in her soul. Such a collapse of emotions would not heal her mother, resurrect her brothers, or mend the expanding void between sisters.

"Rest your body, Mamma, and heal your mind, *please!*"

Her heart aching, she gently kissed Sofia's forehead. The smell of her mother's hair filled Angelina's nose. It was the scent that chased away the pain from any trials, injuries, or bad dreams. There was no need to etch the smell into her memory. It was already permanently embedded in every cell of her body. For a moment, she bathed in the scent of the most loving angel she had ever known.

Angelina whispered into her mother's ear, then placed a simple note on the bedside table.

I love you, Mamma.
Love Always,
Angelina

Standing in the doorway to her father's room, the light from the hall illuminated the serine figure tucked perfectly into the white sheets. It was hard to see her mother severely injured, but to see the man she thought was invincible, barely alive, was soul-crushing.

"Papa, please squeeze my hand if you can hear me."

She waited for a few moments and tried her plea again, but her father remained motionless. Choking back her tears, Angelina squeezed her father's hand.

"Papa, please know I am not abandoning you and Mamma, or Cat, for that matter. If you knew The Don's plan for me, you would immediately usher me out of sight!" Angelina kissed her father's palm, then pressed it to her cheek. "You and Mamma are safe in the convent. For now, Cat is safe, too. I am not." Angelina commanded her tears not to fall. She needed him to know she was still strong. "That is why I must leave. Leave...to return to fight another day!"

Angelina pressed her face against his palm. She did not want to let go, to leave the warmth and safety of Rosario's reach, but the man before her was not her Papa. He was a shell resembling the man Angelina admired her entire life. Beneath the broken bones, bruises, and long gashes lay the man whose words of guidance she longed to hear.

"Rest, Papa. Rest and recover," Angelina whispered and kissed his palm once more.

Resolute in her decision, Angelina placed a note on his bedside table and left the room without looking back.

Quietly walking down the marble-floored hallway, Angelina checked her watch. She had enough time for one more thing.

Following the meandering maze, she took a left at the end of the hallway. Many of the convent's passageways were long galleries for ancient masterpieces. The valuable art was displayed far enough apart, allowing each piece its own glorious space. Sparkling clean marble floors reflected soft hues, making one feel as close to heaven as possible.

Angelina stopped at the last door on the right. She hesitated before deciding it was appropriate to say *thank you*. Softly, she tapped her knuckles on the door. The door immediately popped open, revealing a woman dressed and ready for her day.

"Angelina?"

"Good morning, Francesca."

"I was just on my way to pray in the chapel. Will you walk with me?" Francesca asked after they hugged.

"It is my last stop before I leave."

"How can you be leaving when you just arrived?"

"I've been here for almost an hour."

"After mass, we can visit your parents together." Francesca rambled on, ignoring Angelina's comment. "The doctor said they will mend, but it will take time."

"I already visited them."

"Then we can have breakfast together!"

Angelina placed her hand on Francesca's arm, stopping their progress. "I wanted to thank you for everything you did for me. You are very dear to me. It seems strange how tragedy can bond two lives in such a brief time, but I couldn't leave without at least letting you know."

"Leave? What!"

"Shh," Angelina patted her hands. "Please, no one must know. For *their* safety and *mine*."

"Where will you go?"

Angelina resumed walking in silence, keeping her gaze forward.

"Who is going with you?"

"No one! And no one must know!"

"You cannot go to... *nowhere* by yourself! It is dangerous!"

"It is safer than staying *here* under the command of Don

Salvatore!" Angelina shuddered at the thought. "Thank you for your concern, but I *cannot* stay!"

Francesca arched her brow, glowering at Angelina.

"I will be fine!" Angelina gave Francesca a reassuring pat. "Please look after my parents for me!"

"It is not wise to leave, but if you must..." Francesca sighed, nodding her acceptance.

"Thank you! We will meet again, I promise!"

"Be careful, Angelina. His people are *everywhere!*"

"I know."

Angelina kneeled in the pew beside Francesca and bowed her head to pray. A heavy emotional anchor overpowered her eagerness to depart. The determination that coursed through her veins a few hours before was gone. Now, she felt an overwhelming desire to stay.

"Stay and do what? Be a whore?" she thought.

A rush of heat burned Angelina's core, and a wave of anxiety consumed her. She fidgeted one too many times, breaking Francesca's prayer.

"Stop wiggling like a two-year-old!"

"Sorry!" Angelina bowed her head to pray and commanded her body to remain still.

"Holy Father, help me keep my eyes forward, to live in the present so I may be ready for the future. With your blessing, I release myself from the past, freeing my hands to use the gifts bestowed upon me each day."

As the nuns sang in an ethereal harmony with the organist, the priest assumed his position on the altar. In holy union, everyone made the sign-of-the-cross and bowed their heads for the Penitential Rite. Angelina dipped her fingers in the holy water and slipped out the door before the priest finished asking for God's mercy on his flock.

The sun was in full glory on the horizon when Angelina parked in front of Anna's Café. Stepping out of the car, the smell of fresh pastries and coffee made Angelina's stomach growl. It was tempting to pop in for an espresso and a sweet roll. However, she was pressed for time.

Angelina, dressed in her mother's baggy dress and floppy hat. Her disguise would help her remain hidden for her short walk. She grabbed her luggage and turned down the first alley.

A brisk gust of wind bit at her cheeks, but Angelina remained focused. Not even the chirping birds singing their joy for the bright blue sky or the rising sun's glow drew her attention. Her only thought was reaching the train station without being noticed.

Dozens of travelers stood on the platform awaiting their train, while another dozen waited in line to purchase a ticket. At this early hour, the station was rarely full. However, in two hours, the stone building would be bustling with a hundred passengers and their family members waiting to say farewell.

Angelina joined the line of travelers to purchase her unknown future. Her choice to leave was in its infancy. Though she chose *to go*, she had yet to select the *where*. She stared at the train's arrival times and destinations. That morning, four trains would arrive before noon. Having never ventured far from her hometown, each place held a unique adventure for her.

An elderly couple who, with great adoration, greeted Rosario every Sunday at Mass stood in front of Angelina. Because of their size, the Beretta family was hard to miss. Only two other families outnumbered the Berettas; the Severino's had eight children, and the Stallone's had twelve. Given the small town, it would be difficult to avoid running into someone who knew her, so she kept her head down, hoping the elderly couple would not notice her.

"Two for Bergamo," the elderly man requested as he removed his wallet.

A photograph fell from his pocket, landing next to

Angelina's shoe. Staring up at her were three pairs of eyes, pleading for her to pick up the image and return it to the lovely couple. Angelina recognized the siblings. She attended school with the girl, Lucinda. Her brothers were standing behind Lucinda in the photo. They went to school with Anton and Ricardo. The connection to Angelina's brothers and the tie to a dear friend resurfaced her desire to stay.

You are not leaving forever. You will come back! Angelina thought.

It was tempting to keep the picture, but it would put an innocent family in danger if she were caught by Don Salvatore's men.

"You dropped this," Angelina whispered.

"Here are your tickets. The platform is to your right," the attendant stated before yelling, "Next!"

Unable to listen to two people, the elderly couple became confused and frustrated. The old man snapped the picture out of Angelina's hand and grabbed the tickets from the attendant.

"Where do we go?" the old lady asked her husband.

"This way, over here," he grumbled, juggling his wallet, the photo, and the tickets.

"Where to?" the attendant snapped at Angelina.

Angelina looked at her options and quickly ruled out two trains based on the long wait for their arrival. Her eyes darted back and forth, trying to decide between her remaining two options. The attendant's condescending look and the ever-increasing number of people filling the area added to her anxiety. She did not know why picking was so difficult, but she needed to pick one and move on!

Angelina leaned forward and whispered her choice.

"Speak up! Where to?"

The attendant's abruptness made Angelina flinch. She did not want anyone overhearing her destination. She tapped her throat, insinuating she couldn't speak louder, then whispered her destination again.

The attendant rolled her eyes and barked the price to Angelina.

"Here's your ticket and your change. The platform is over there. Next!"

Angelina winced again at the attendant's brash attitude but was grateful she didn't announce her train's destination.

"Thank you," Angelina whispered, taking her ticket.

Even though the train was due to arrive in fifteen minutes, it felt like two hours. Angelina's nerves begged her to pace across the wooden platform, but she was determined not to show any anxiety. Today, she was just another traveler waiting on a train.

In the distance, a loud whistle blew, announcing the locomotive's arrival. As the steel machine rounded the corner, a white cloud billowed out of the smokestack, and a chug-chug echoed down the track. Closing in on the station, the screech of metal on metal and the whistle of steam sent a chill down Angelina's spine. Excitement and fear danced a jig in her heart; this was her last chance to stay in Brusnengo.

Taking a cue from the other women, Angelina held her hat firmly against her head until the gust of wind dissipated.

"Good morning, Signorina. May I take your bags?" Asked a large man dressed in a dark coat, his highly polished brass buttons twinkling in the sunlight.

"Um... Si, thank you."

Smiling, the man carried Angelina's luggage to the end of the aisle and placed the hard suitcase on the rack above her seat. Before he lifted the soft bag, Angelina grabbed the straps and pulled it close to her feet.

"May I keep this one here with me?"

"If you wish, Signorina," the conductor replied.

Settled into her seat, the conductor gave her a pleasant nod, tipped his hat, and returned to help other passengers.

Her emotions surged and receded with the force of a changing tide. Her excitement faded to apprehension, back to excitement several times, while a hundred butterflies performed gymnastics in her stomach.

Stop it! Focus on something else, or it will be a long trip!

The conductor seated her with her back against the far wall, giving her a perfect view of every passenger entering the train. With a slight bow and a smile, the conductor greeted each passenger.

"If I may," the conductor's deep voice bellowed kindly. "Very well. Enjoy your trip."

The conductor repeated his line a dozen times before Angelina noticed something unusual. His accent and tall, round stature made him seem out of place. Given this line ran across several countries, it was plausible to think he could be from anywhere. Yet, something else about the man didn't fit. The way he spoke and his enthusiasm for his job was the opposite of the man behind the ticket counter. The conductor was considerably older, too, which added to the oddity of his persona.

"Does he work for The Don?" The thought sickened her.

Don Salvatore's power was vast, but Angelina never quantified the distance of his reach. The expansiveness of the world made Angelina feel insignificant. She was a bug easily swatted by the enormity of powerful hands far more experienced than her. Doubting the wisdom of her choice, Angelina kept her head down and took out her anxiety on the lace of her handkerchief.

"Oh, dear God, help me!" she whispered.

"He will," a voice replied.

Stunned, Angelina didn't move. It was not unreasonable to think someone would engage with her, but she really had not prepared her mind for such an encounter. Struck by fear, Angelina remained with her eyes down on the white lace of the hankie.

"Angelina?"

Unsure which was more shocking, knowing the owner of the voice or that the owner knew where to find her?

Angelina swallowed hard. "How did you know which train?"

"I followed you."

"But I... How could you..."

"I couldn't let you go alone."

A tear rolled down Angelina's cheek as she looked up at her traveling companion.

"But what about?"

"Women like us are always ready to pick up and run," Francesca explained as she placed her hand on Angelina's. "And... you drive slow!" Francesca added with a giggle.

"Thank you!" Angelina muttered. "You didn't have to..."

"I know, but I figured you could use some company."

Still befuddled, Angelina asked again, "How did you know which train to get on?"

"I know you think this dress hides you, but really it is eye-catchingly ugly!" Francesca teased. "And that hat!"

The playful insult made Angelina relax enough to laugh.

"Thank you."

Francesca's cheerful demeanor flipped to terror.

"Don't thank me yet!" she said, grabbing Angelina's hand.

"What do you mean?"

A pale stone statue, Francesca stared straight ahead.

"What?" Angelina followed her gaze but saw nothing.

"Not what...*who*!" Francesca visibly shuddered. "Those men walking toward us killed my dear Alberto!"

Angelina's head snapped to the right, her eyes falling on a tall, thin man with a devilish grin strutting toward them. Following close behind, with a ravenous glare, was a man about two inches taller and a hundred pounds heavier. The closer they came, the harder Francesca squeezed Angelina's hand. At first, Angelina didn't notice the vice crushing her fingers until the men were two steps away.

"Easy, you will break my..."

"Good morning, ladies! You don't mind if my friend and I sit across from you?"Antonio asked rhetorically. "Oh, good!"

Settling into the seats across from the ladies, the men sighed as if they were finally sitting down after a long, arduous day of work.

Bruno's enormous feet and long legs left little room for Francesca's dainty form. Though Antonio barely invaded Angelina's space, she felt the pressure of his ominous persona on her chest.

"You ever have a day when you had something in your hands, and for a brief second, you set it down but then can't find it?"

Antonio chatted as he offered a cigarette to his three companions; only Bruno accepted. He lit his cigarette and handed Antonio the small box of matches.

"It really grates my nerves when things sprout legs and run!" Antonio taunted playfully as he rolled the box of matches across his knuckles with the ease of a magician rolling a coin.

He flashed a playful smile and winked at Francesca before placing the cigarette between his lips. He slowly drew the match across the box; it sizzled into a flame. Antonio held the matchstick near the tobacco but did not light it. The flame's playful bounce on the stick was a mesmerizing dance, keeping everyone's gaze.

Angelina's eyes widened. Beyond the flame, the glow illuminated a horror. In Antonio's haunting eyes, she saw two dark portals to hell. She shuddered. He wanted her to know the depth of evil within him. To understand his evil was far more ominous than Don Salvatore's.

Antonio's smile widened. His point made, he lit his cigarette, gently pulling the polluted air into his lungs.

"I am sorry, ladies! How rude of me to just plop down and not introduce myself." Antonio released a few smoke rings into the air. "My name is Antonio, and this is my business partner, Bruno. This trip is all business for us, but sometimes pleasure blends perfectly with our line of work, so who knows. Maybe this will be a short but thrilling adventure.

Tell me, what takes you lovely ladies to Alessandria? Signorina Beretta, are you on your way to strike a deal with a customer? Hmm? Francesca, are you headed to see an old friend?"

Angelina struggled to breathe. Carlos warned her about these men. How did they know her plan? She had not decided *where* to go until standing at the ticket window. Her mind volleyed between "how did they know which train" to "what will they do to us."

To imagine what the devils would do over the next several hours was grim. Antonio was having fun batting the trapped mice between his paws. Given there were no chances of fleeing his grasp, Francesca and Angelina would endure whatever torture Antonio could deliver in public. In private... Angelina refused to allow her mind to imagine it.

"Cat got your tongue?" Antonio asked when neither lady replied. "Take your time. We have hours and hours to discuss *where and why.*'"

Finding Antonio's comment funny, Bruno laughed. The deep, haunting bellow echoed around the small space.

"That is an excellent idea, Bruno!" Antonio exclaimed as he patted his partner's forearm. "We should play a little game to pass the time! I will tell you what the little birdie chirped in my ear. You will tell me if the feathered snitch was right!" He savored another drag from his cigarette. "Until your tongues thaw, a simple nod is an acceptable answer." Antonio, quite amused with himself, chuckled. "Of course, like any good book, I will not divulge the fate of our heroines until the end."

A lurch of the train and a scream from the whistle nixed Angelina's idea to run. Though jumping from a moving train was an option, it could be far deadlier than conversing with the enemy. Her immediate death was not part of Don Salvatore's plan.

You are a fool, Angelina," She thought. *"Did Giorgio's hand clamped around your throat kill every brain cell in your head!*

"Francesca, let's start with your storyline, shall we?" Antonio asked.

Angelina panicked when Francesca's breathing became abnormal, and all the color in her face drained away. Francesca was diagnosed with a weak heart. The doctor was adamant she must avoid stress. Their escalating predicament was precisely what the doctor insisted she avoid. Francesca was on the verge of a heart attack.

Angelina's *plan* was rapidly spiraling downward. After one week of experiencing the *real world*, Angelina's self-confidence plummeted. Now, she questioned her ability to read people. Her family and friends raved about her talent; she was a charmer like no other. Were their words true, or hot air to inflate her ego? Did her abilities reach no farther than the vineyard's edge? Was she merely the talented daughter of a renowned vintner and a peddler of wine. The truth, *her truth*, was grim. Angelina was like all women in the male-dominated world outside of Beretta Vineyards. She was weak.

In accepting her fragility, Angelina understood Cat's decision to stay in her current position. At least there, Catalina had some control, even if only for a brief period.

"Bruno, how did our birdie put it?"

"She ran," Bruno grunted.

"In short, Si. But this is a long train ride, and the least we can do is entertain our lovely companions! Let's see... Signor Tweet-tweet said, "Francesca sold her train ticket, stole a car, and drove to Naples." How am I doing? Am I right so far?" Antonio asked the pale Francesca.

Waiting for a response, he released four smoke rings into the air above Angelina's head. His vial breath, the stench of smoke, and the blatant gloating as he danced on their graves overwhelmed Angelina. Her eyes rolled back as her body wilted. The warmth of Antonio's hand on her knee pulled her from the black abyss.

"Don't sleep now. The fun is just getting started!"

Angelina gasped at the demon's touch and pulled her legs closer to her seat. Her head snapped up to bark an insult, but a movement across the way made her pause. The conductor who helped her with her luggage was strolling toward her seat. He smiled a comforting smile and gave Angelina a wink. However, it wasn't his protective gesture that filled her eyes with tears and her heart with hope. It was the person seated at the opposite end of the car, wearing a familiar smile. Her fears were calmed, and she knew she was *not* alone.

BOOK CLUBS & MORE
Ask The Author

Dear Reader,

Have you ever wondered how or why the author wrote the story? What inspired them to use specific names and locations? Do you believe the tiniest detail has a deeper meaning? I will tell you the answers to these questions and more. Simply invite me to your next meeting!

Visiting with readers is one of the best parts of writing. It gives you a chance to learn more about me and the reason behind the novel. (I use lots of symbolism, and most details are not happenstance!) I, too, benefit because I ask you questions, too! Learning what inspires you, why scenes ensnared you, and what you think will happen next are all gratifying and help stir my creativity. Who knows, you may find yourself in my next novel!

Writing is more than telling a story. It is a conversation that doesn't end on the last page. I look forward to the next chapter in our discussion! Connect with me through social media or www.theitalianrose.com. Please be sure to like, share, and leave reviews!

Very Truly Yours,
Christina R Mitchell

Get YOUR NAME in my NEXT BOOK!
FOLLOW on Socail Media or Subscribe for one entry
WRITE A REVIEW for two entries.

'

TheItalianRose
TheItalianRose
@TheItalianRose
TheItalianRose.com
papillonebooks.com

THE *WHO,* THE *WHERE,* & THE *WHY:*

As an author, I get to decide every aspect, from character names to locations. Below, I explain why I picked specific names and settings for my mafia series. *Enjoy!*

Rosario—Ever have a dream that seemed real? When I was *ten years old*, I had such a dream. Every element was vivid enough to be reality. I mean, *freakishly* real!

An older man took my brother, Stephen, and me to a boardwalk carnival. A Ferris wheel spun in the distance, and a weird organ played as we walked hand-in-hand across the wooden planks. The old man spoke in a foreign language, but I understood him. He told us stories and asked us if we liked this or that. I felt an intense love and bond for this stranger as if we were family. He offered to buy us peanuts. Timidly, we nodded our heads. He hurried to the cart and purchased a white paper bag full of freshly roasted peanuts. With a big smile, he encouraged us to try them. The smell and heat from the peanuts were incredibly vivid. When I woke, I described the old man in my dream to my mother and told her it felt more lifelike than any dream. Mom showed me a picture of her grandfather, Rosario. Instantly, I said, "That's him!" My Great-Grandfather Rosario spoke Italian and broken English. He died when my mother was *ten years old*.

Catalina—I derived her name from my grandmother, Katherine. I changed the spelling to keep as close to authentic Italian names as possible. However, I kept the love and endearment for a woman I adored. Angelina's Nonna tells the parable of 'The Italian Rose.' At the end of her tale, Nonna blesses Angelina by saying, "Bouna Cosa Sempré," the Sicilian slang for cose buone sempre. This was Grandma Katherine's blessing to guests as they left her home. With tremendous respect and adoration for an extraordinary woman, my mother and I continue to share this blessing through different facets of our lives, including our inspirational workshops and writings. In my heart and soul, Grandma's love will always be the catalyst for *Bouna Cosa Sempré*.

Angelina—My Grandma Katherine's half-sister was Aunt Angelina, a hardworking woman who walked to work instead of taking the bus. This frugal choice was not self-serving. The money she saved was used to purchase food for her half-brother, Sam, and half-sister, Katherine. In her 100 years, she lived through many tragic situations, yet remained strong and resilient. In my life, few women measure up to Aunt Angelina.

Sofia—When pregnant with my sons, I picked out three girl names; Alexandra, Katherine, and Sofia. Sofia seemed the most fitting for Rosario's bride.

Dr. Andriano—My brother Andrew is a Dermatology P.A. Thus, it seemed appropriate to use a similar name for a doctor. I haven't found the perfect characters to name after my other brothers, but rest assured, their names will appear in one of my novels.

Brusnengo, Italy—In choosing the setting, the place had to meet a particular set of criteria; a familial tie, an actual town in Italy, a place free of preconceived ideas (unfamiliar to most), and a place where having a vineyard was plausible. My family is from Sicily, but most of the known mafia stories are tied to the island. Brusnengo met every criterion; a real town in Northern Italy, a region known for producing wine, wasn't tainted by preconceived notions and was the origin of my husband's family. My only concern, was there a mafia presence in the Northern part of the boot? After a bit of research, I found my answer: Si! Though the mafia was more prevalent in the Southern regions, like most crime, it spread in all directions, including the North.

Beretta—This is the last name of my husband's family from Brusnengo.

Bella Anna Caffè—After one of my beautiful nieces.

Alessandria—Chosen for two reasons; another darling niece's name is similar to this actual city, and Brusnengo is not far from Alessandria.

Bergamo—My maiden name is 'Berg,' and this is another city near Brusnengo—what a coincidence!

The Italian Rose—Since this is a mafia series set in Italy, the 'Italian' is a given. Rose, however, is not just my favorite flower. It is my middle name, my mother's middle name and that of my *paternal* great-grandmother and grandmother! Rose also means strength. As with most themes and names that I pick, there is a deeper meaning, and 'Italian Rose' falls into this category. When I created this book, no mafia movie portrayed a feminine character as the leader. Women (especially in the Italian culture) are typically portrayed as obedient pawns in a man's world. I know of several instances where this subordinate cliché is inaccurate. From my Italian heritage, four women provided me this template of strength: my Mother, Grandmother Katherine, Great-Aunt Angelina, and Great-Aunt Vita. These resilient women, a rose's meaning, and the desire to crush the stigma of a 'weak woman' propelled me to write The Italian Rose.

(Three names did not appear in The Italian Rose, first edition)

Stallone—My grandmother Katherine's maiden name.

Severino—My husband's grandfather's middle name.

Lucinda—My Bestest Bestie's name is Cindy Lou.

LEGAL'S NOTE

Though some names are family names, the character traits and actions do not reflect those individuals. This story, in its entirety, is pure fiction.

Yours Truly,
David R. Mitchell, Esq.
www.MitchellandAssociates.com

AUTHOR'S NOTE

Please leave a review on the website on which you purchased this book. Like, share, and follow us on all social media platforms.
@theitalianrose
The few seconds it takes to do this provides tremendous, lasting support, plus encourages me to type faster. ☺
I hope you enjoyed the book!
Want the 'Who, Where, and Why, for this book?

Get YOUR NAME in my **NEXT BOOK!**
FOLLOW on Socail Media or Subscribe for one entry
WRITE A REVIEW for two entries.
See your name in print!
Subscribe at www.theitalianrose.com.

For more inside scoops, invite me to your book club!
It has been a pleasure to entertain you!

Buono Cosa Sempre'
C. R. Mitchell

Join the family at www.theitalianrose.com.

C. R. MITCHELL

C. R. Mitchell's author journey began in 2008 when her husband encouraged her to channel her natural storytelling talent to inspire others. Intrigued, she began writing. In 2014, an illness drastically changed her life, turning her from a workaholic and active in the community into an unemployed hermit.

Despite feeling broken, she clung to her faith, convinced that her life path shifted so she could inspire others by writing. From her personal experience with chronic pain and depression, she wrote a nonfiction book on managing these invisible monsters to encourage others to embrace a victorious mindset.

Her debut novel, The Italian Rose Mafia Series, honors the formidable women in her life, particularly her mother, who triumphed in the sexist Italian culture.

Mitchell excels at crafting vivid scenes with realistic characters that readers can fall in love with or despise. She believes that a novel achieves an artistic level when it evokes strong emotions within her during the final read-through.

She and her husband started GolfWithLiz.com – The ODP Foundation after their daughter died in a car accident. Ten months later, they hosted their first golf tournament. With the help of family and friends, their annual golf tournament, held the first Sunday in May, raises money to fund annual scholarships for young women. In three years, the foundation has awarded over $20,000 in scholarships.

Christina is a member of P.E.O., Chapter KH. P.E.O. has awarded over $435 million to support women's education.

Mitchell resides in Blue Springs, MO. She cherishes time with her husband, children, family, and friends. She enjoys snuggling with her Papillon puppy, Enzo, playing the piano, and the occasional faceplant into chocolate.